"Did you expect Hell to be something other than pain? It's just a matter of finding what hurts.

"This hurts, doesn't it?"

—The Devil

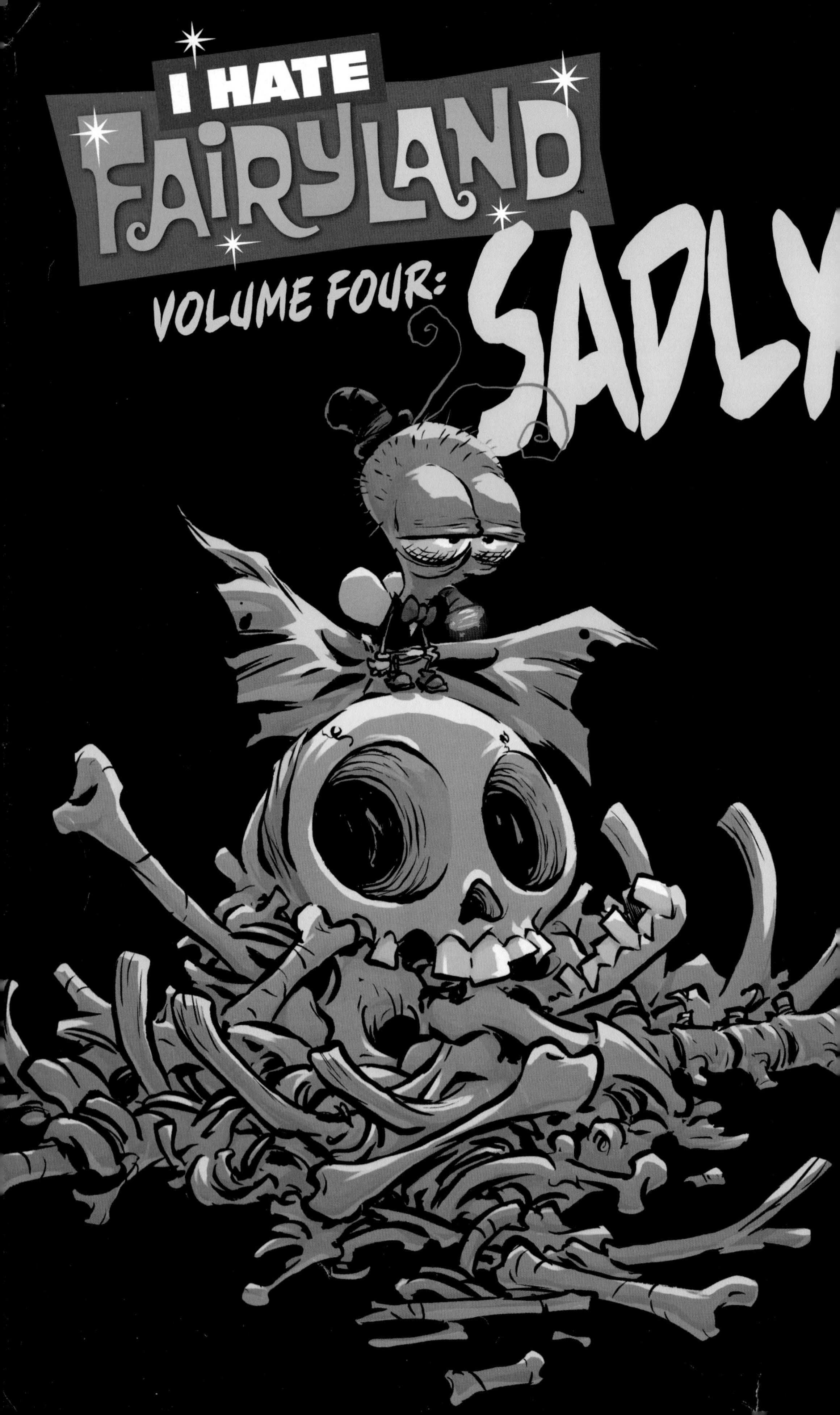
I HATE
FAIRYLAND
VOLUME FOUR:
SADLY

NEVER AFTER

Written and Drawn by
SKOTTIE YOUNG

Coloring by
JEAN-FRANCOIS BEAULIEU

Lettering & Design by
NATE PIEKOS OF BLAMBOT®

Edited by
KENT WAGENSCHUTZ

Logo Design by
RIAN HUGHES

Volume Four Book Design by
CAREY HALL

Additional Development
JASON YOUNG

IMAGE COMICS, INC.
Robert Kirkman — Chief Operating Officer
Erik Larsen — Chief Financial Officer
Todd McFarlane — President
Marc Silvestri — Chief Executive Officer
Jim Valentino — Vice President
Eric Stephenson — Publisher / Chief Creative Officer
Corey Hart — Director of Sales
Jeff Boison — Director of Publishing Planning & Book Trade Sales
Chris Ross — Director of Digital Sales
Jeff Stang — Director of Specialty Sales
Kat Salazar — Director of PR & Marketing
Drew Gill — Art Director
Heather Doornink — Production Director
Nicole Lapalme — Controller
IMAGECOMICS.COM

REGULAR EDITION ISBN: 978-1-5343-0680-6
FORBIDDEN PLANET/BIG BANG COMICS
EXCLUSIVE EDITION ISBN: 978-1-5343-1102-2

SIXTEEN

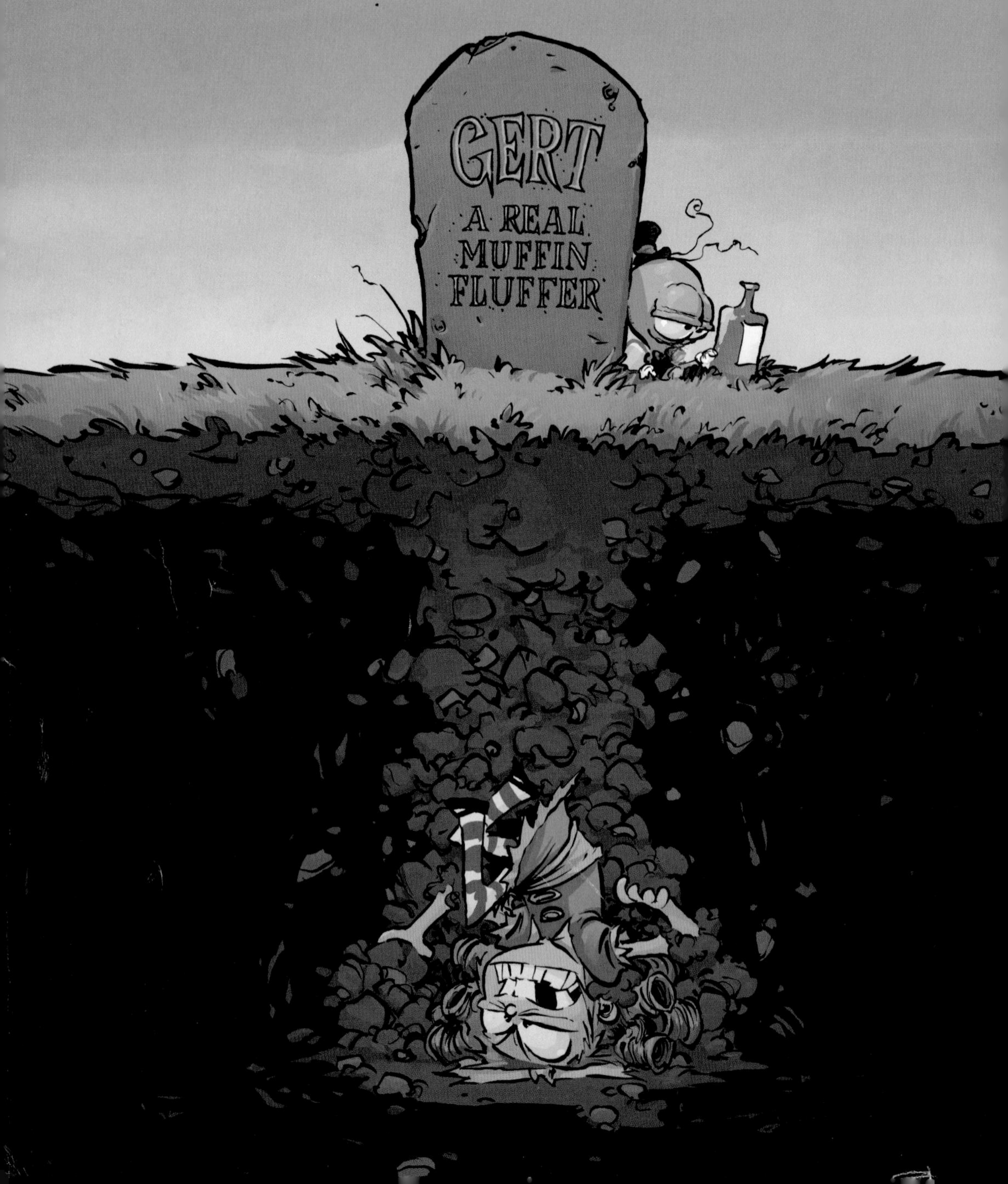
GERT
A REAL MUFFIN FLUFFER

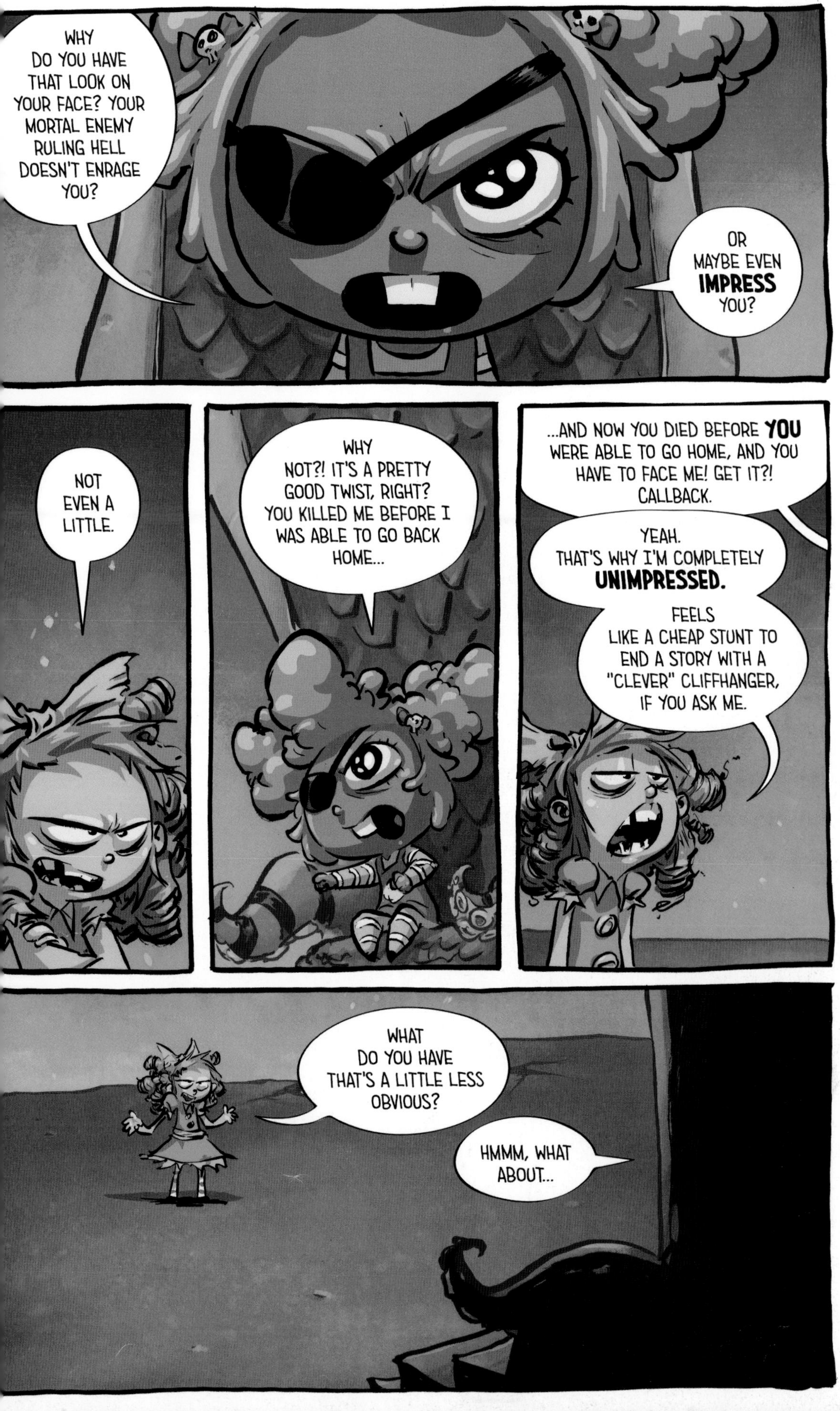

WHY DO YOU HAVE THAT LOOK ON YOUR FACE? YOUR MORTAL ENEMY RULING HELL DOESN'T ENRAGE YOU?
OR MAYBE EVEN **IMPRESS** YOU?
NOT EVEN A LITTLE.
WHY NOT?! IT'S A PRETTY GOOD TWIST, RIGHT? YOU KILLED ME BEFORE I WAS ABLE TO GO BACK HOME...
...AND NOW YOU DIED BEFORE **YOU** WERE ABLE TO GO HOME, AND YOU HAVE TO FACE ME! GET IT?! CALLBACK.
YEAH. THAT'S WHY I'M COMPLETELY **UNIMPRESSED.**
FEELS LIKE A CHEAP STUNT TO END A STORY WITH A "CLEVER" CLIFFHANGER, IF YOU ASK ME.
WHAT DO YOU HAVE THAT'S A LITTLE LESS OBVIOUS?
HMMM, WHAT ABOUT...

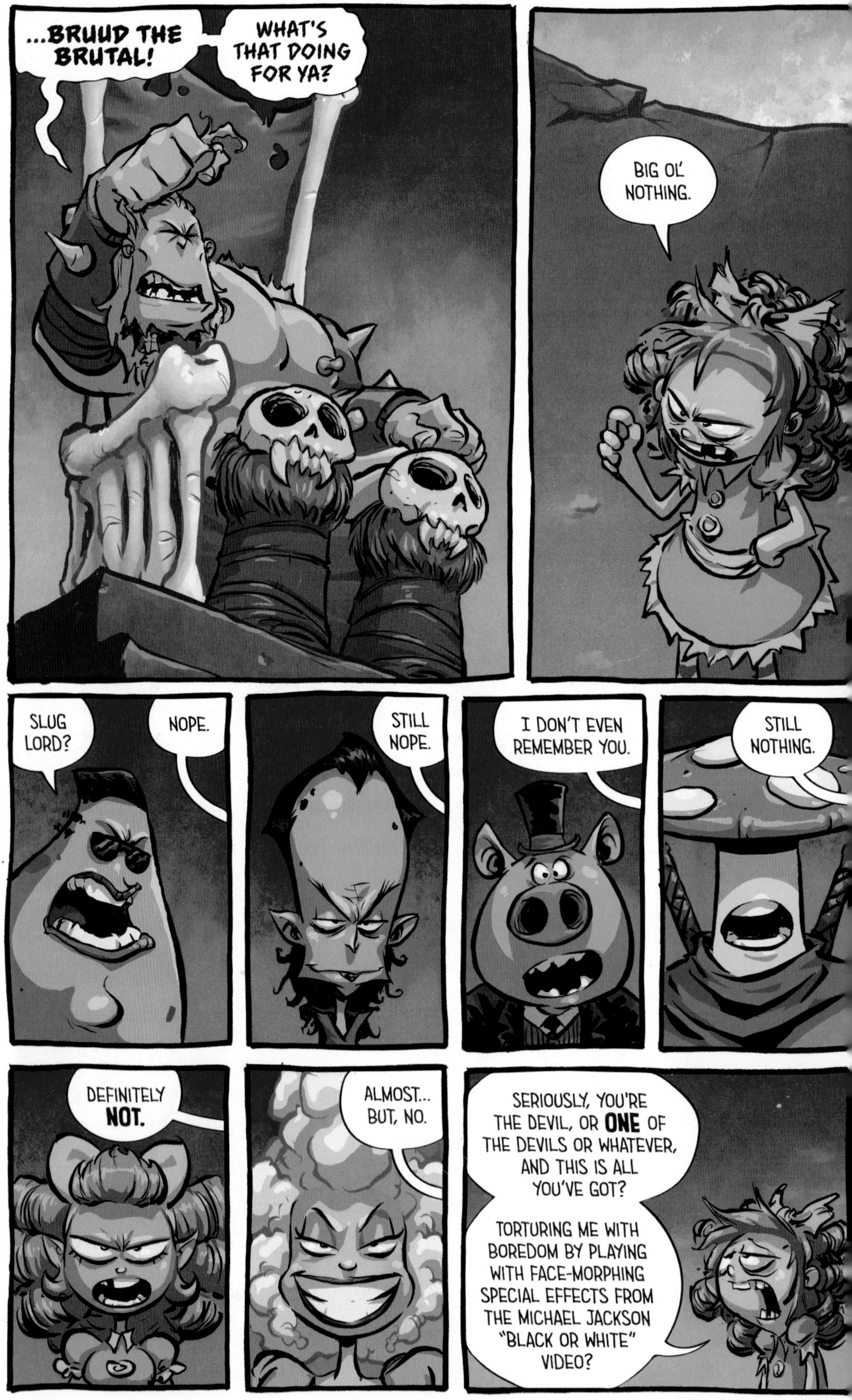
...BRUUD THE BRUTAL!
WHAT'S THAT DOING FOR YA?
BIG OL' NOTHING.
SLUG LORD?
NOPE.
STILL NOPE.
I DON'T EVEN REMEMBER YOU.
STILL NOTHING.
DEFINITELY **NOT.**
ALMOST... BUT, NO.
SERIOUSLY, YOU'RE THE DEVIL, OR **ONE** OF THE DEVILS OR WHATEVER, AND THIS IS ALL YOU'VE GOT?
TORTURING ME WITH BOREDOM BY PLAYING WITH FACE-MORPHING SPECIAL EFFECTS FROM THE MICHAEL JACKSON "BLACK OR WHITE" VIDEO?

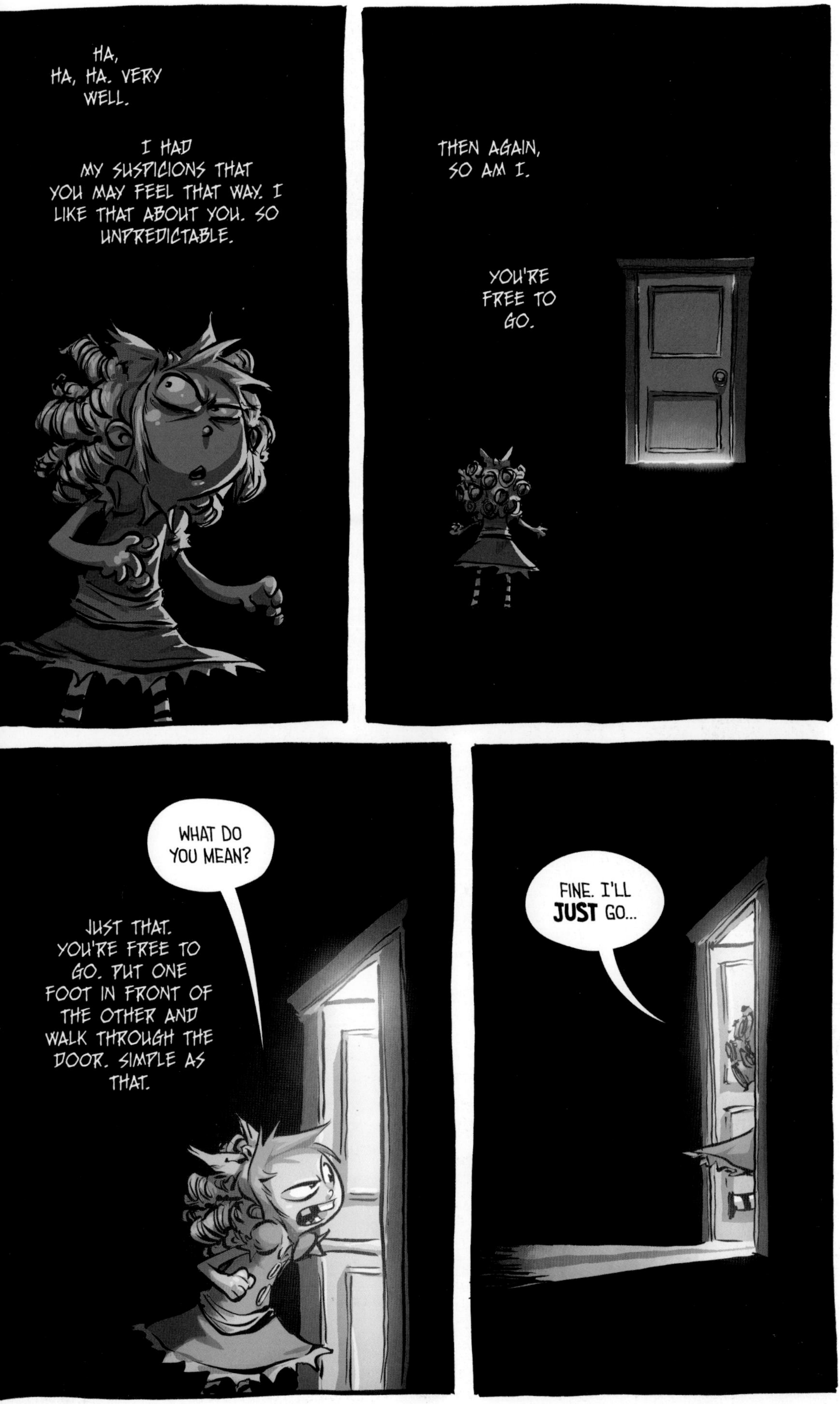
HA, HA, HA. VERY WELL.
I HAD MY SUSPICIONS THAT YOU MAY FEEL THAT WAY. I LIKE THAT ABOUT YOU. SO UNPREDICTABLE.
THEN AGAIN, SO AM I.
YOU'RE FREE TO GO.
WHAT DO YOU MEAN?
JUST THAT. YOU'RE FREE TO GO. PUT ONE FOOT IN FRONT OF THE OTHER AND WALK THROUGH THE DOOR. SIMPLE AS THAT.
FINE. I'LL **JUST** GO...

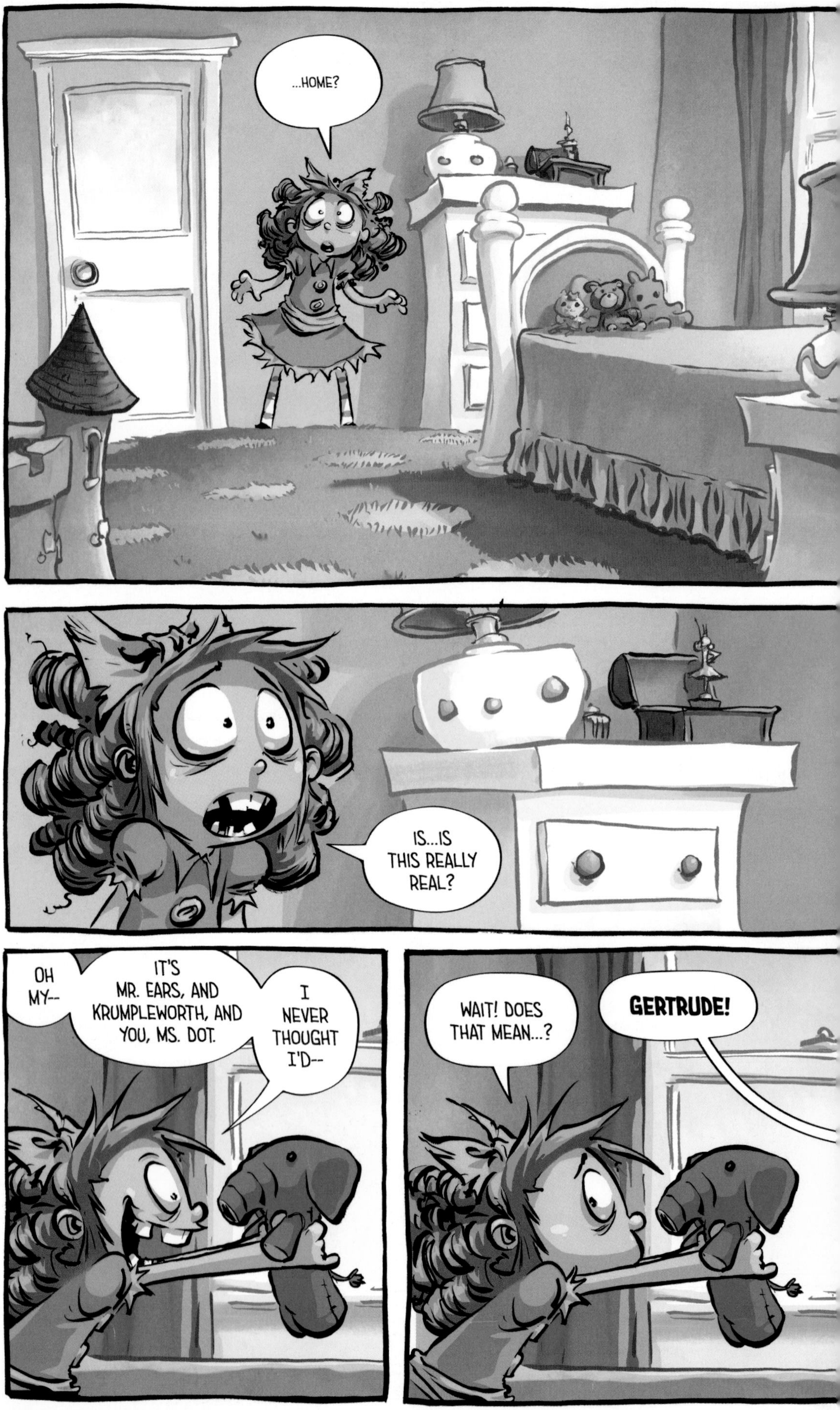
...HOME?
IS...IS THIS REALLY REAL?
OH MY--
IT'S MR. EARS, AND KRUMPLEWORTH, AND YOU, MS. DOT.
I NEVER THOUGHT I'D--
WAIT! DOES THAT MEAN...?
GERTRUDE!

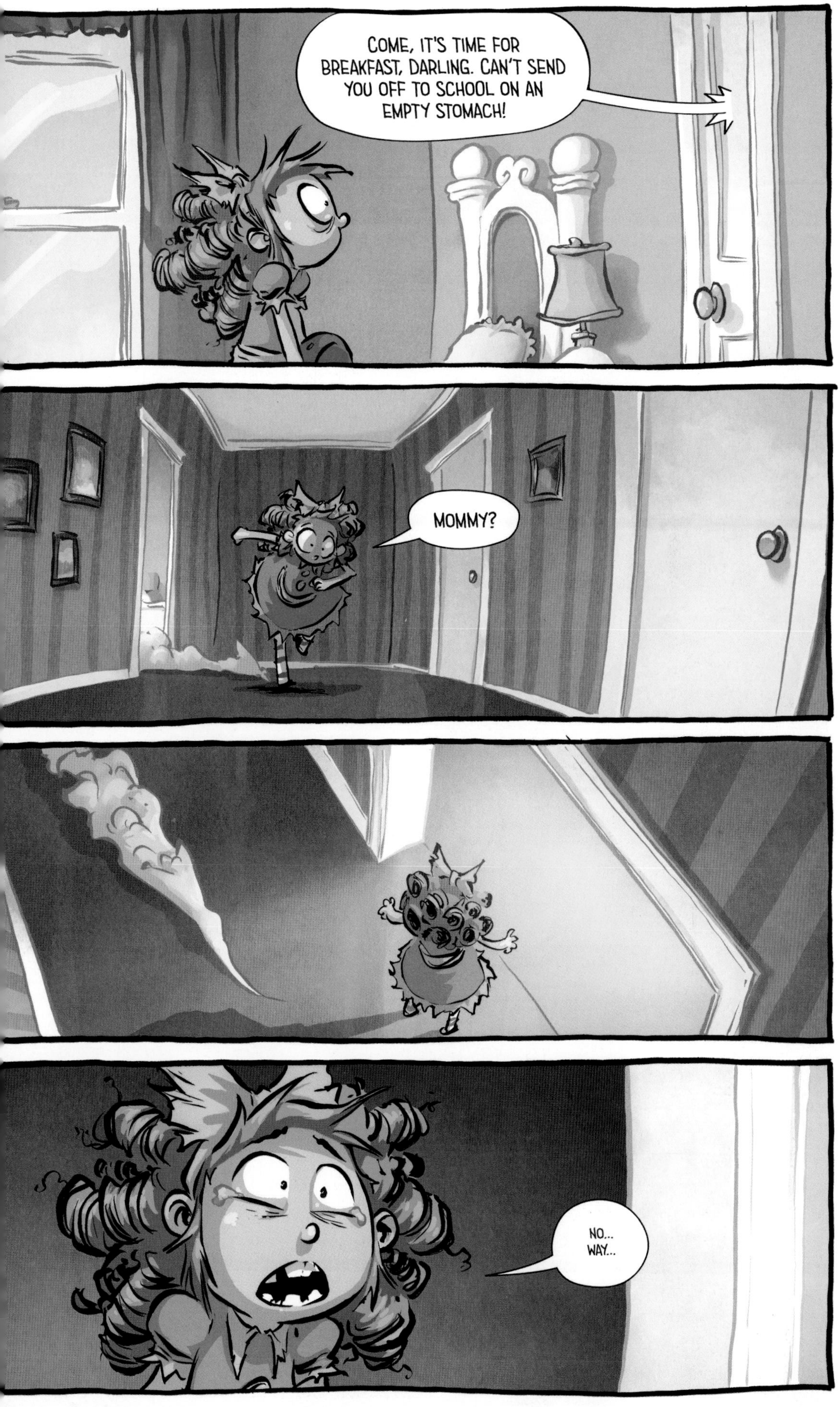
COME, IT'S TIME FOR BREAKFAST, DARLING. CAN'T SEND YOU OFF TO SCHOOL ON AN EMPTY STOMACH!
MOMMY?
NO... WAY...

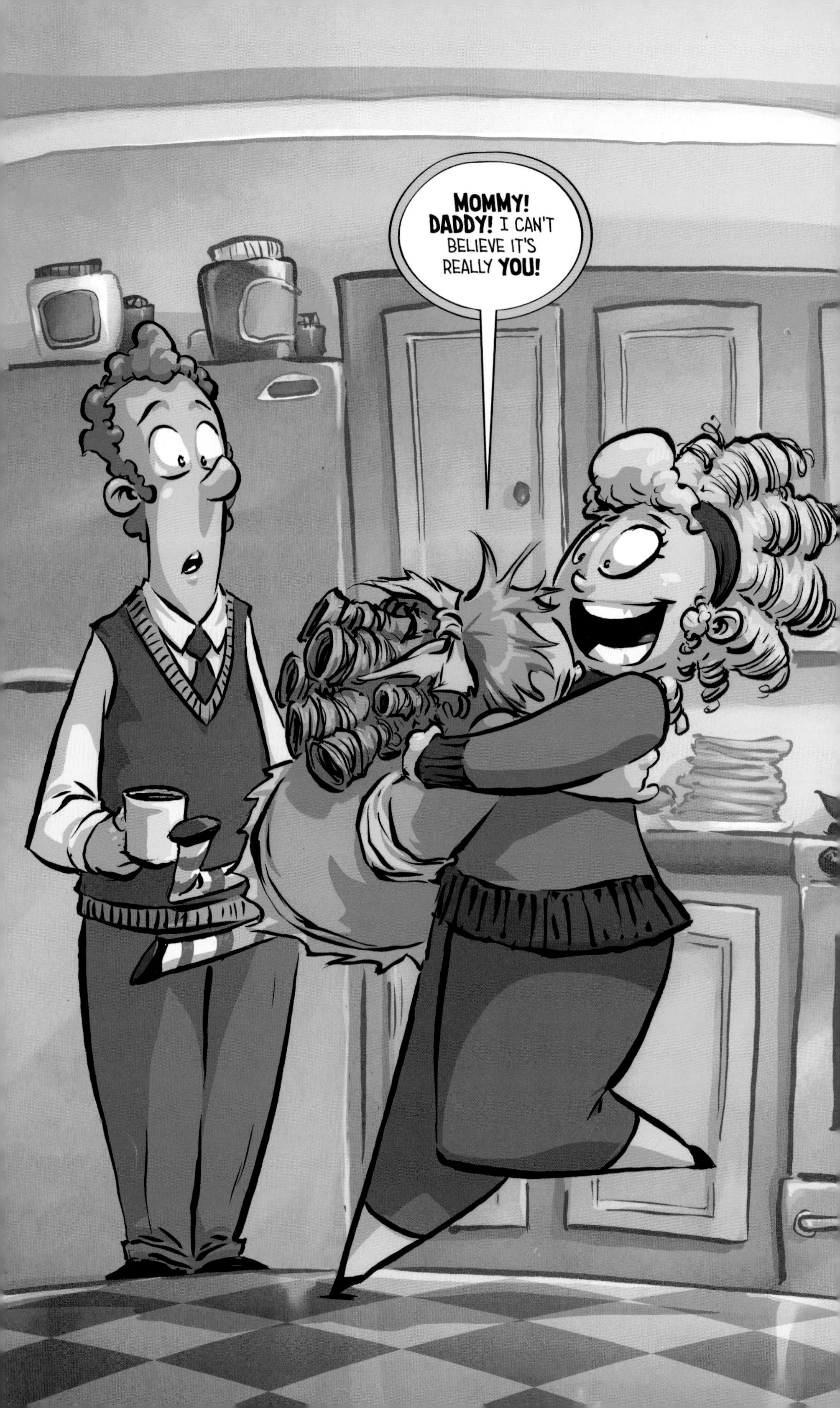
MOMMY! DADDY! I CAN'T BELIEVE IT'S REALLY YOU!

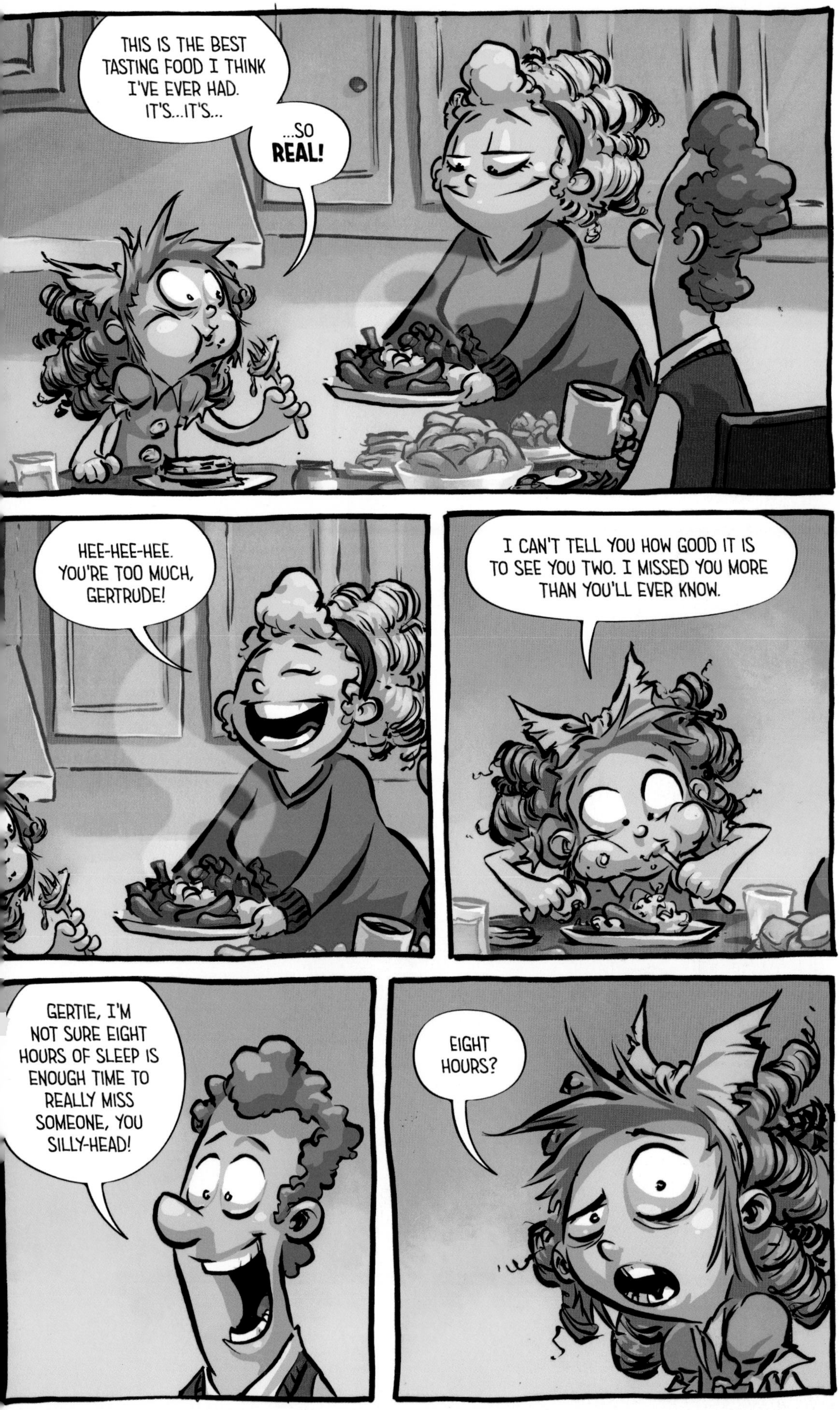
THIS IS THE BEST TASTING FOOD I THINK I'VE EVER HAD. IT'S...IT'S...
...SO **REAL!**
HEE-HEE-HEE. YOU'RE TOO MUCH, GERTRUDE!
I CAN'T TELL YOU HOW GOOD IT IS TO SEE YOU TWO. I MISSED YOU MORE THAN YOU'LL EVER KNOW.
GERTIE, I'M NOT SURE EIGHT HOURS OF SLEEP IS ENOUGH TIME TO REALLY MISS SOMEONE, YOU SILLY-HEAD!
EIGHT HOURS?

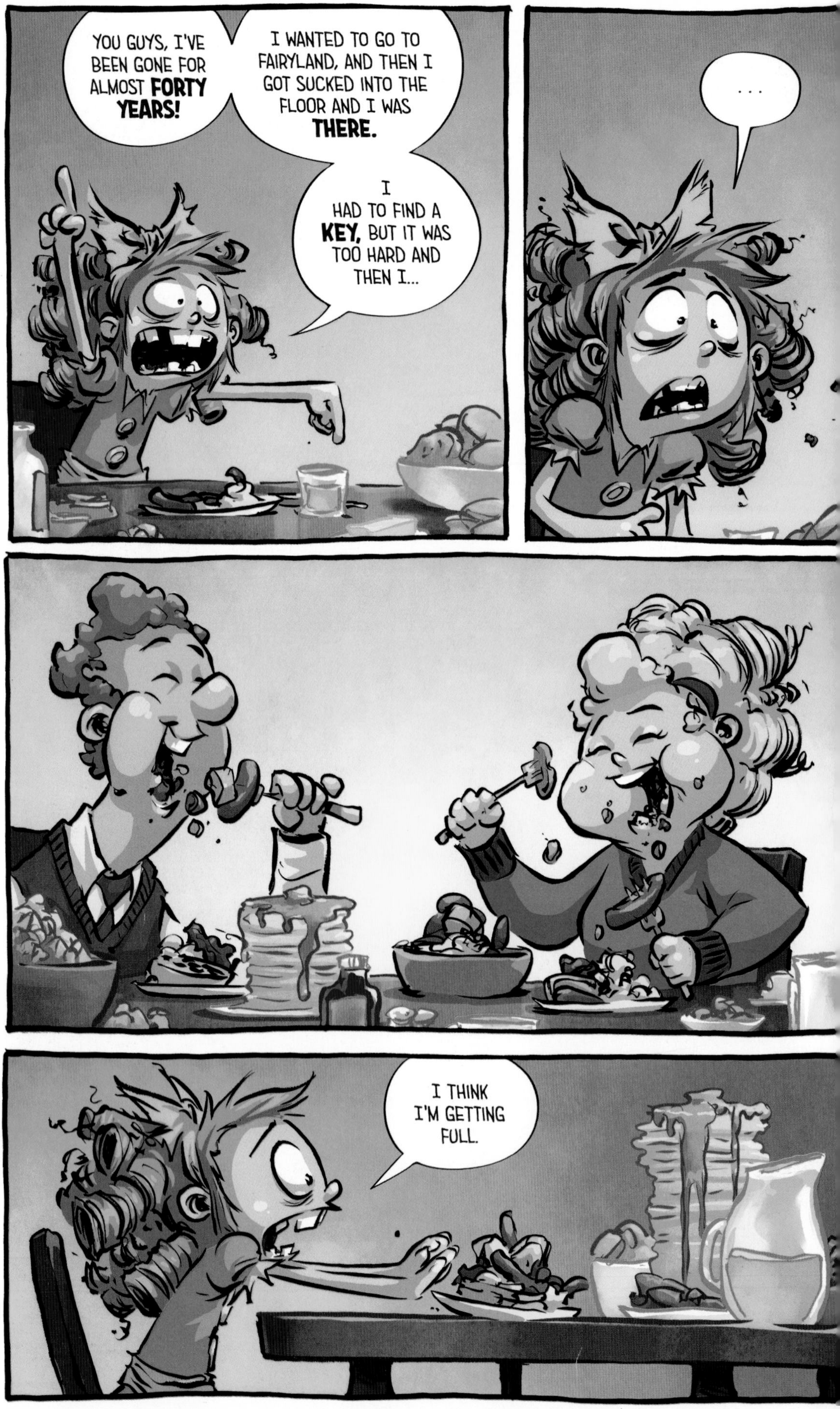

YOU GUYS, I'VE BEEN GONE FOR ALMOST **FORTY YEARS!**
I WANTED TO GO TO FAIRYLAND, AND THEN I GOT SUCKED INTO THE FLOOR AND I WAS **THERE.**
I HAD TO FIND A **KEY,** BUT IT WAS TOO HARD AND THEN I...
. . .
I THINK I'M GETTING FULL.

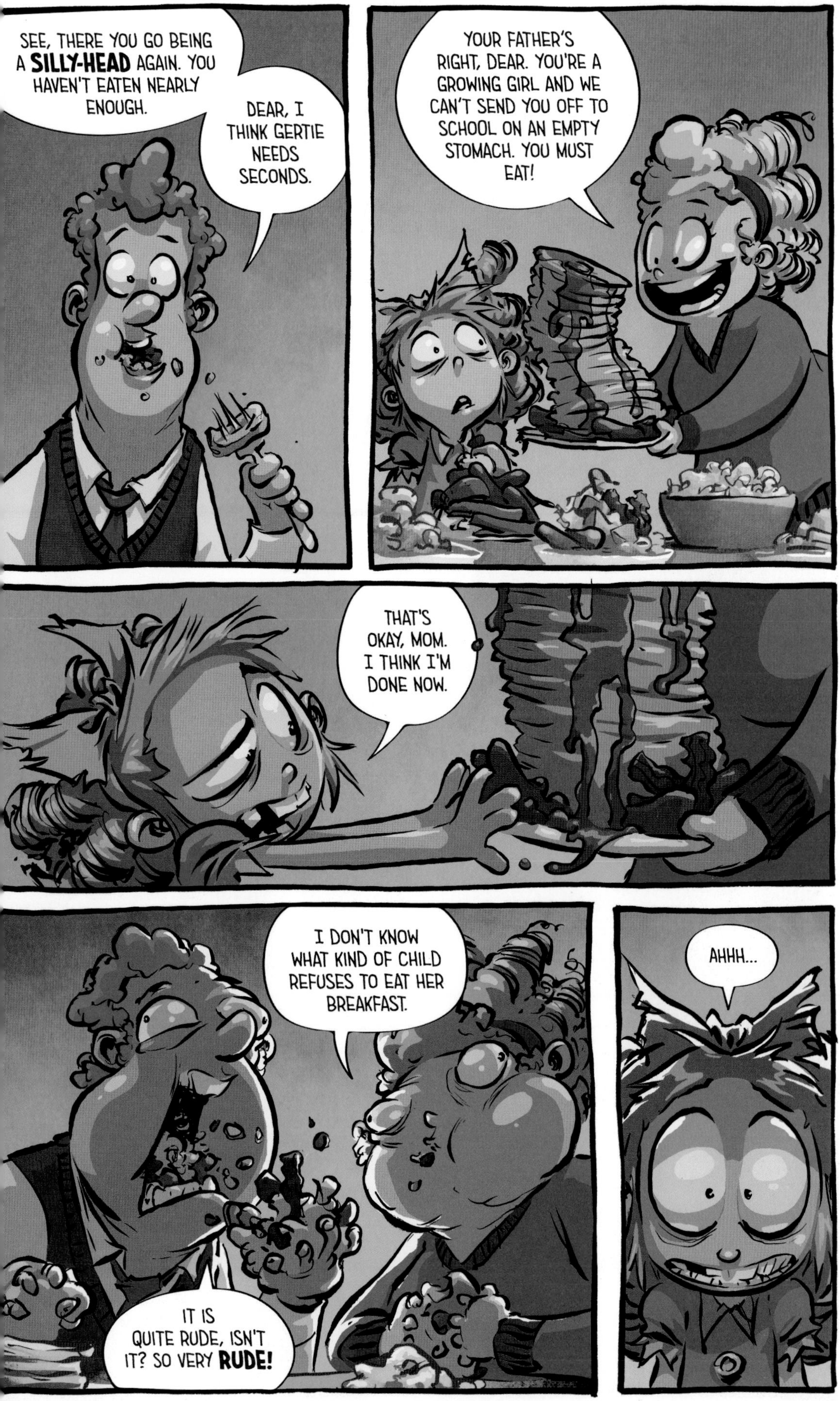
SEE, THERE YOU GO BEING A **SILLY-HEAD** AGAIN. YOU HAVEN'T EATEN NEARLY ENOUGH.
DEAR, I THINK GERTIE NEEDS SECONDS.
YOUR FATHER'S RIGHT, DEAR. YOU'RE A GROWING GIRL AND WE CAN'T SEND YOU OFF TO SCHOOL ON AN EMPTY STOMACH. YOU MUST EAT!
THAT'S OKAY, MOM. I THINK I'M DONE NOW.
I DON'T KNOW WHAT KIND OF CHILD REFUSES TO EAT HER BREAKFAST.
IT IS QUITE RUDE, ISN'T IT? SO VERY **RUDE!**
AHHH...

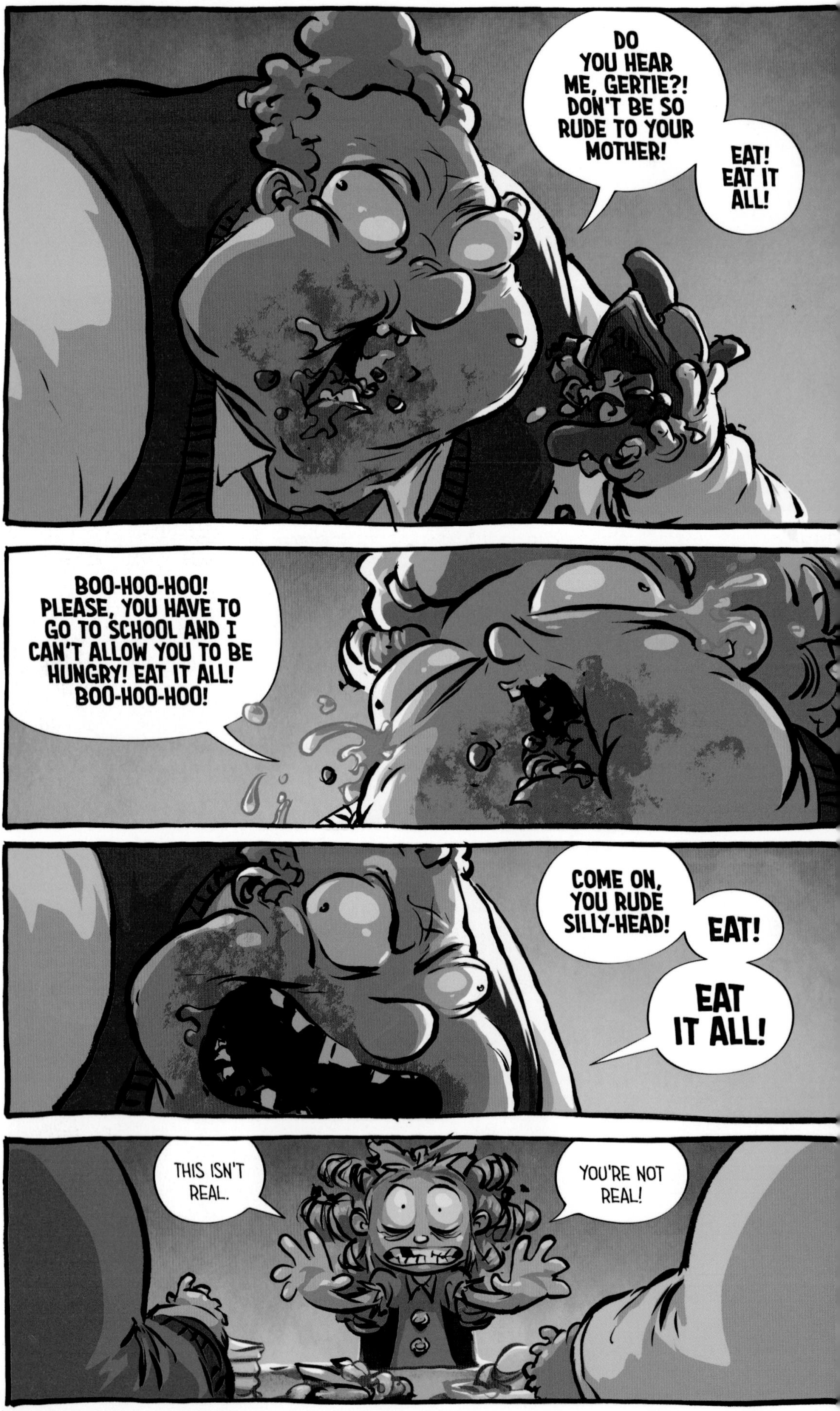

DO YOU HEAR ME, GERTIE?! DON'T BE SO RUDE TO YOUR MOTHER!
EAT! EAT IT ALL!
BOO-HOO-HOO! PLEASE, YOU HAVE TO GO TO SCHOOL AND I CAN'T ALLOW YOU TO BE HUNGRY! EAT IT ALL! BOO-HOO-HOO!
COME ON, YOU RUDE SILLY-HEAD!
EAT!
EAT IT ALL!
THIS ISN'T REAL.
YOU'RE NOT REAL!

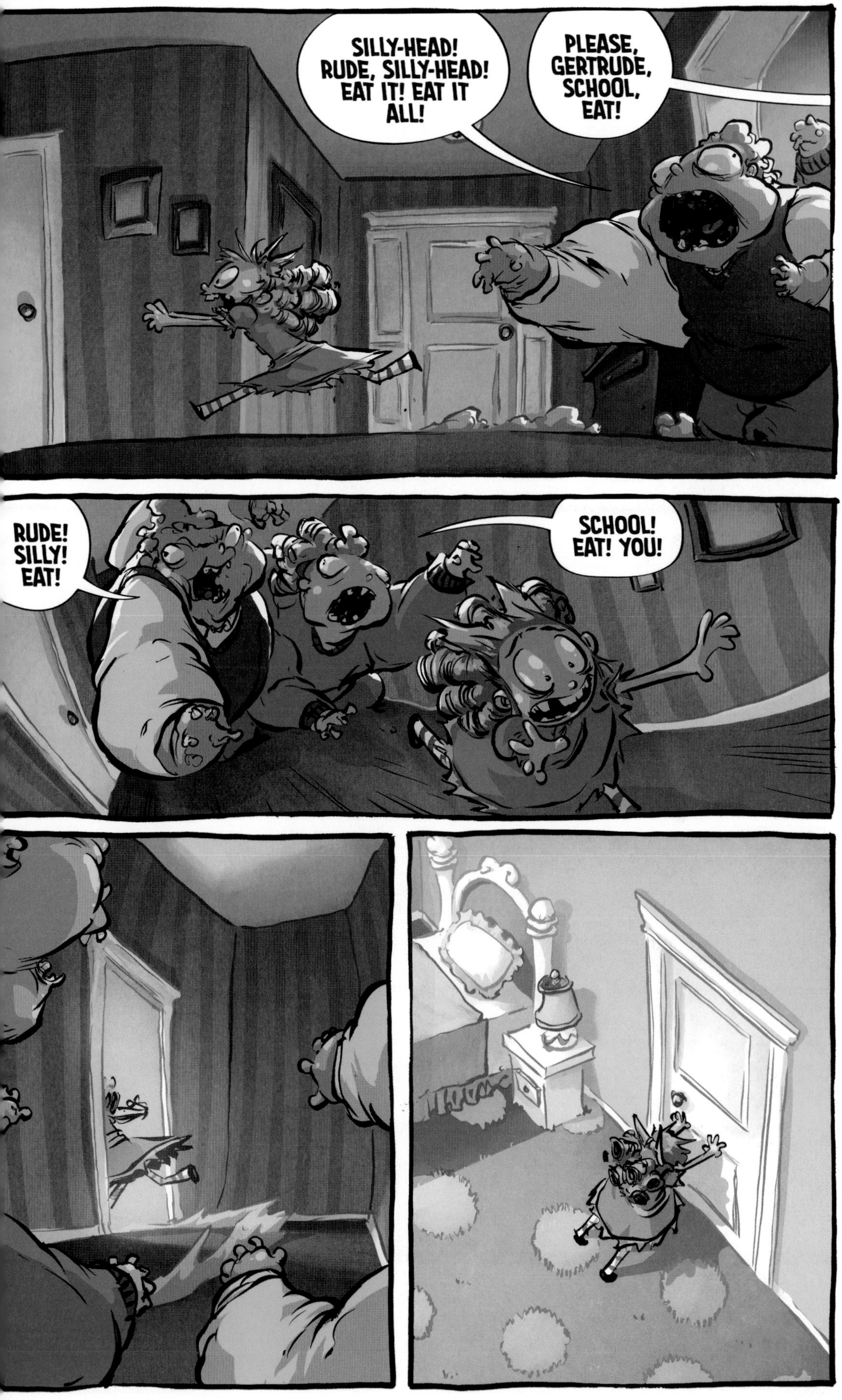
SILLY-HEAD! RUDE, SILLY-HEAD! EAT IT! EAT IT ALL!
PLEASE, GERTRUDE, SCHOOL, EAT!
RUDE! SILLY! EAT!
SCHOOL! EAT! YOU!

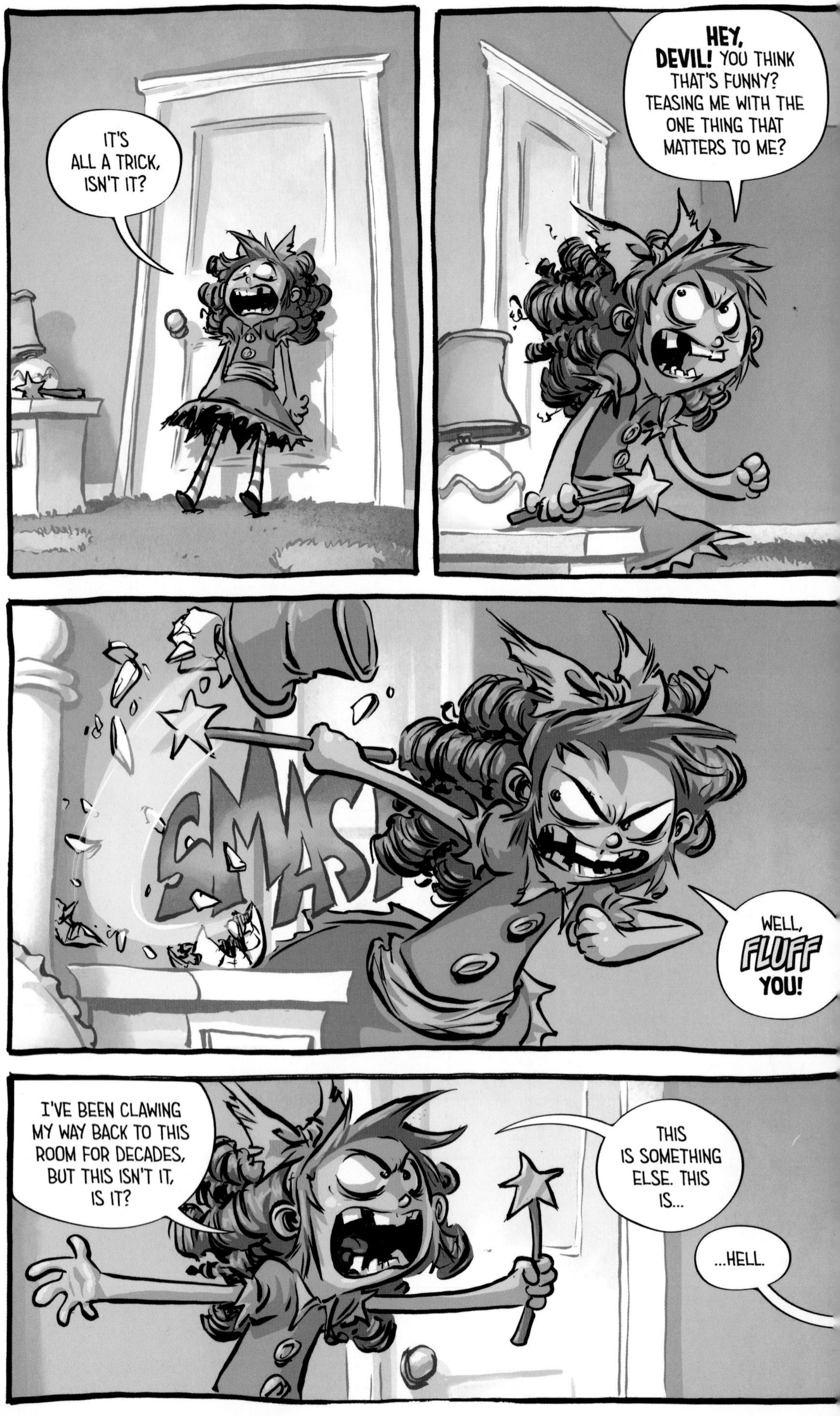
IT'S ALL A TRICK, ISN'T IT?
HEY, DEVIL! YOU THINK THAT'S FUNNY? TEASING ME WITH THE ONE THING THAT MATTERS TO ME?
SMASH
WELL, FLUFF YOU!
I'VE BEEN CLAWING MY WAY BACK TO THIS ROOM FOR DECADES, BUT THIS ISN'T IT, IS IT?
THIS IS SOMETHING ELSE. THIS IS...
...HELL.

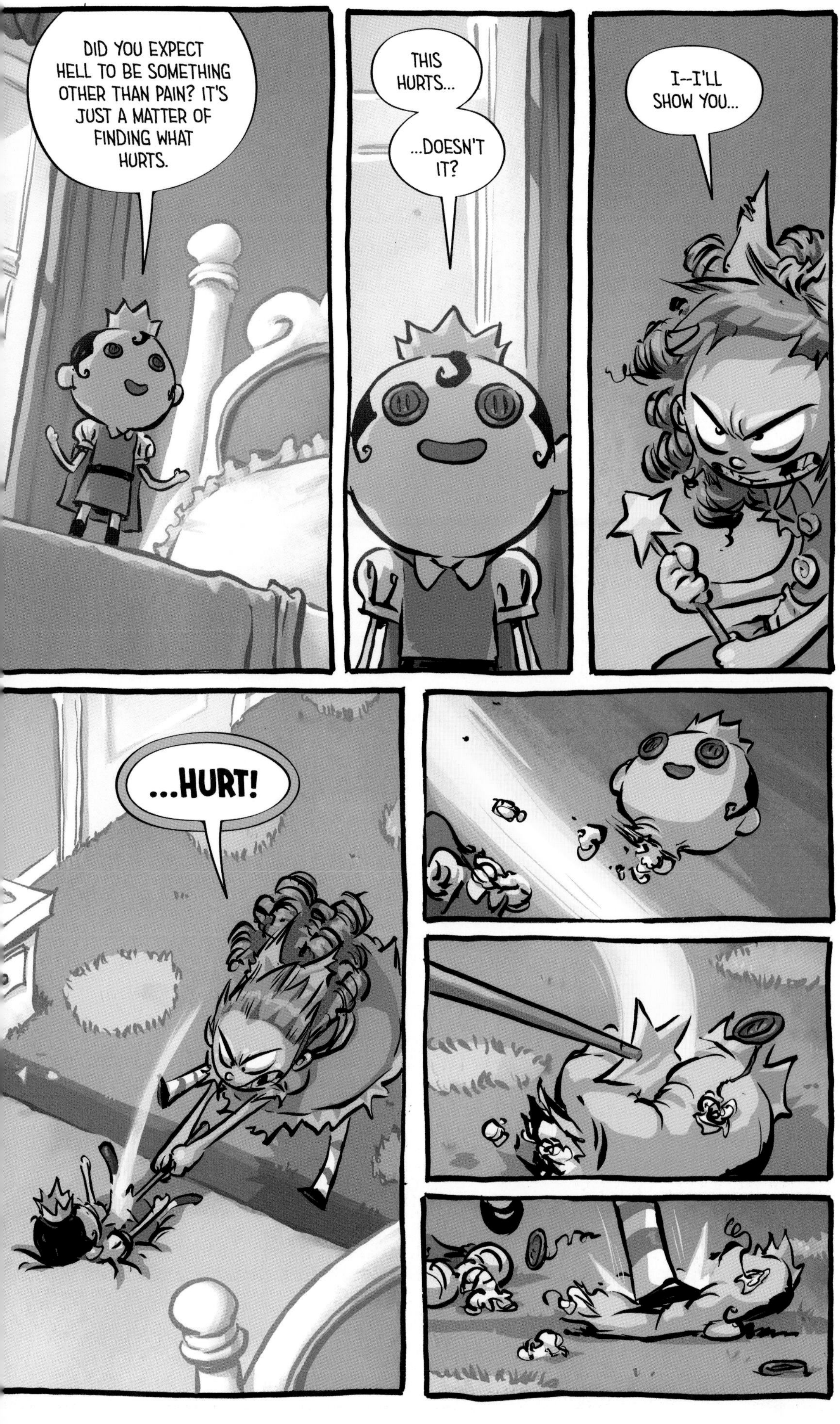

DID YOU EXPECT HELL TO BE SOMETHING OTHER THAN PAIN? IT'S JUST A MATTER OF FINDING WHAT HURTS.
THIS HURTS...
...DOESN'T IT?
I--I'LL SHOW YOU...
...HURT!

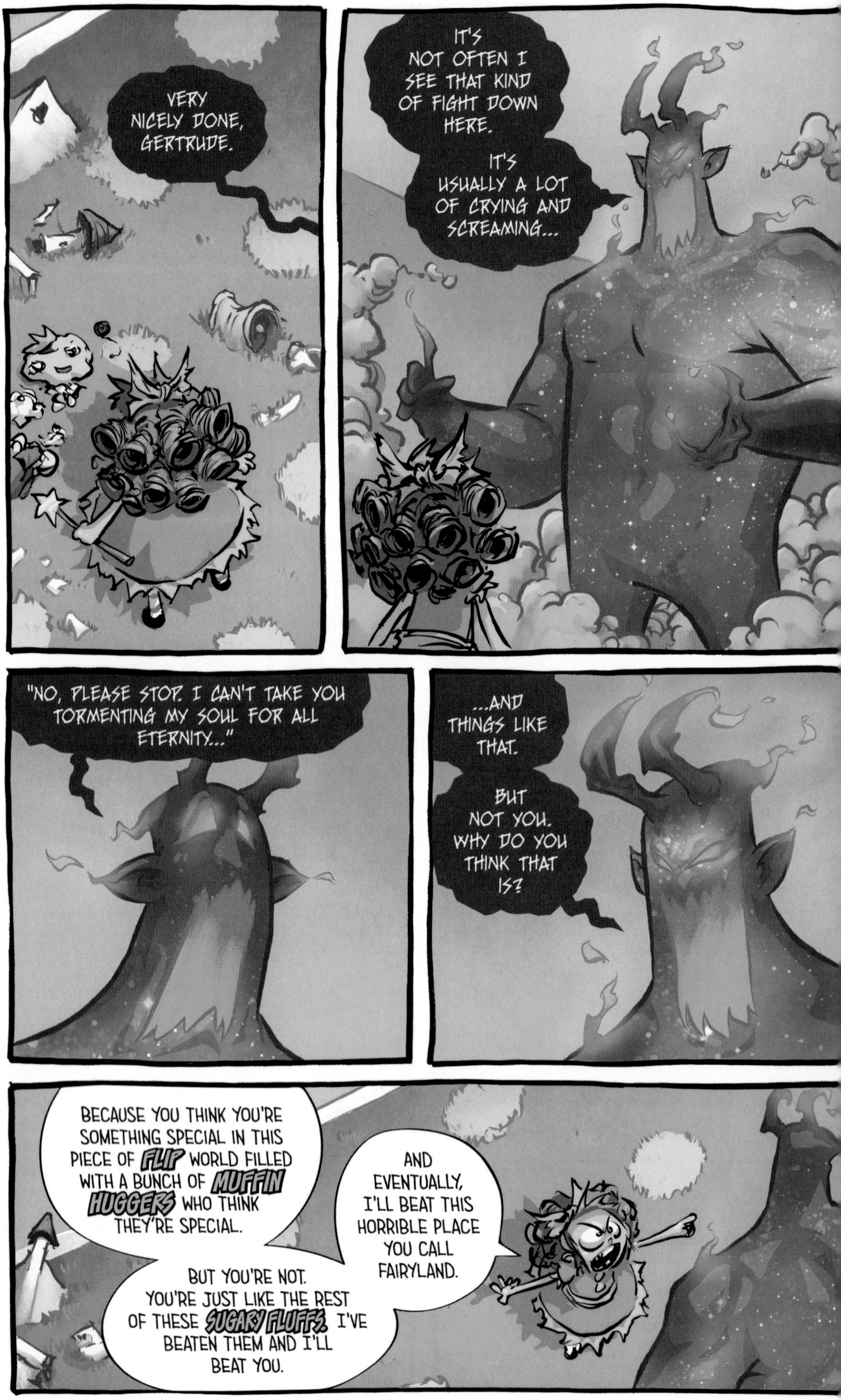
VERY NICELY DONE, GERTRUDE.
IT'S NOT OFTEN I SEE THAT KIND OF FIGHT DOWN HERE.
IT'S USUALLY A LOT OF CRYING AND SCREAMING...
"NO, PLEASE STOP. I CAN'T TAKE YOU TORMENTING MY SOUL FOR ALL ETERNITY..."
...AND THINGS LIKE THAT.
BUT NOT YOU. WHY DO YOU THINK THAT IS?
BECAUSE YOU THINK YOU'RE SOMETHING SPECIAL IN THIS PIECE OF FLIP WORLD FILLED WITH A BUNCH OF MUFFIN HUGGERS WHO THINK THEY'RE SPECIAL.
BUT YOU'RE NOT. YOU'RE JUST LIKE THE REST OF THESE SUGARY FLUFFS. I'VE BEATEN THEM AND I'LL BEAT YOU.
AND EVENTUALLY, I'LL BEAT THIS HORRIBLE PLACE YOU CALL FAIRYLAND.

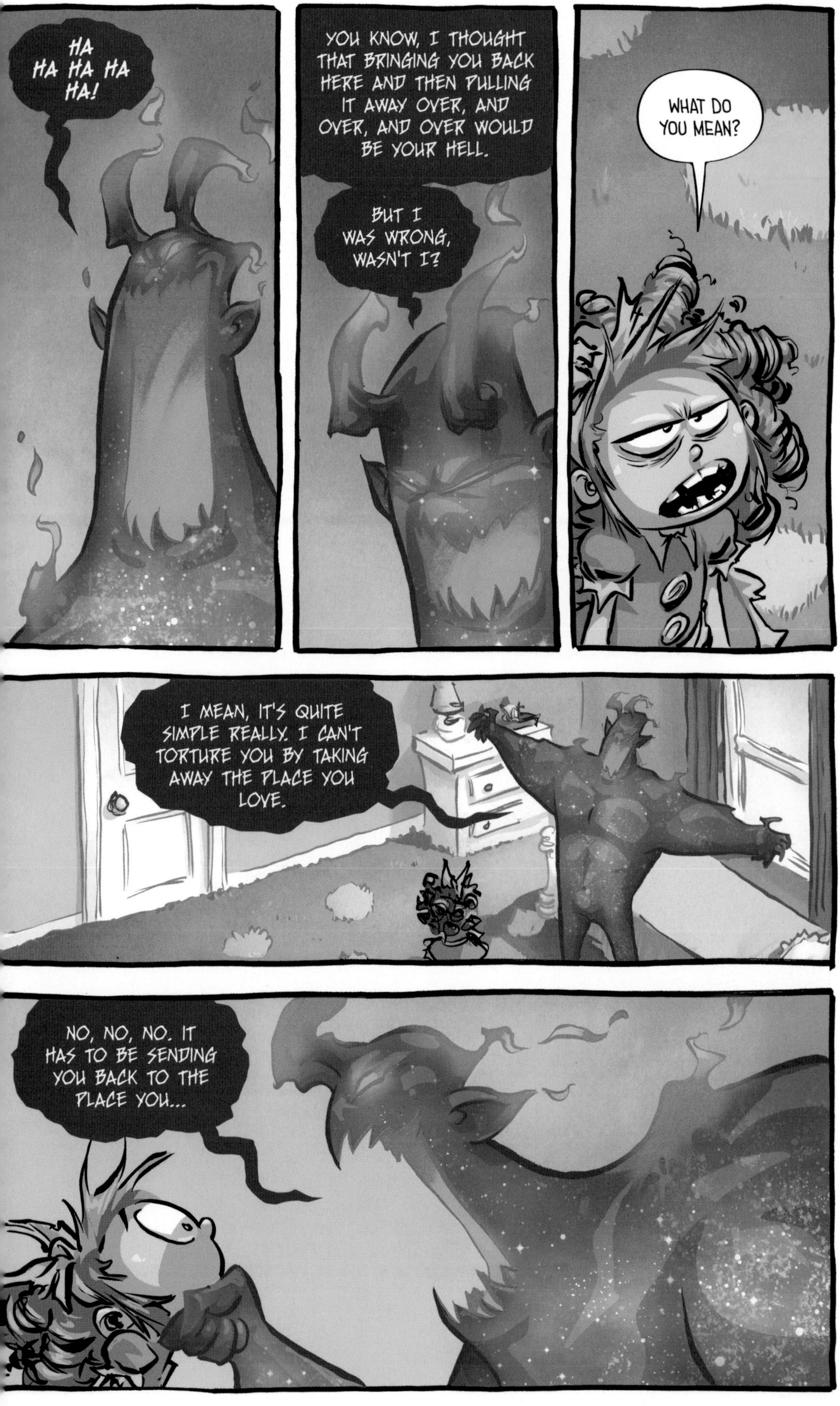
HA HA HA HA HA!
YOU KNOW, I THOUGHT THAT BRINGING YOU BACK HERE AND THEN PULLING IT AWAY OVER, AND OVER, AND OVER WOULD BE YOUR HELL.
BUT I WAS WRONG, WASN'T I?
WHAT DO YOU MEAN?
I MEAN, IT'S QUITE SIMPLE REALLY. I CAN'T TORTURE YOU BY TAKING AWAY THE PLACE YOU LOVE.
NO, NO, NO. IT HAS TO BE SENDING YOU BACK TO THE PLACE YOU...

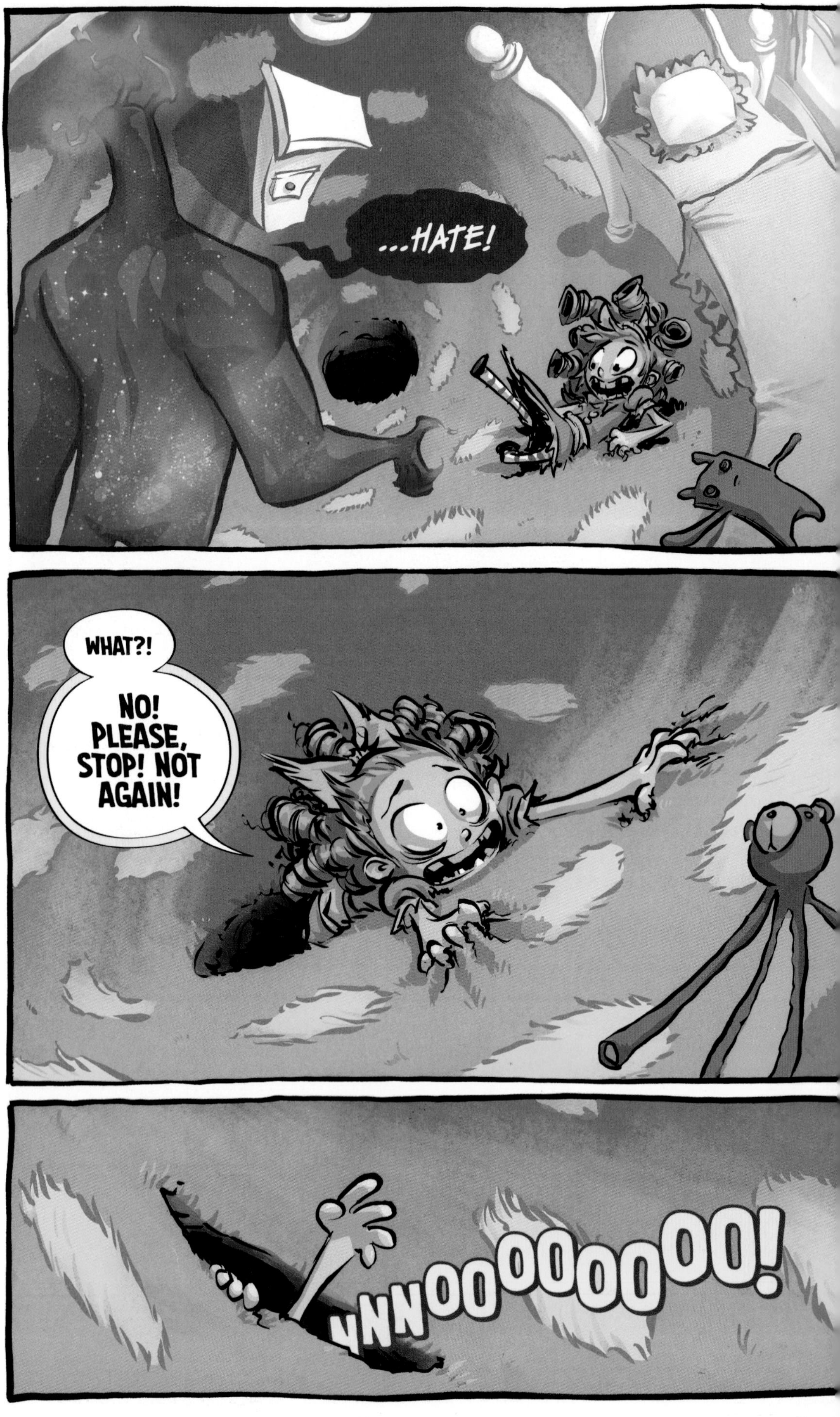
...HATE!
WHAT?!
NO! PLEASE, STOP! NOT AGAIN!
NNOOOOOOOOOO!

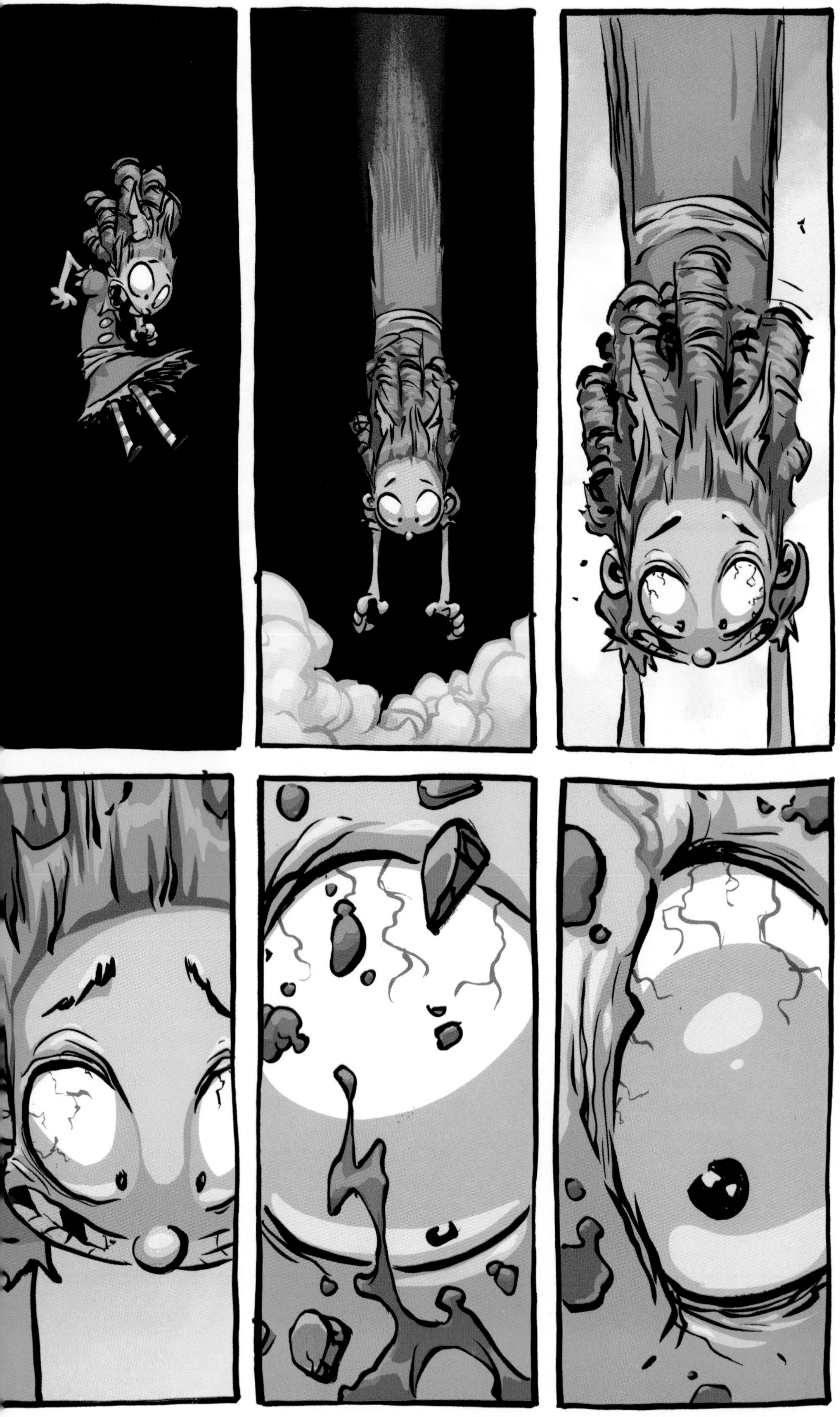

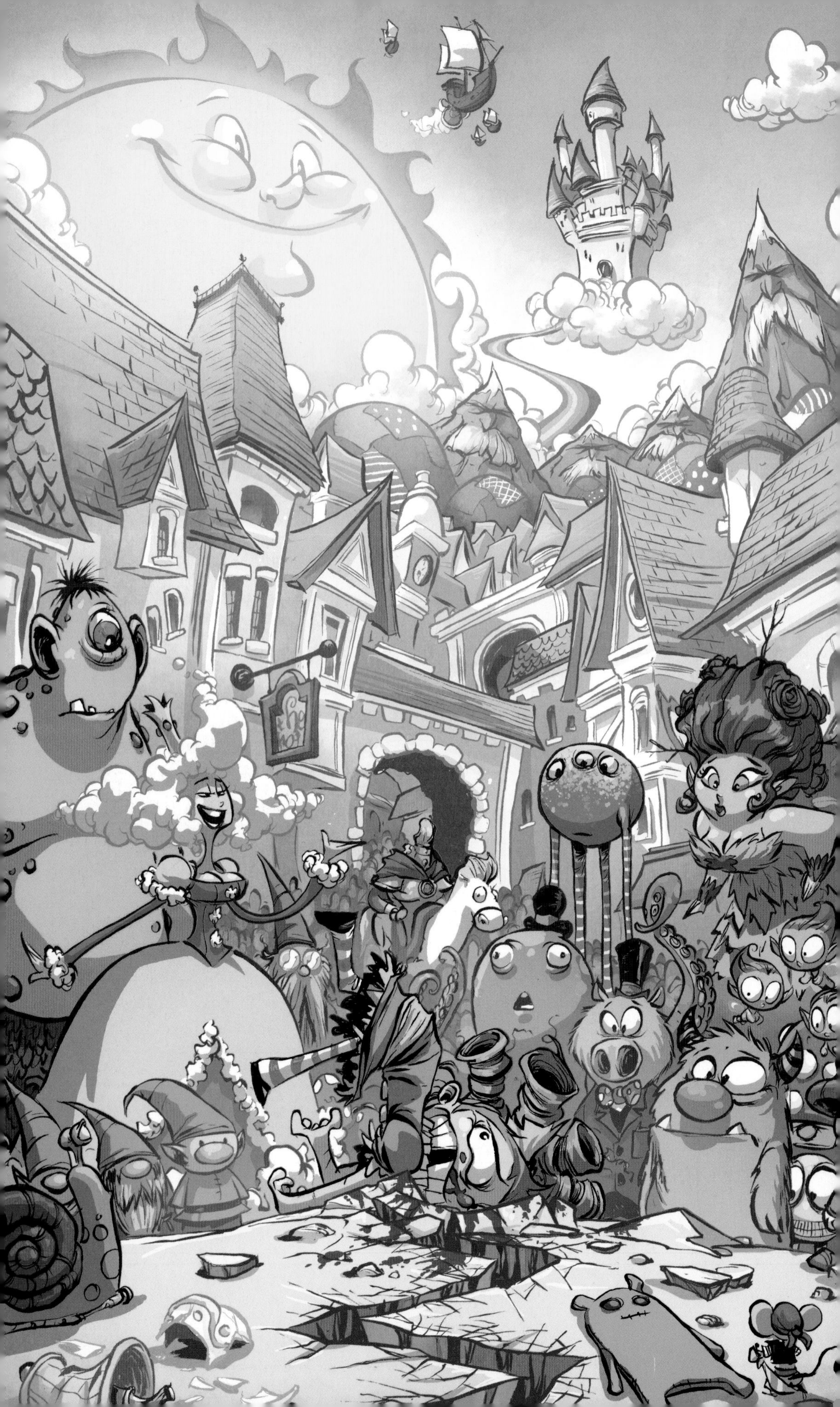

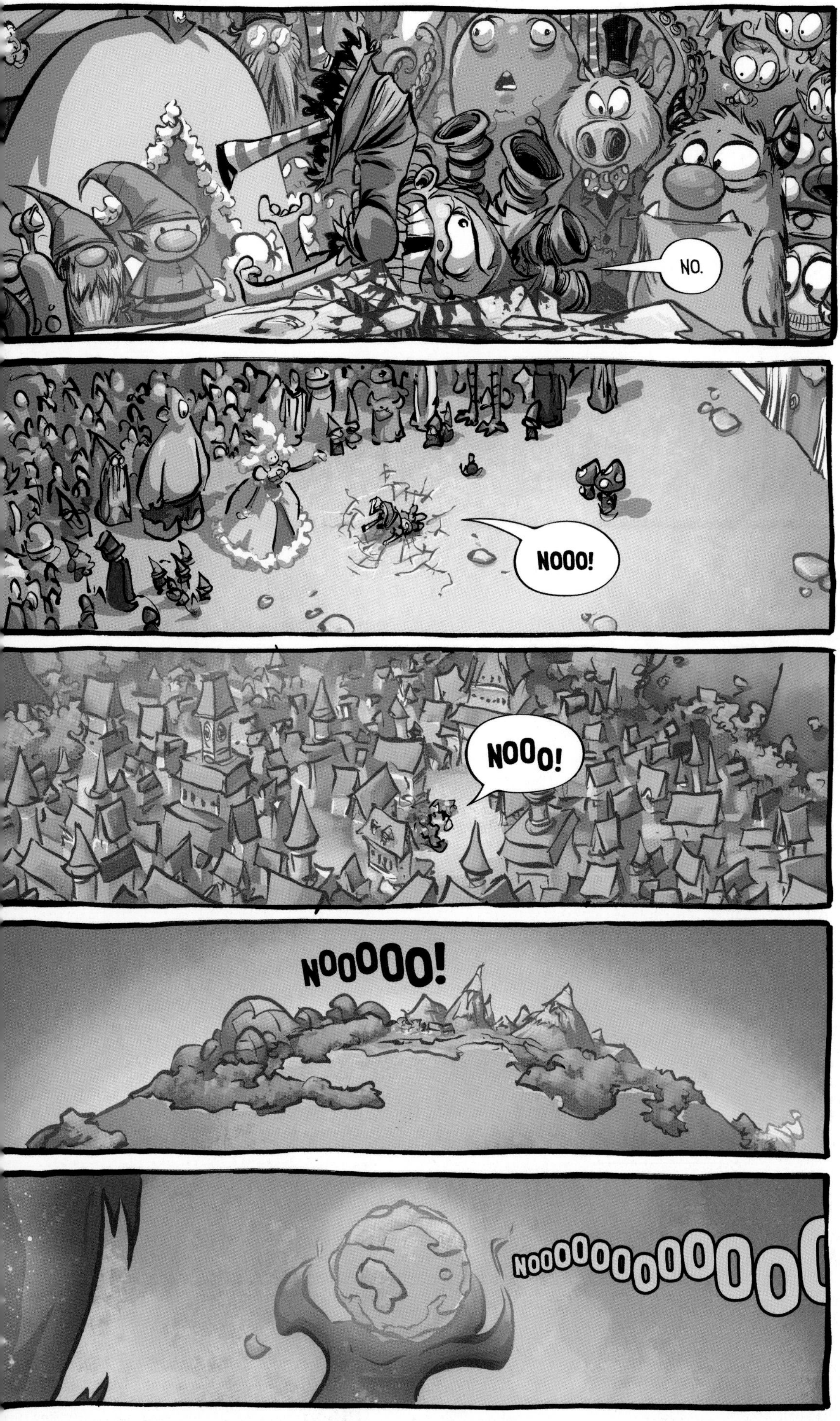
NO.
NOOO!
NOOO!
NOOOOO!
NOOOOOOOOOOOOO

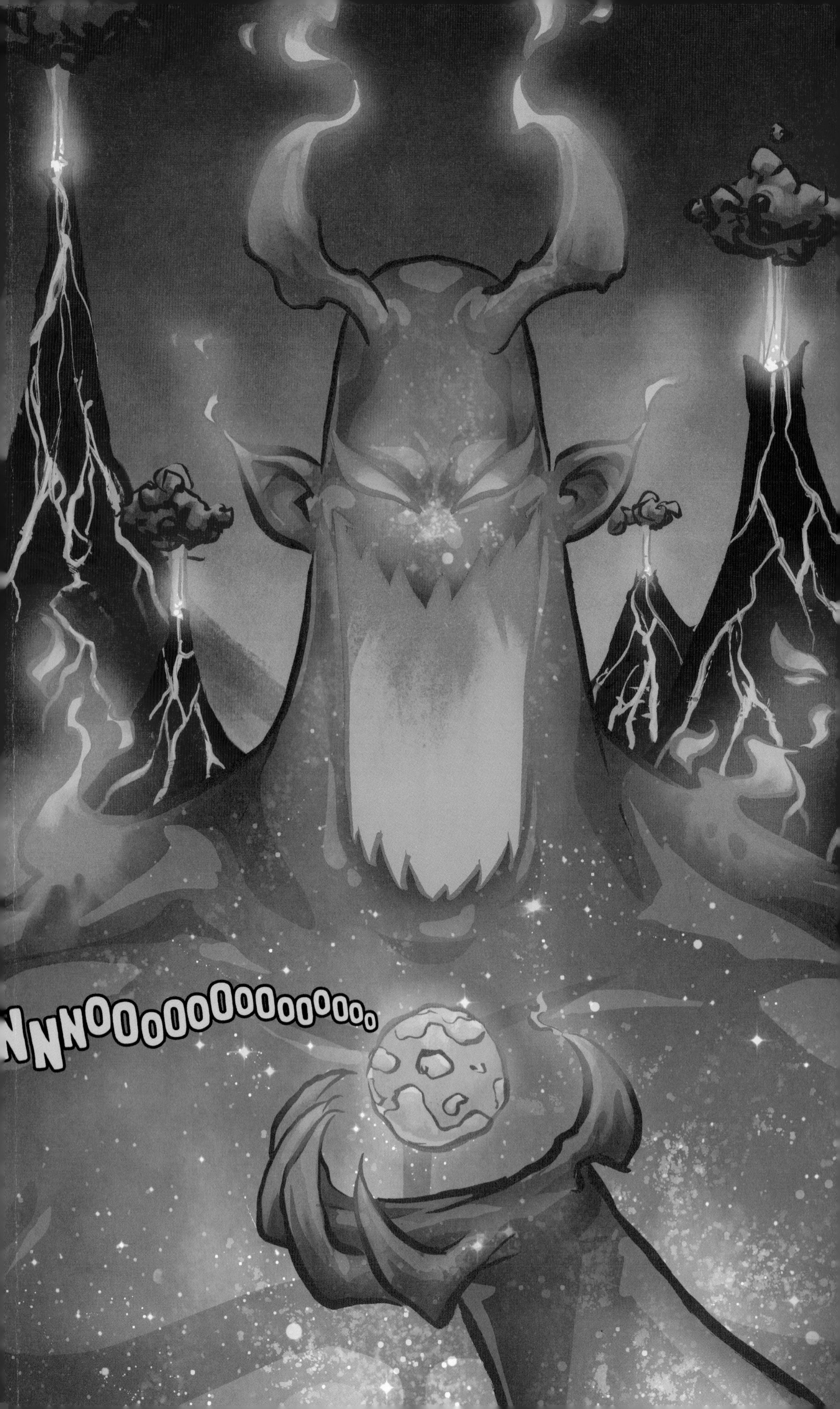
NNNOOOOOOOOOOOOOOOo

SEVENTEEN

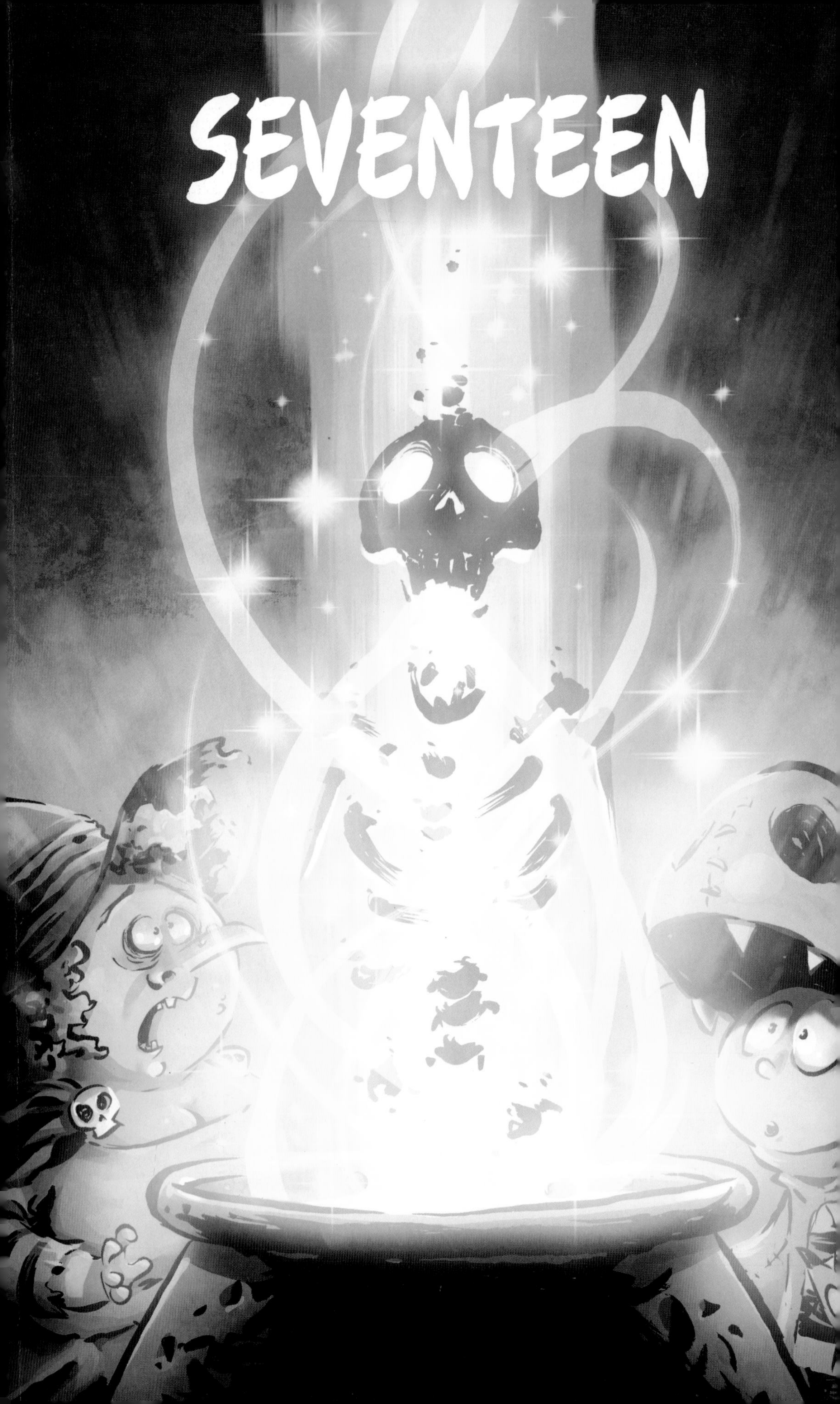

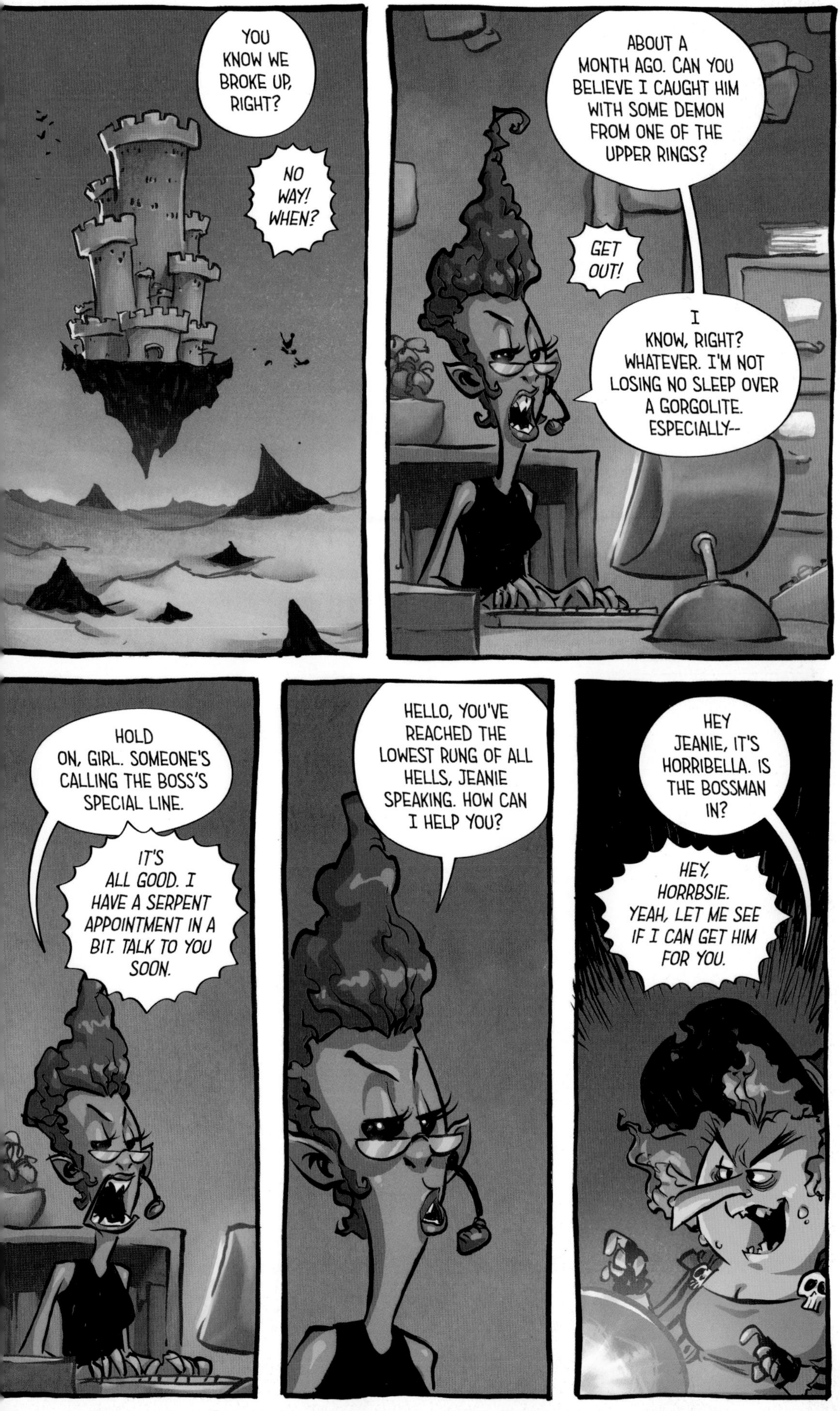
YOU KNOW WE BROKE UP, RIGHT?
NO WAY! WHEN?
ABOUT A MONTH AGO. CAN YOU BELIEVE I CAUGHT HIM WITH SOME DEMON FROM ONE OF THE UPPER RINGS?
GET OUT!
I KNOW, RIGHT? WHATEVER. I'M NOT LOSING NO SLEEP OVER A GORGOLITE. ESPECIALLY--
HOLD ON, GIRL. SOMEONE'S CALLING THE BOSS'S SPECIAL LINE.
IT'S ALL GOOD. I HAVE A SERPENT APPOINTMENT IN A BIT. TALK TO YOU SOON.
HELLO, YOU'VE REACHED THE LOWEST RUNG OF ALL HELLS, JEANIE SPEAKING. HOW CAN I HELP YOU?
HEY JEANIE, IT'S HORRIBELLA. IS THE BOSSMAN IN?
HEY, HORRBSIE. YEAH, LET ME SEE IF I CAN GET HIM FOR YOU.

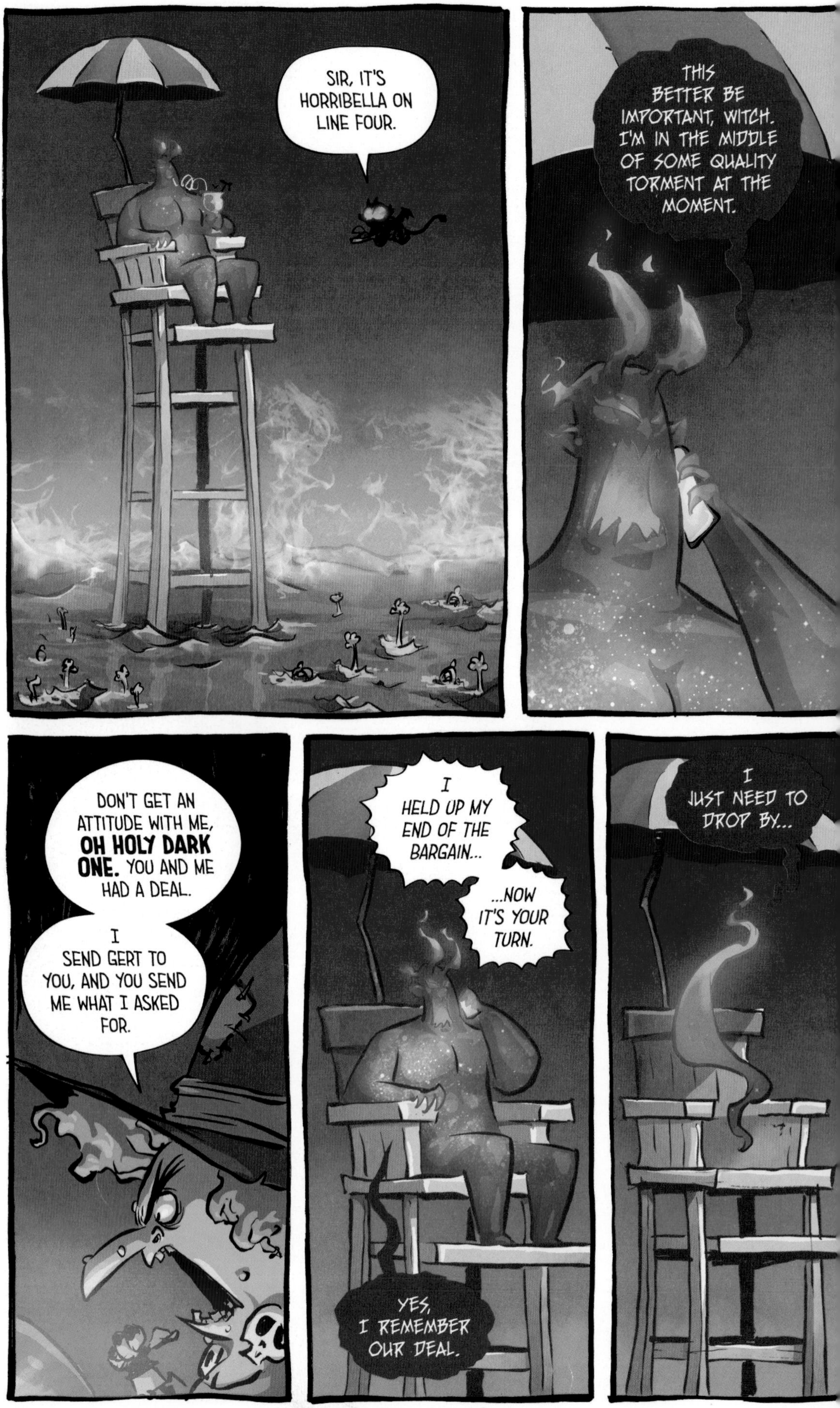
SIR, IT'S HORRIBELLA ON LINE FOUR.
THIS BETTER BE IMPORTANT, WITCH. I'M IN THE MIDDLE OF SOME QUALITY TORMENT AT THE MOMENT.
DON'T GET AN ATTITUDE WITH ME, OH HOLY DARK ONE. YOU AND ME HAD A DEAL.
I SEND GERT TO YOU, AND YOU SEND ME WHAT I ASKED FOR.
I HELD UP MY END OF THE BARGAIN...
...NOW IT'S YOUR TURN.
YES, I REMEMBER OUR DEAL.
I JUST NEED TO DROP BY...

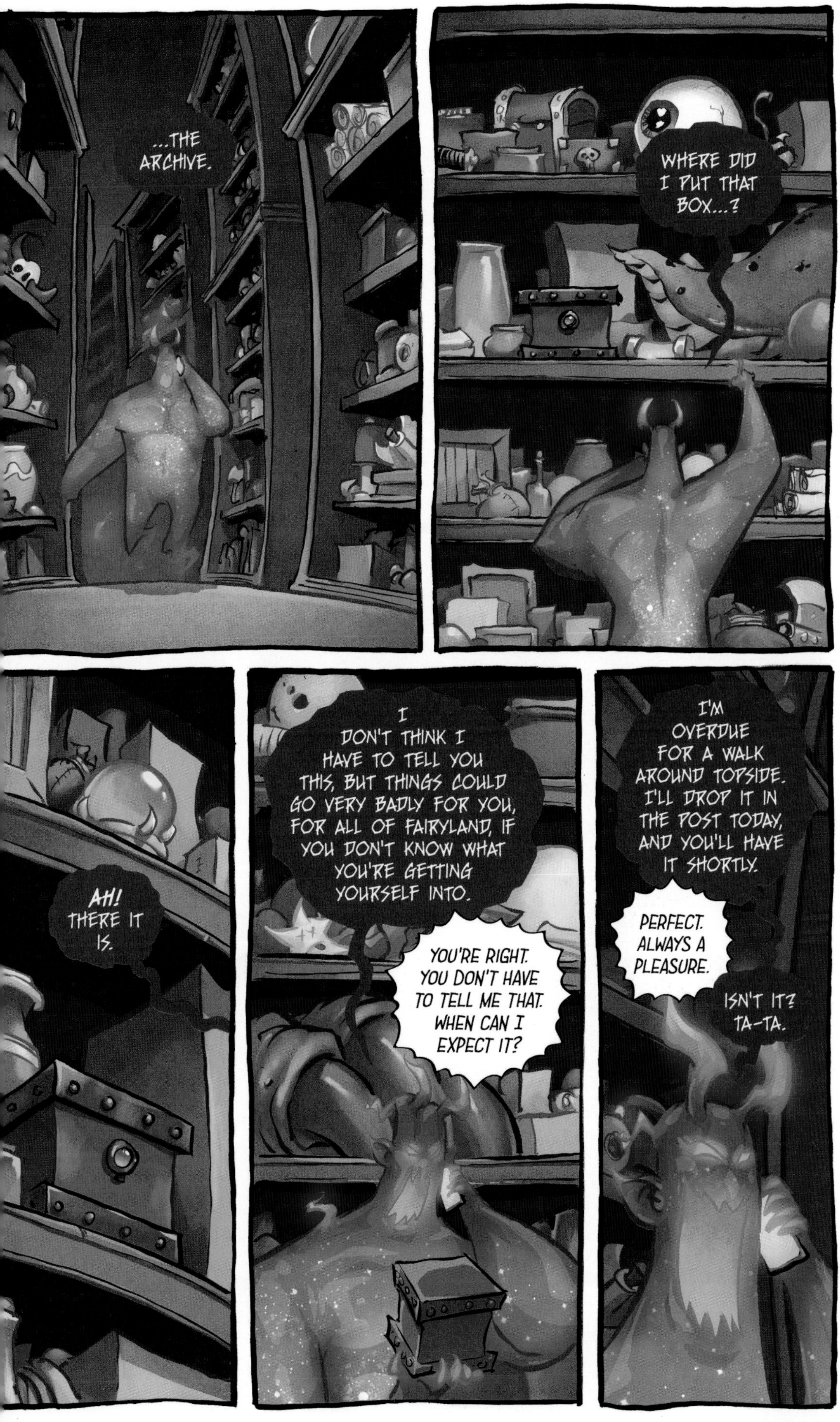
...THE ARCHIVE.
WHERE DID I PUT THAT BOX...?
AH! THERE IT IS.
I DON'T THINK I HAVE TO TELL YOU THIS, BUT THINGS COULD GO VERY BADLY FOR YOU, FOR ALL OF FAIRYLAND, IF YOU DON'T KNOW WHAT YOU'RE GETTING YOURSELF INTO.
YOU'RE RIGHT. YOU DON'T HAVE TO TELL ME THAT. WHEN CAN I EXPECT IT?
I'M OVERDUE FOR A WALK AROUND TOPSIDE. I'LL DROP IT IN THE POST TODAY, AND YOU'LL HAVE IT SHORTLY.
PERFECT. ALWAYS A PLEASURE.
ISN'T IT? TA-TA.

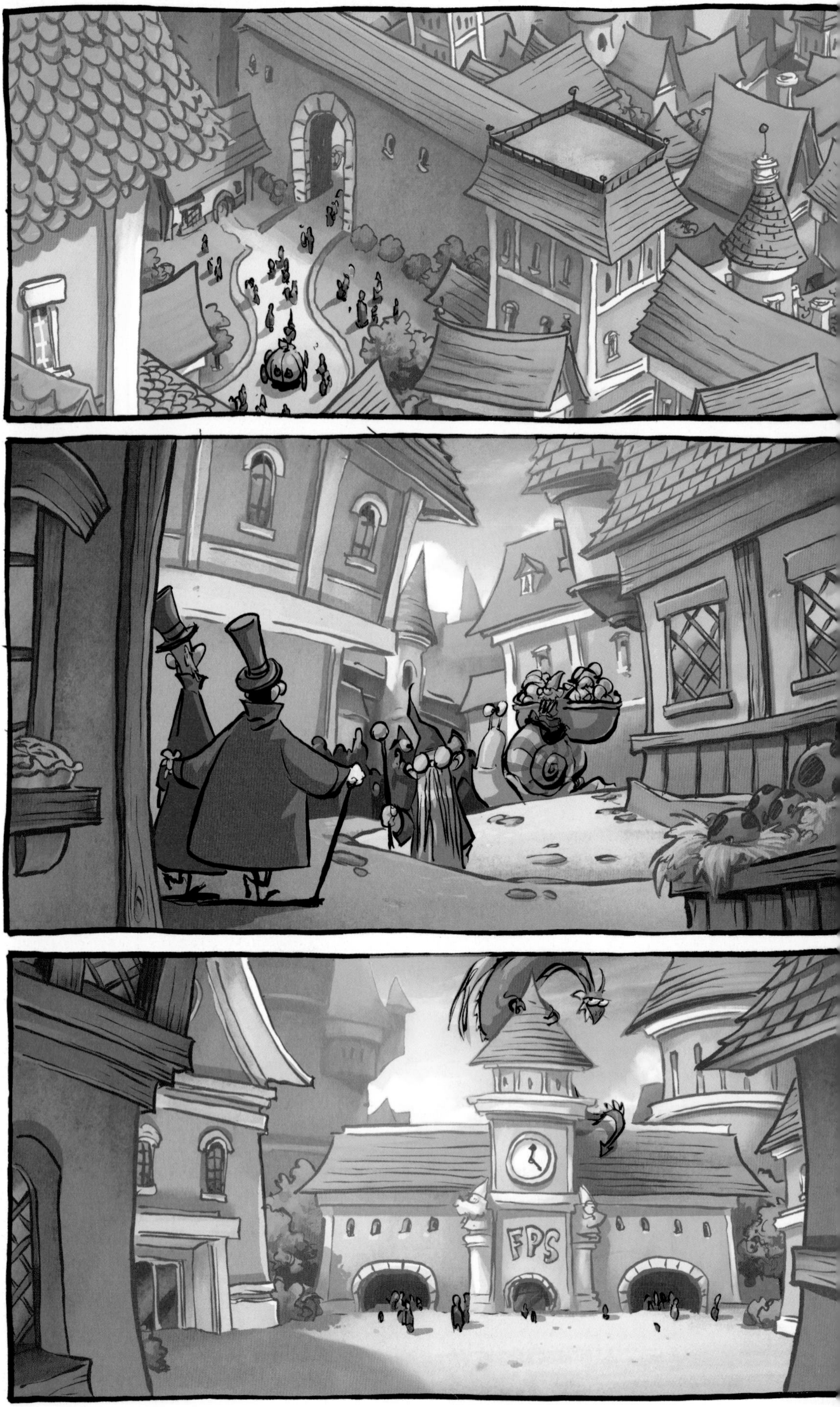
FPS

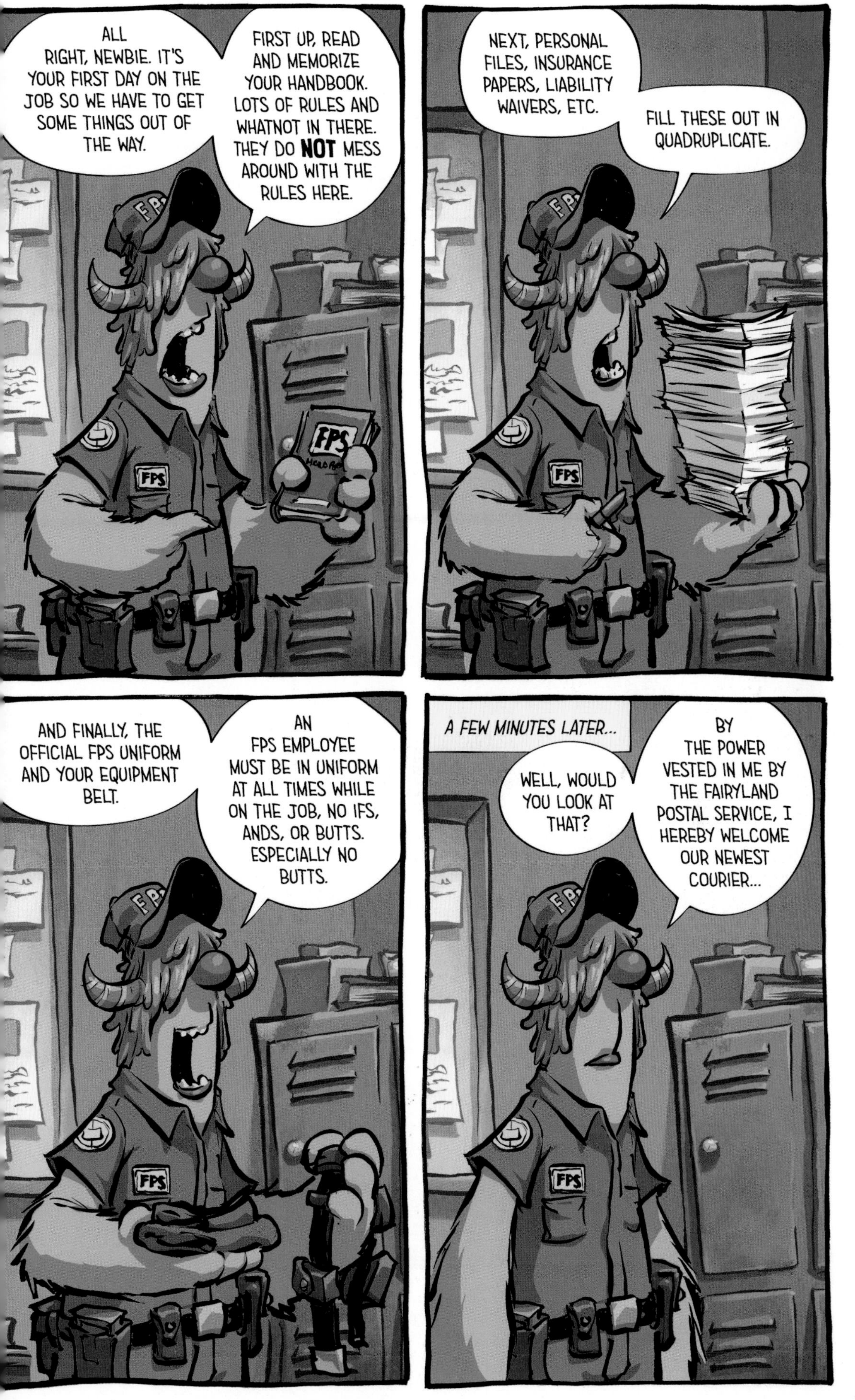

ALL RIGHT, NEWBIE. IT'S YOUR FIRST DAY ON THE JOB SO WE HAVE TO GET SOME THINGS OUT OF THE WAY.
FIRST UP, READ AND MEMORIZE YOUR HANDBOOK. LOTS OF RULES AND WHATNOT IN THERE. THEY DO **NOT** MESS AROUND WITH THE RULES HERE.
FPS
FPS
NEXT, PERSONAL FILES, INSURANCE PAPERS, LIABILITY WAIVERS, ETC.
FILL THESE OUT IN QUADRUPLICATE.
FPS
FPS
AND FINALLY, THE OFFICIAL FPS UNIFORM AND YOUR EQUIPMENT BELT.
AN FPS EMPLOYEE MUST BE IN UNIFORM AT ALL TIMES WHILE ON THE JOB, NO IFS, ANDS, OR BUTTS. ESPECIALLY NO BUTTS.
FPS
FPS
A FEW MINUTES LATER...
WELL, WOULD YOU LOOK AT THAT?
BY THE POWER VESTED IN ME BY THE FAIRYLAND POSTAL SERVICE, I HEREBY WELCOME OUR NEWEST COURIER...
FPS
FPS

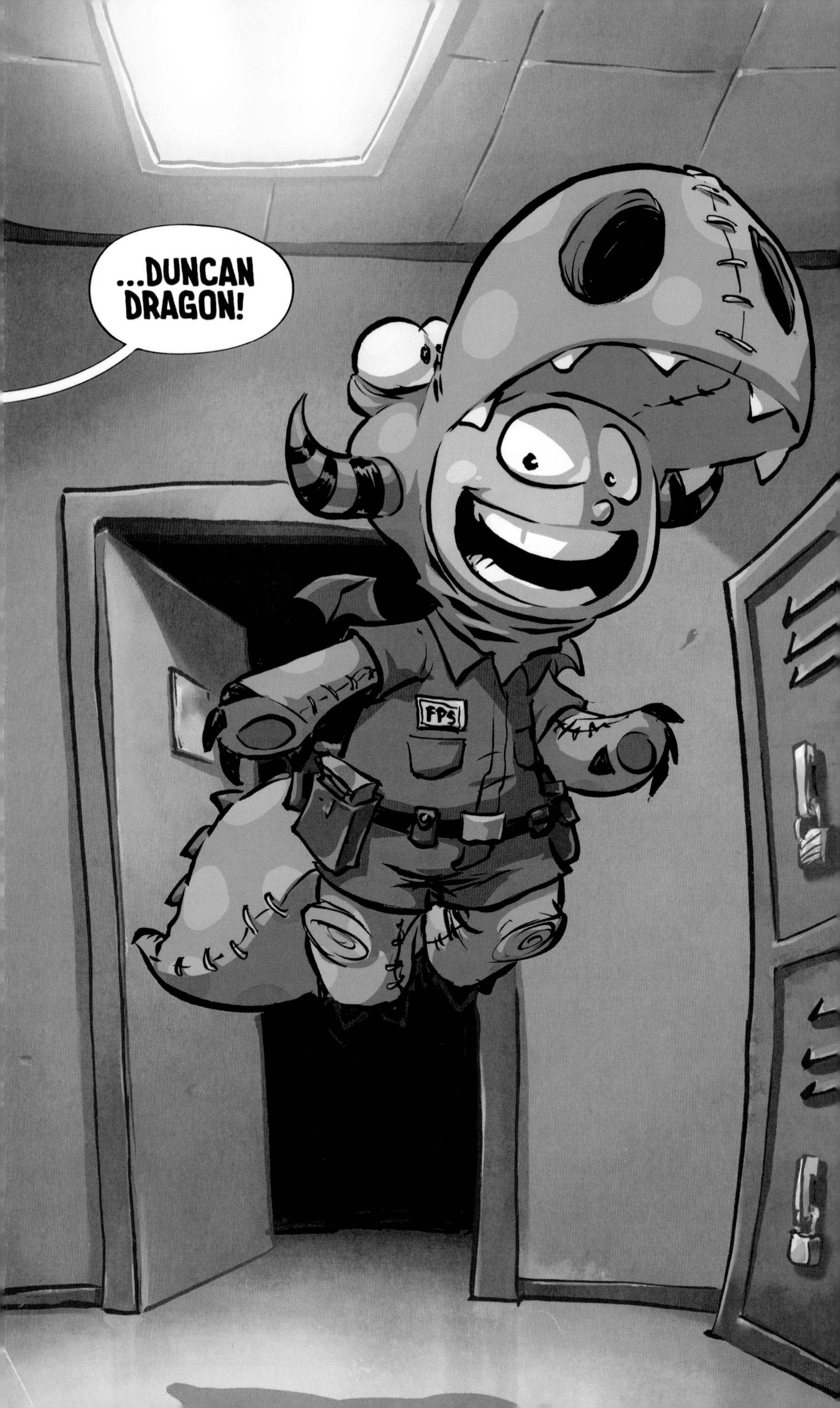
...DUNCAN DRAGON!
FPS

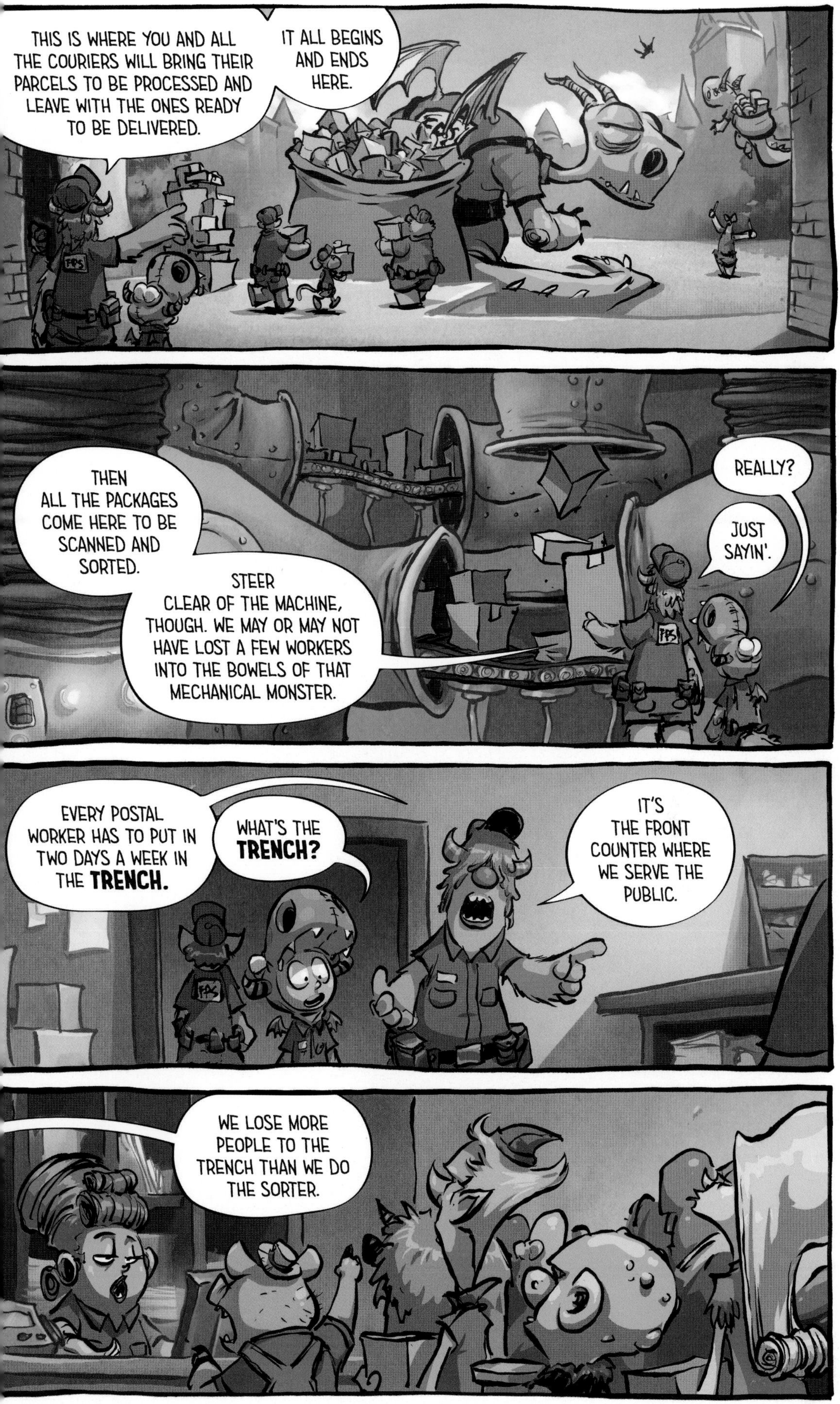
THIS IS WHERE YOU AND ALL THE COURIERS WILL BRING THEIR PARCELS TO BE PROCESSED AND LEAVE WITH THE ONES READY TO BE DELIVERED.
IT ALL BEGINS AND ENDS HERE.
FPS
THEN ALL THE PACKAGES COME HERE TO BE SCANNED AND SORTED.
STEER CLEAR OF THE MACHINE, THOUGH. WE MAY OR MAY NOT HAVE LOST A FEW WORKERS INTO THE BOWELS OF THAT MECHANICAL MONSTER.
REALLY?
JUST SAYIN'.
EVERY POSTAL WORKER HAS TO PUT IN TWO DAYS A WEEK IN THE **TRENCH.**
WHAT'S THE **TRENCH?**
IT'S THE FRONT COUNTER WHERE WE SERVE THE PUBLIC.
WE LOSE MORE PEOPLE TO THE TRENCH THAN WE DO THE SORTER.

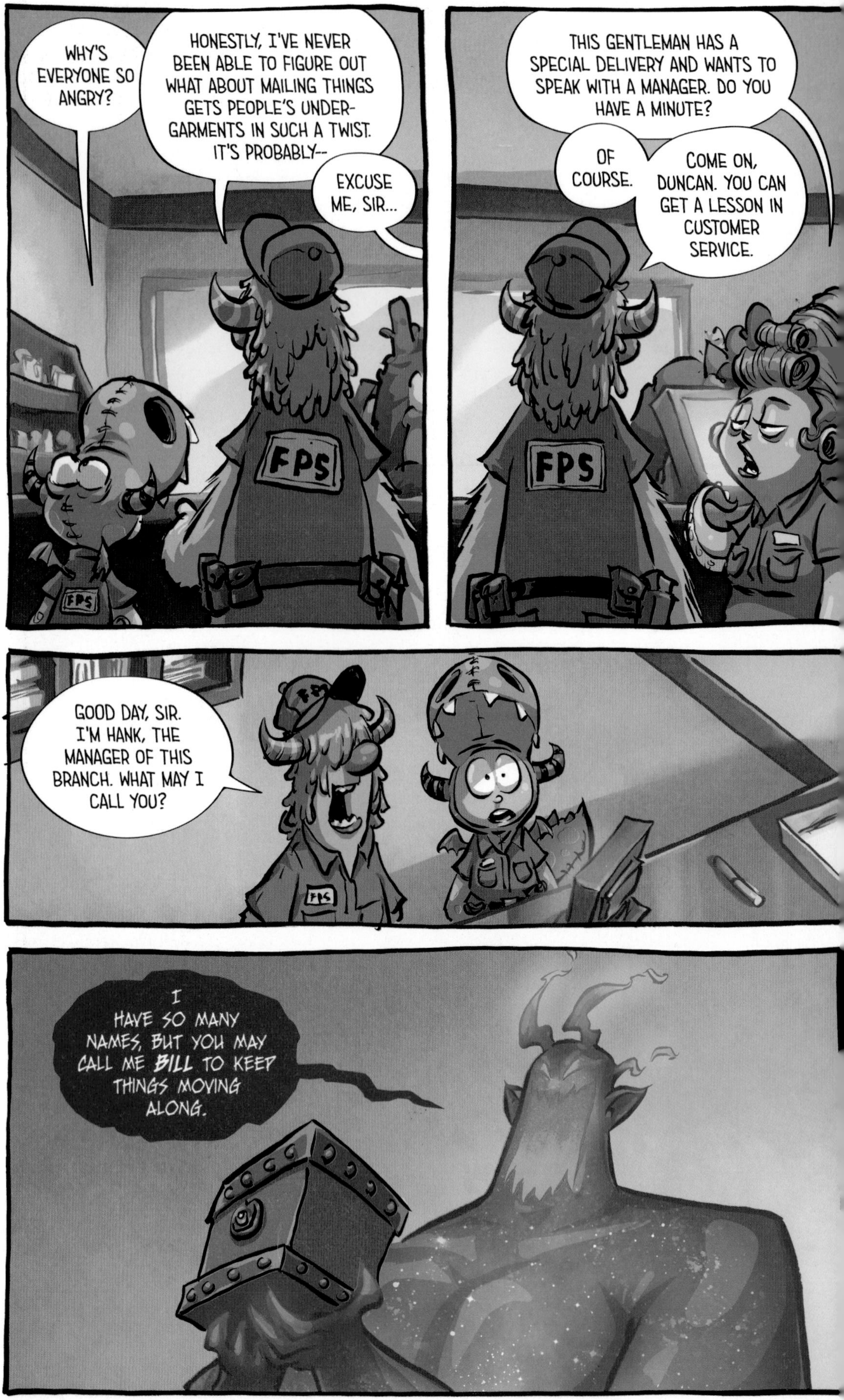
WHY'S EVERYONE SO ANGRY?
HONESTLY, I'VE NEVER BEEN ABLE TO FIGURE OUT WHAT ABOUT MAILING THINGS GETS PEOPLE'S UNDER-GARMENTS IN SUCH A TWIST. IT'S PROBABLY--
EXCUSE ME, SIR...
FPS
THIS GENTLEMAN HAS A SPECIAL DELIVERY AND WANTS TO SPEAK WITH A MANAGER. DO YOU HAVE A MINUTE?
OF COURSE.
COME ON, DUNCAN. YOU CAN GET A LESSON IN CUSTOMER SERVICE.
FPS
GOOD DAY, SIR. I'M HANK, THE MANAGER OF THIS BRANCH. WHAT MAY I CALL YOU?
I HAVE SO MANY NAMES, BUT YOU MAY CALL ME **BILL** TO KEEP THINGS MOVING ALONG.

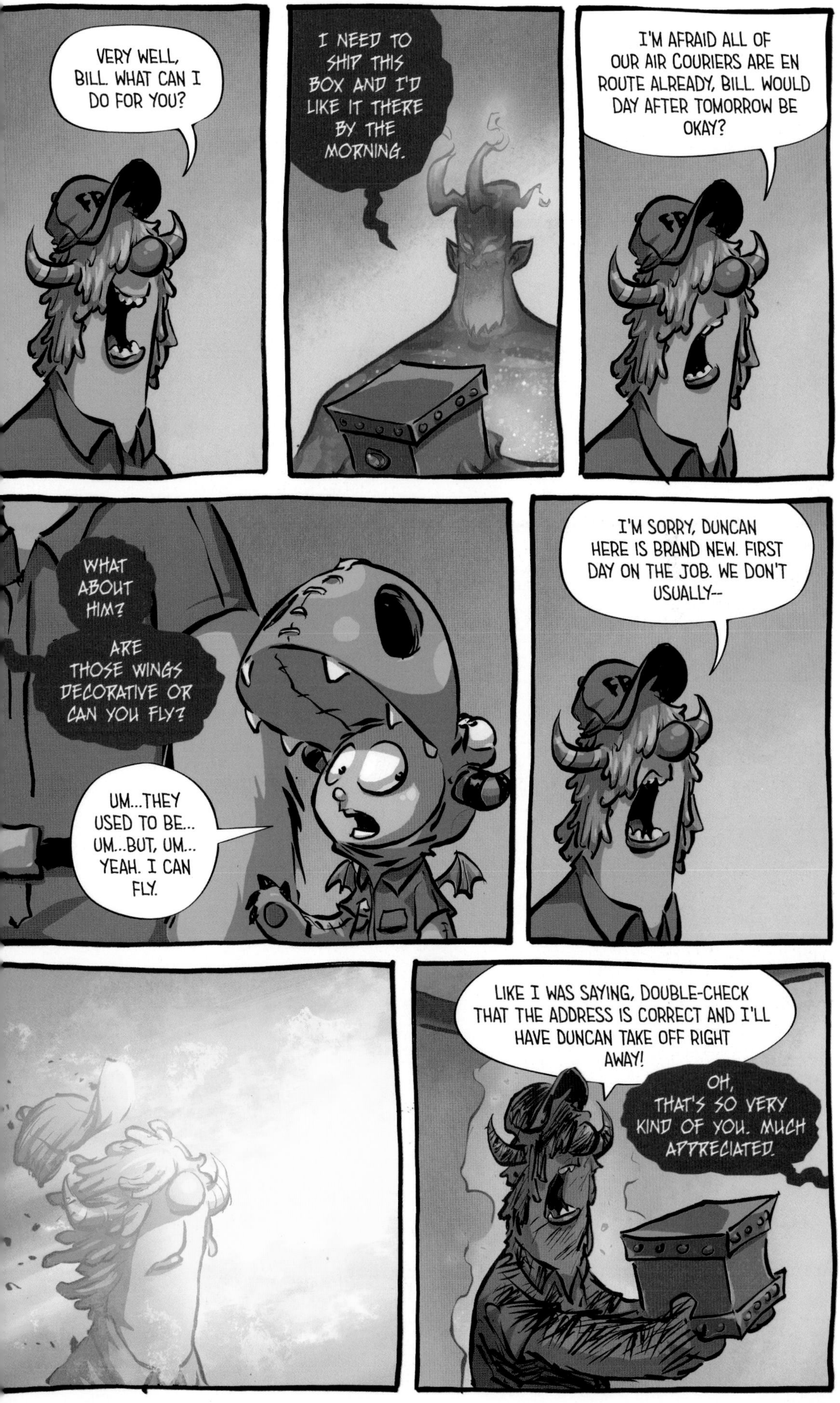
VERY WELL, BILL. WHAT CAN I DO FOR YOU?
I NEED TO SHIP THIS BOX AND I'D LIKE IT THERE BY THE MORNING.
I'M AFRAID ALL OF OUR AIR COURIERS ARE EN ROUTE ALREADY, BILL. WOULD DAY AFTER TOMORROW BE OKAY?
WHAT ABOUT HIM?
ARE THOSE WINGS DECORATIVE OR CAN YOU FLY?
UM...THEY USED TO BE... UM...BUT, UM... YEAH. I CAN FLY.
I'M SORRY, DUNCAN HERE IS BRAND NEW. FIRST DAY ON THE JOB. WE DON'T USUALLY--
LIKE I WAS SAYING, DOUBLE-CHECK THAT THE ADDRESS IS CORRECT AND I'LL HAVE DUNCAN TAKE OFF RIGHT AWAY!
OH, THAT'S SO VERY KIND OF YOU. MUCH APPRECIATED.

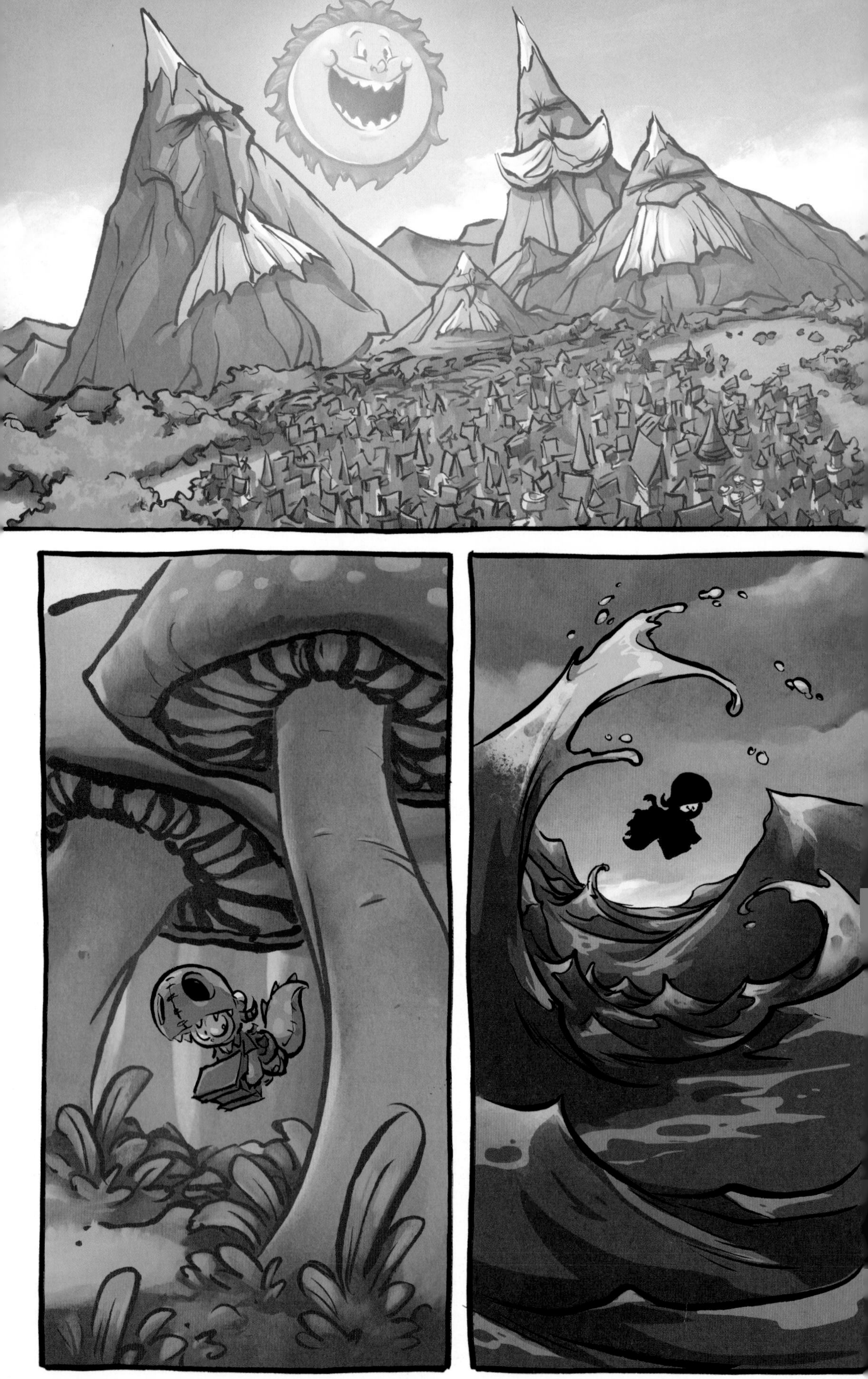

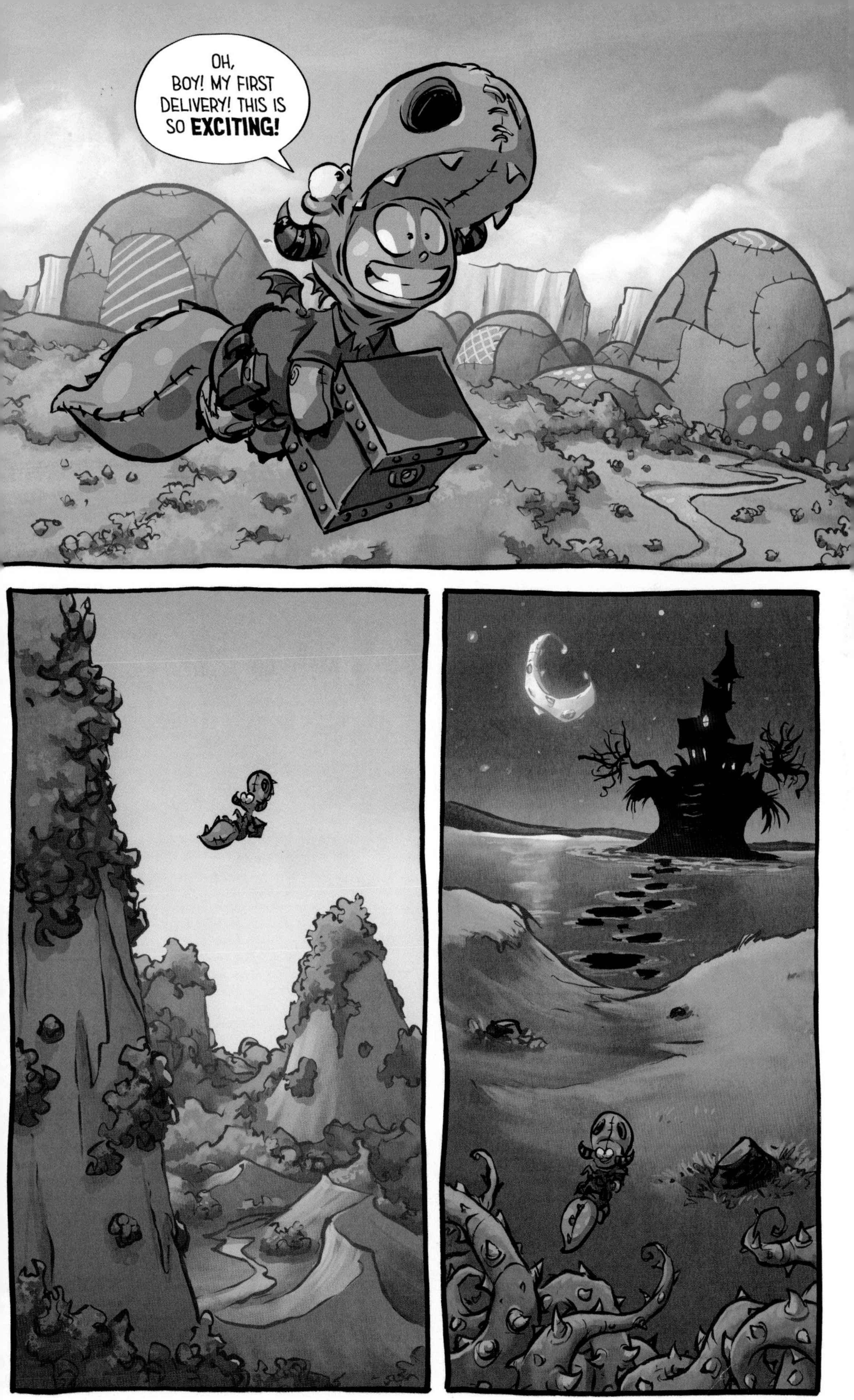
OH, BOY! MY FIRST DELIVERY! THIS IS SO **EXCITING!**

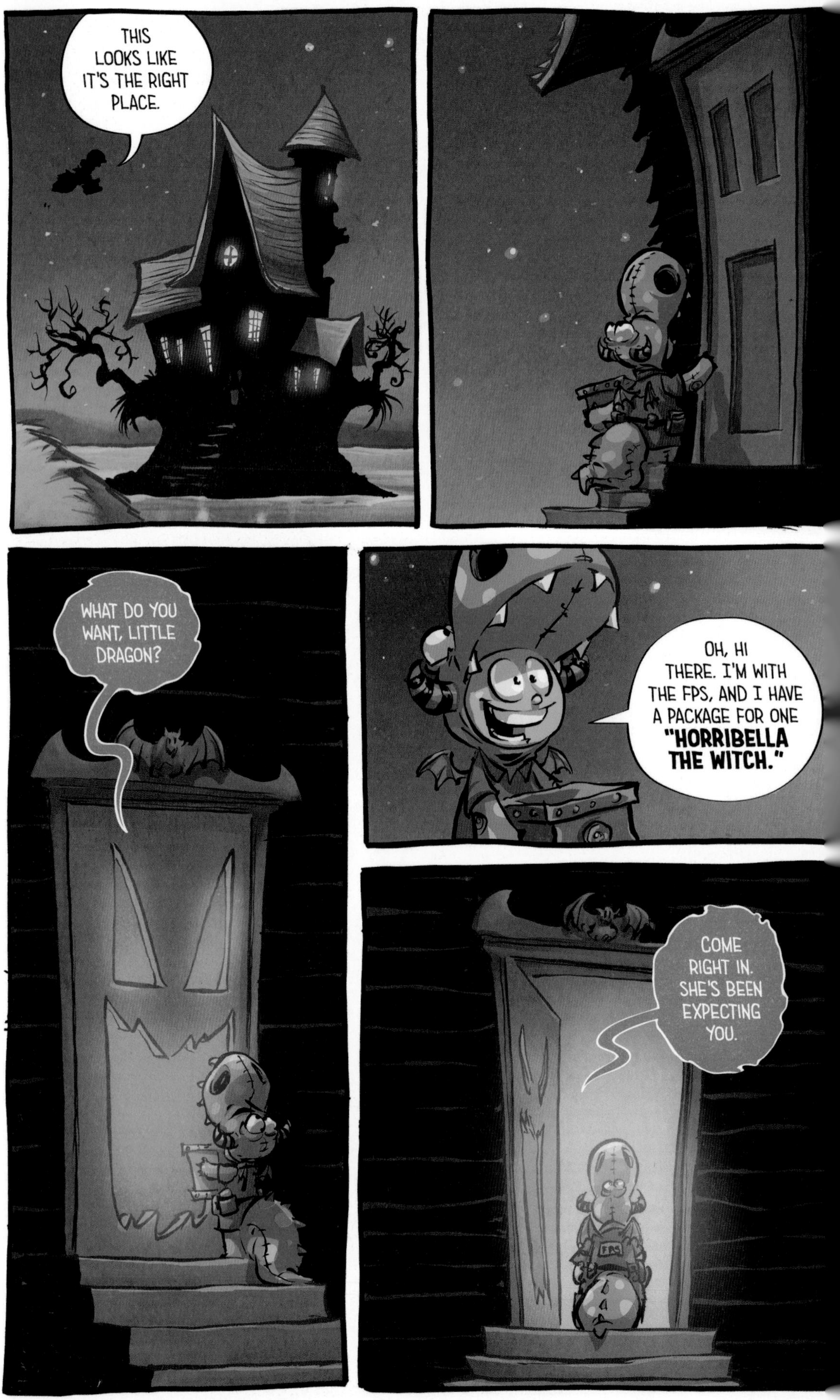
THIS LOOKS LIKE IT'S THE RIGHT PLACE.
WHAT DO YOU WANT, LITTLE DRAGON?
OH, HI THERE. I'M WITH THE FPS, AND I HAVE A PACKAGE FOR ONE **"HORRIBELLA THE WITCH."**
COME RIGHT IN. SHE'S BEEN EXPECTING YOU.

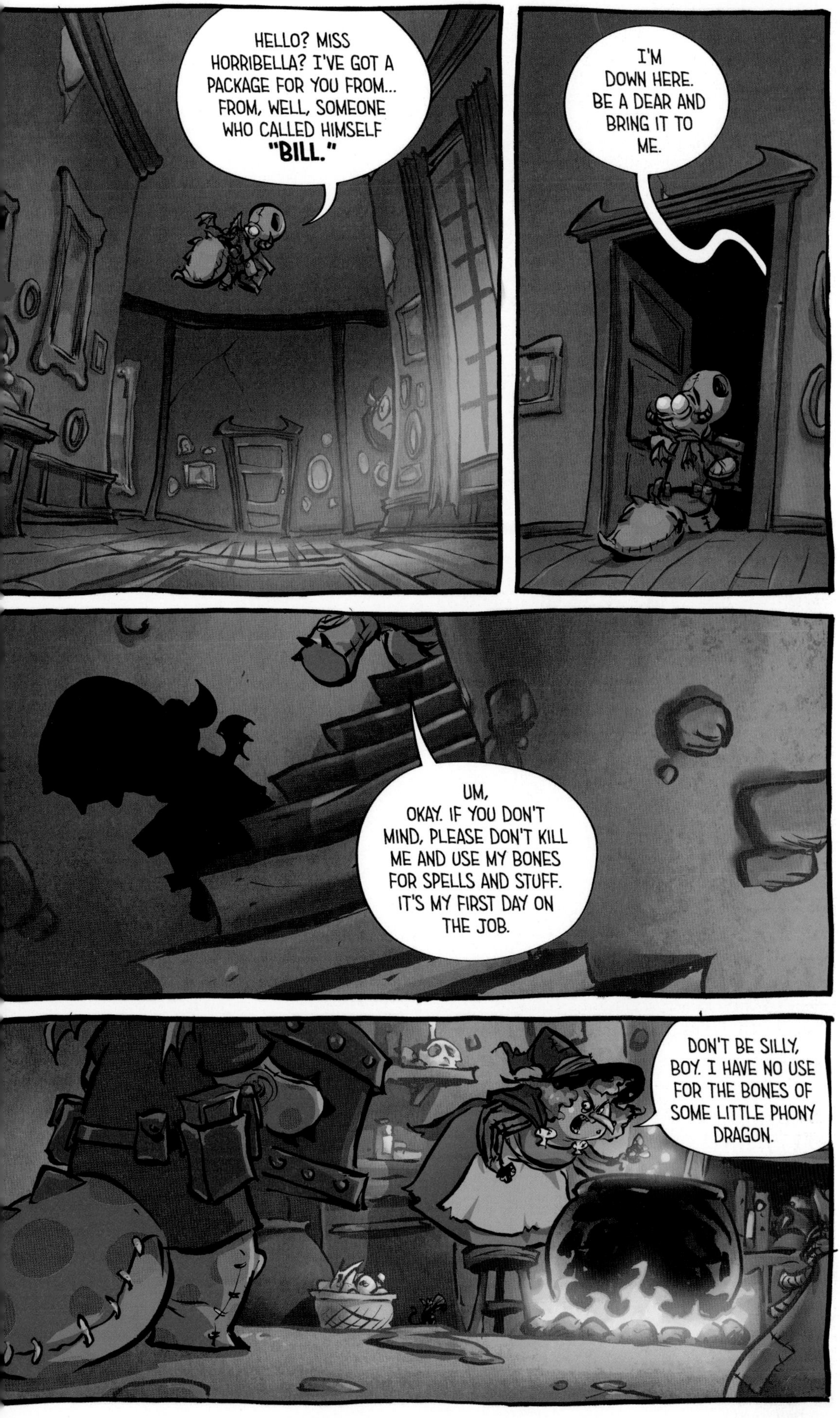
HELLO? MISS HORRIBELLA? I'VE GOT A PACKAGE FOR YOU FROM... FROM, WELL, SOMEONE WHO CALLED HIMSELF **"BILL."**
I'M DOWN HERE. BE A DEAR AND BRING IT TO ME.
UM, OKAY. IF YOU DON'T MIND, PLEASE DON'T KILL ME AND USE MY BONES FOR SPELLS AND STUFF. IT'S MY FIRST DAY ON THE JOB.
DON'T BE SILLY, BOY. I HAVE NO USE FOR THE BONES OF SOME LITTLE PHONY DRAGON.

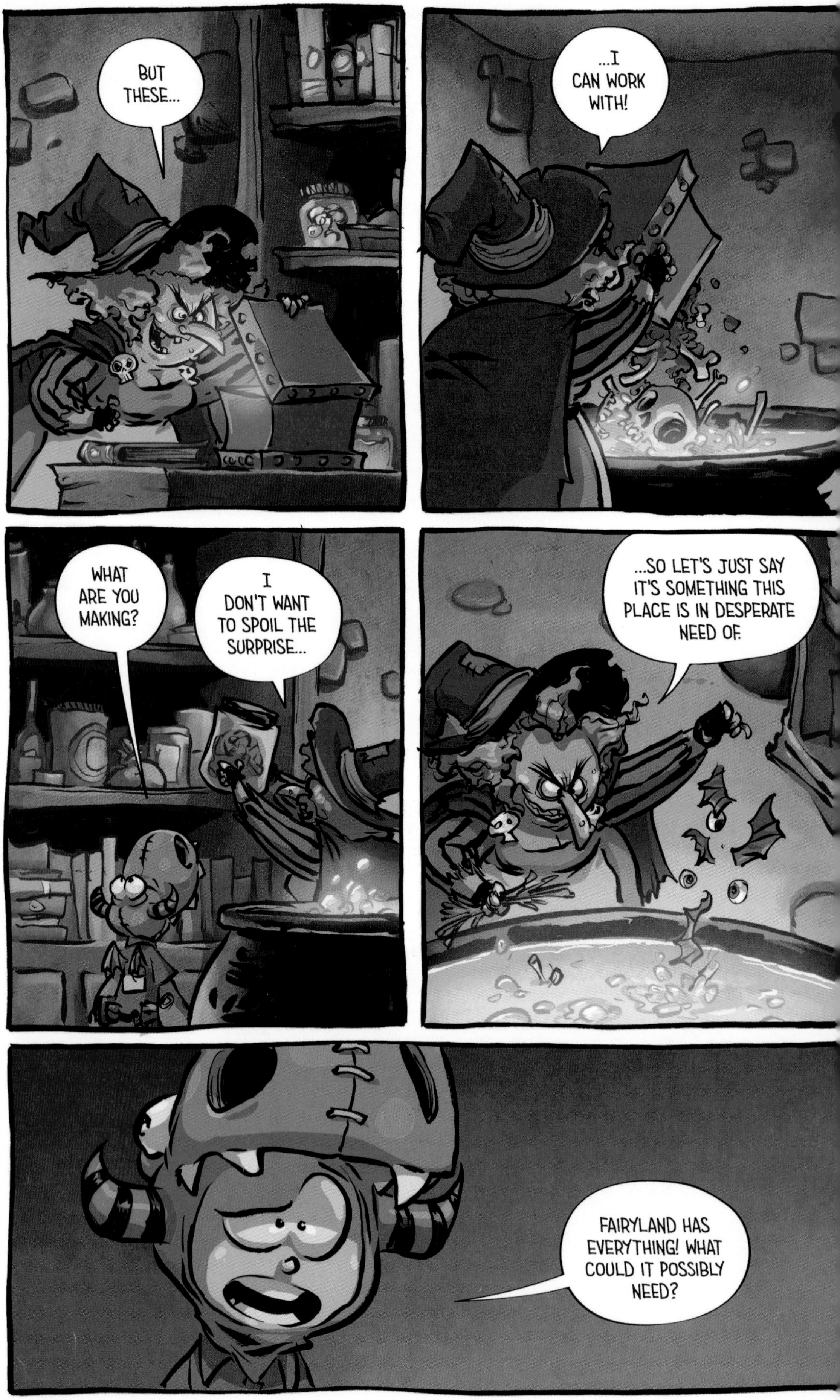
BUT THESE...
...I CAN WORK WITH!
WHAT ARE YOU MAKING?
I DON'T WANT TO SPOIL THE SURPRISE...
...SO LET'S JUST SAY IT'S SOMETHING THIS PLACE IS IN DESPERATE NEED OF.
FAIRYLAND HAS EVERYTHING! WHAT COULD IT POSSIBLY NEED?

YES, FAIRYLAND HAS EVERYTHING ONE'S MIND CAN IMAGINE AND EVEN MORE THAT IT CANNOT.

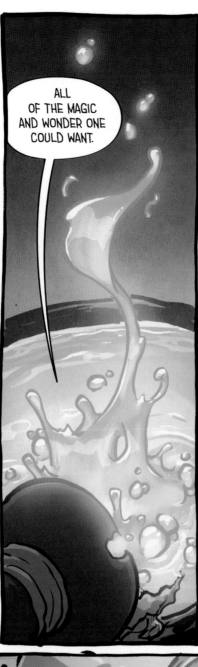

ALL OF THE MAGIC AND WONDER ONE COULD WANT.

STILL, SEARCH AS FAR AND AS LONG AS YOU'RE ABLE AND YOU'LL DISCOVER THERE IS **ONE** THING MISSING.

W-W-WHAT'S THAT?!

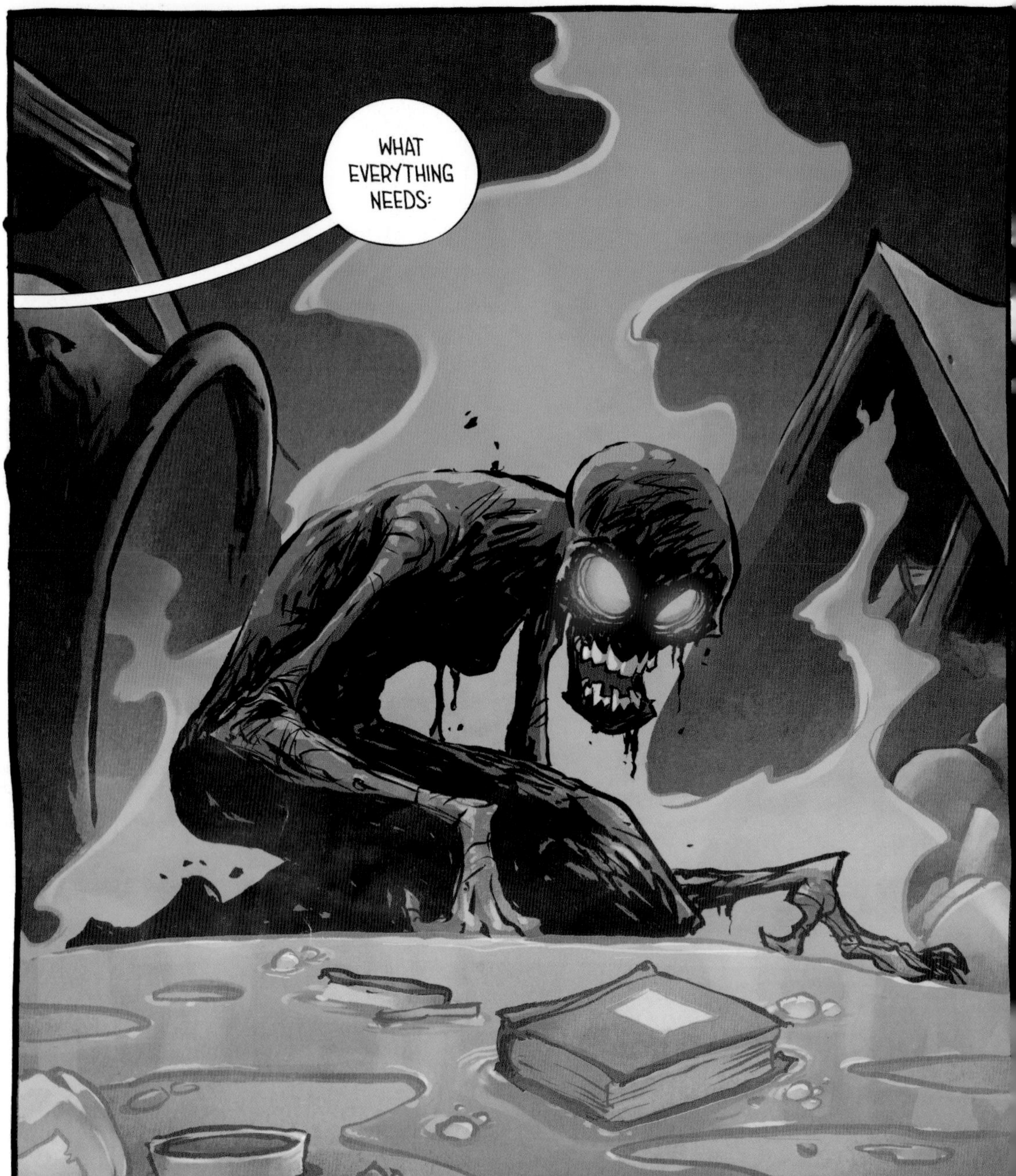
WHAT EVERYTHING NEEDS:

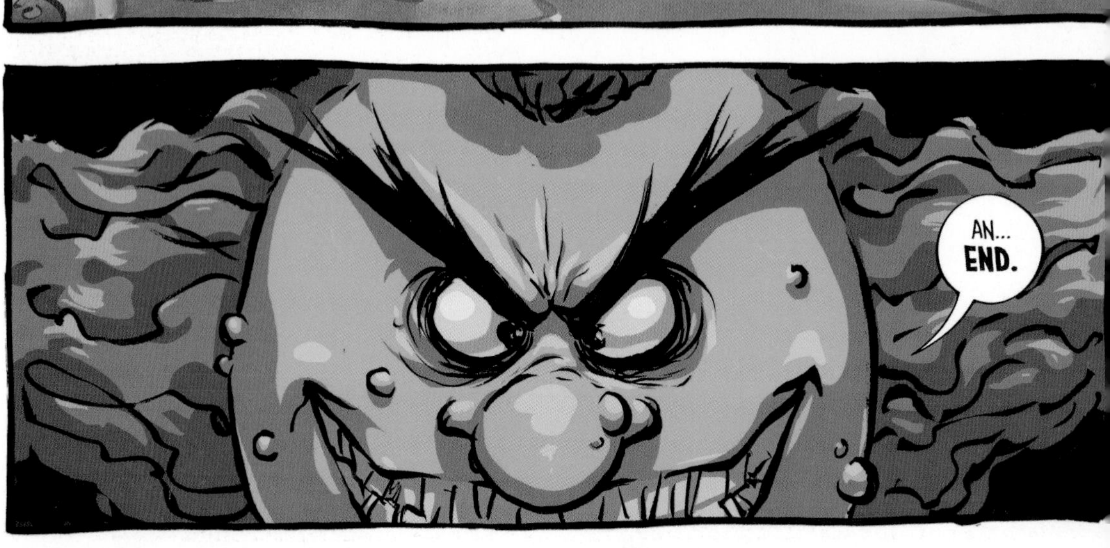
AN... **END.**

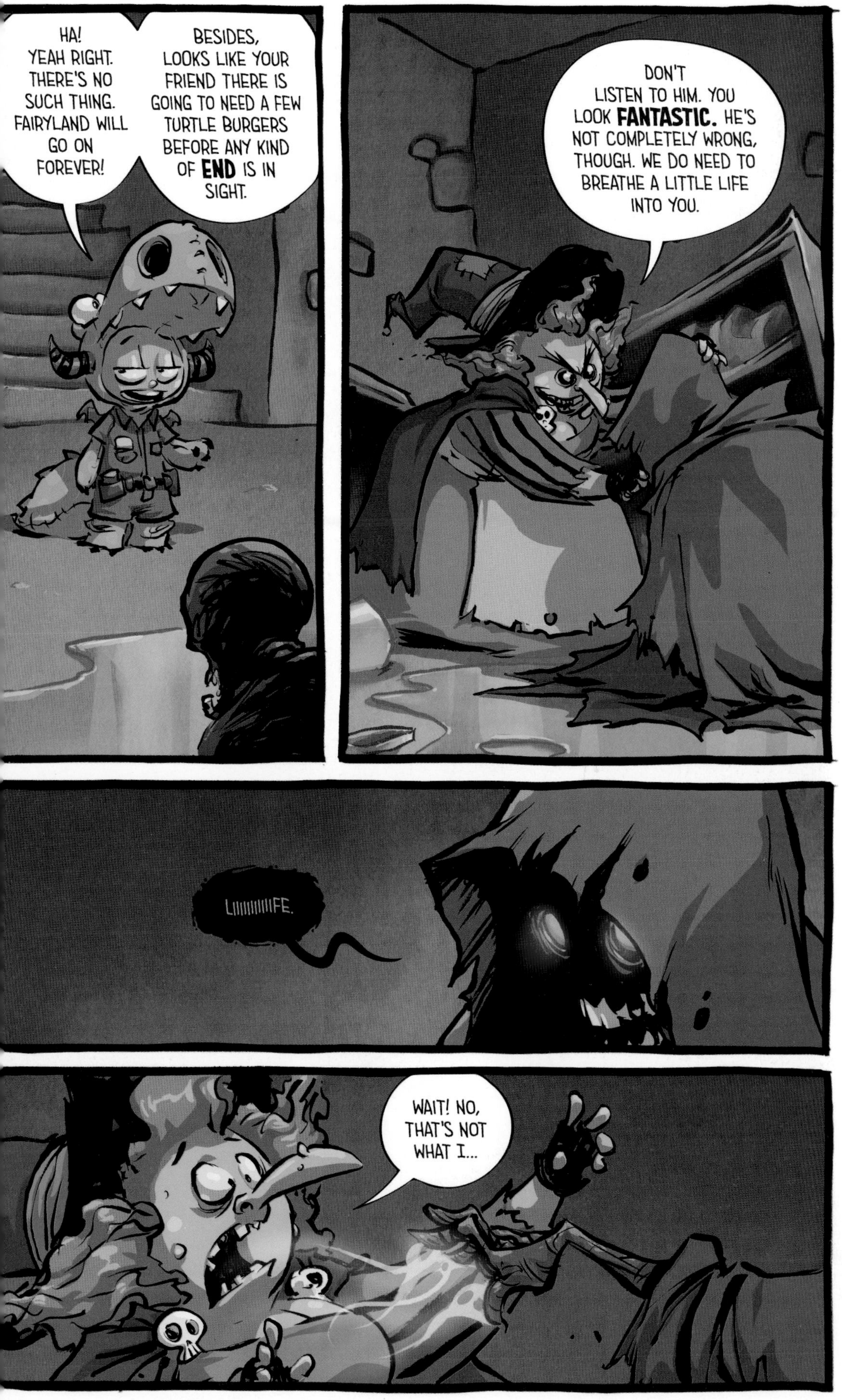
HA! YEAH RIGHT. THERE'S NO SUCH THING. FAIRYLAND WILL GO ON FOREVER!
BESIDES, LOOKS LIKE YOUR FRIEND THERE IS GOING TO NEED A FEW TURTLE BURGERS BEFORE ANY KIND OF **END** IS IN SIGHT.
DON'T LISTEN TO HIM. YOU LOOK **FANTASTIC.** HE'S NOT COMPLETELY WRONG, THOUGH. WE DO NEED TO BREATHE A LITTLE LIFE INTO YOU.
LIIIIIIIIIFE.
WAIT! NO, THAT'S NOT WHAT I...

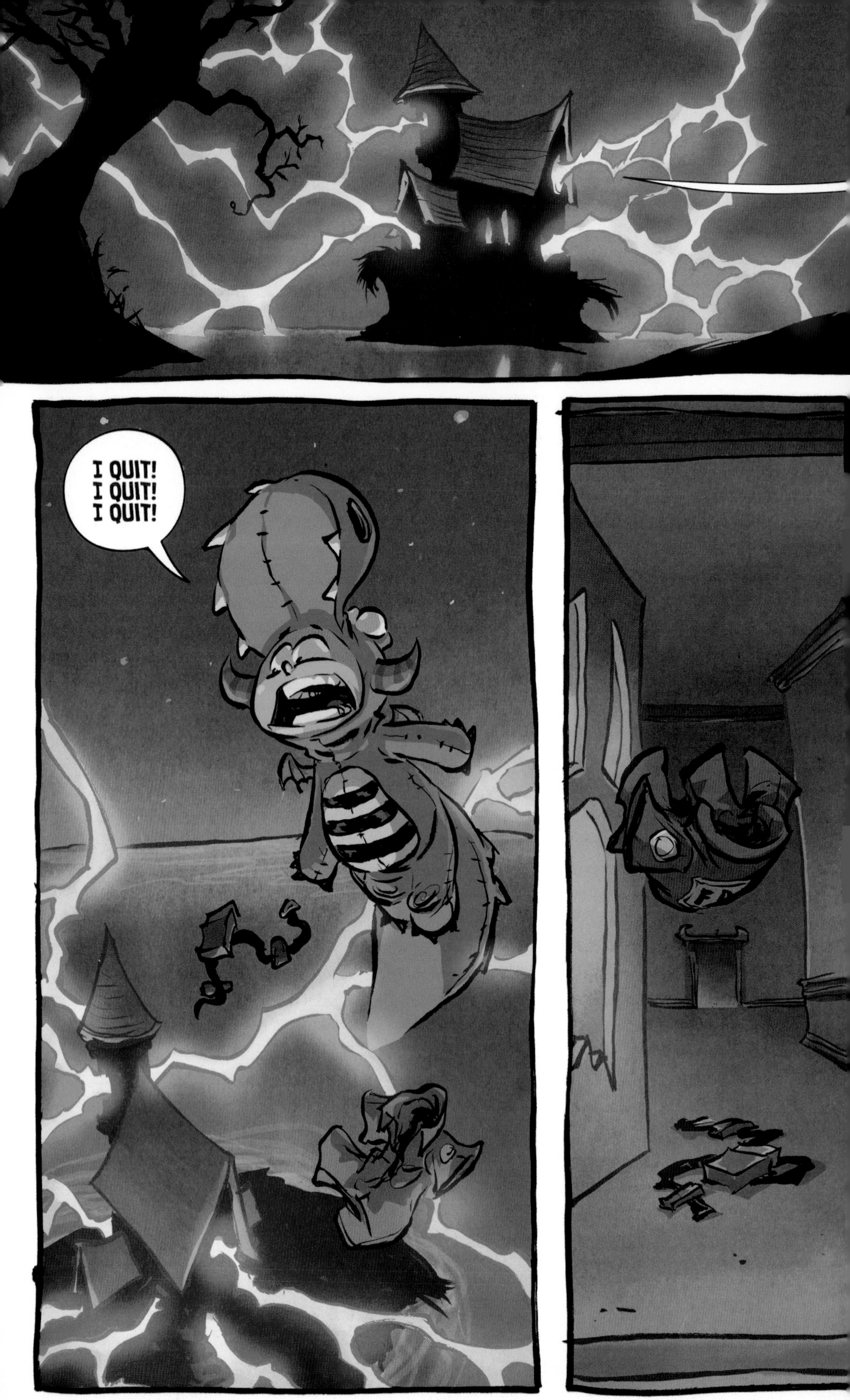
I QUIT! I QUIT! I QUIT!

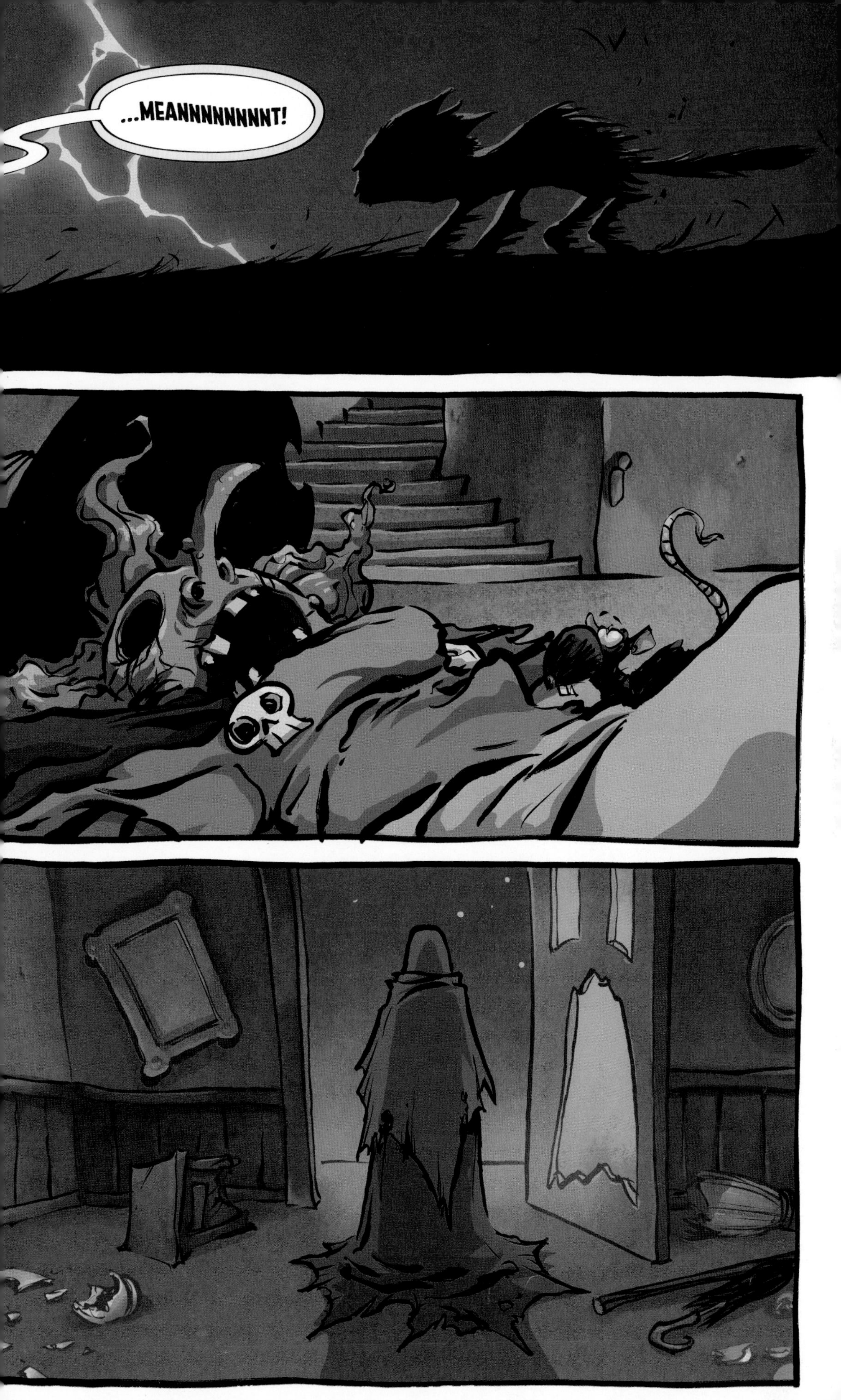
...MEANNNNNNNNT!

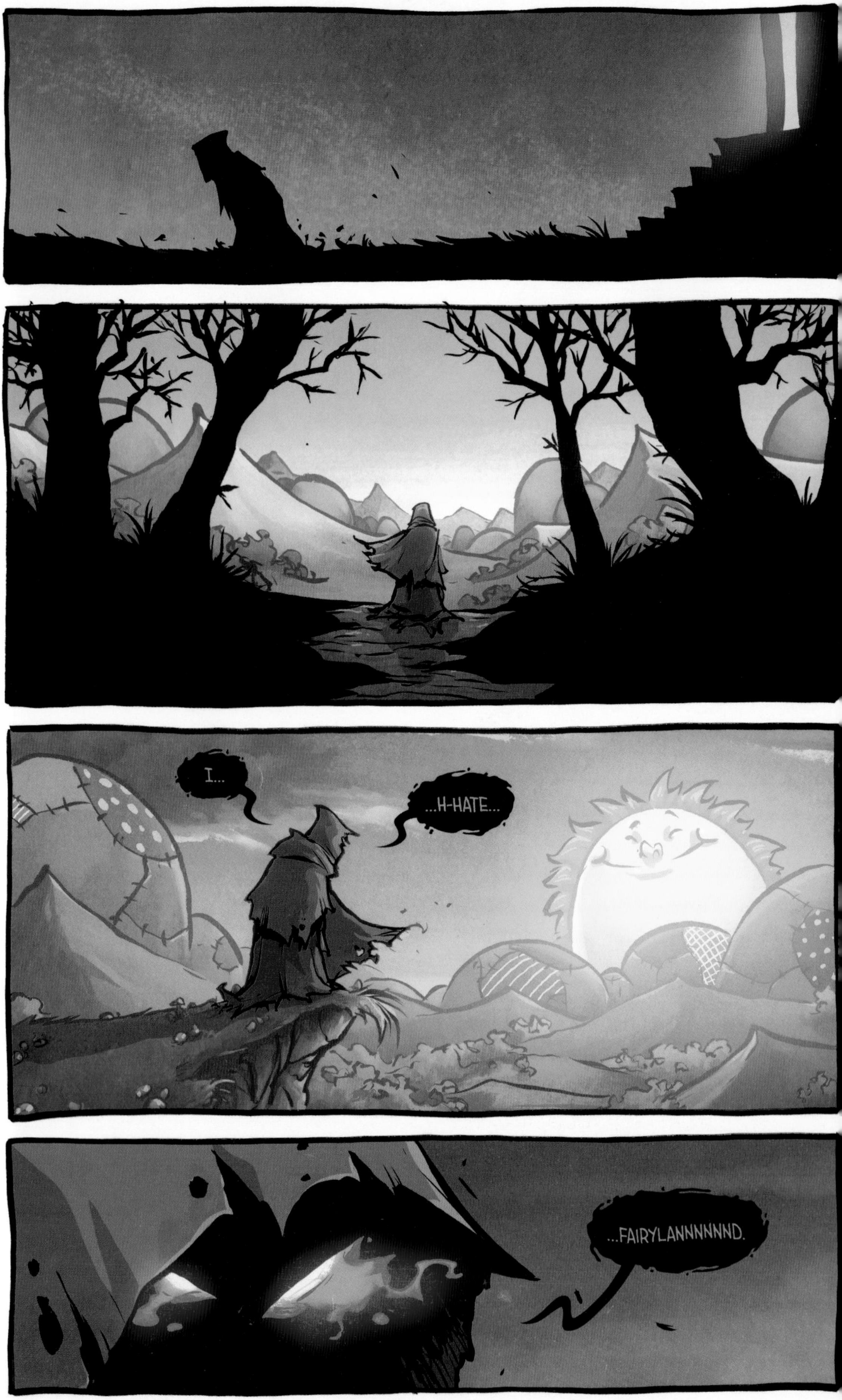
I...
...H-HATE...
...FAIRYLANNNNNND.

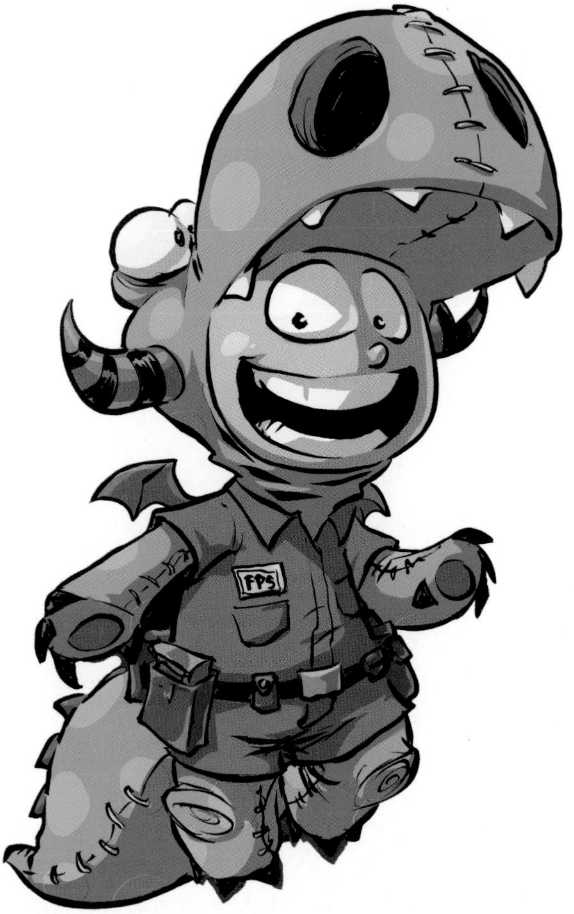
FPS

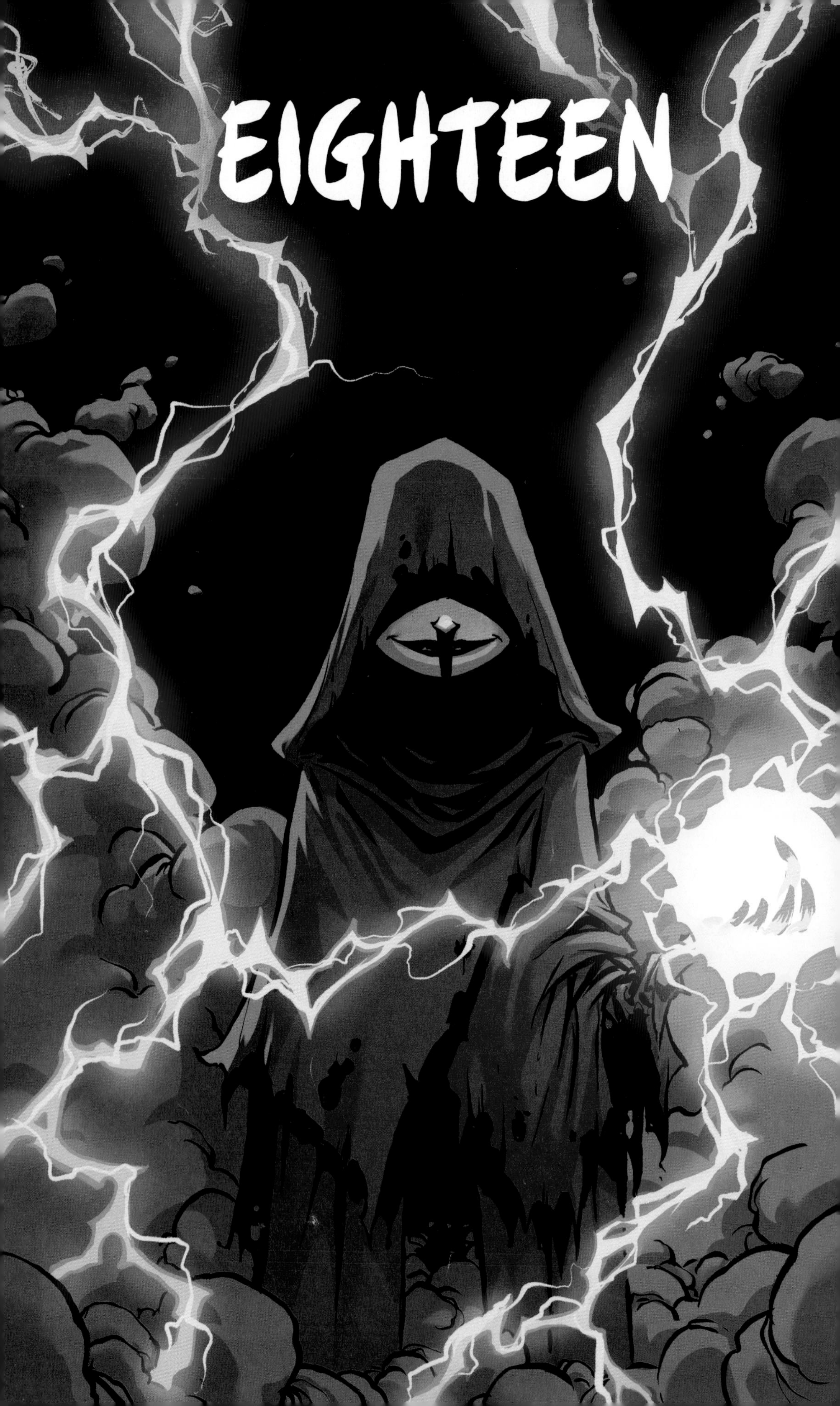
EIGHTEEN

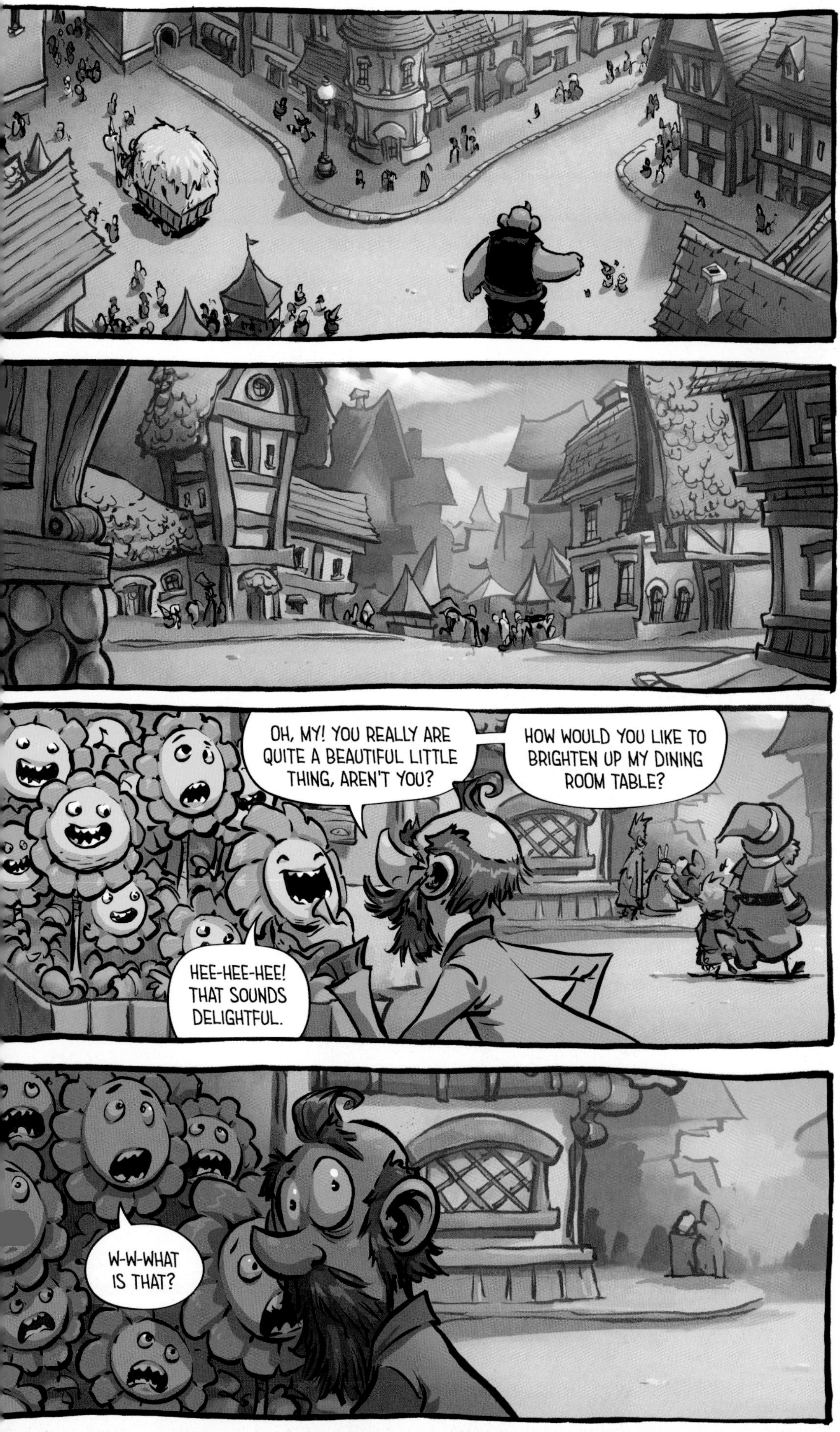
OH, MY! YOU REALLY ARE QUITE A BEAUTIFUL LITTLE THING, AREN'T YOU?
HOW WOULD YOU LIKE TO BRIGHTEN UP MY DINING ROOM TABLE?
HEE-HEE-HEE! THAT SOUNDS DELIGHTFUL.
W-W-WHAT IS THAT?

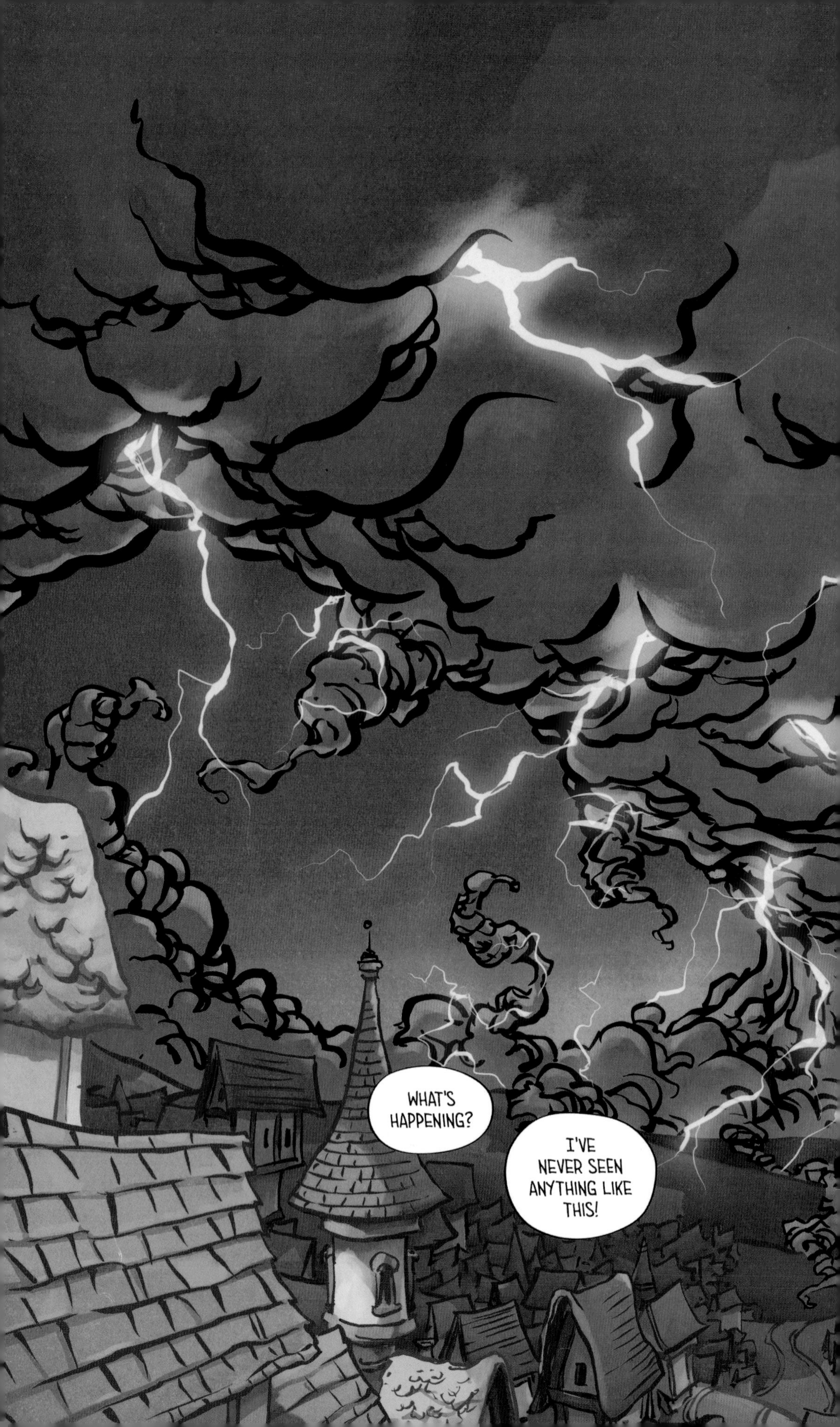
WHAT'S HAPPENING?
I'VE NEVER SEEN ANYTHING LIKE THIS!

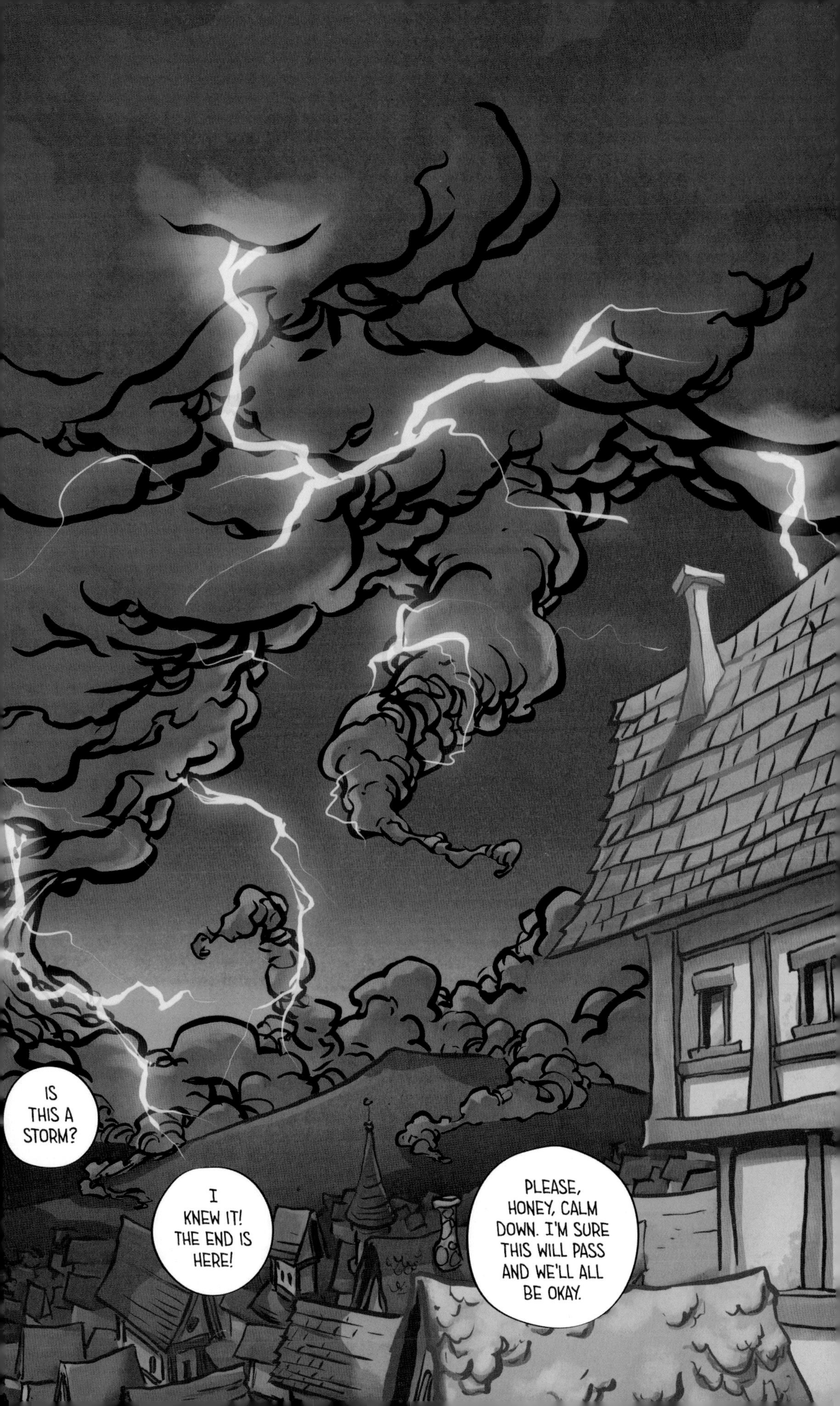
IS THIS A STORM?
I KNEW IT! THE END IS HERE!
PLEASE, HONEY, CALM DOWN. I'M SURE THIS WILL PASS AND WE'LL ALL BE OKAY.

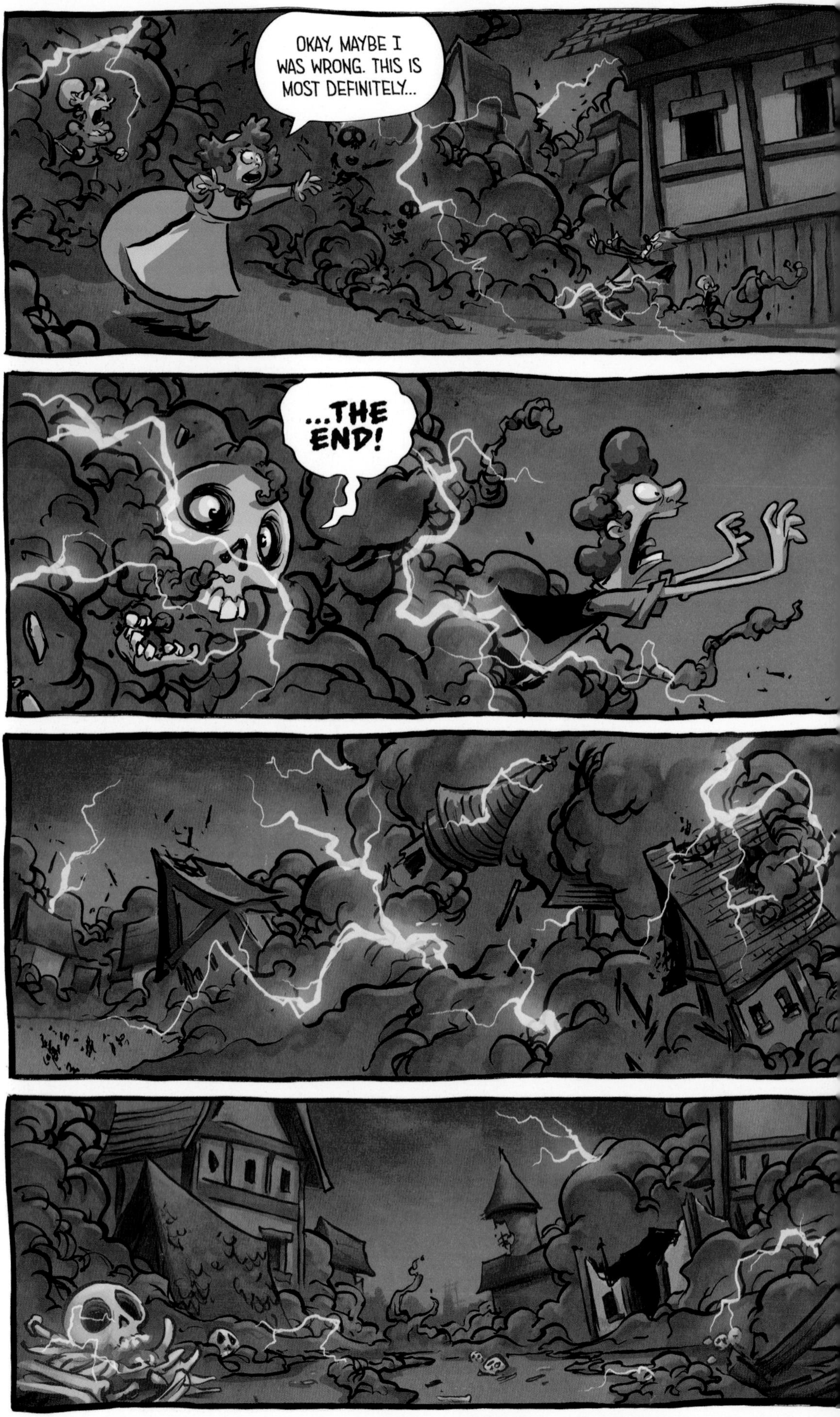
OKAY, MAYBE I WAS WRONG. THIS IS MOST DEFINITELY...
...THE END!

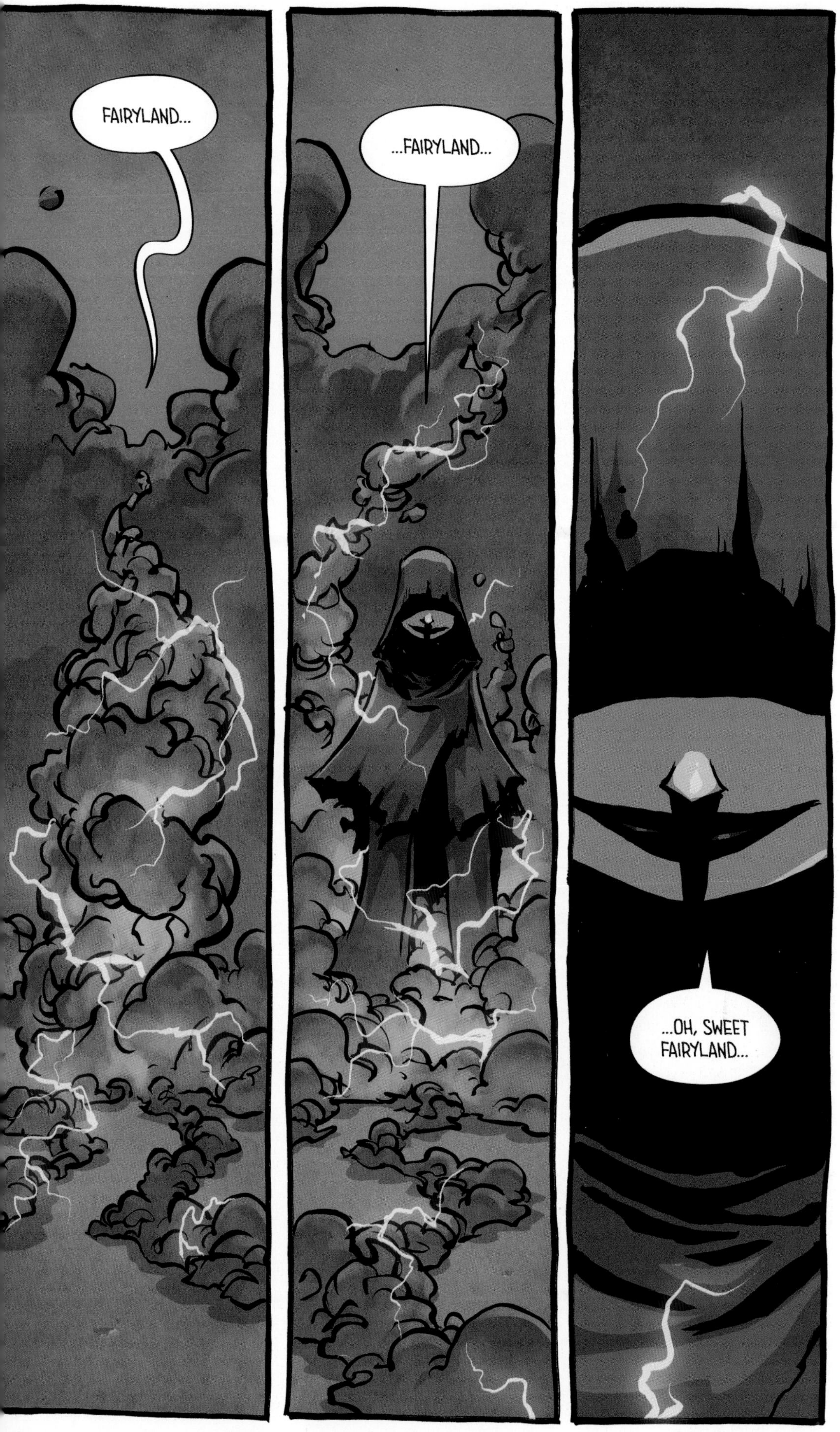
FAIRYLAND...
...FAIRYLAND...
...OH, SWEET FAIRYLAND...

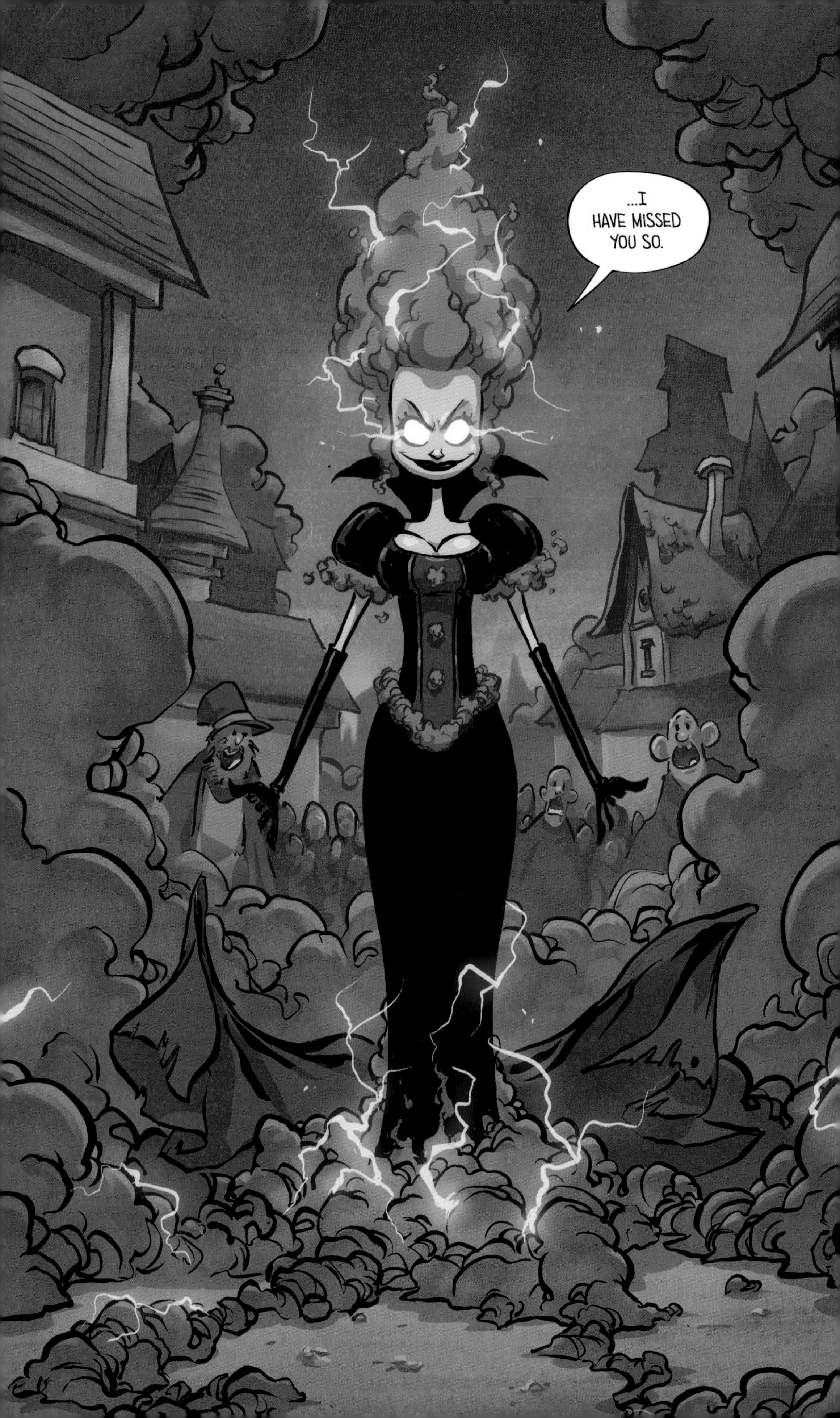
...I HAVE MISSED YOU SO.

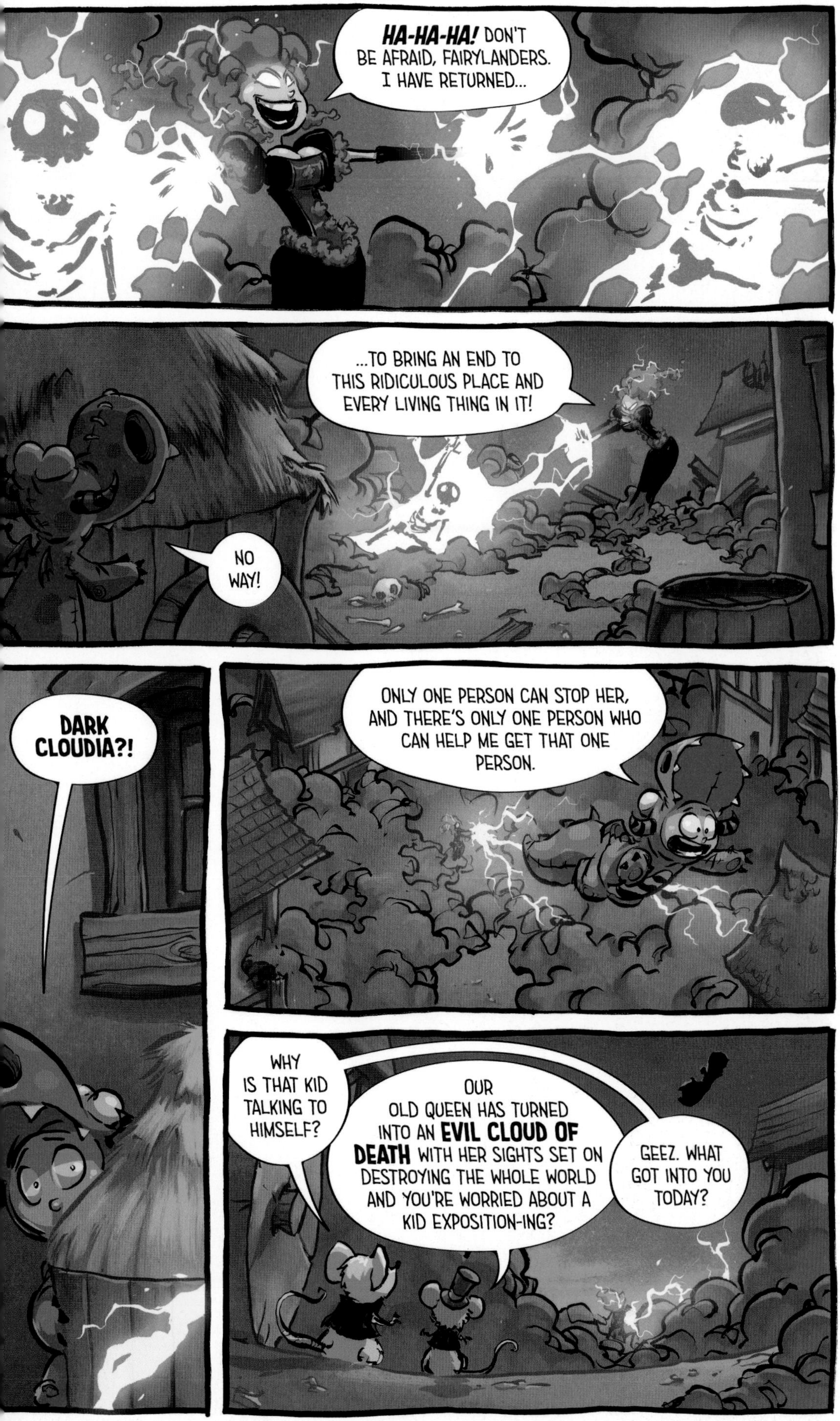
HA-HA-HA! DON'T BE AFRAID, FAIRYLANDERS. I HAVE RETURNED...
...TO BRING AN END TO THIS RIDICULOUS PLACE AND EVERY LIVING THING IN IT!
NO WAY!
DARK CLOUDIA?!
ONLY ONE PERSON CAN STOP HER, AND THERE'S ONLY ONE PERSON WHO CAN HELP ME GET THAT ONE PERSON.
WHY IS THAT KID TALKING TO HIMSELF?
OUR OLD QUEEN HAS TURNED INTO AN EVIL CLOUD OF DEATH WITH HER SIGHTS SET ON DESTROYING THE WHOLE WORLD AND YOU'RE WORRIED ABOUT A KID EXPOSITION-ING?
GEEZ. WHAT GOT INTO YOU TODAY?

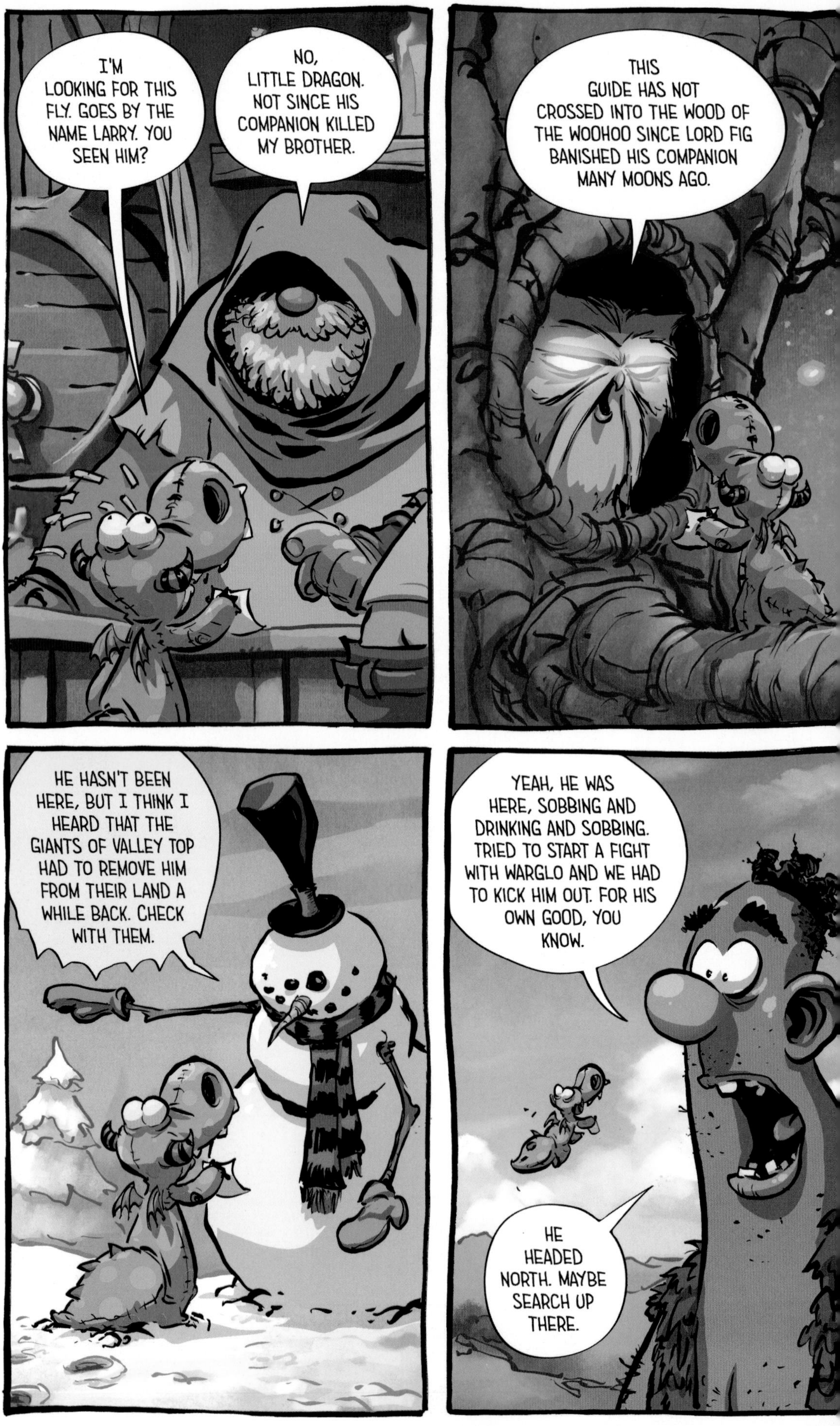
I'M LOOKING FOR THIS FLY. GOES BY THE NAME LARRY. YOU SEEN HIM?
NO, LITTLE DRAGON. NOT SINCE HIS COMPANION KILLED MY BROTHER.
THIS GUIDE HAS NOT CROSSED INTO THE WOOD OF THE WOOHOO SINCE LORD FIG BANISHED HIS COMPANION MANY MOONS AGO.
HE HASN'T BEEN HERE, BUT I THINK I HEARD THAT THE GIANTS OF VALLEY TOP HAD TO REMOVE HIM FROM THEIR LAND A WHILE BACK. CHECK WITH THEM.
YEAH, HE WAS HERE, SOBBING AND DRINKING AND SOBBING. TRIED TO START A FIGHT WITH WARGLO AND WE HAD TO KICK HIM OUT. FOR HIS OWN GOOD, YOU KNOW.
HE HEADED NORTH. MAYBE SEARCH UP THERE.

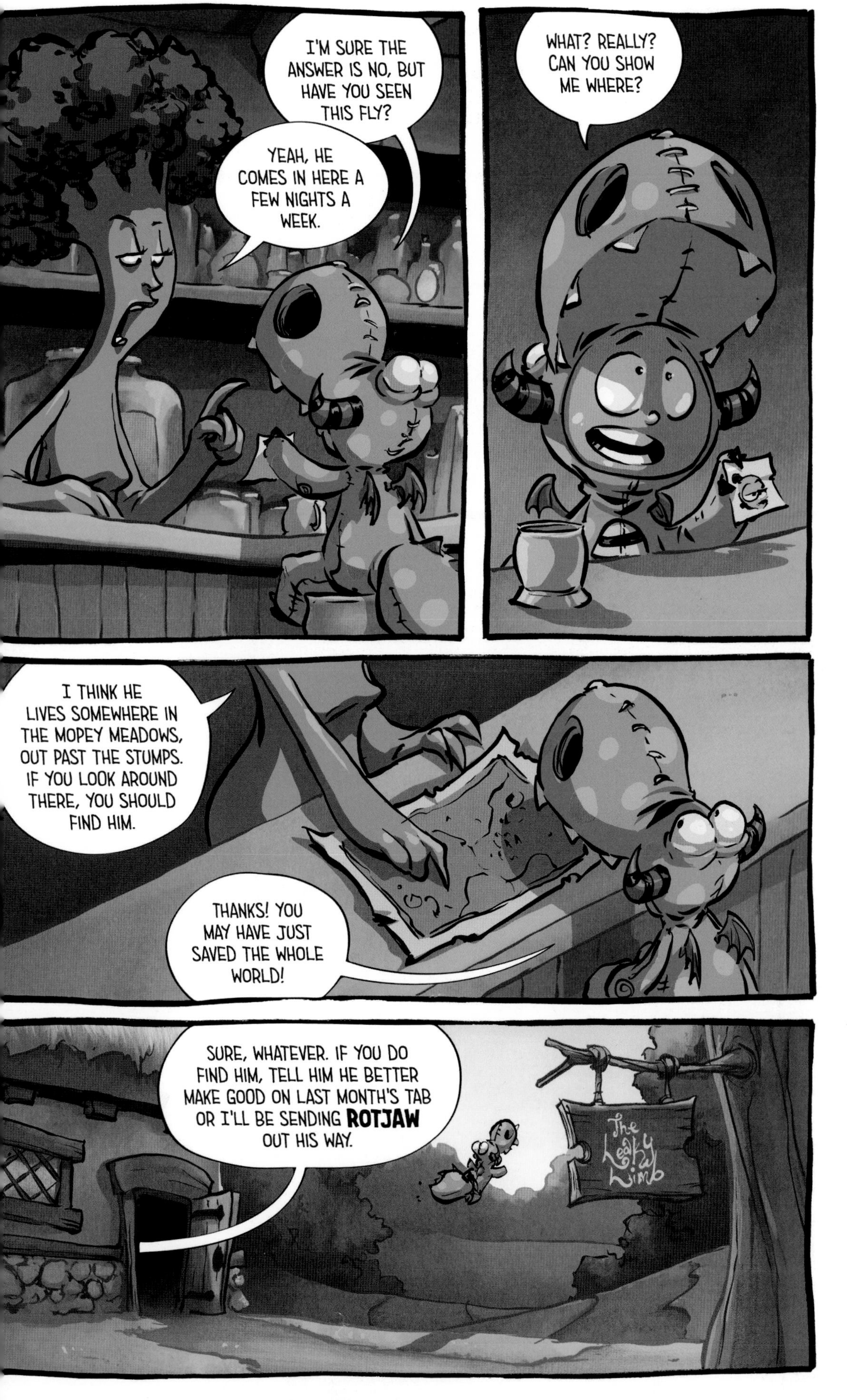
I'M SURE THE ANSWER IS NO, BUT HAVE YOU SEEN THIS FLY?
YEAH, HE COMES IN HERE A FEW NIGHTS A WEEK.
WHAT? REALLY? CAN YOU SHOW ME WHERE?
I THINK HE LIVES SOMEWHERE IN THE MOPEY MEADOWS, OUT PAST THE STUMPS. IF YOU LOOK AROUND THERE, YOU SHOULD FIND HIM.
THANKS! YOU MAY HAVE JUST SAVED THE WHOLE WORLD!
SURE, WHATEVER. IF YOU DO FIND HIM, TELL HIM HE BETTER MAKE GOOD ON LAST MONTH'S TAB OR I'LL BE SENDING **ROTJAW** OUT HIS WAY.
The Leaky Limb

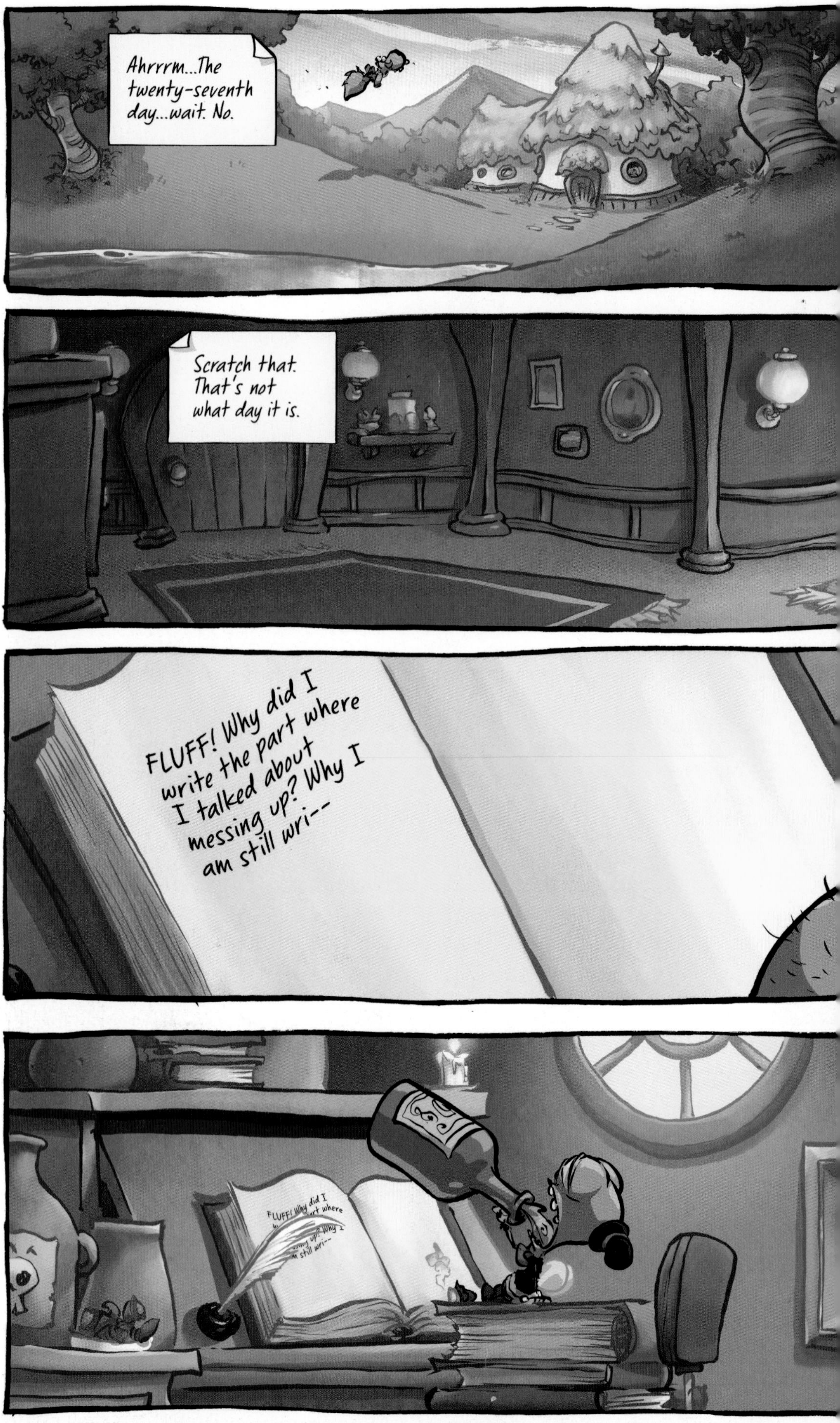

Ahrrrm...The twenty-seventh day...wait. No.
Scratch that. That's not what day it is.
FLUFF! Why did I write the part where I talked about messing up? Why I am still wri--

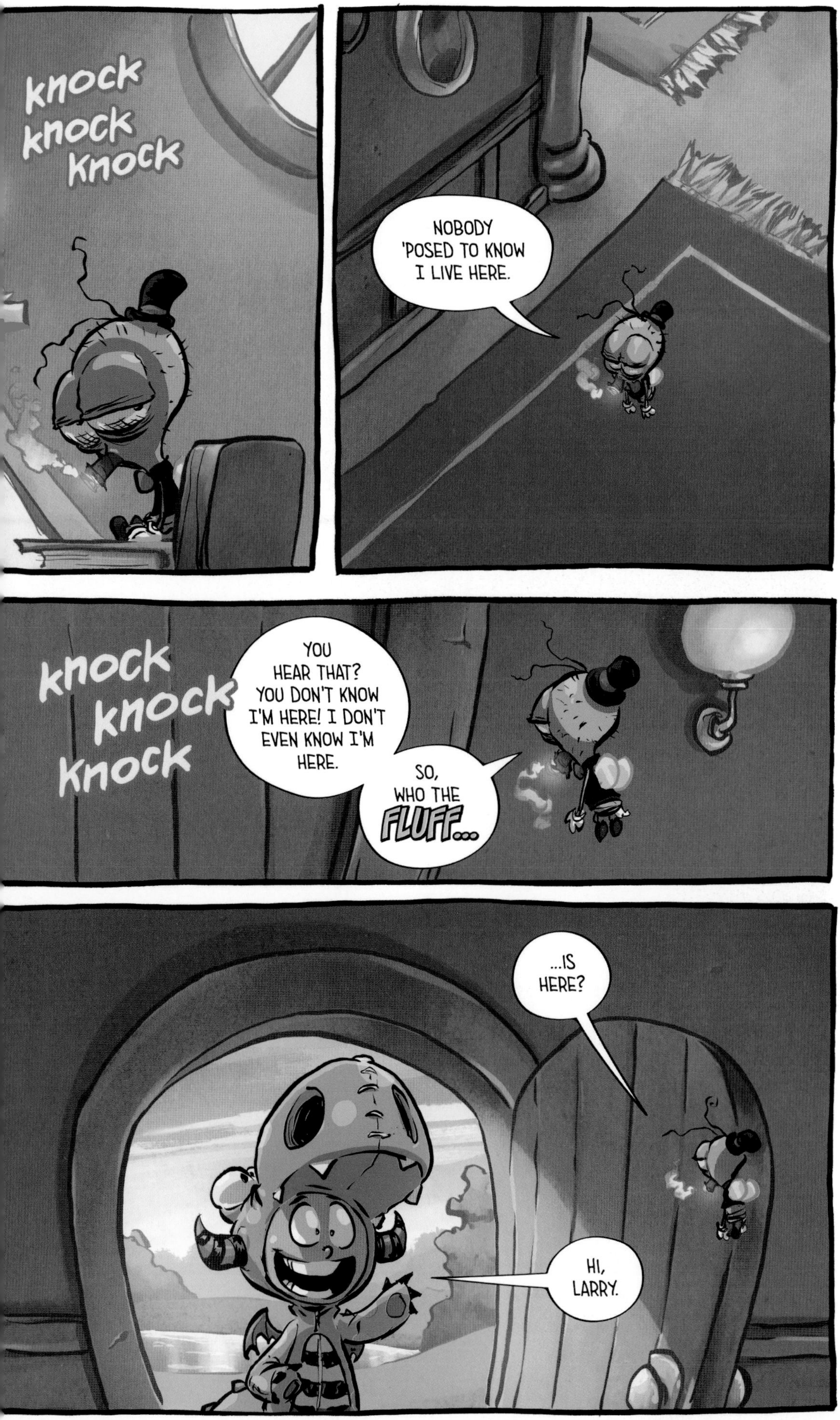
knock
knock
knock
NOBODY 'POSED TO KNOW I LIVE HERE.
knock
knock
knock
YOU HEAR THAT? YOU DON'T KNOW I'M HERE! I DON'T EVEN KNOW I'M HERE.
SO, WHO THE FLUFF...
...IS HERE?
HI, LARRY.

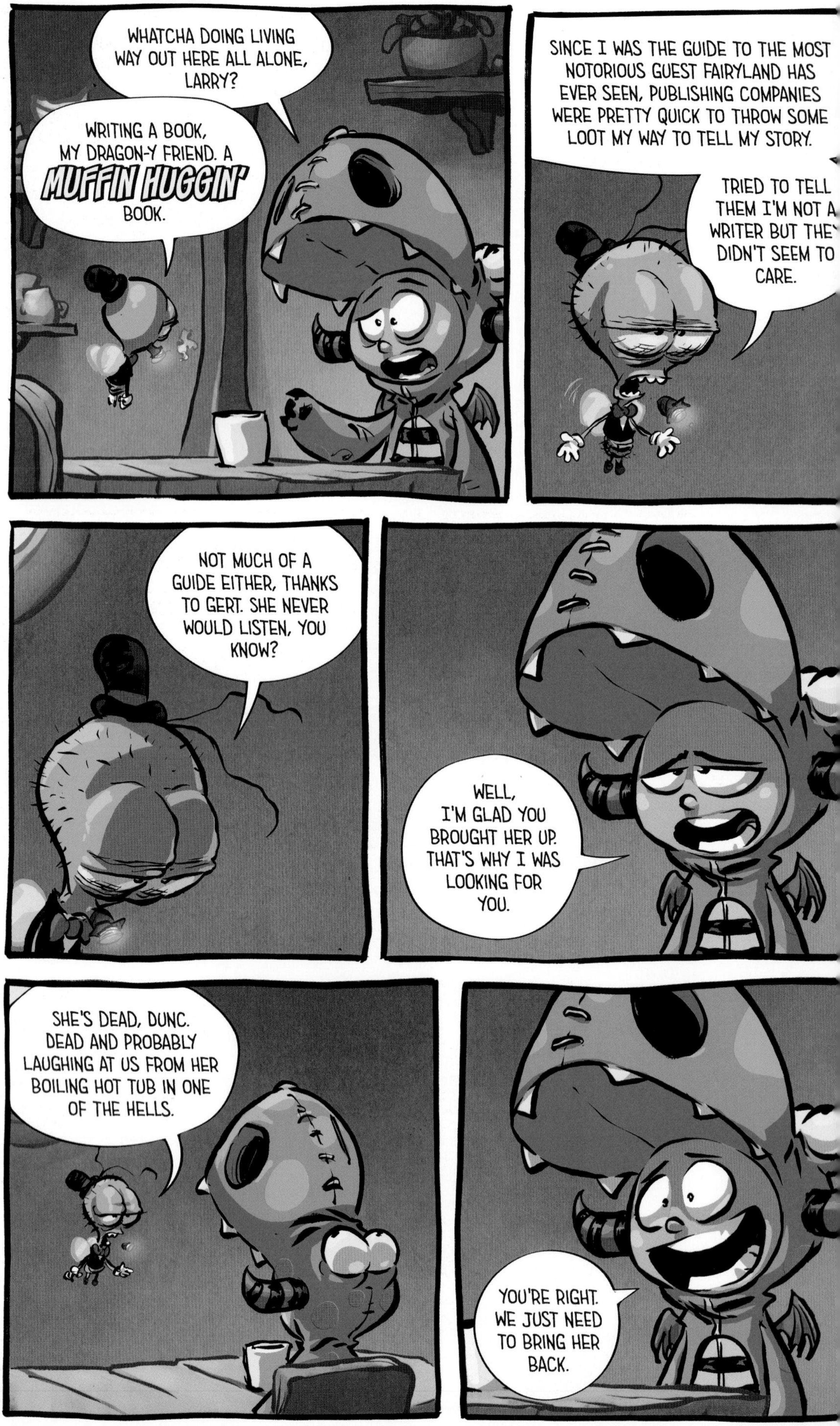
WHATCHA DOING LIVING WAY OUT HERE ALL ALONE, LARRY?
WRITING A BOOK, MY DRAGON-Y FRIEND. A MUFFIN HUGGIN' BOOK.
SINCE I WAS THE GUIDE TO THE MOST NOTORIOUS GUEST FAIRYLAND HAS EVER SEEN, PUBLISHING COMPANIES WERE PRETTY QUICK TO THROW SOME LOOT MY WAY TO TELL MY STORY.
TRIED TO TELL THEM I'M NOT A WRITER BUT THEY DIDN'T SEEM TO CARE.
NOT MUCH OF A GUIDE EITHER, THANKS TO GERT. SHE NEVER WOULD LISTEN, YOU KNOW?
WELL, I'M GLAD YOU BROUGHT HER UP. THAT'S WHY I WAS LOOKING FOR YOU.
SHE'S DEAD, DUNC. DEAD AND PROBABLY LAUGHING AT US FROM HER BOILING HOT TUB IN ONE OF THE HELLS.
YOU'RE RIGHT. WE JUST NEED TO BRING HER BACK.

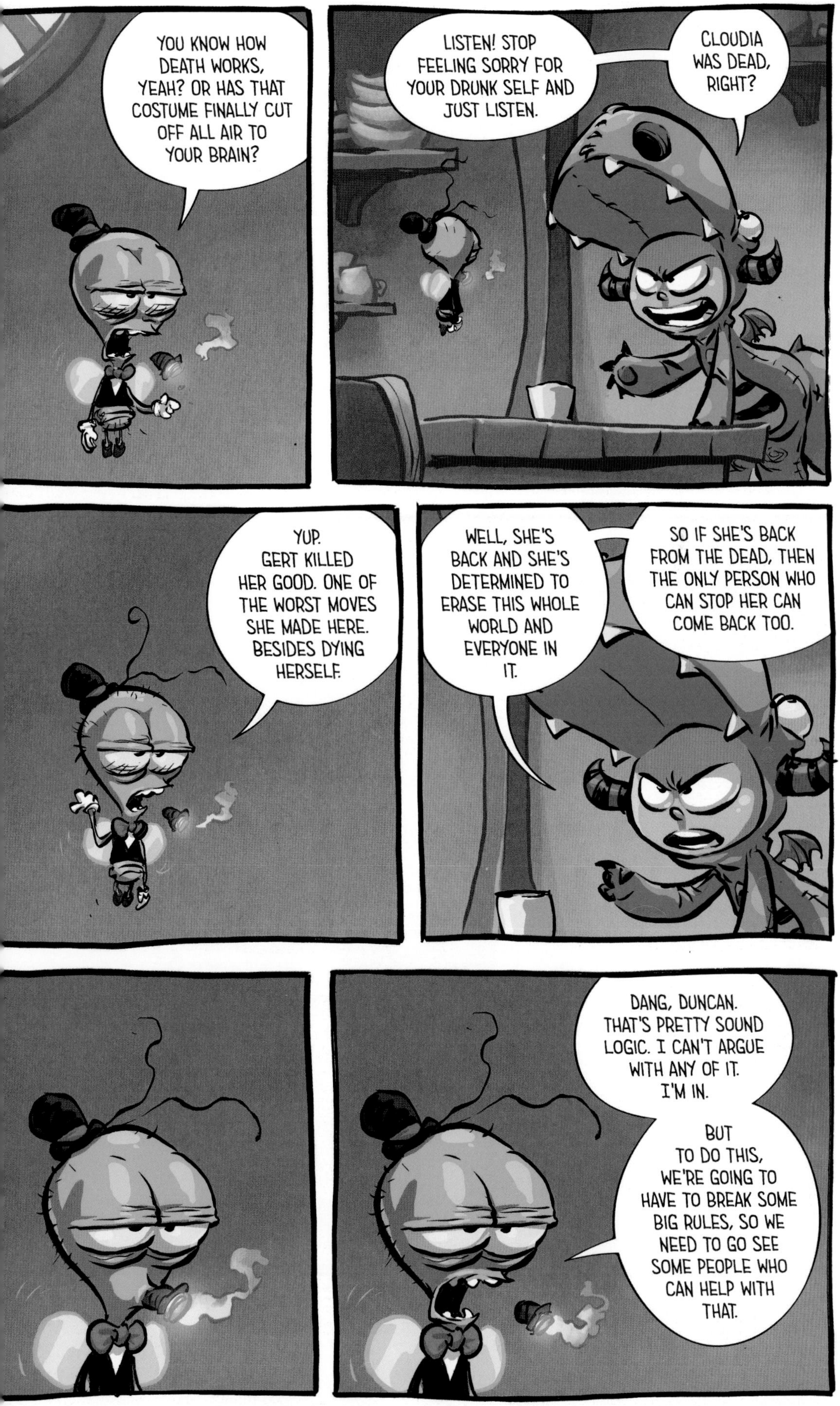
YOU KNOW HOW DEATH WORKS, YEAH? OR HAS THAT COSTUME FINALLY CUT OFF ALL AIR TO YOUR BRAIN?
LISTEN! STOP FEELING SORRY FOR YOUR DRUNK SELF AND JUST LISTEN.
CLOUDIA WAS DEAD, RIGHT?
YUP. GERT KILLED HER GOOD. ONE OF THE WORST MOVES SHE MADE HERE. BESIDES DYING HERSELF.
WELL, SHE'S BACK AND SHE'S DETERMINED TO ERASE THIS WHOLE WORLD AND EVERYONE IN IT.
SO IF SHE'S BACK FROM THE DEAD, THEN THE ONLY PERSON WHO CAN STOP HER CAN COME BACK TOO.
DANG, DUNCAN. THAT'S PRETTY SOUND LOGIC. I CAN'T ARGUE WITH ANY OF IT. I'M IN.
BUT TO DO THIS, WE'RE GOING TO HAVE TO BREAK SOME BIG RULES, SO WE NEED TO GO SEE SOME PEOPLE WHO CAN HELP WITH THAT.

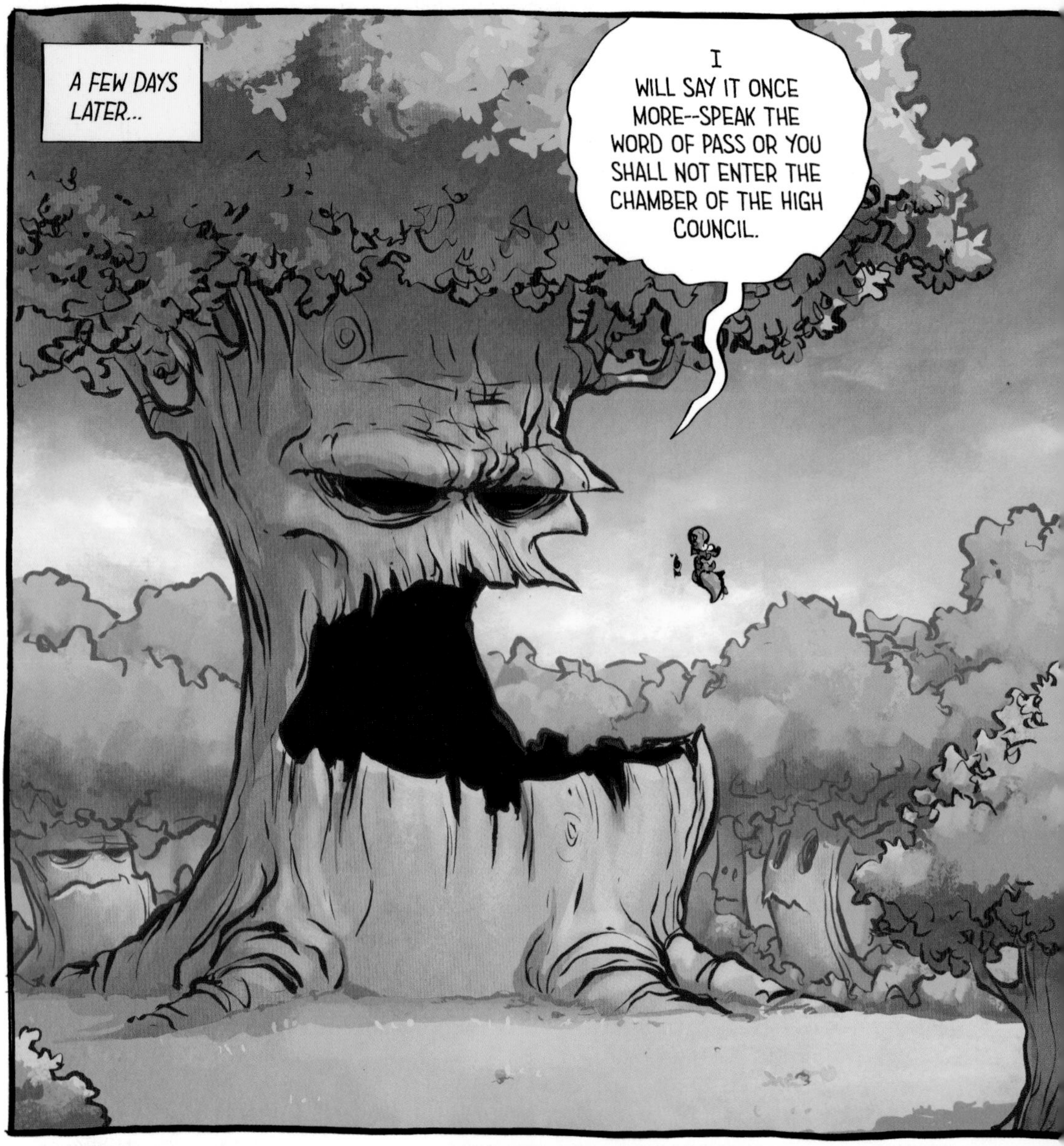
A FEW DAYS LATER...
I WILL SAY IT ONCE MORE--SPEAK THE WORD OF PASS OR YOU SHALL NOT ENTER THE CHAMBER OF THE HIGH COUNCIL.

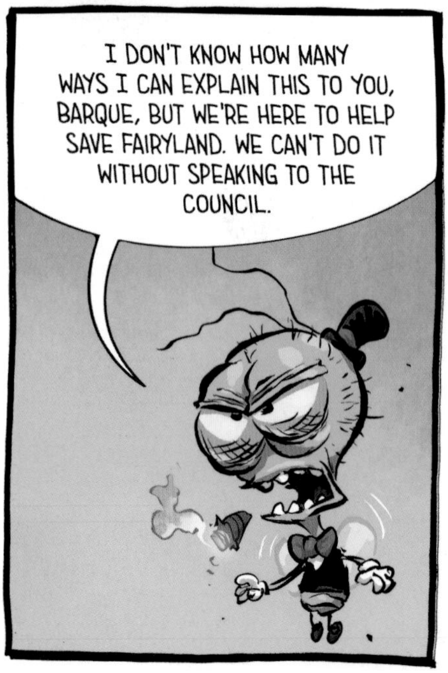
I DON'T KNOW HOW MANY WAYS I CAN EXPLAIN THIS TO YOU, BARQUE, BUT WE'RE HERE TO HELP SAVE FAIRYLAND. WE CAN'T DO IT WITHOUT SPEAKING TO THE COUNCIL.

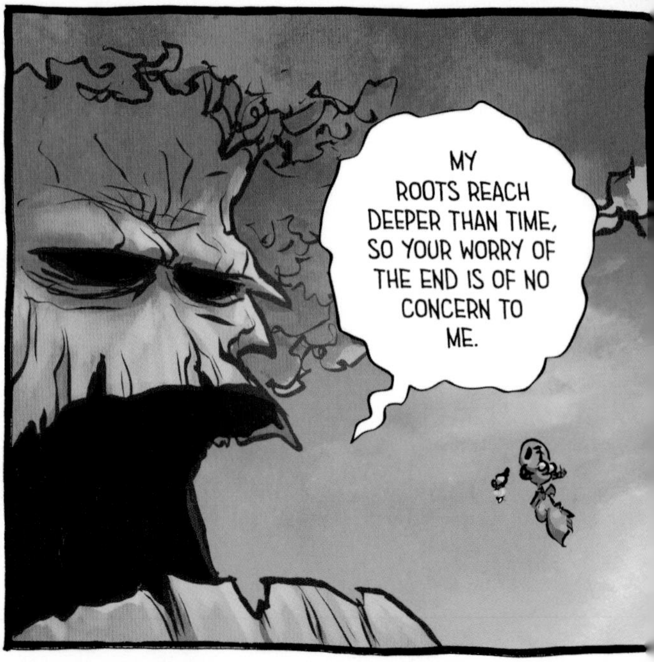
MY ROOTS REACH DEEPER THAN TIME, SO YOUR WORRY OF THE END IS OF NO CONCERN TO ME.

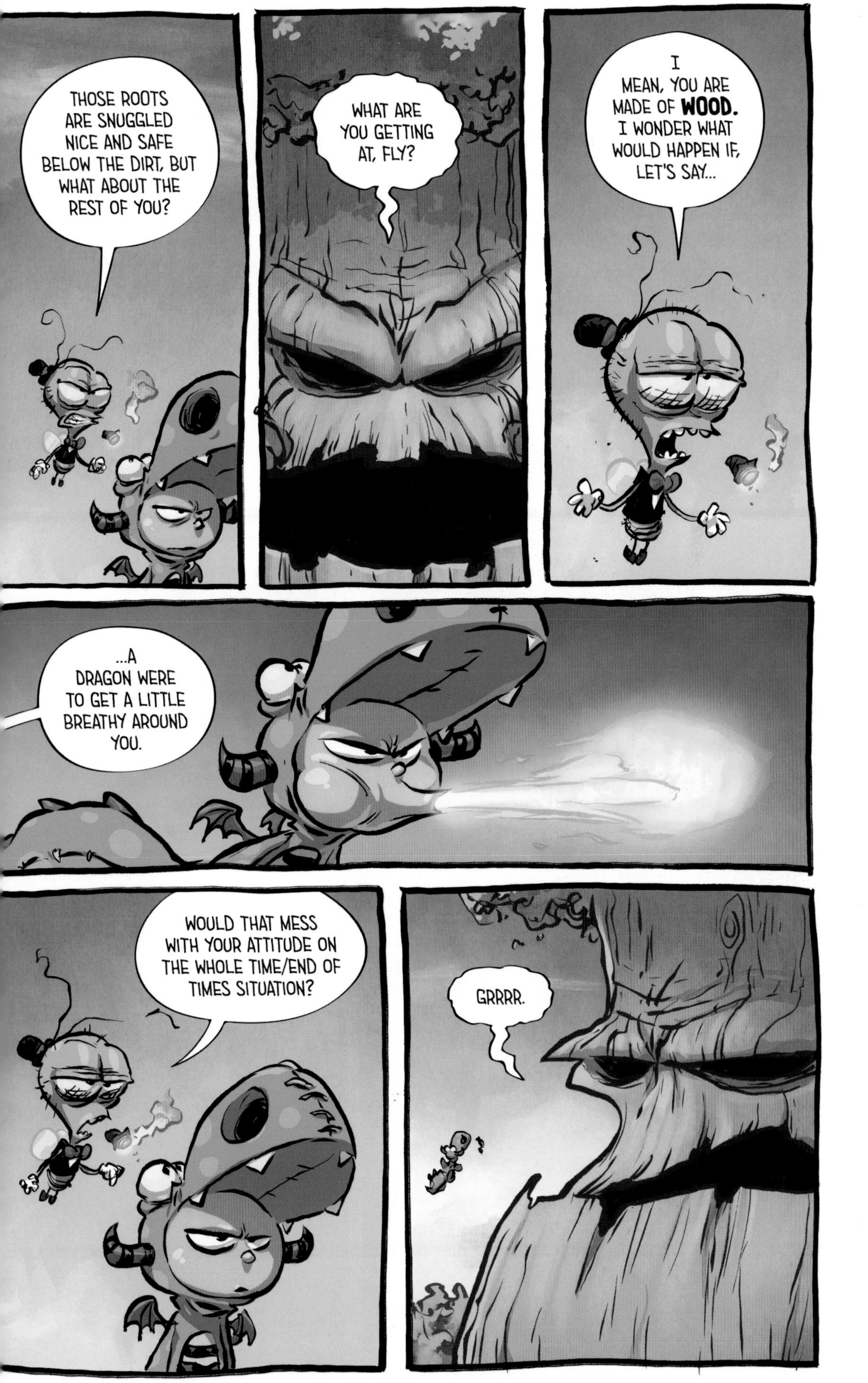
THOSE ROOTS ARE SNUGGLED NICE AND SAFE BELOW THE DIRT, BUT WHAT ABOUT THE REST OF YOU?
WHAT ARE YOU GETTING AT, FLY?
I MEAN, YOU ARE MADE OF **WOOD.** I WONDER WHAT WOULD HAPPEN IF, LET'S SAY...
...A DRAGON WERE TO GET A LITTLE BREATHY AROUND YOU.
WOULD THAT MESS WITH YOUR ATTITUDE ON THE WHOLE TIME/END OF TIMES SITUATION?
GRRRR.

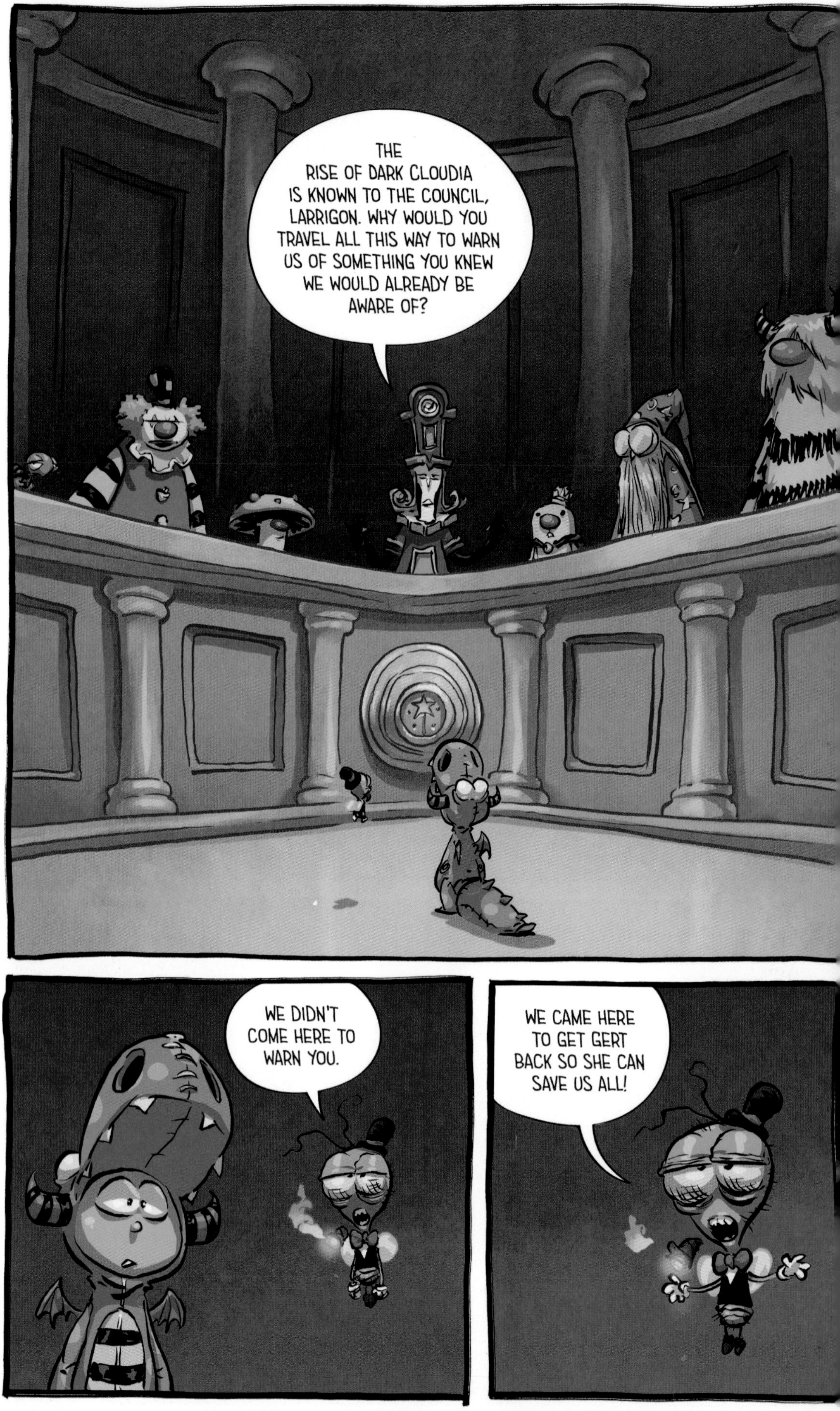
THE RISE OF DARK CLOUDIA IS KNOWN TO THE COUNCIL, LARRIGON. WHY WOULD YOU TRAVEL ALL THIS WAY TO WARN US OF SOMETHING YOU KNEW WE WOULD ALREADY BE AWARE OF?
WE DIDN'T COME HERE TO WARN YOU.
WE CAME HERE TO GET GERT BACK SO SHE CAN SAVE US ALL!

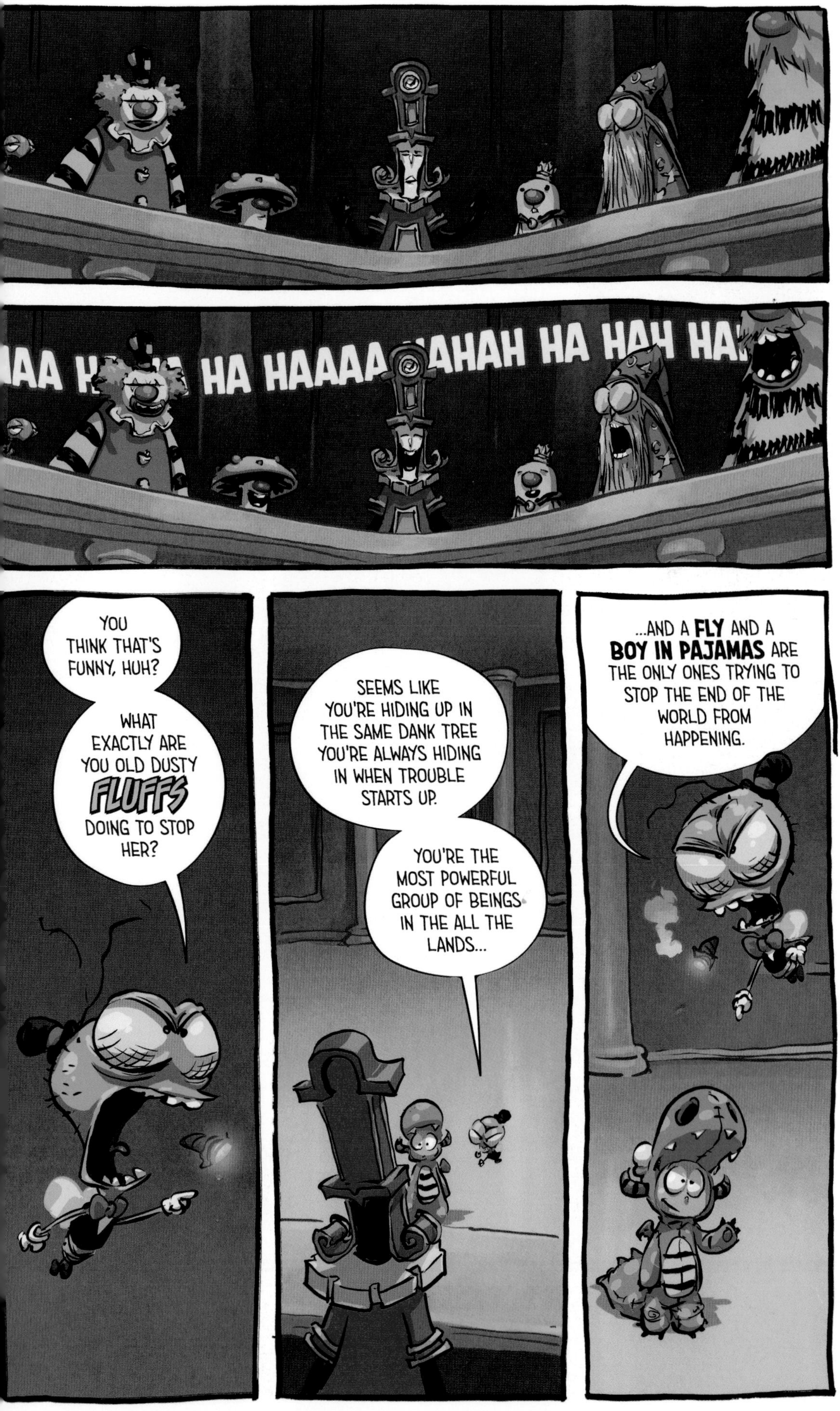

HA HAAAA HAHAH HA HAH
YOU THINK THAT'S FUNNY, HUH?
WHAT EXACTLY ARE YOU OLD DUSTY FLUFFS DOING TO STOP HER?
SEEMS LIKE YOU'RE HIDING UP IN THE SAME DANK TREE YOU'RE ALWAYS HIDING IN WHEN TROUBLE STARTS UP.
YOU'RE THE MOST POWERFUL GROUP OF BEINGS IN THE ALL THE LANDS...
...AND A FLY AND A BOY IN PAJAMAS ARE THE ONLY ONES TRYING TO STOP THE END OF THE WORLD FROM HAPPENING.

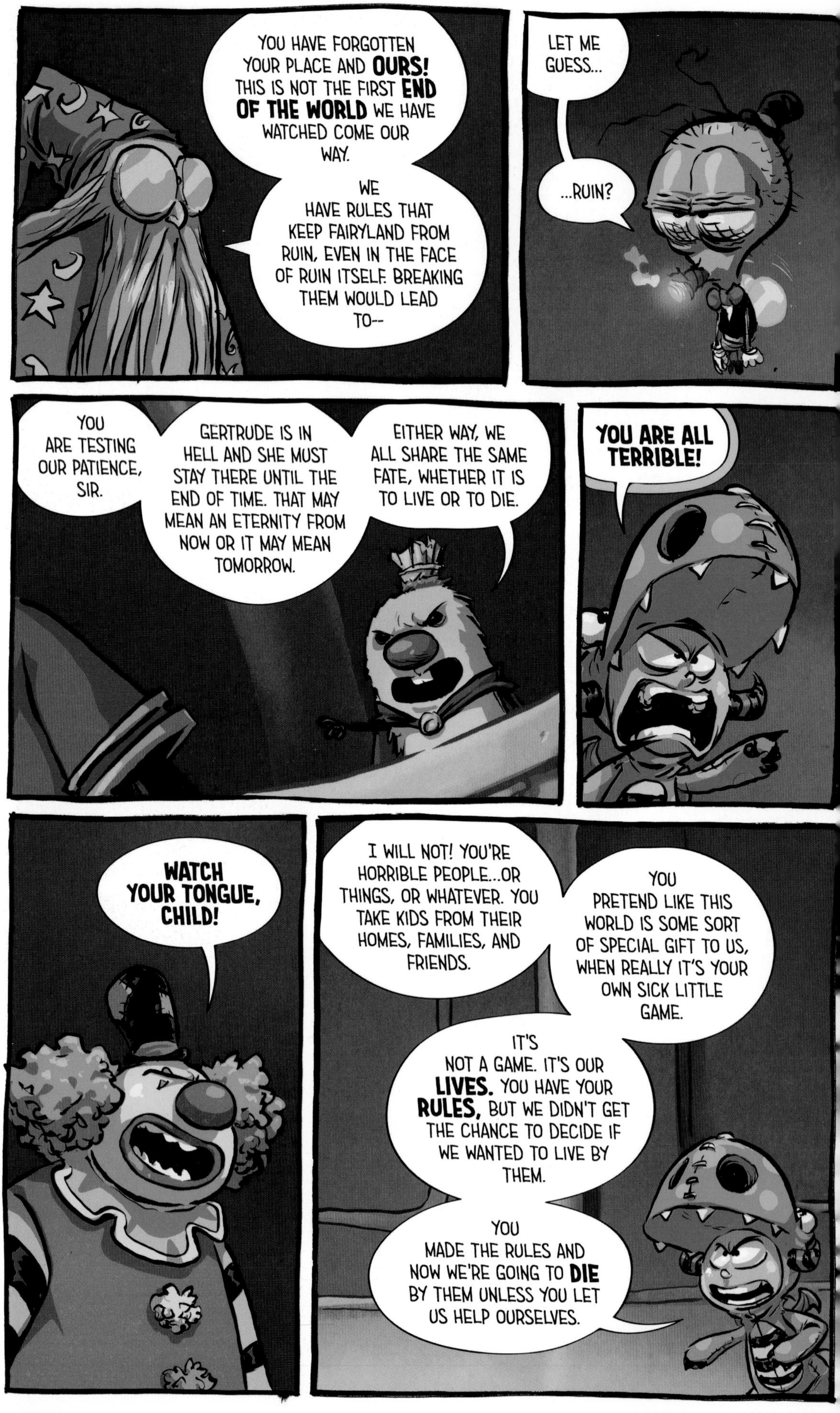

YOU HAVE FORGOTTEN YOUR PLACE AND **OURS!** THIS IS NOT THE FIRST **END OF THE WORLD** WE HAVE WATCHED COME OUR WAY.
WE HAVE RULES THAT KEEP FAIRYLAND FROM RUIN, EVEN IN THE FACE OF RUIN ITSELF. BREAKING THEM WOULD LEAD TO--
LET ME GUESS...
...RUIN?
YOU ARE TESTING OUR PATIENCE, SIR.
GERTRUDE IS IN HELL AND SHE MUST STAY THERE UNTIL THE END OF TIME. THAT MAY MEAN AN ETERNITY FROM NOW OR IT MAY MEAN TOMORROW.
EITHER WAY, WE ALL SHARE THE SAME FATE, WHETHER IT IS TO LIVE OR TO DIE.
YOU ARE ALL TERRIBLE!
WATCH YOUR TONGUE, CHILD!
I WILL NOT! YOU'RE HORRIBLE PEOPLE...OR THINGS, OR WHATEVER. YOU TAKE KIDS FROM THEIR HOMES, FAMILIES, AND FRIENDS.
YOU PRETEND LIKE THIS WORLD IS SOME SORT OF SPECIAL GIFT TO US, WHEN REALLY IT'S YOUR OWN SICK LITTLE GAME.
IT'S NOT A GAME. IT'S OUR **LIVES.** YOU HAVE YOUR **RULES,** BUT WE DIDN'T GET THE CHANCE TO DECIDE IF WE WANTED TO LIVE BY THEM.
YOU MADE THE RULES AND NOW WE'RE GOING TO **DIE** BY THEM UNLESS YOU LET US HELP OURSELVES.

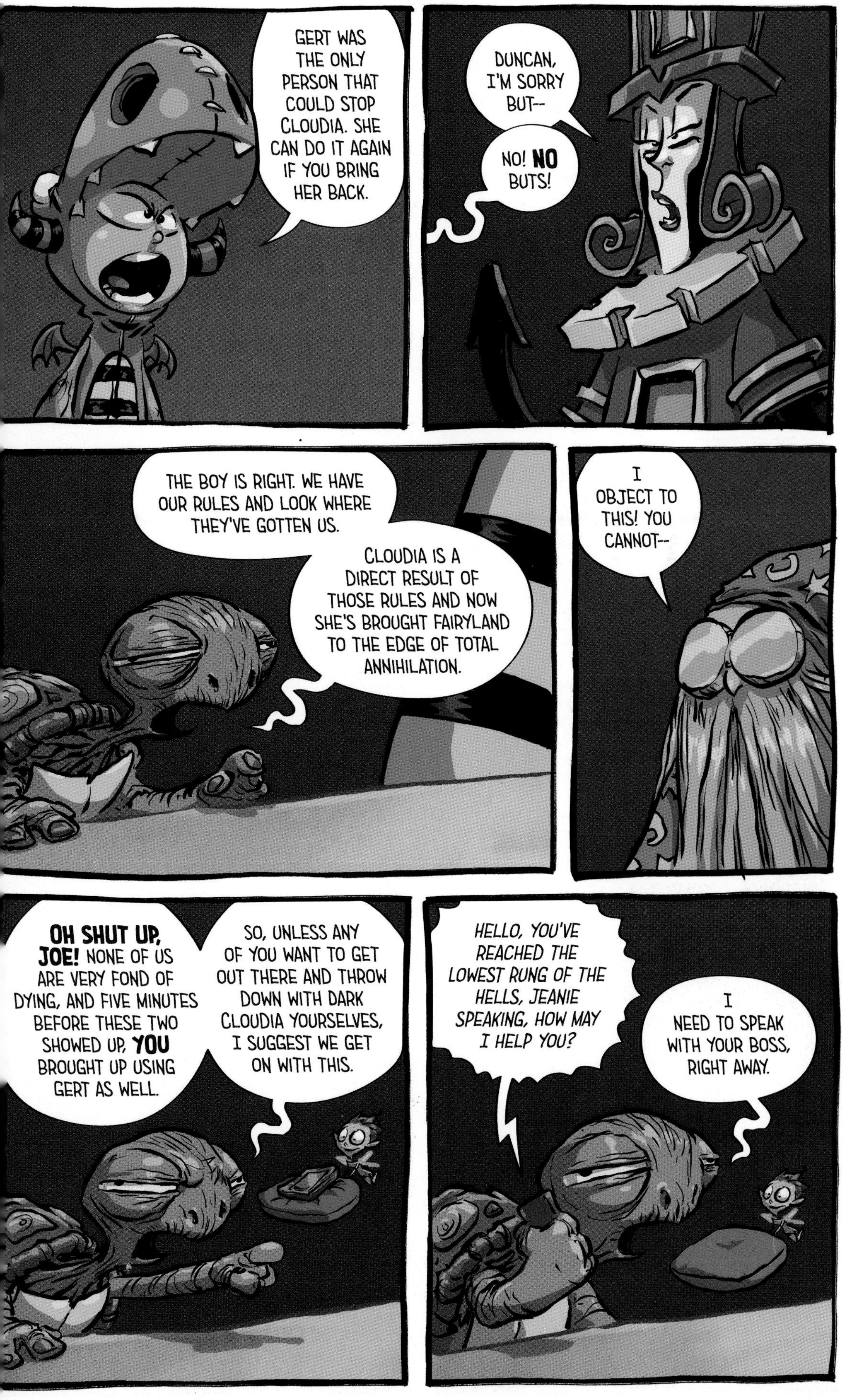
GERT WAS THE ONLY PERSON THAT COULD STOP CLOUDIA. SHE CAN DO IT AGAIN IF YOU BRING HER BACK.
DUNCAN, I'M SORRY BUT--
NO! **NO** BUTS!
THE BOY IS RIGHT. WE HAVE OUR RULES AND LOOK WHERE THEY'VE GOTTEN US.
CLOUDIA IS A DIRECT RESULT OF THOSE RULES AND NOW SHE'S BROUGHT FAIRYLAND TO THE EDGE OF TOTAL ANNIHILATION.
I OBJECT TO THIS! YOU CANNOT--
OH SHUT UP, JOE! NONE OF US ARE VERY FOND OF DYING, AND FIVE MINUTES BEFORE THESE TWO SHOWED UP, **YOU** BROUGHT UP USING GERT AS WELL.
SO, UNLESS ANY OF YOU WANT TO GET OUT THERE AND THROW DOWN WITH DARK CLOUDIA YOURSELVES, I SUGGEST WE GET ON WITH THIS.
HELLO, YOU'VE REACHED THE LOWEST RUNG OF THE HELLS, JEANIE SPEAKING, HOW MAY I HELP YOU?
I NEED TO SPEAK WITH YOUR BOSS, RIGHT AWAY.

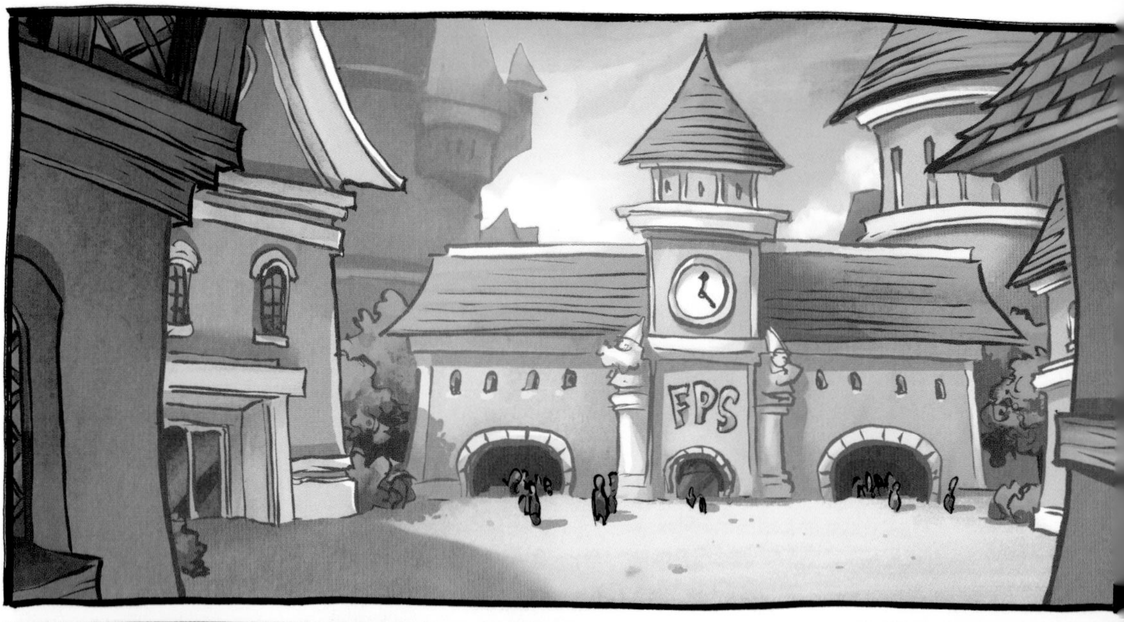

FPS

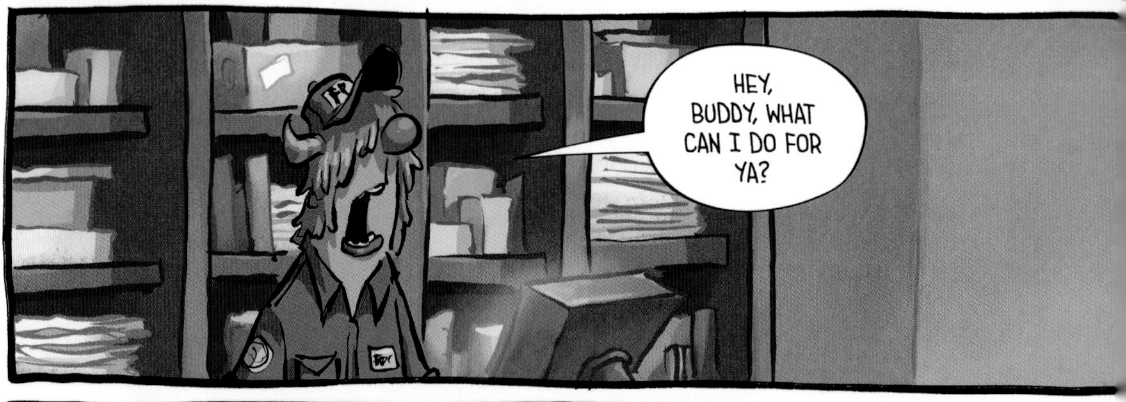

HEY, BUDDY, WHAT CAN I DO FOR YA?

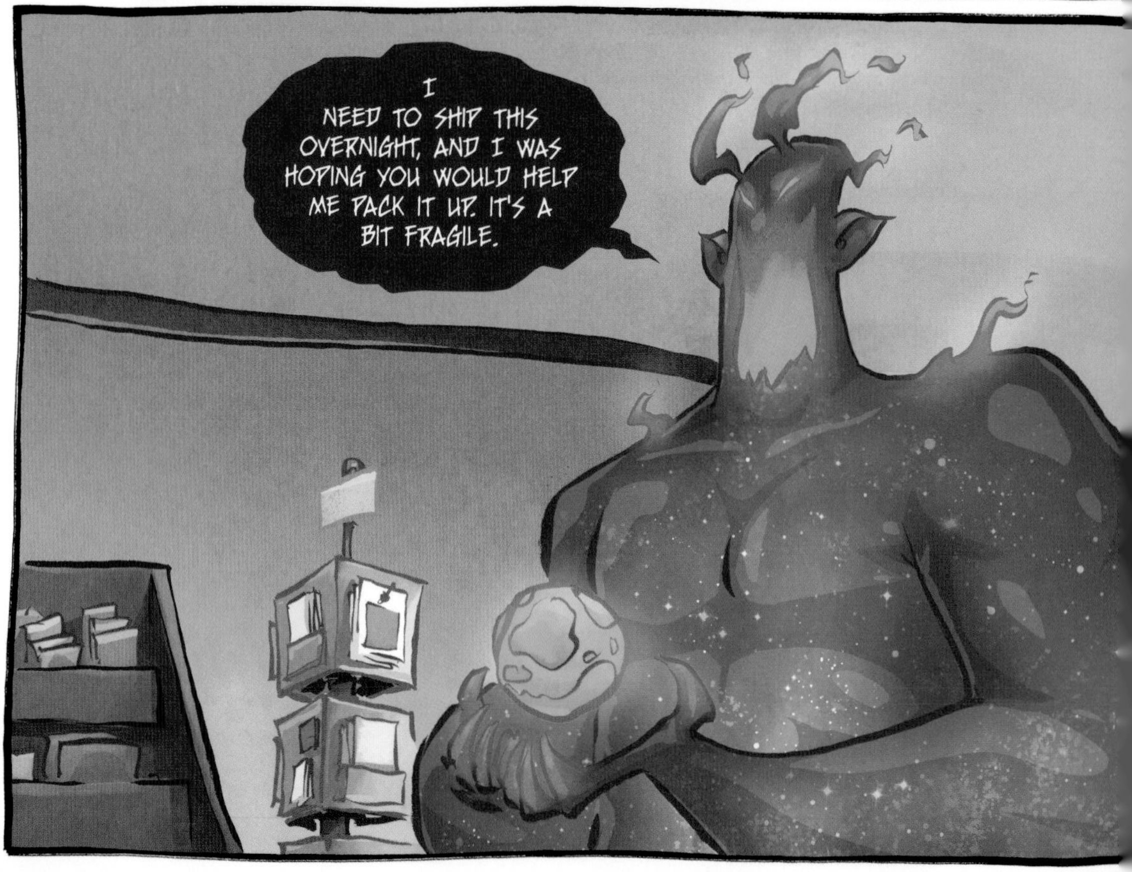

I NEED TO SHIP THIS OVERNIGHT, AND I WAS HOPING YOU WOULD HELP ME PACK IT UP. IT'S A BIT FRAGILE.

NINETEEN

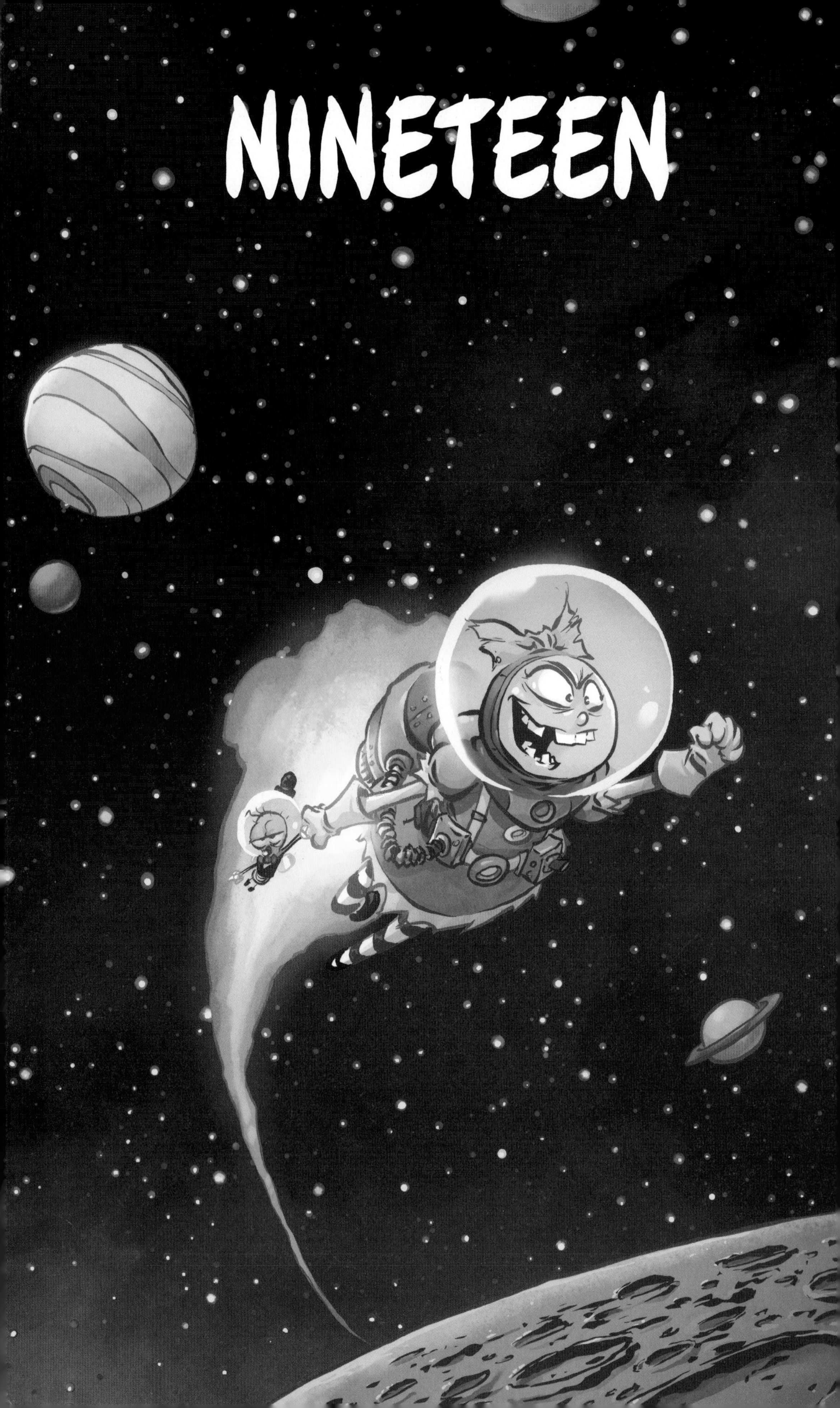

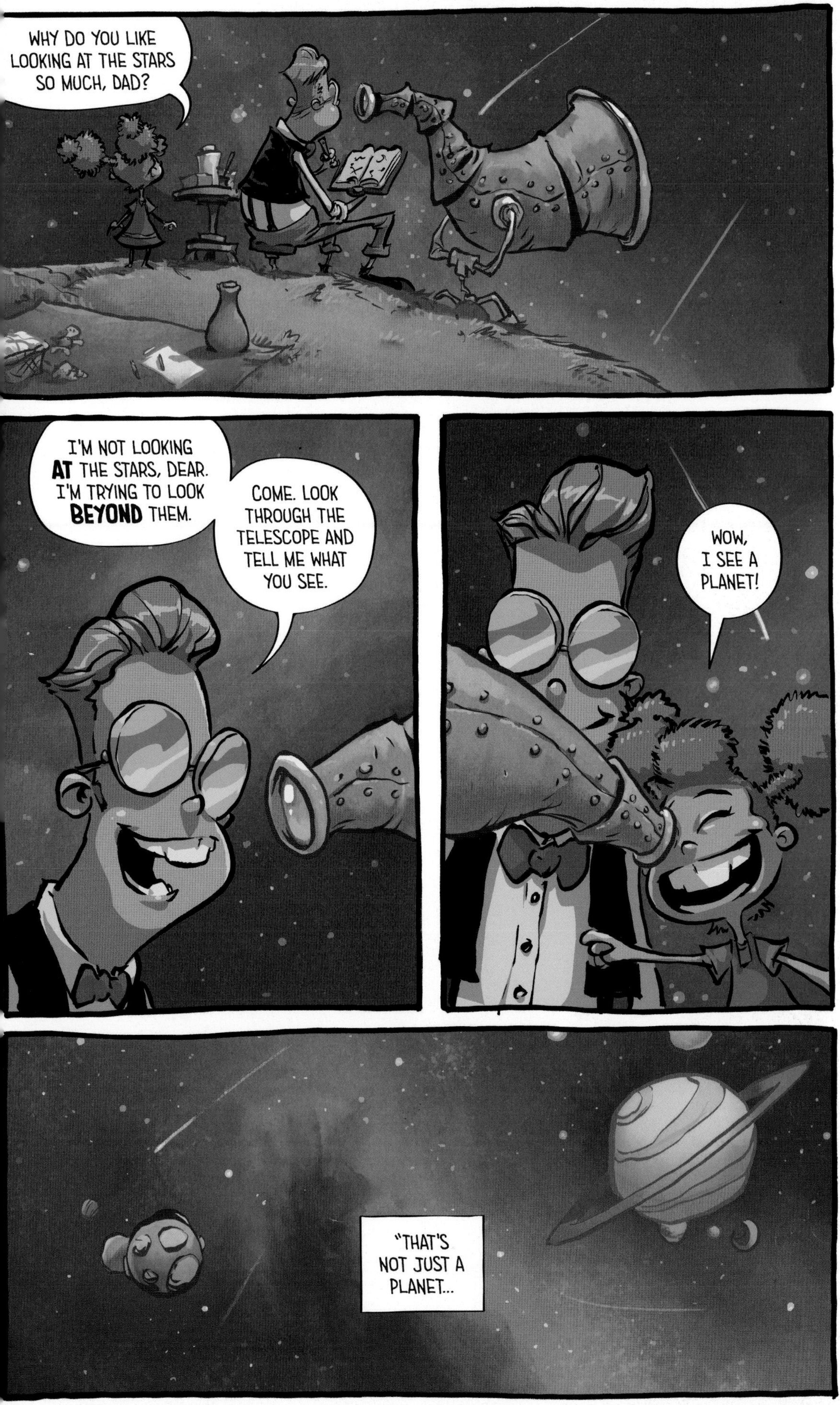
WHY DO YOU LIKE LOOKING AT THE STARS SO MUCH, DAD?
I'M NOT LOOKING **AT** THE STARS, DEAR. I'M TRYING TO LOOK **BEYOND** THEM.
COME. LOOK THROUGH THE TELESCOPE AND TELL ME WHAT YOU SEE.
WOW, I SEE A PLANET!
"THAT'S NOT JUST A PLANET...

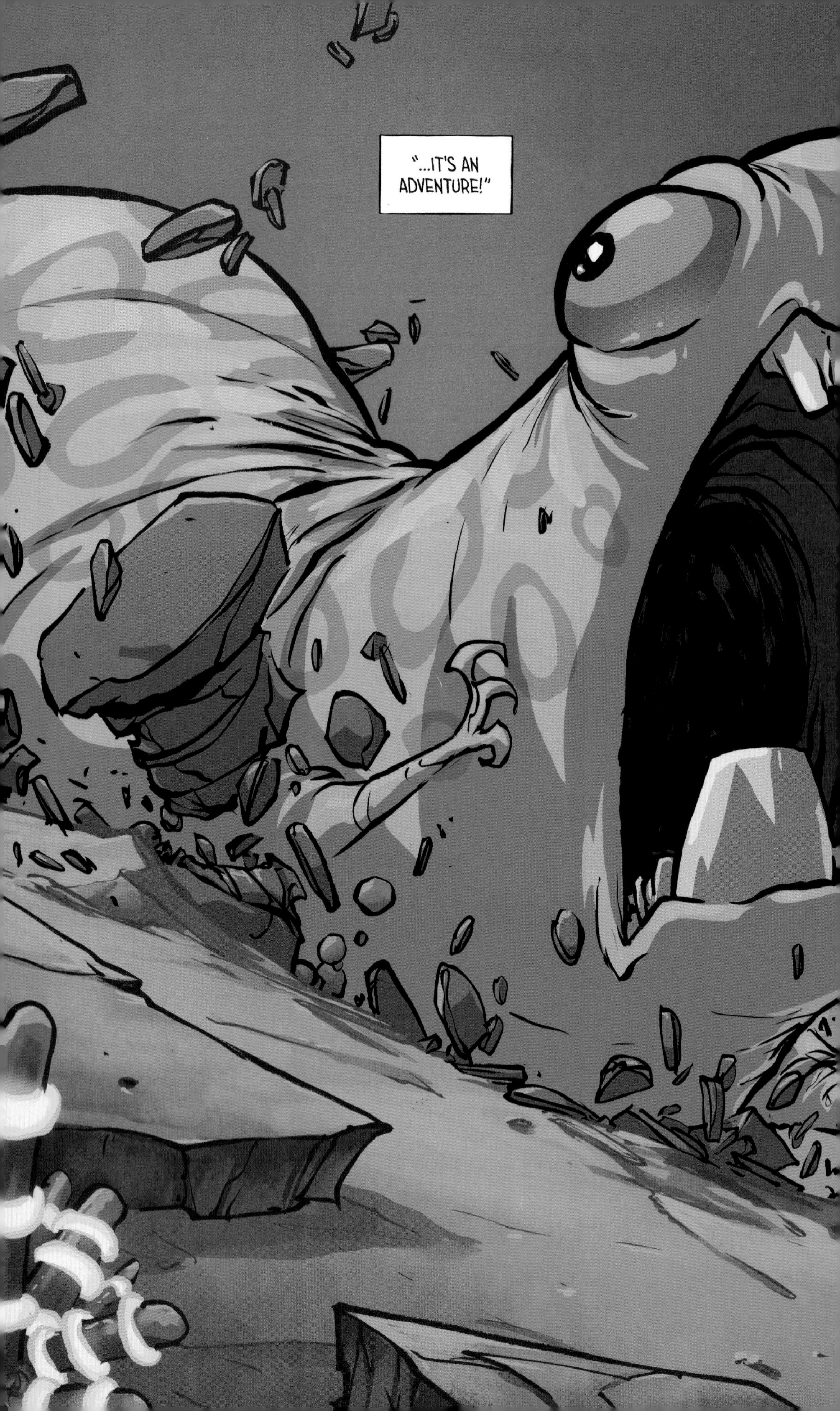
"...IT'S AN ADVENTURE!"

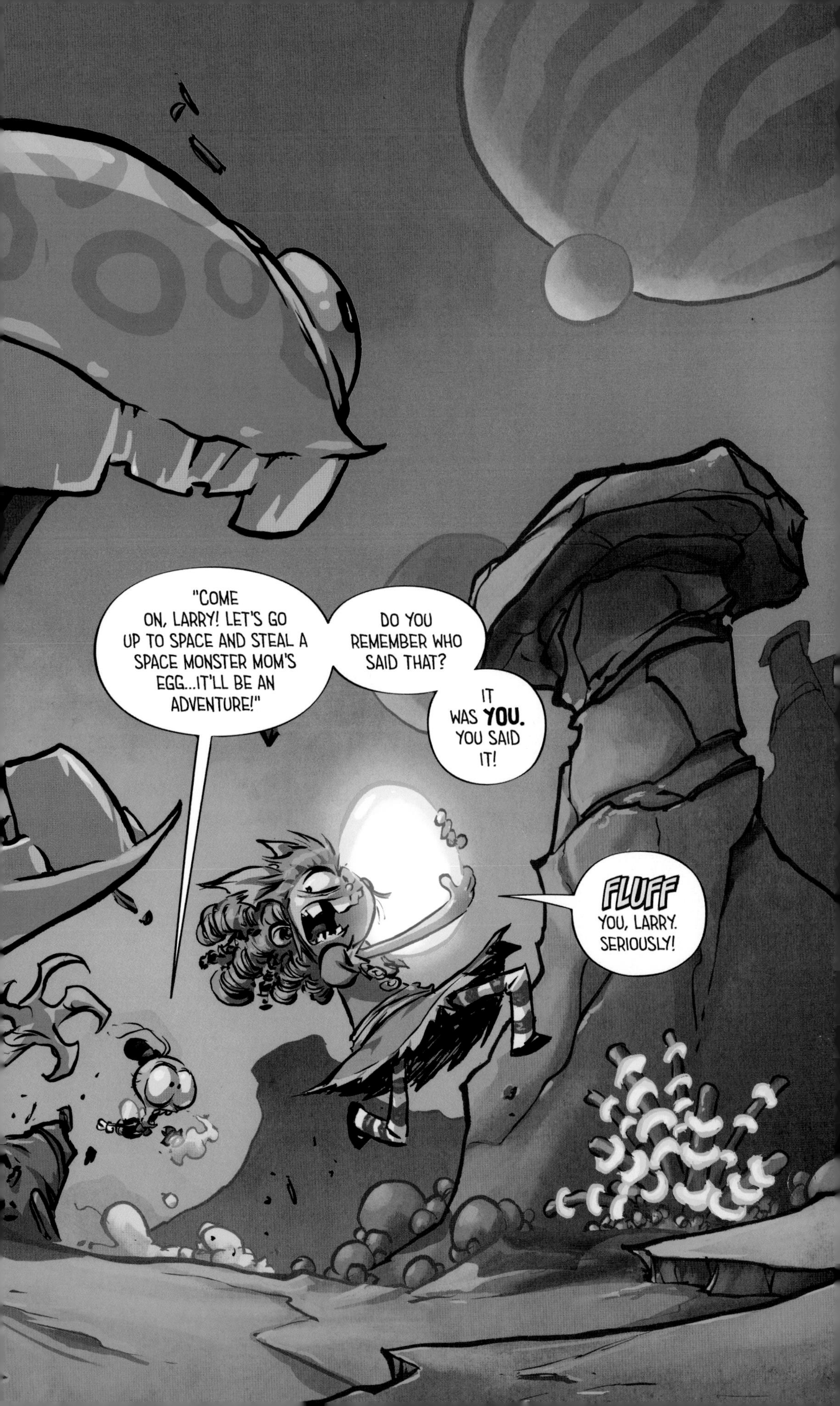
"COME ON, LARRY! LET'S GO UP TO SPACE AND STEAL A SPACE MONSTER MOM'S EGG...IT'LL BE AN ADVENTURE!"
DO YOU REMEMBER WHO SAID THAT?
IT WAS **YOU.** YOU SAID IT!
FLUFF YOU, LARRY. SERIOUSLY!

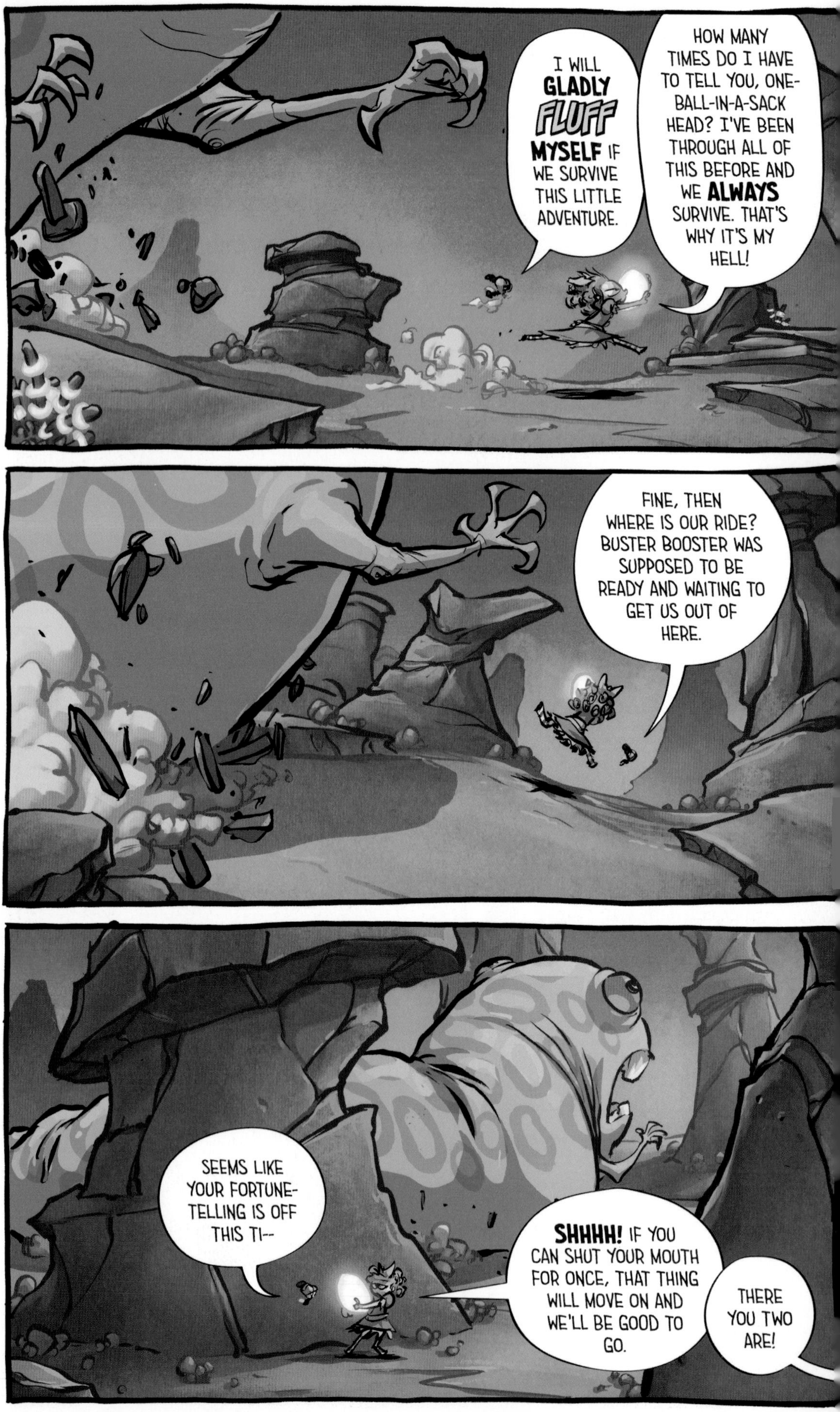
I WILL **GLADLY** FLUFF **MYSELF** IF WE SURVIVE THIS LITTLE ADVENTURE.
HOW MANY TIMES DO I HAVE TO TELL YOU, ONE-BALL-IN-A-SACK HEAD? I'VE BEEN THROUGH ALL OF THIS BEFORE AND WE **ALWAYS** SURVIVE. THAT'S WHY IT'S MY HELL!
FINE, THEN WHERE IS OUR RIDE? BUSTER BOOSTER WAS SUPPOSED TO BE READY AND WAITING TO GET US OUT OF HERE.
SEEMS LIKE YOUR FORTUNE-TELLING IS OFF THIS TI--
SHHHH! IF YOU CAN SHUT YOUR MOUTH FOR ONCE, THAT THING WILL MOVE ON AND WE'LL BE GOOD TO GO.
THERE YOU TWO ARE!

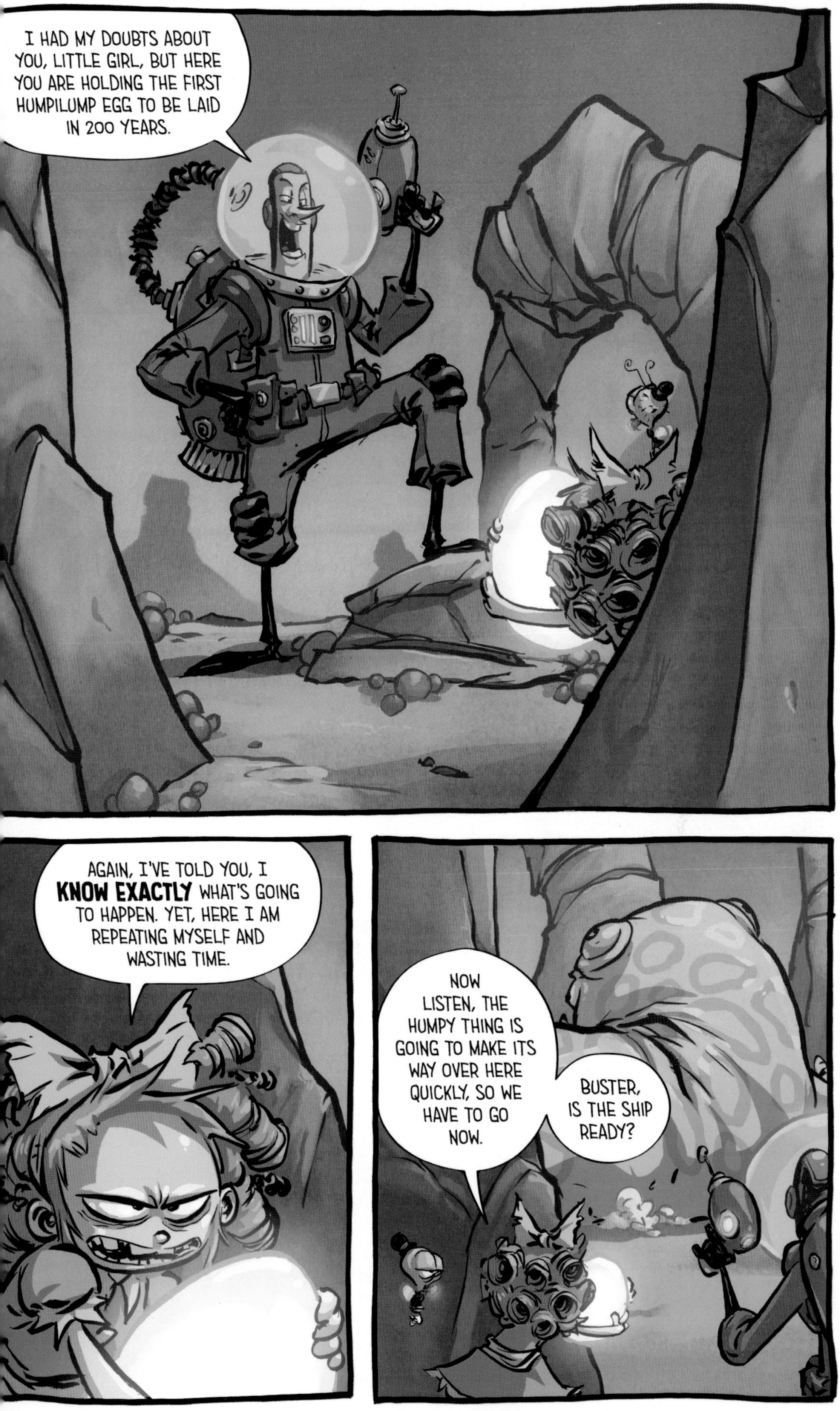
I HAD MY DOUBTS ABOUT YOU, LITTLE GIRL, BUT HERE YOU ARE HOLDING THE FIRST HUMPILUMP EGG TO BE LAID IN 200 YEARS.
AGAIN, I'VE TOLD YOU, I **KNOW EXACTLY** WHAT'S GOING TO HAPPEN. YET, HERE I AM REPEATING MYSELF AND WASTING TIME.
NOW LISTEN, THE HUMPY THING IS GOING TO MAKE ITS WAY OVER HERE QUICKLY, SO WE HAVE TO GO NOW.
BUSTER, IS THE SHIP READY?

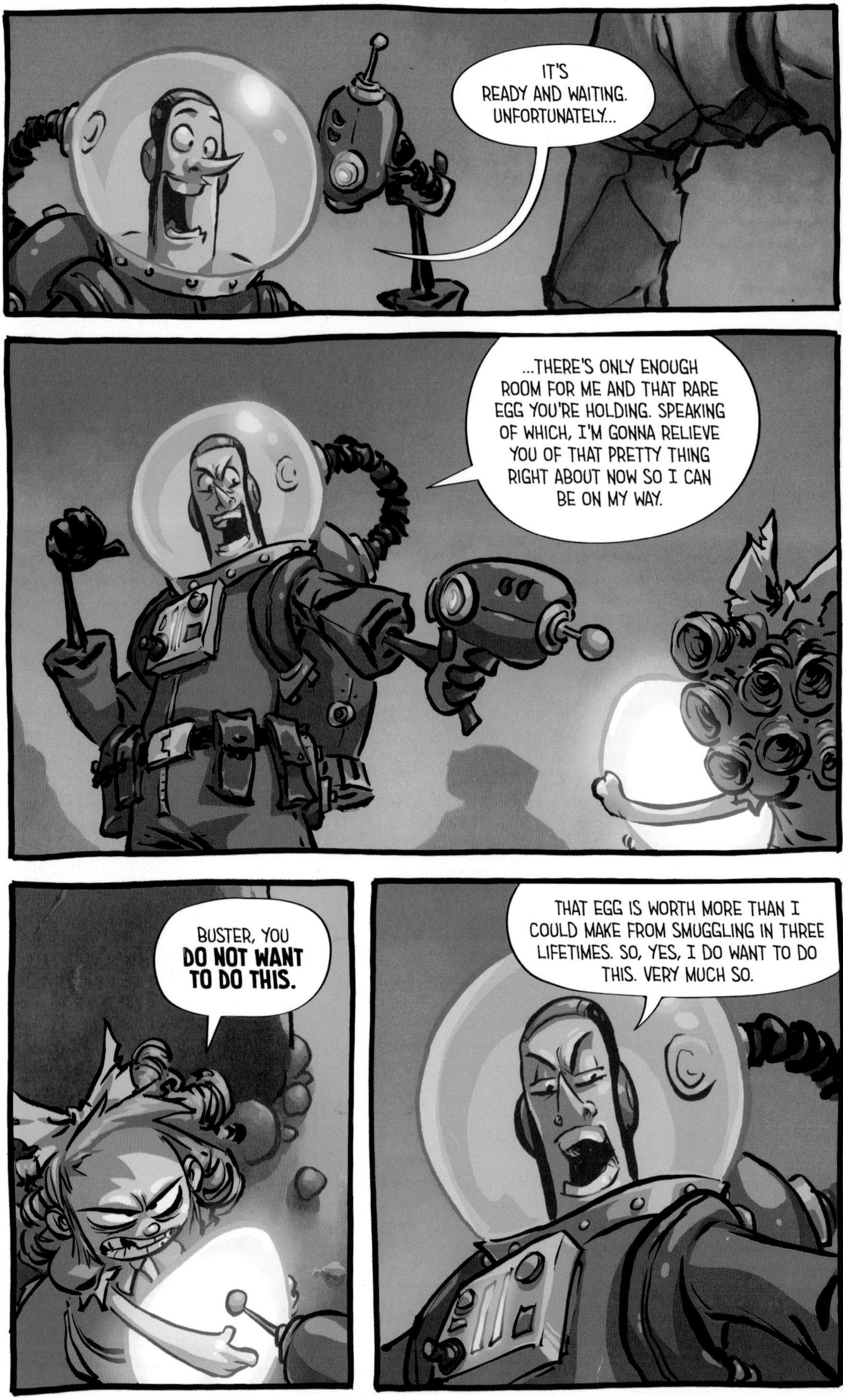

IT'S READY AND WAITING. UNFORTUNATELY...
...THERE'S ONLY ENOUGH ROOM FOR ME AND THAT RARE EGG YOU'RE HOLDING. SPEAKING OF WHICH, I'M GONNA RELIEVE YOU OF THAT PRETTY THING RIGHT ABOUT NOW SO I CAN BE ON MY WAY.
BUSTER, YOU **DO NOT WANT TO DO THIS.**
THAT EGG IS WORTH MORE THAN I COULD MAKE FROM SMUGGLING IN THREE LIFETIMES. SO, YES, I DO WANT TO DO THIS. VERY MUCH SO.

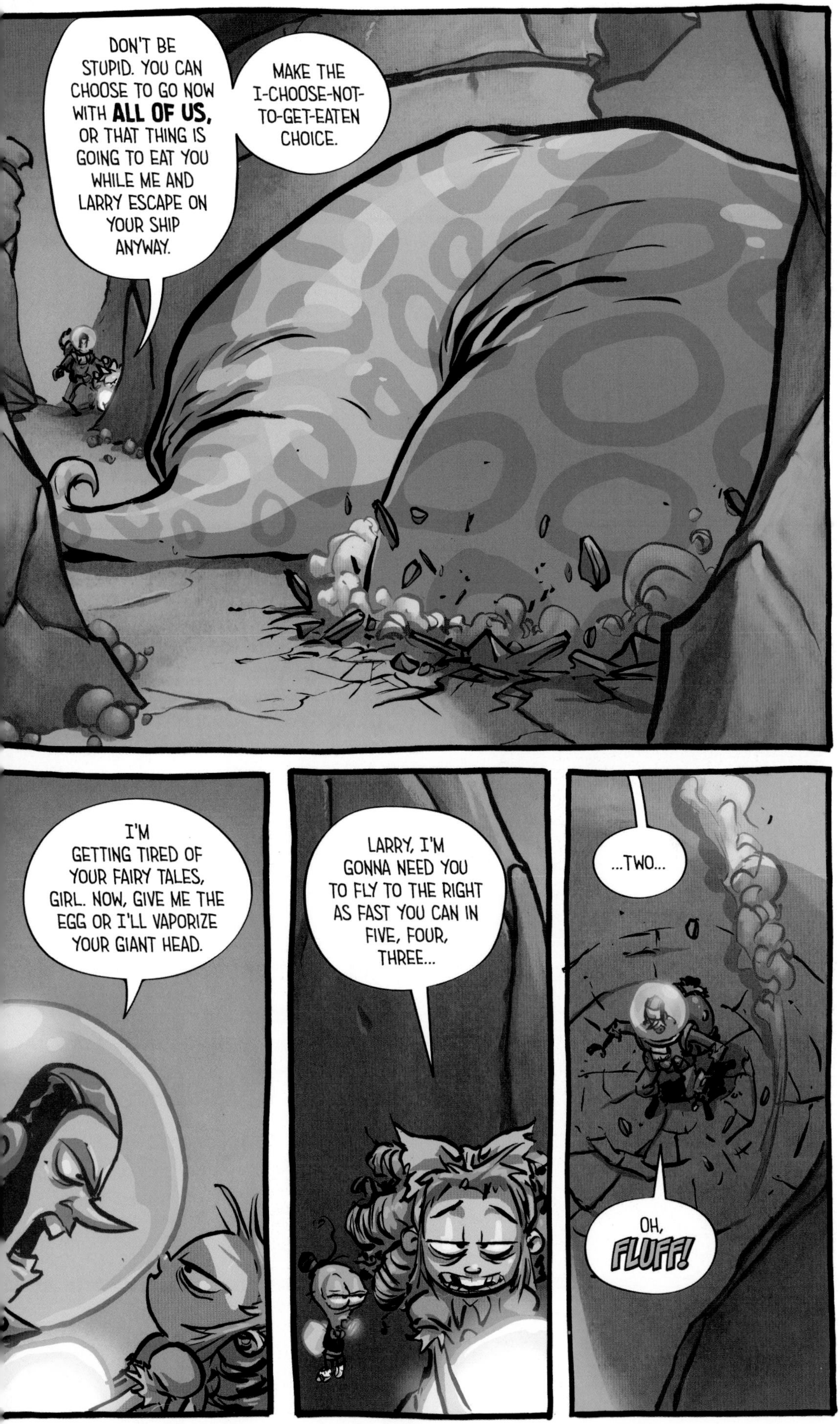
DON'T BE STUPID. YOU CAN CHOOSE TO GO NOW WITH ALL OF US, OR THAT THING IS GOING TO EAT YOU WHILE ME AND LARRY ESCAPE ON YOUR SHIP ANYWAY.
MAKE THE I-CHOOSE-NOT-TO-GET-EATEN CHOICE.
I'M GETTING TIRED OF YOUR FAIRY TALES, GIRL. NOW, GIVE ME THE EGG OR I'LL VAPORIZE YOUR GIANT HEAD.
LARRY, I'M GONNA NEED YOU TO FLY TO THE RIGHT AS FAST YOU CAN IN FIVE, FOUR, THREE...
...TWO...
OH, FLUFF!

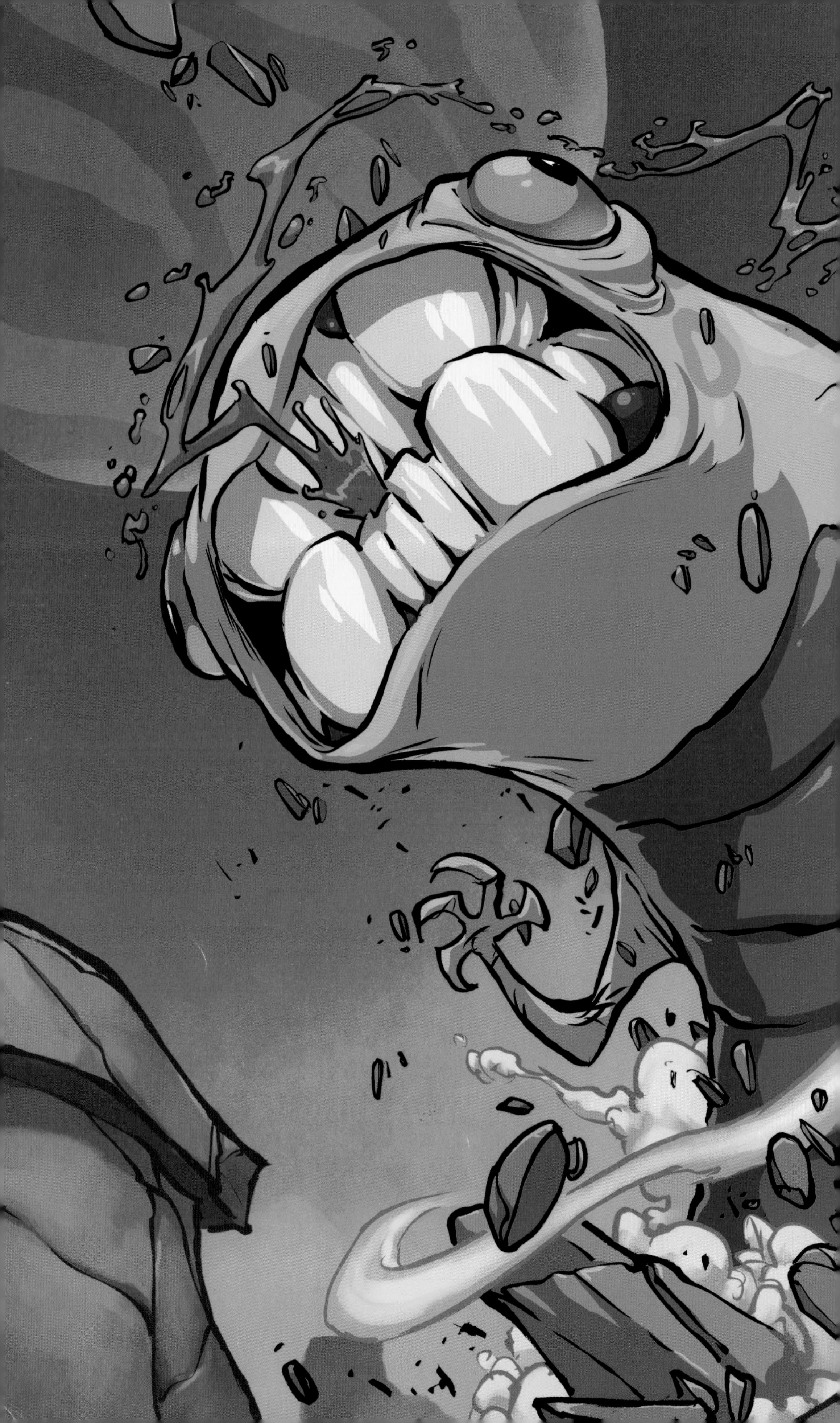

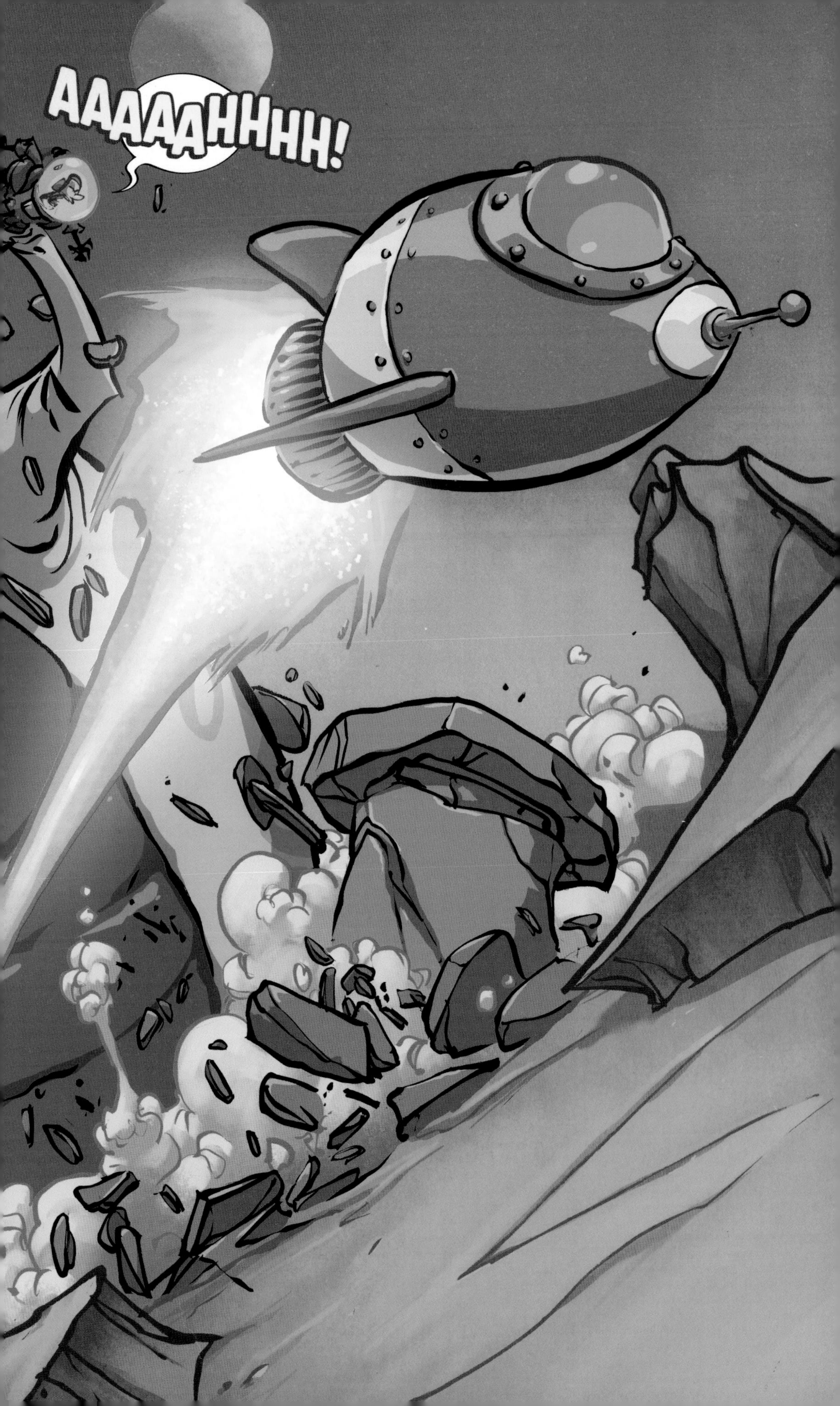
AAAAAHHHH!

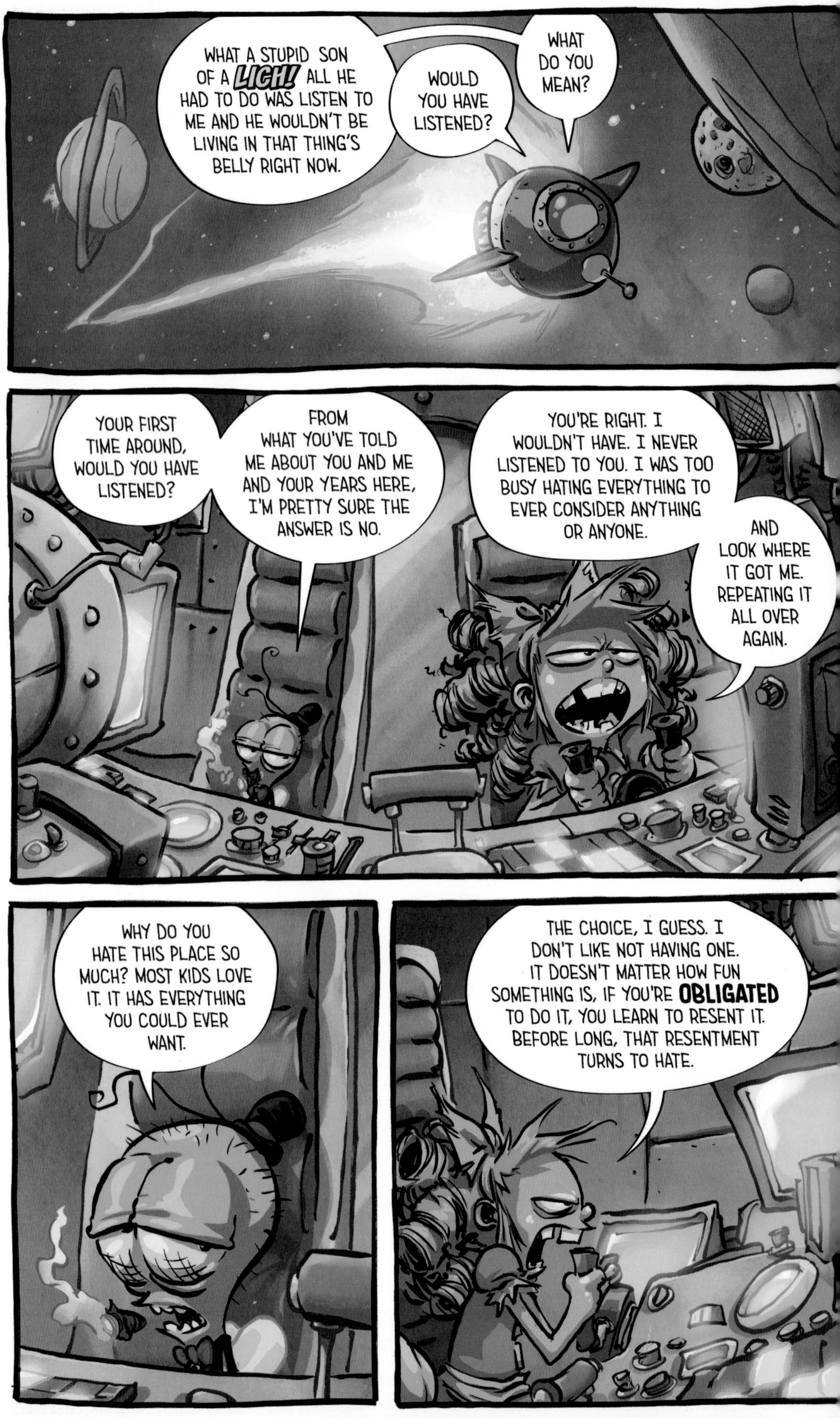
WHAT A STUPID SON OF A LICH! ALL HE HAD TO DO WAS LISTEN TO ME AND HE WOULDN'T BE LIVING IN THAT THING'S BELLY RIGHT NOW.
WHAT DO YOU MEAN?
WOULD YOU HAVE LISTENED?
YOUR FIRST TIME AROUND, WOULD YOU HAVE LISTENED?
FROM WHAT YOU'VE TOLD ME ABOUT YOU AND ME AND YOUR YEARS HERE, I'M PRETTY SURE THE ANSWER IS NO.
YOU'RE RIGHT. I WOULDN'T HAVE. I NEVER LISTENED TO YOU. I WAS TOO BUSY HATING EVERYTHING TO EVER CONSIDER ANYTHING OR ANYONE.
AND LOOK WHERE IT GOT ME. REPEATING IT ALL OVER AGAIN.
WHY DO YOU HATE THIS PLACE SO MUCH? MOST KIDS LOVE IT. IT HAS EVERYTHING YOU COULD EVER WANT.
THE CHOICE, I GUESS. I DON'T LIKE NOT HAVING ONE. IT DOESN'T MATTER HOW FUN SOMETHING IS, IF YOU'RE OBLIGATED TO DO IT, YOU LEARN TO RESENT IT. BEFORE LONG, THAT RESENTMENT TURNS TO HATE.

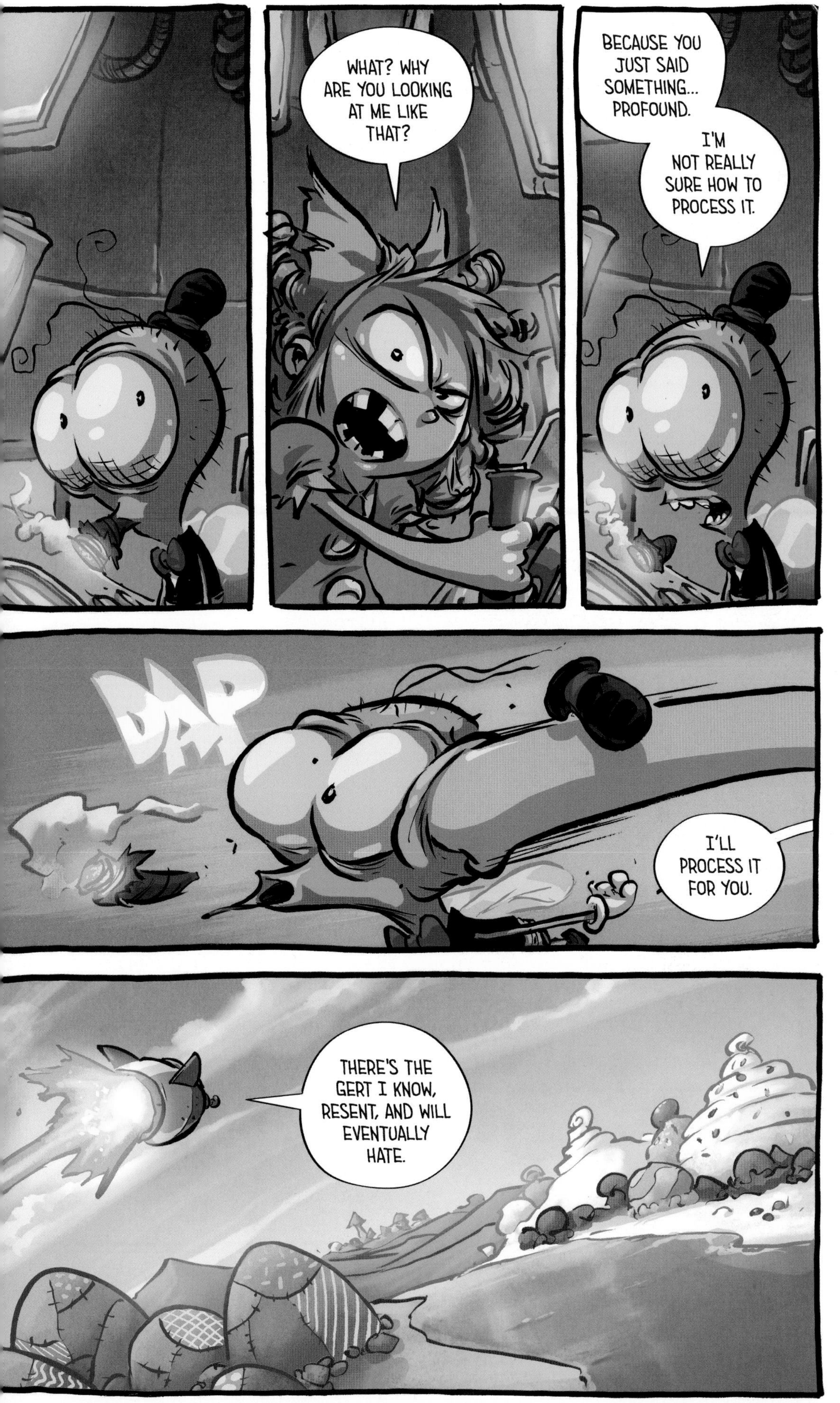
WHAT? WHY ARE YOU LOOKING AT ME LIKE THAT?
BECAUSE YOU JUST SAID SOMETHING... PROFOUND.
I'M NOT REALLY SURE HOW TO PROCESS IT.
DAP
I'LL PROCESS IT FOR YOU.
THERE'S THE GERT I KNOW, RESENT, AND WILL EVENTUALLY HATE.

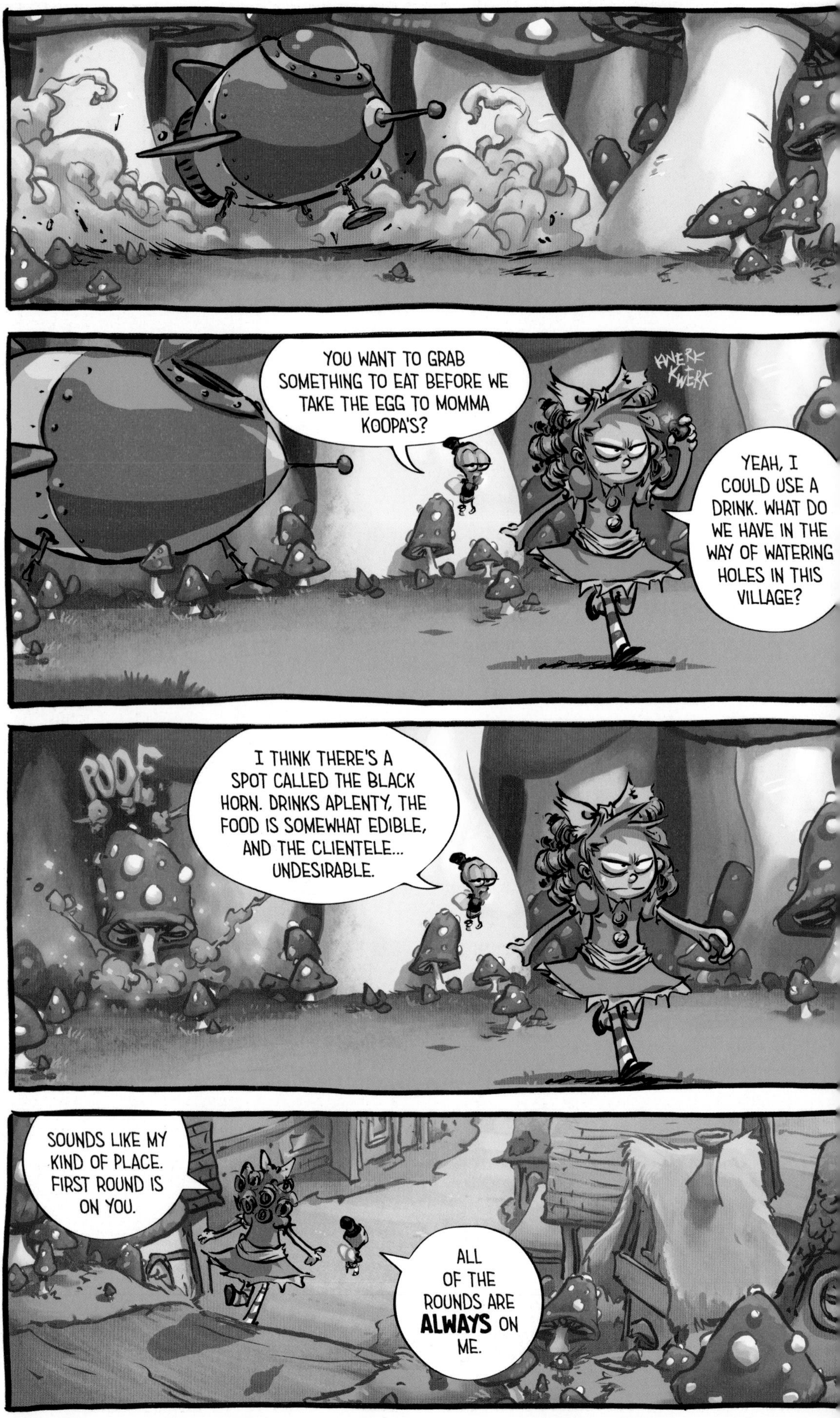
YOU WANT TO GRAB SOMETHING TO EAT BEFORE WE TAKE THE EGG TO MOMMA KOOPA'S?
KWERK KWERK
YEAH, I COULD USE A DRINK. WHAT DO WE HAVE IN THE WAY OF WATERING HOLES IN THIS VILLAGE?
POOF
I THINK THERE'S A SPOT CALLED THE BLACK HORN. DRINKS APLENTY, THE FOOD IS SOMEWHAT EDIBLE, AND THE CLIENTELE... UNDESIRABLE.
SOUNDS LIKE MY KIND OF PLACE. FIRST ROUND IS ON YOU.
ALL OF THE ROUNDS ARE **ALWAYS** ON ME.

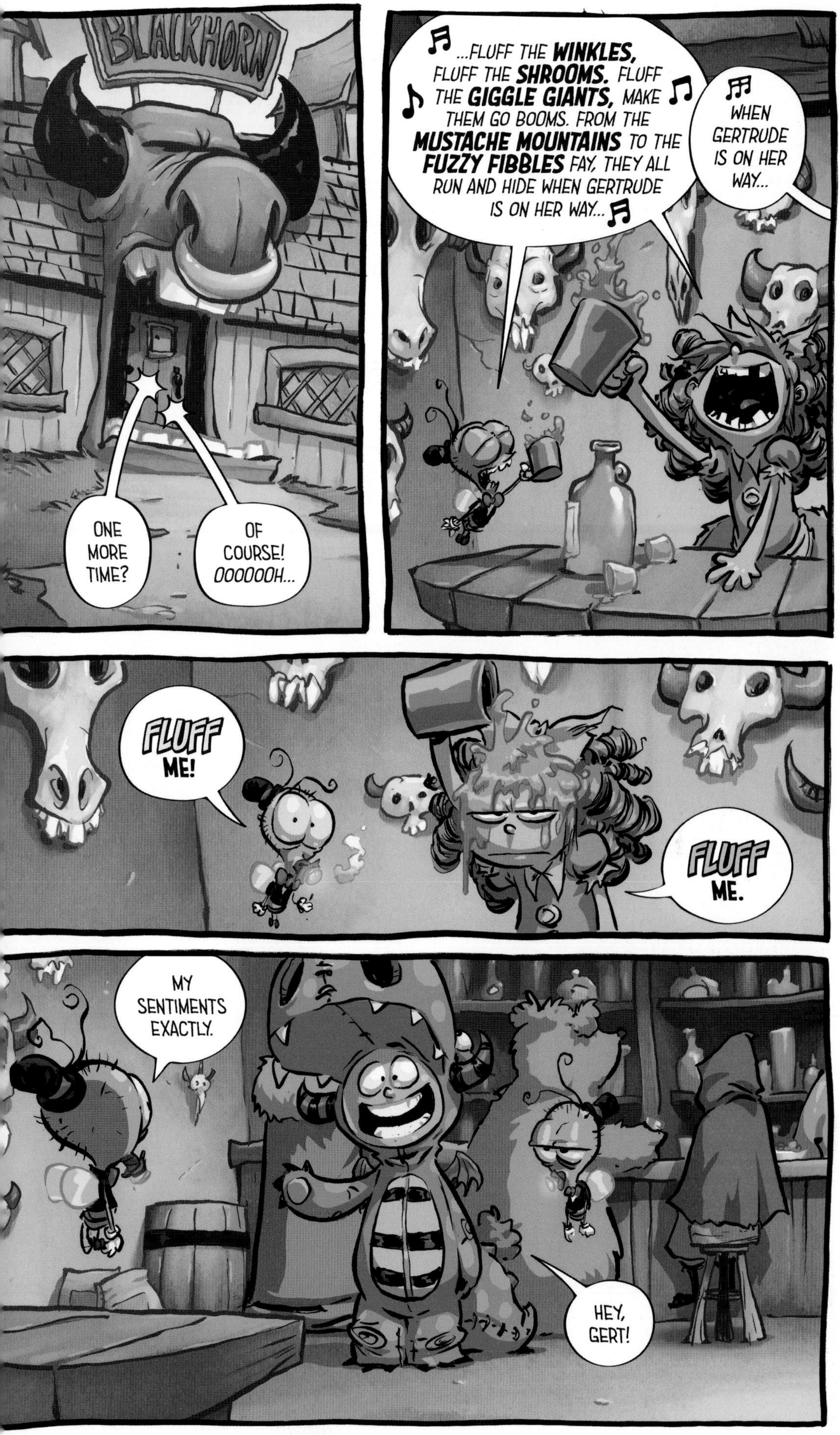
BLACKHORN
ONE MORE TIME?
OF COURSE! OOOOOOH...
...FLUFF THE WINKLES, FLUFF THE SHROOMS. FLUFF THE GIGGLE GIANTS, MAKE THEM GO BOOMS. FROM THE MUSTACHE MOUNTAINS TO THE FUZZY FIBBLES FAY, THEY ALL RUN AND HIDE WHEN GERTRUDE IS ON HER WAY...
WHEN GERTRUDE IS ON HER WAY...
FLUFF ME!
FLUFF ME.
MY SENTIMENTS EXACTLY.
HEY, GERT!

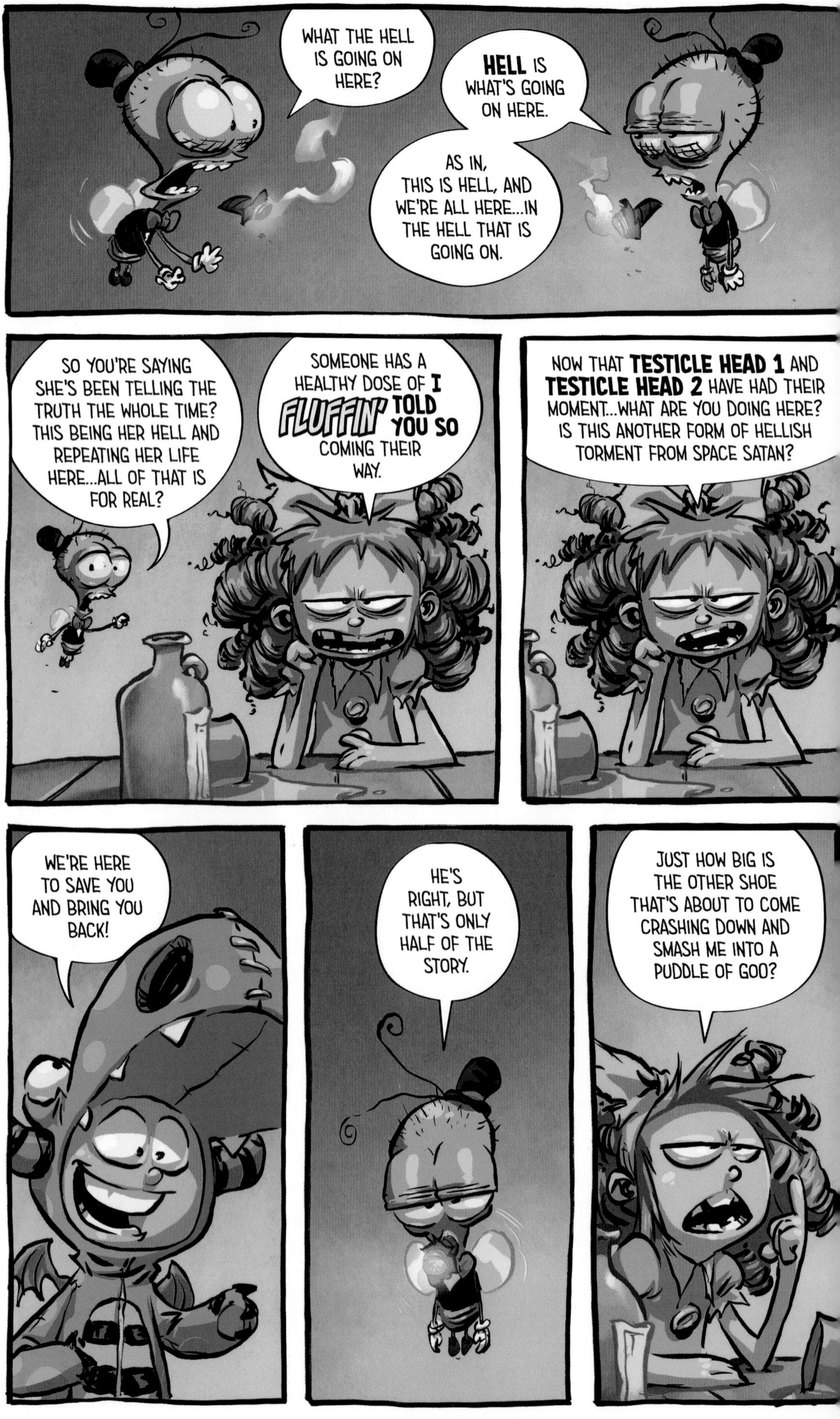
WHAT THE HELL IS GOING ON HERE?
HELL IS WHAT'S GOING ON HERE.
AS IN, THIS IS HELL, AND WE'RE ALL HERE...IN THE HELL THAT IS GOING ON.
SO YOU'RE SAYING SHE'S BEEN TELLING THE TRUTH THE WHOLE TIME? THIS BEING HER HELL AND REPEATING HER LIFE HERE...ALL OF THAT IS FOR REAL?
SOMEONE HAS A HEALTHY DOSE OF **I FLUFFIN' TOLD YOU SO** COMING THEIR WAY.
NOW THAT **TESTICLE HEAD 1** AND **TESTICLE HEAD 2** HAVE HAD THEIR MOMENT...WHAT ARE YOU DOING HERE? IS THIS ANOTHER FORM OF HELLISH TORMENT FROM SPACE SATAN?
WE'RE HERE TO SAVE YOU AND BRING YOU BACK!
HE'S RIGHT, BUT THAT'S ONLY HALF OF THE STORY.
JUST HOW BIG IS THE OTHER SHOE THAT'S ABOUT TO COME CRASHING DOWN AND SMASH ME INTO A PUDDLE OF GOO?

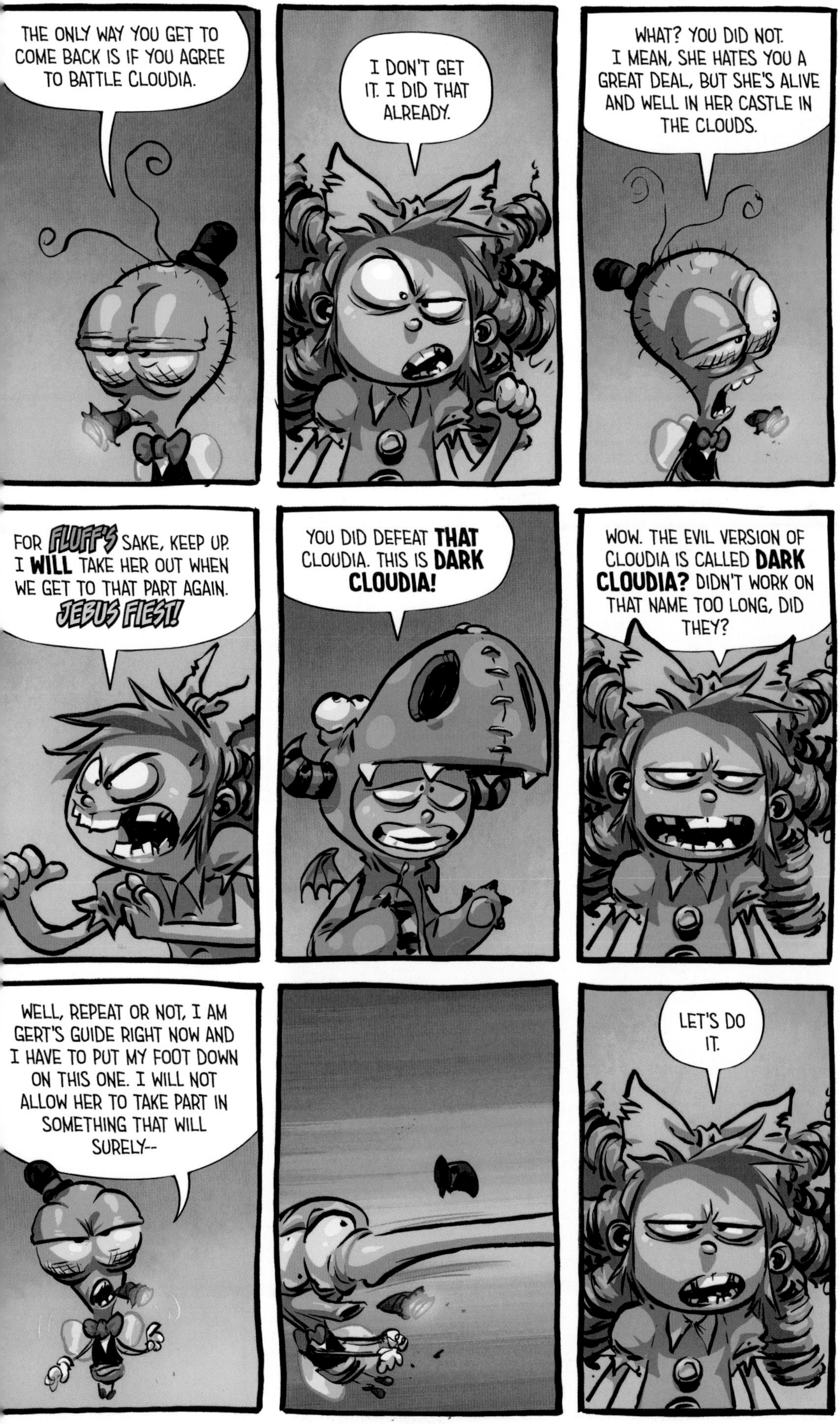
THE ONLY WAY YOU GET TO COME BACK IS IF YOU AGREE TO BATTLE CLOUDIA.
I DON'T GET IT. I DID THAT ALREADY.
WHAT? YOU DID NOT. I MEAN, SHE HATES YOU A GREAT DEAL, BUT SHE'S ALIVE AND WELL IN HER CASTLE IN THE CLOUDS.
FOR FLUFF'S SAKE, KEEP UP. I **WILL** TAKE HER OUT WHEN WE GET TO THAT PART AGAIN. JEBUS FIEST!
YOU DID DEFEAT **THAT** CLOUDIA. THIS IS **DARK CLOUDIA!**
WOW. THE EVIL VERSION OF CLOUDIA IS CALLED **DARK CLOUDIA?** DIDN'T WORK ON THAT NAME TOO LONG, DID THEY?
WELL, REPEAT OR NOT, I AM GERT'S GUIDE RIGHT NOW AND I HAVE TO PUT MY FOOT DOWN ON THIS ONE. I WILL NOT ALLOW HER TO TAKE PART IN SOMETHING THAT WILL SURELY--
LET'S DO IT.

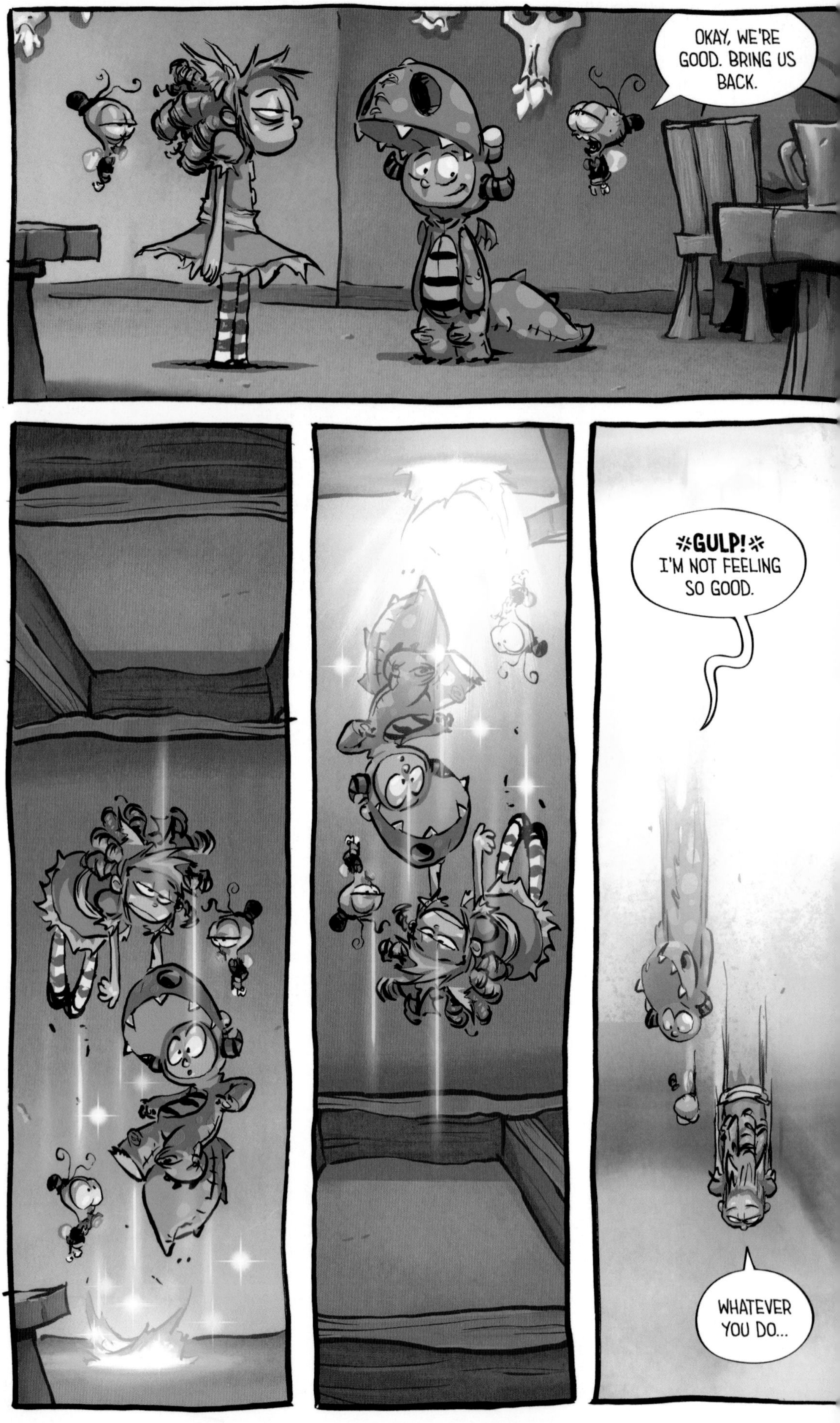
OKAY, WE'RE GOOD. BRING US BACK.
GULP! I'M NOT FEELING SO GOOD.
WHATEVER YOU DO...

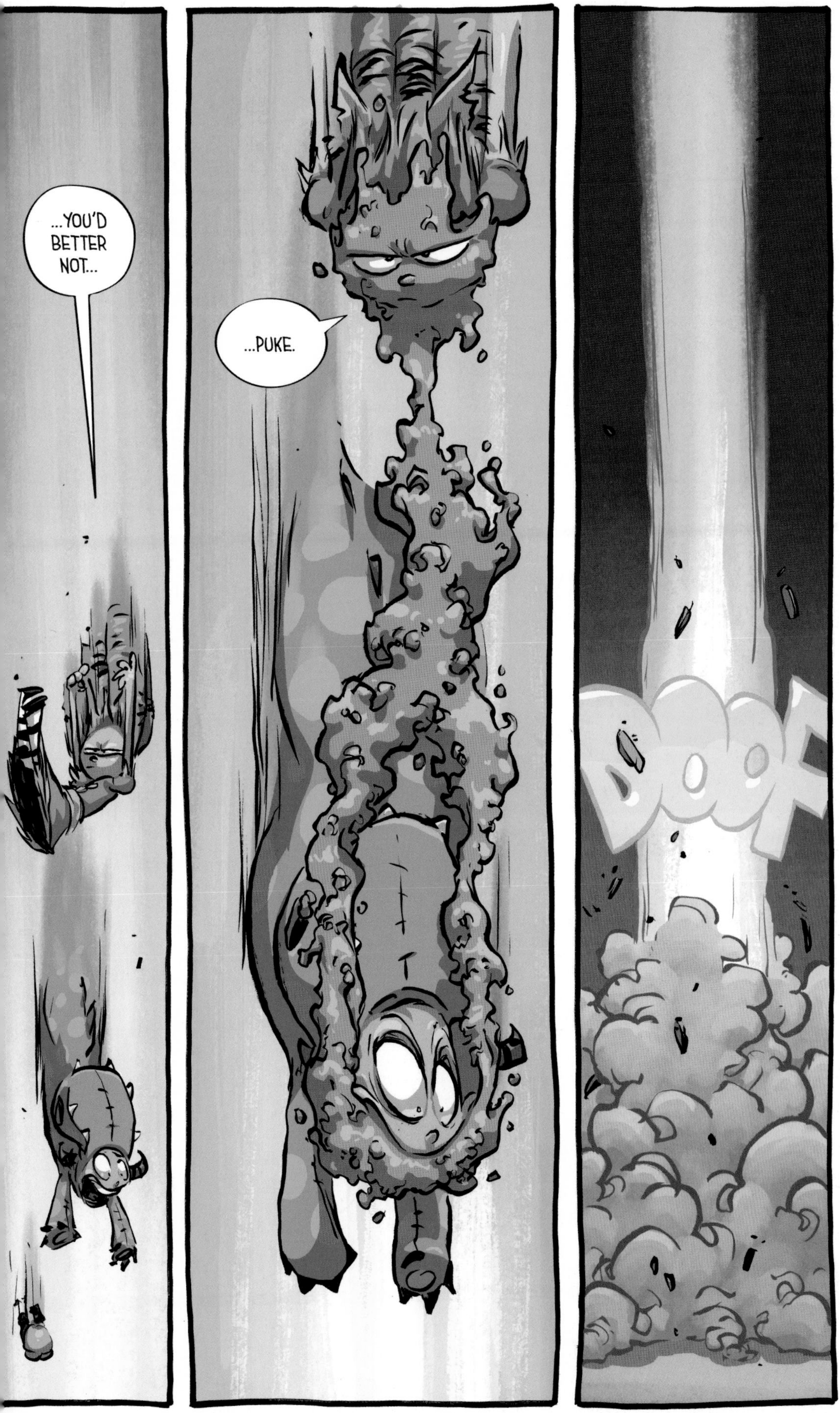
...YOU'D BETTER NOT...
...PUKE.
DOOF

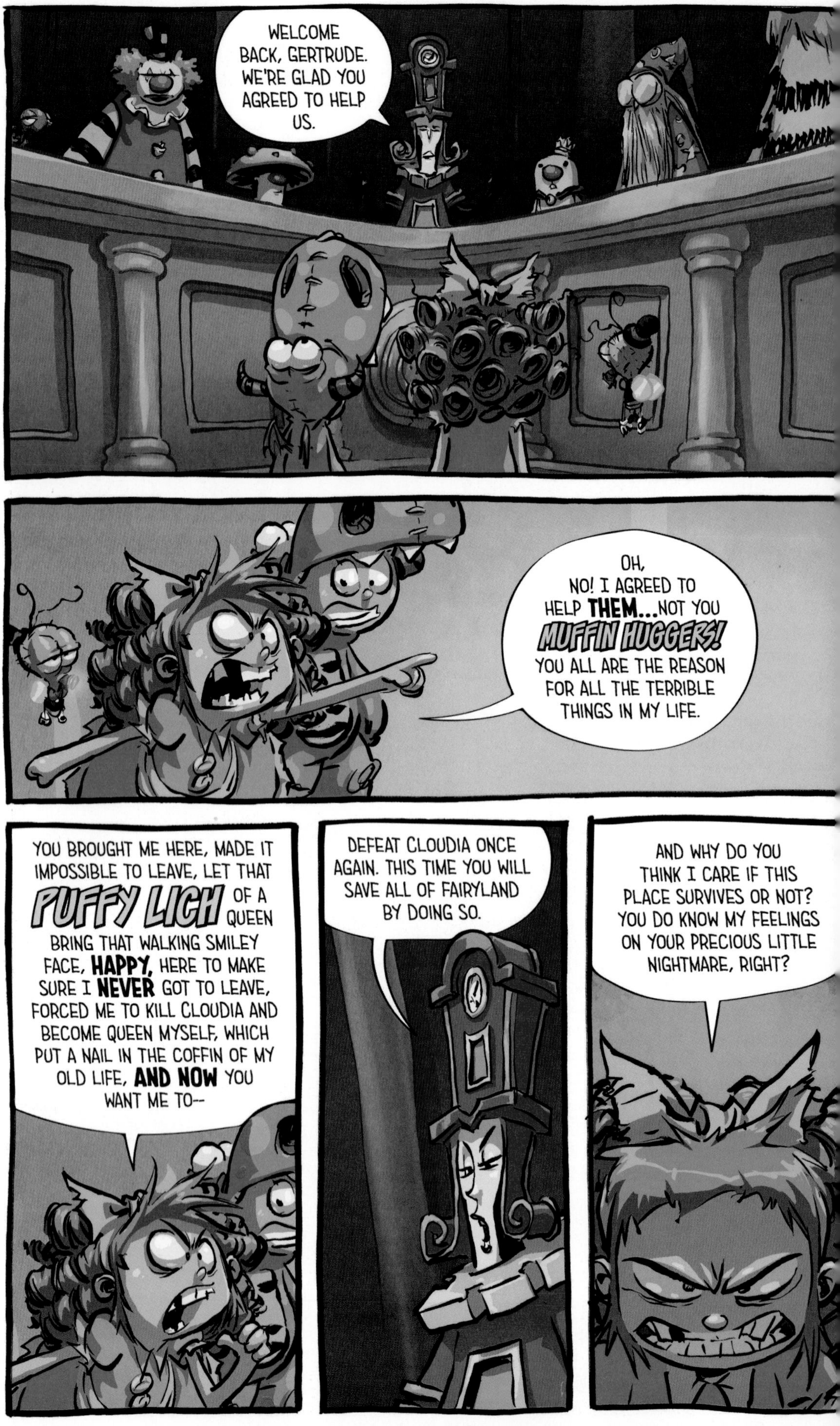
WELCOME BACK, GERTRUDE. WE'RE GLAD YOU AGREED TO HELP US.
OH, NO! I AGREED TO HELP THEM...NOT YOU MUFFIN HUGGERS! YOU ALL ARE THE REASON FOR ALL THE TERRIBLE THINGS IN MY LIFE.
YOU BROUGHT ME HERE, MADE IT IMPOSSIBLE TO LEAVE, LET THAT PUFFY LICH OF A QUEEN BRING THAT WALKING SMILEY FACE, HAPPY, HERE TO MAKE SURE I NEVER GOT TO LEAVE, FORCED ME TO KILL CLOUDIA AND BECOME QUEEN MYSELF, WHICH PUT A NAIL IN THE COFFIN OF MY OLD LIFE, AND NOW YOU WANT ME TO--
DEFEAT CLOUDIA ONCE AGAIN. THIS TIME YOU WILL SAVE ALL OF FAIRYLAND BY DOING SO.
AND WHY DO YOU THINK I CARE IF THIS PLACE SURVIVES OR NOT? YOU DO KNOW MY FEELINGS ON YOUR PRECIOUS LITTLE NIGHTMARE, RIGHT?

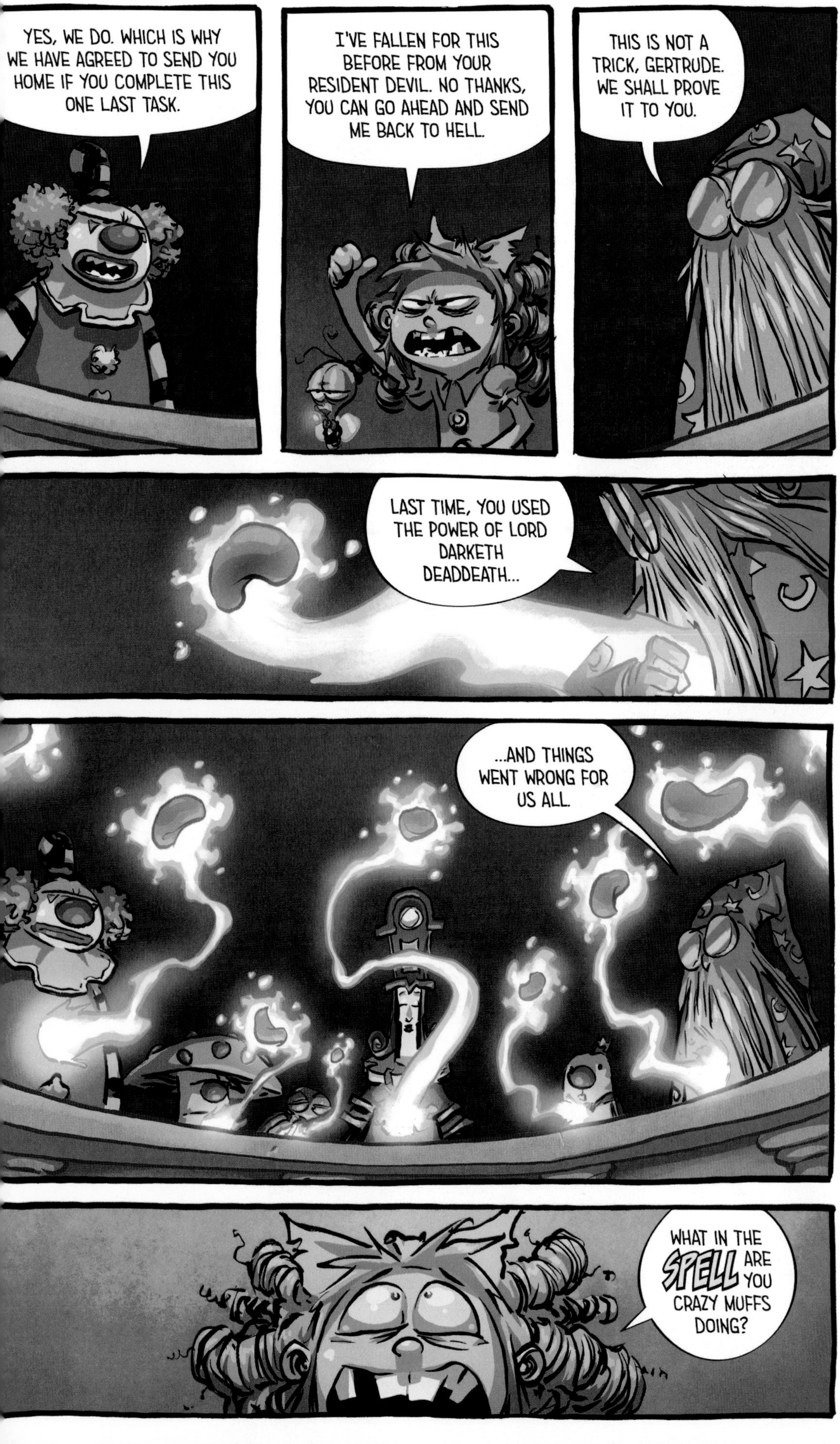
YES, WE DO. WHICH IS WHY WE HAVE AGREED TO SEND YOU HOME IF YOU COMPLETE THIS ONE LAST TASK.
I'VE FALLEN FOR THIS BEFORE FROM YOUR RESIDENT DEVIL. NO THANKS, YOU CAN GO AHEAD AND SEND ME BACK TO HELL.
THIS IS NOT A TRICK, GERTRUDE. WE SHALL PROVE IT TO YOU.
LAST TIME, YOU USED THE POWER OF LORD DARKETH DEADDEATH...
...AND THINGS WENT WRONG FOR US ALL.
WHAT IN THE SPELL ARE YOU CRAZY MUFFS DOING?

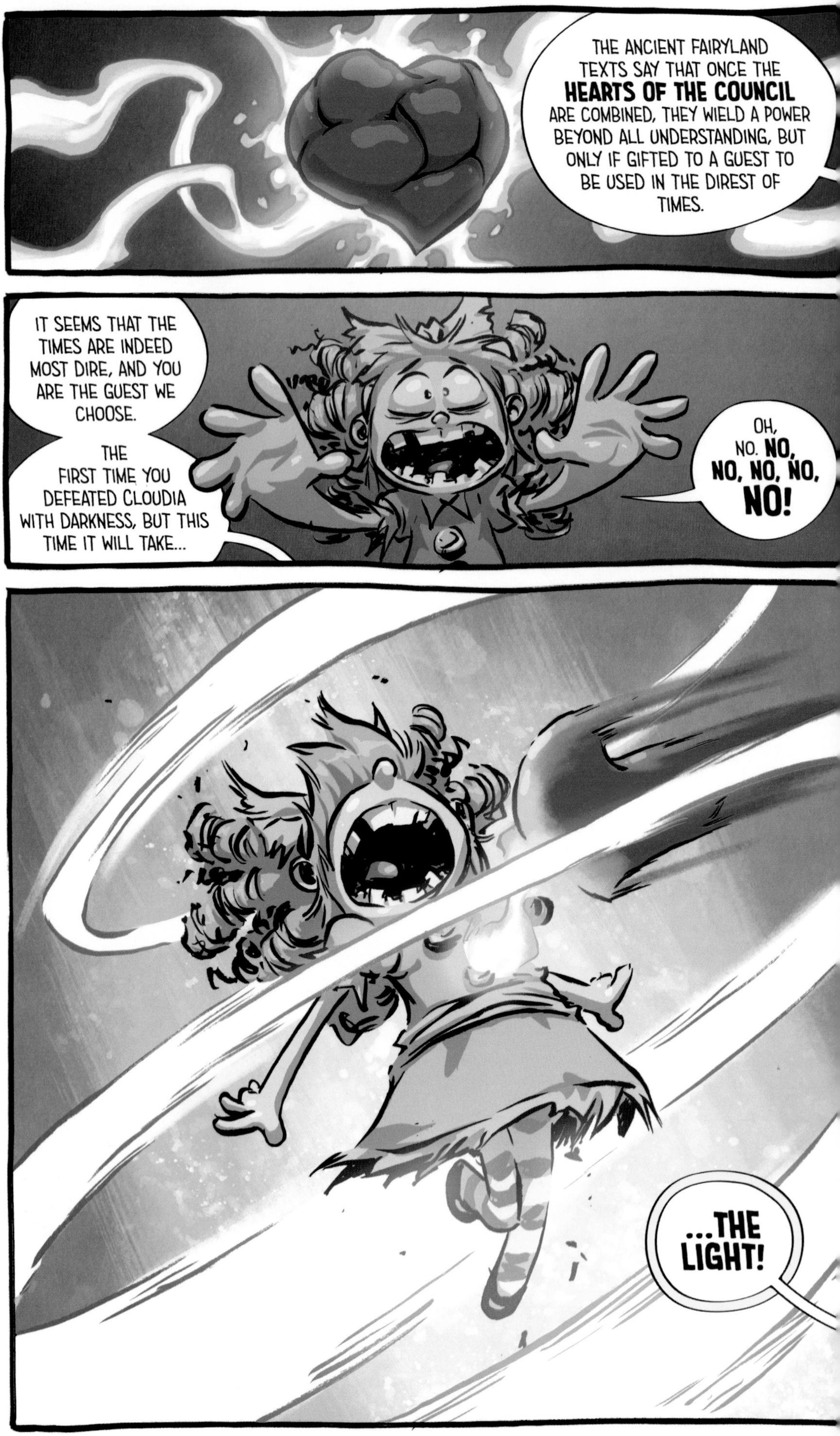
THE ANCIENT FAIRYLAND TEXTS SAY THAT ONCE THE **HEARTS OF THE COUNCIL** ARE COMBINED, THEY WIELD A POWER BEYOND ALL UNDERSTANDING, BUT ONLY IF GIFTED TO A GUEST TO BE USED IN THE DIREST OF TIMES.
IT SEEMS THAT THE TIMES ARE INDEED MOST DIRE, AND YOU ARE THE GUEST WE CHOOSE.
THE FIRST TIME YOU DEFEATED CLOUDIA WITH DARKNESS, BUT THIS TIME IT WILL TAKE...
OH, NO. **NO, NO, NO, NO, NO!**
...THE LIGHT!

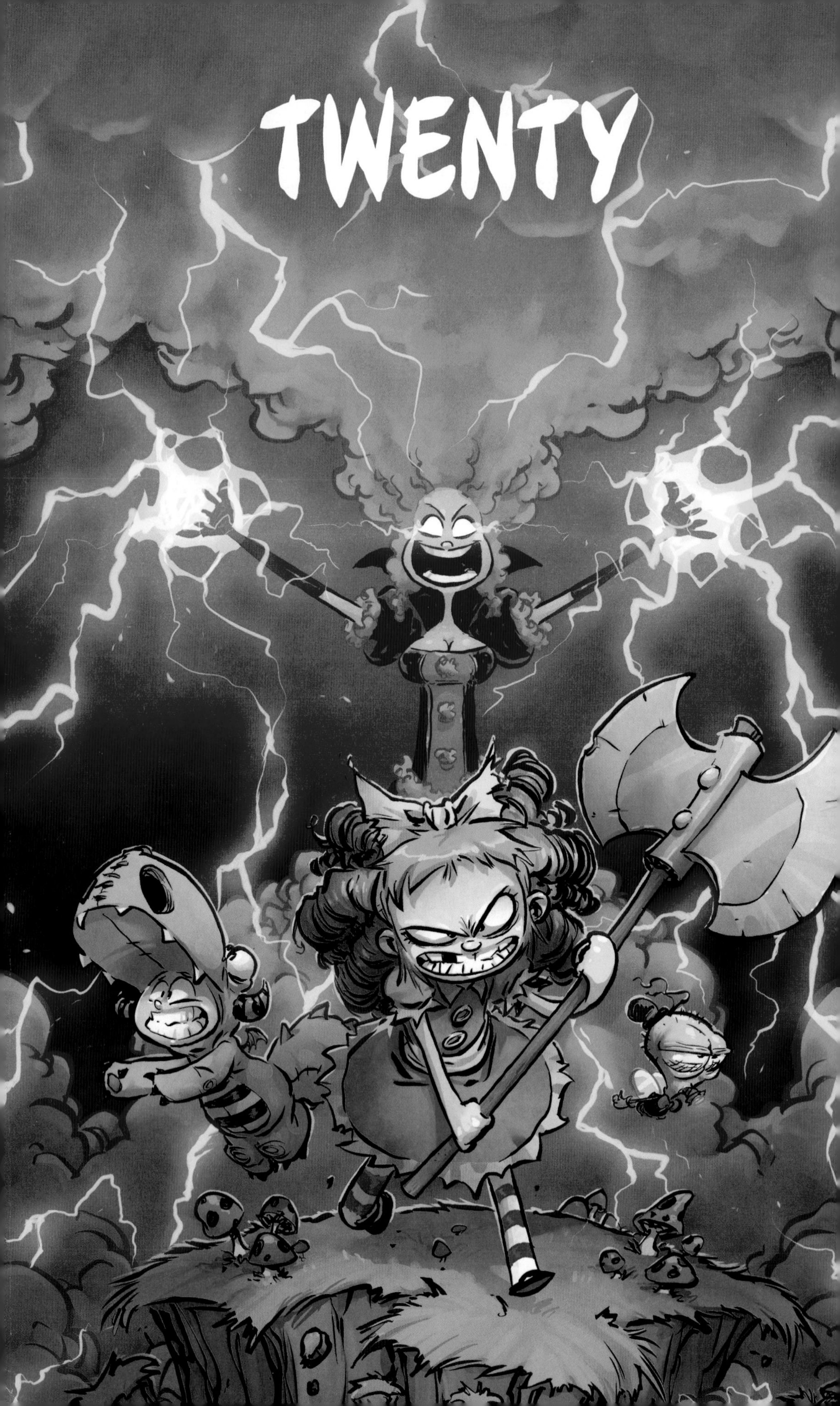
TWENTY

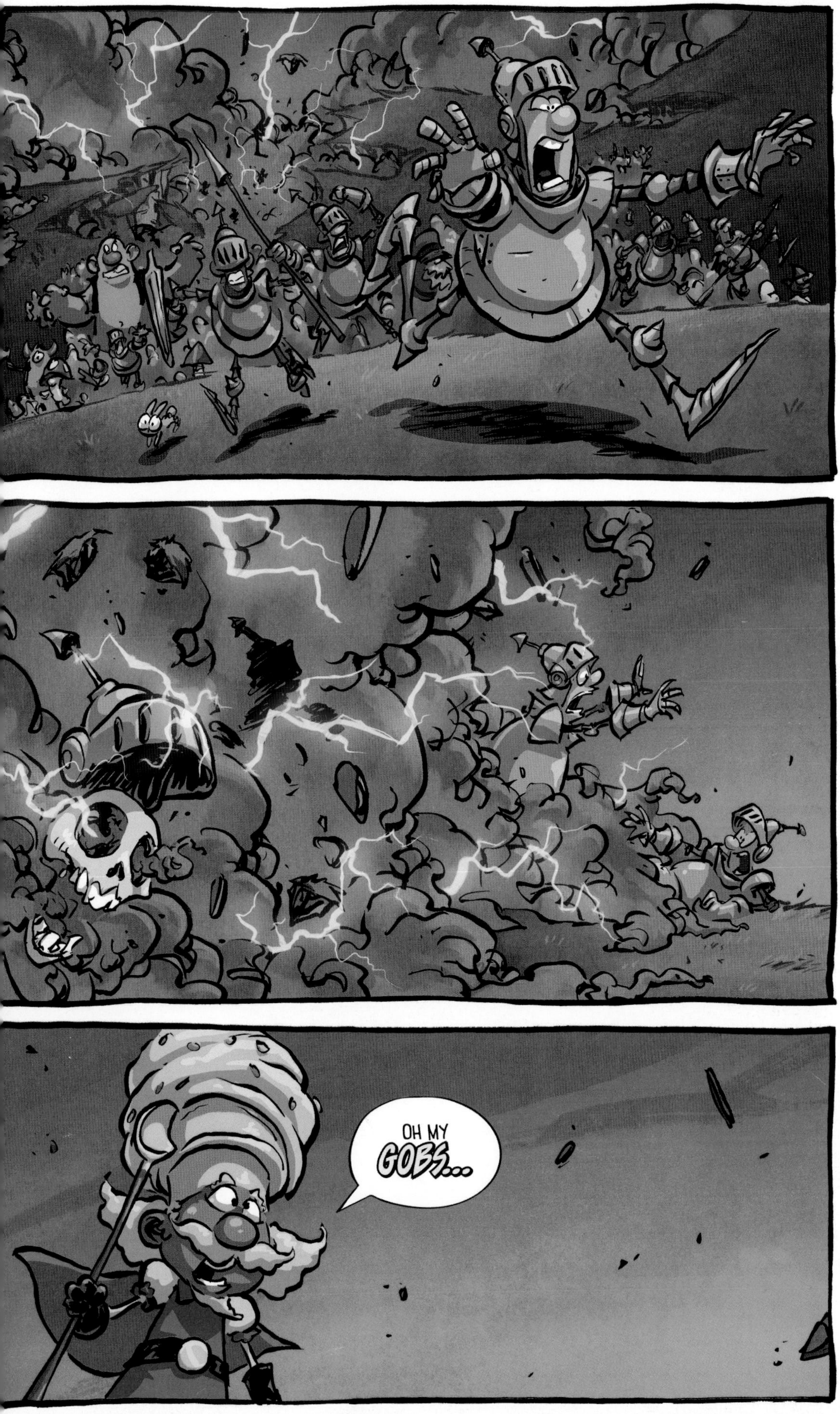
OH MY GOBS...

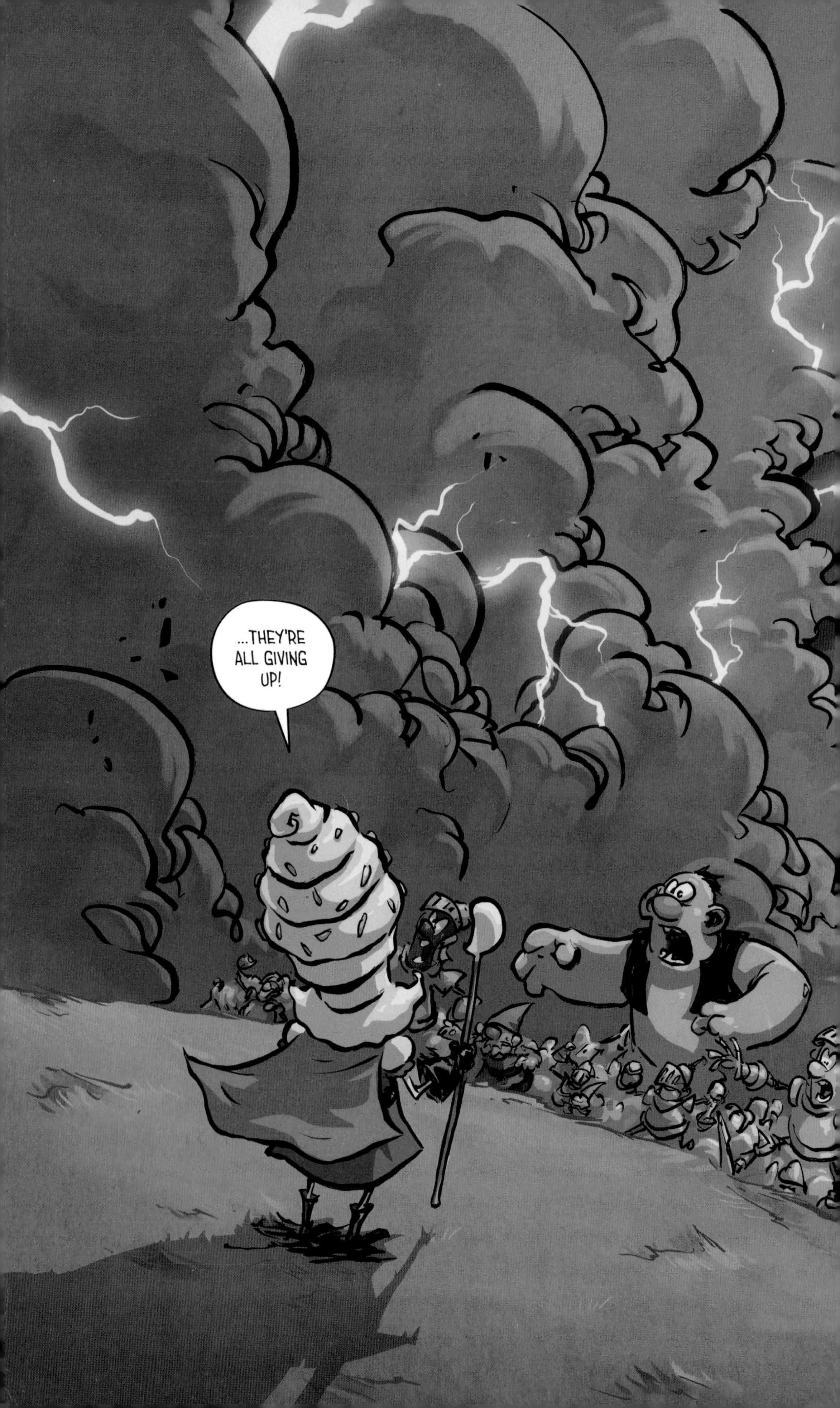
...THEY'RE ALL GIVING UP!

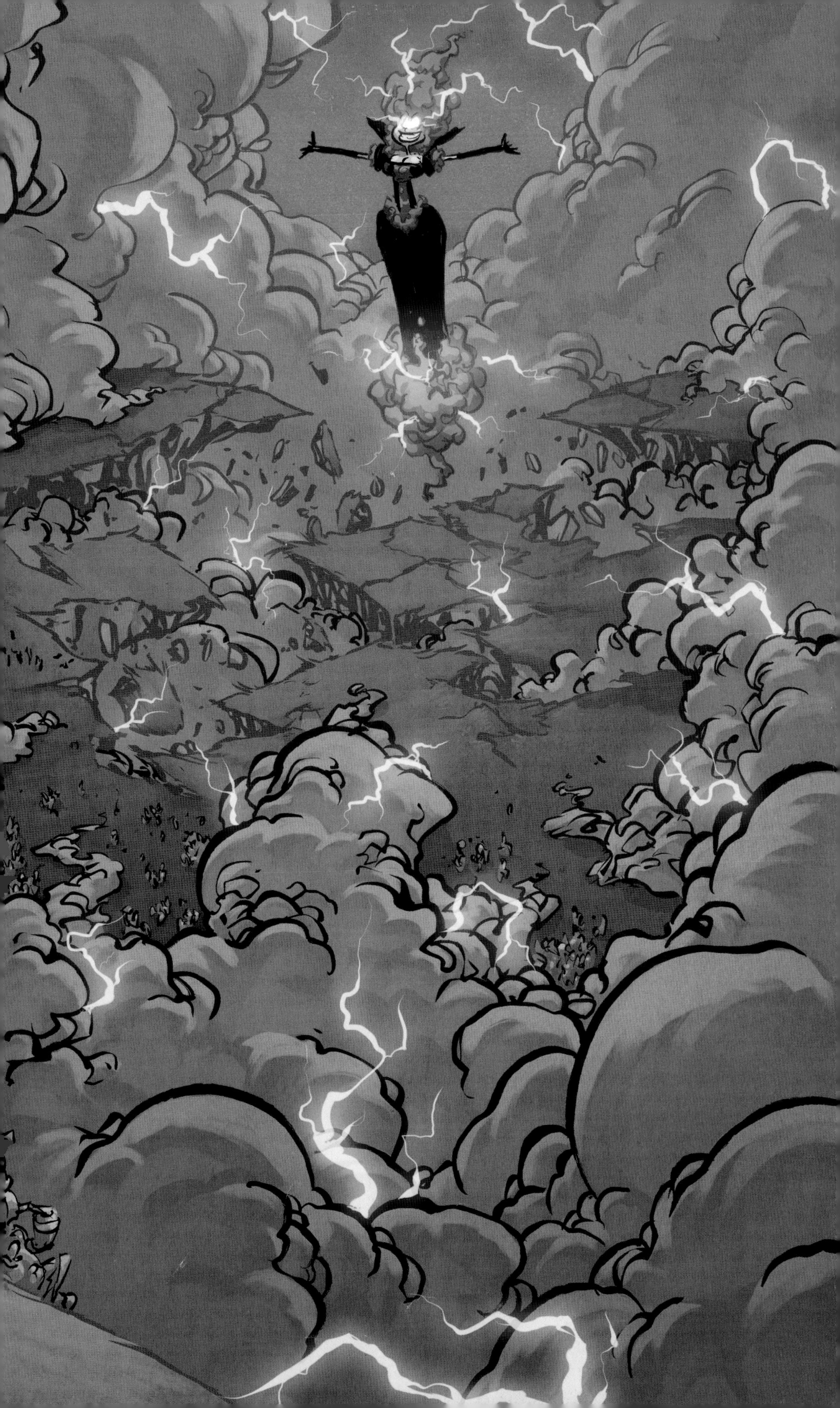

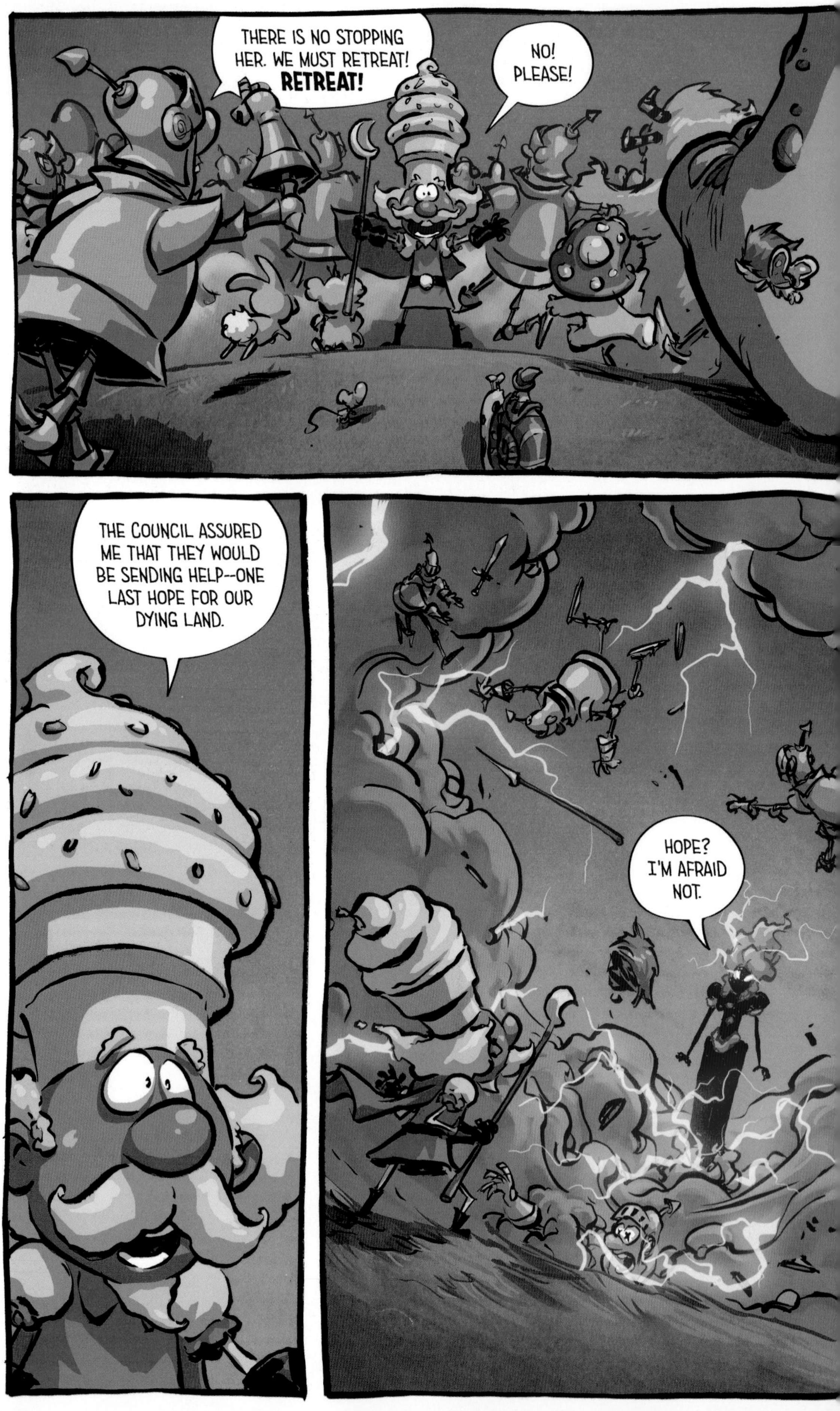
THERE IS NO STOPPING HER. WE MUST RETREAT! **RETREAT!**
NO! PLEASE!
THE COUNCIL ASSURED ME THAT THEY WOULD BE SENDING HELP--ONE LAST HOPE FOR OUR DYING LAND.
HOPE? I'M AFRAID NOT.

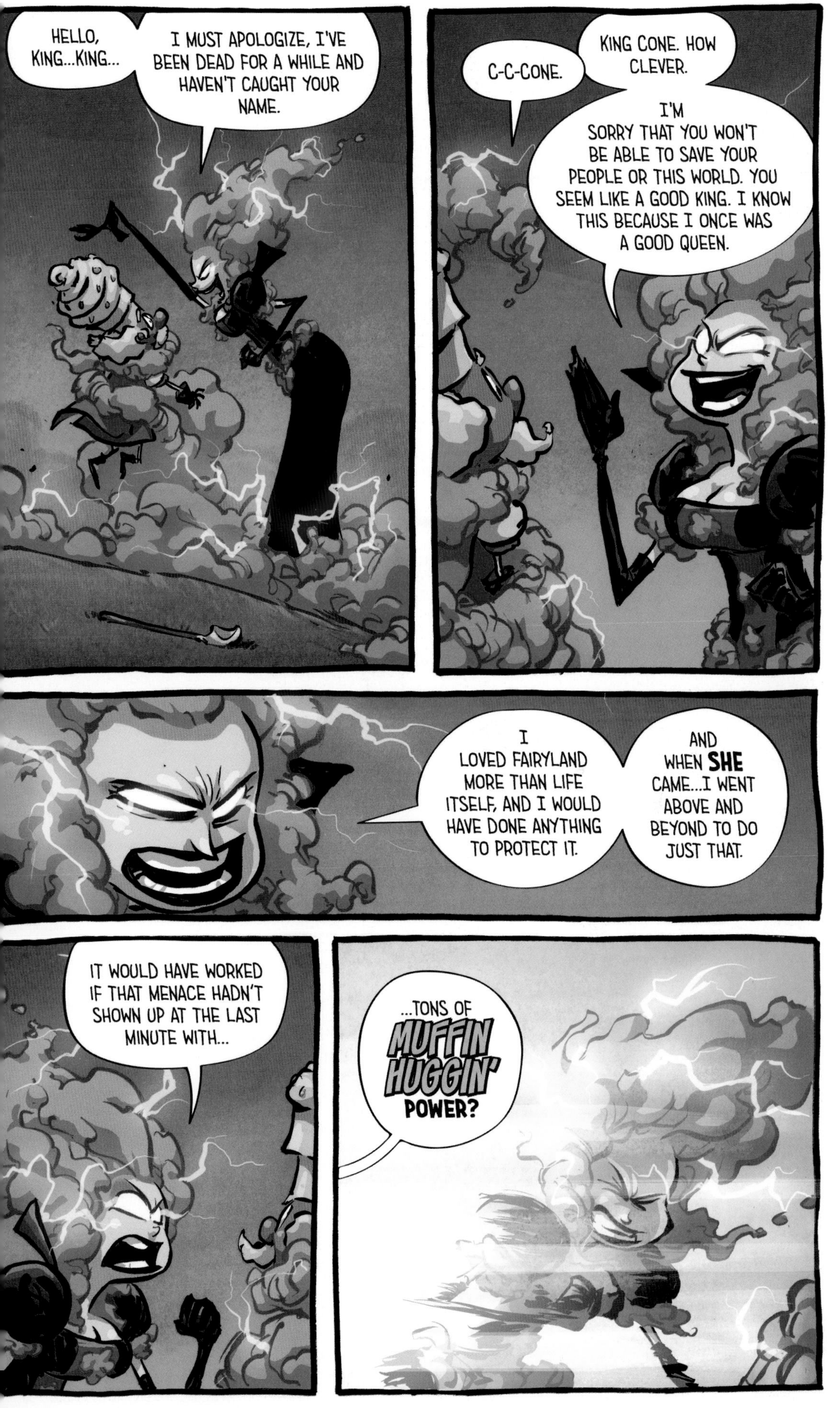
HELLO, KING...KING...
I MUST APOLOGIZE, I'VE BEEN DEAD FOR A WHILE AND HAVEN'T CAUGHT YOUR NAME.
C-C-CONE.
KING CONE. HOW CLEVER.
I'M SORRY THAT YOU WON'T BE ABLE TO SAVE YOUR PEOPLE OR THIS WORLD. YOU SEEM LIKE A GOOD KING. I KNOW THIS BECAUSE I ONCE WAS A GOOD QUEEN.
I LOVED FAIRYLAND MORE THAN LIFE ITSELF, AND I WOULD HAVE DONE ANYTHING TO PROTECT IT.
AND WHEN SHE CAME...I WENT ABOVE AND BEYOND TO DO JUST THAT.
IT WOULD HAVE WORKED IF THAT MENACE HADN'T SHOWN UP AT THE LAST MINUTE WITH...
...TONS OF MUFFIN HUGGIN' POWER?

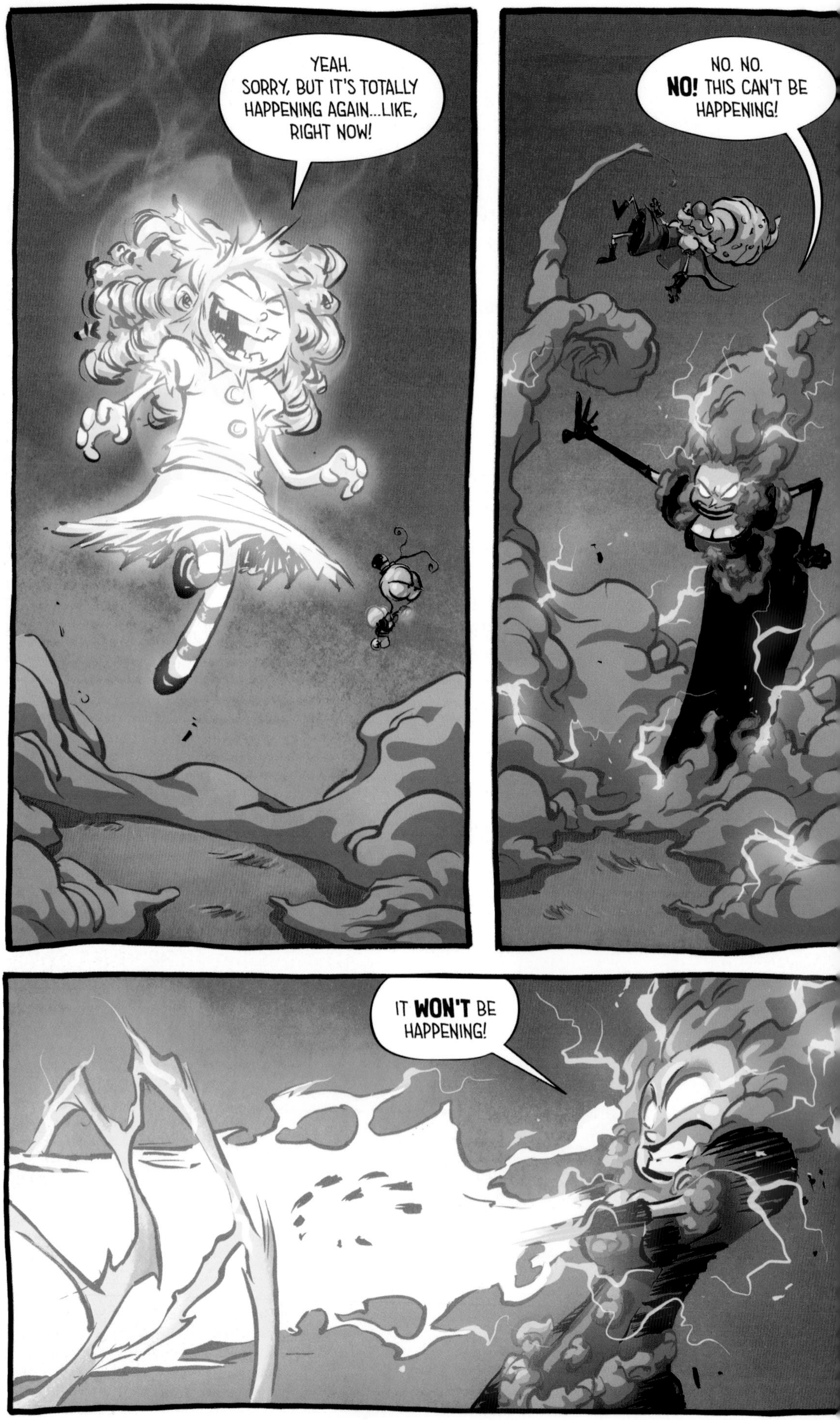
YEAH.
SORRY, BUT IT'S TOTALLY HAPPENING AGAIN...LIKE, RIGHT NOW!
NO. NO. **NO!** THIS CAN'T BE HAPPENING!
IT **WON'T** BE HAPPENING!

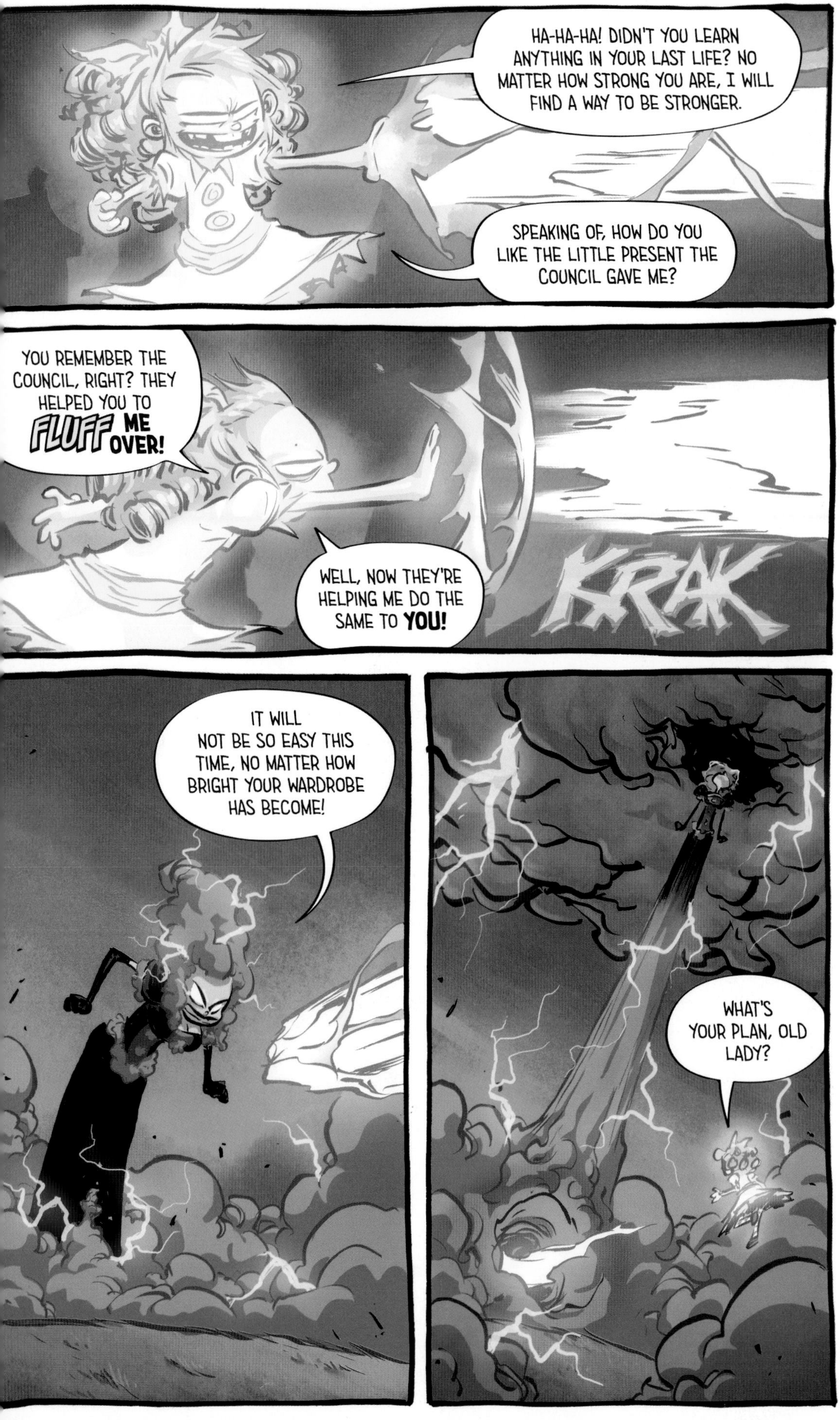
HA-HA-HA! DIDN'T YOU LEARN ANYTHING IN YOUR LAST LIFE? NO MATTER HOW STRONG YOU ARE, I WILL FIND A WAY TO BE STRONGER.
SPEAKING OF, HOW DO YOU LIKE THE LITTLE PRESENT THE COUNCIL GAVE ME?
YOU REMEMBER THE COUNCIL, RIGHT? THEY HELPED YOU TO FLUFF ME OVER!
WELL, NOW THEY'RE HELPING ME DO THE SAME TO YOU!
KRAK
IT WILL NOT BE SO EASY THIS TIME, NO MATTER HOW BRIGHT YOUR WARDROBE HAS BECOME!
WHAT'S YOUR PLAN, OLD LADY?

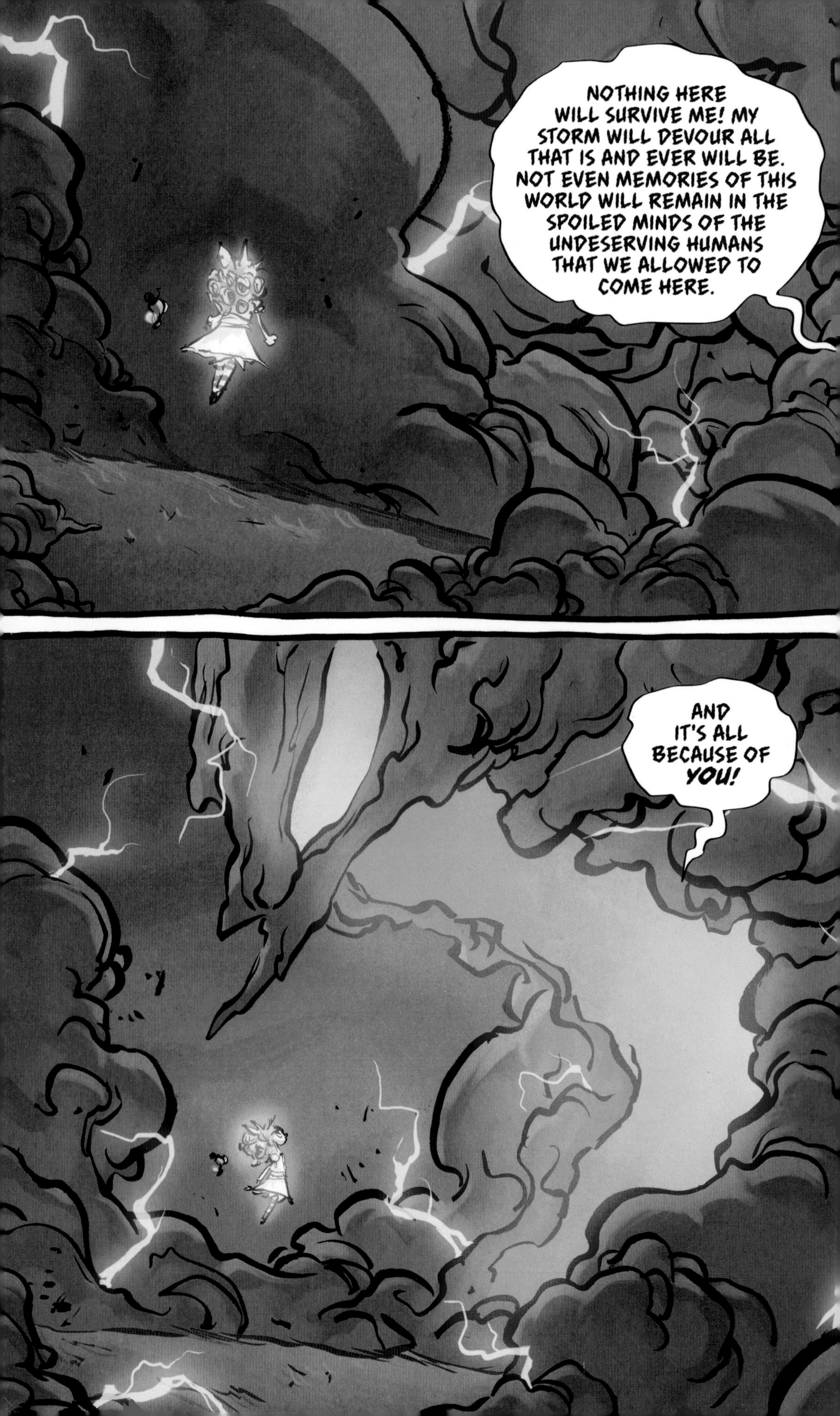
NOTHING HERE WILL SURVIVE ME! MY STORM WILL DEVOUR ALL THAT IS AND EVER WILL BE. NOT EVEN MEMORIES OF THIS WORLD WILL REMAIN IN THE SPOILED MINDS OF THE UNDESERVING HUMANS THAT WE ALLOWED TO COME HERE.
AND IT'S ALL BECAUSE OF *YOU!*

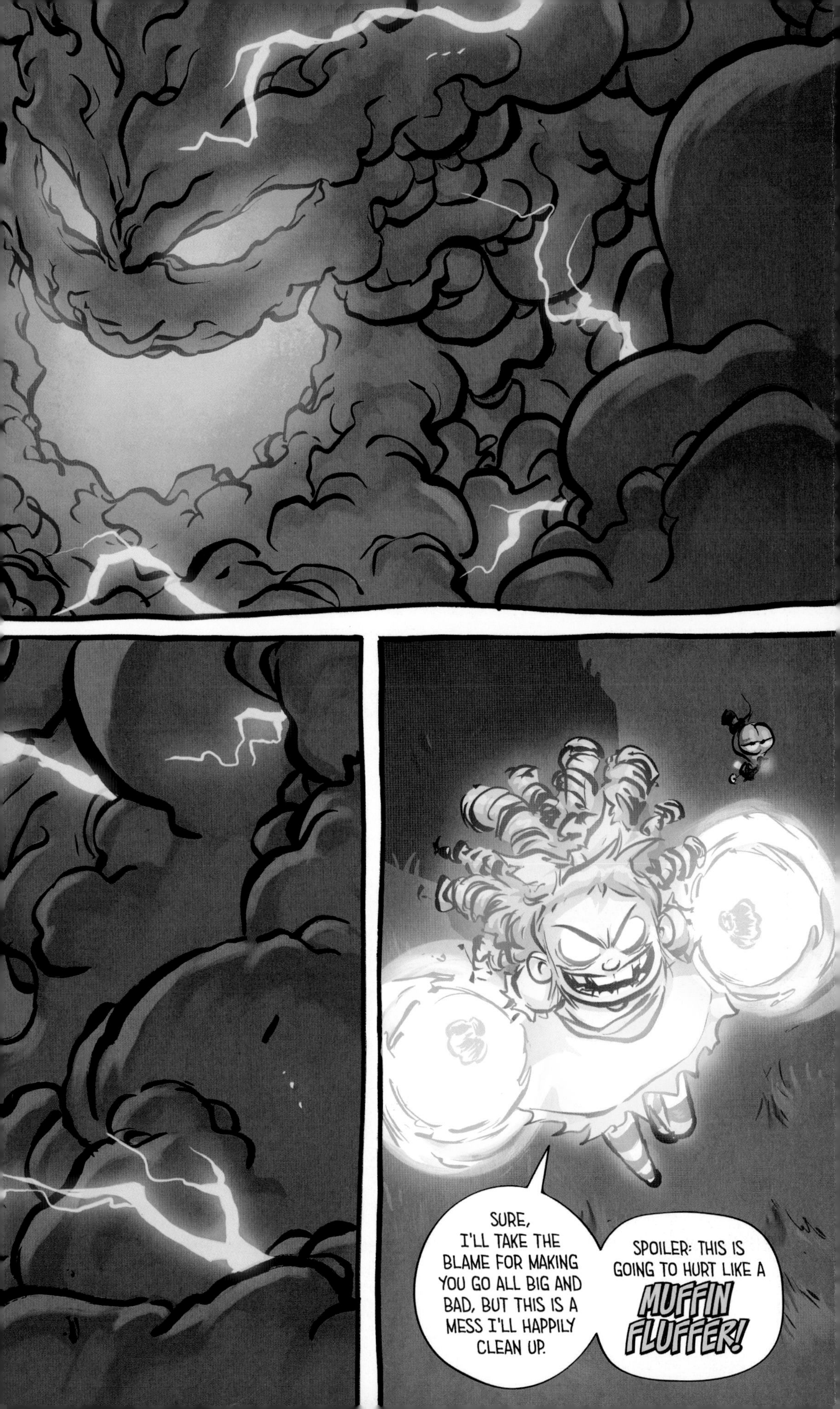
SURE, I'LL TAKE THE BLAME FOR MAKING YOU GO ALL BIG AND BAD, BUT THIS IS A MESS I'LL HAPPILY CLEAN UP.
SPOILER: THIS IS GOING TO HURT LIKE A MUFFIN FLUFFER!

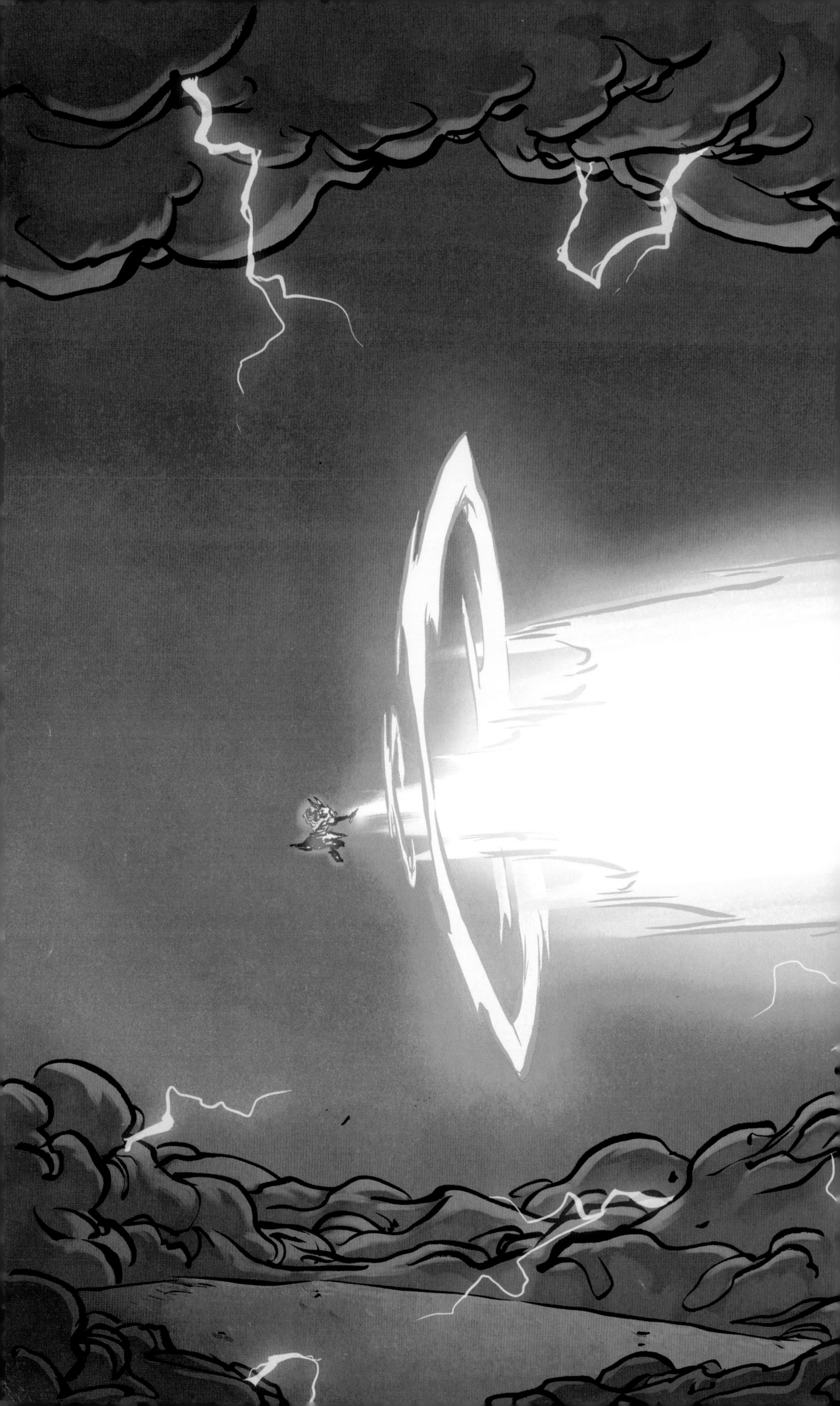

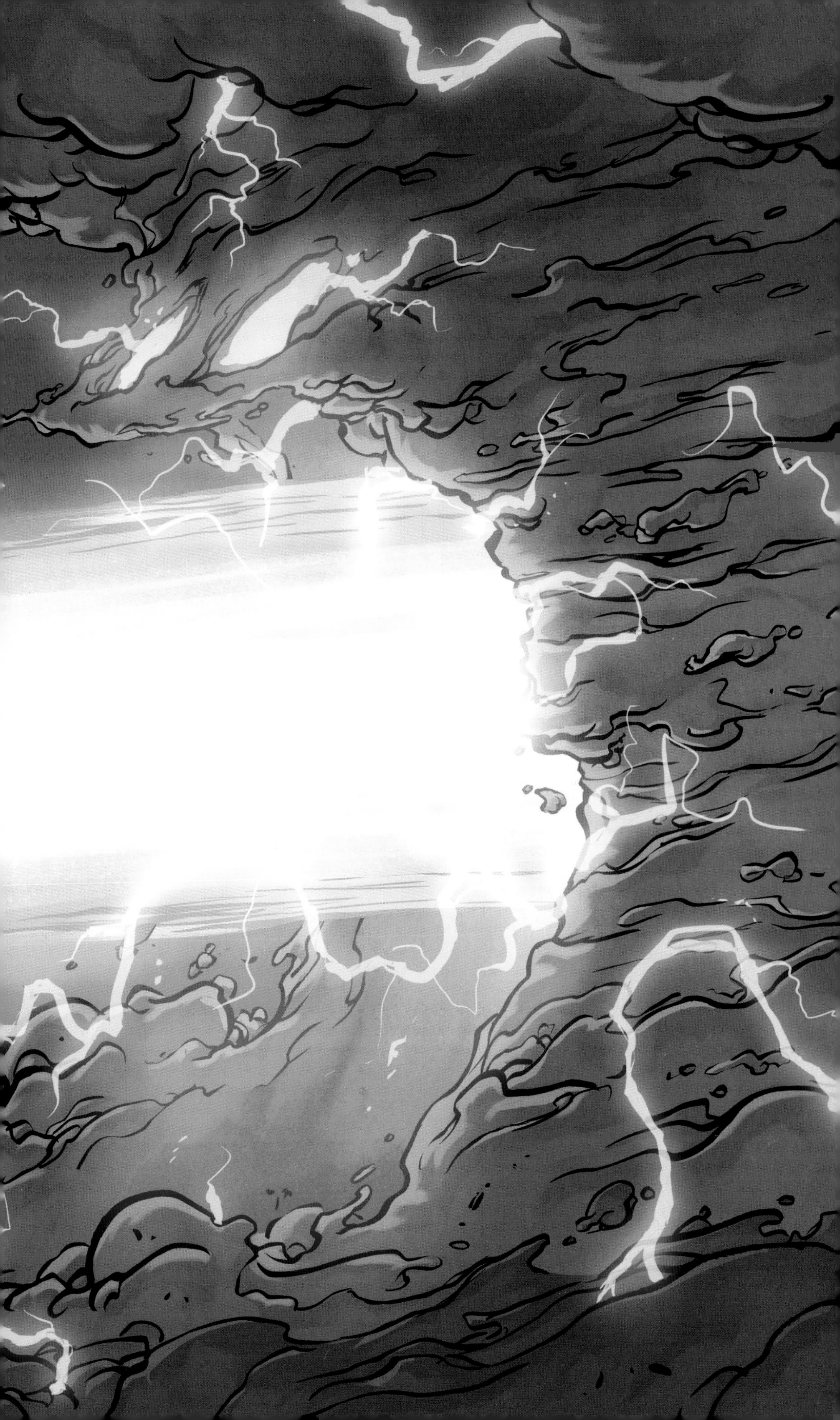

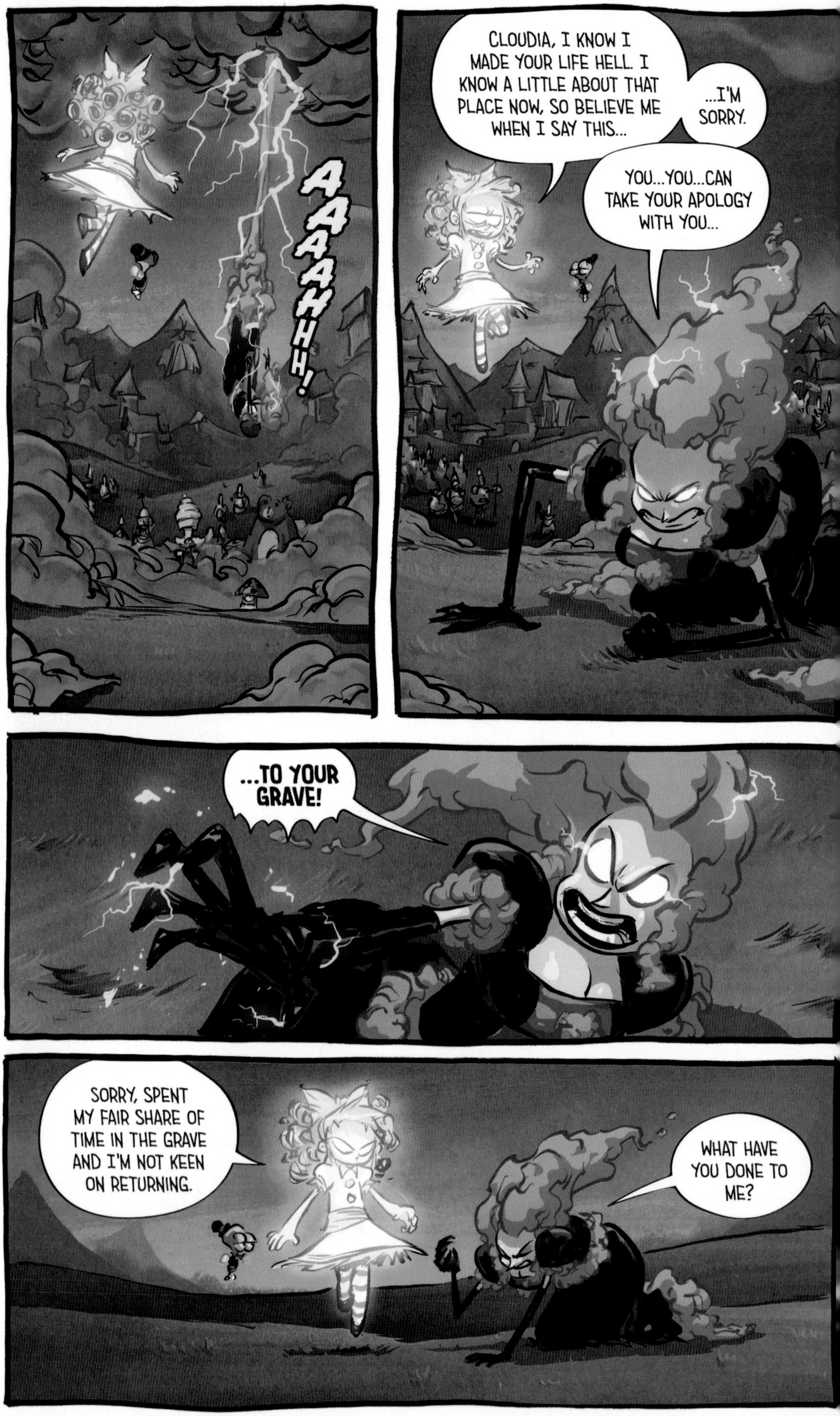
AAAAAHHH!
CLOUDIA, I KNOW I MADE YOUR LIFE HELL. I KNOW A LITTLE ABOUT THAT PLACE NOW, SO BELIEVE ME WHEN I SAY THIS...
...I'M SORRY.
YOU...YOU...CAN TAKE YOUR APOLOGY WITH YOU...
...TO YOUR GRAVE!
SORRY, SPENT MY FAIR SHARE OF TIME IN THE GRAVE AND I'M NOT KEEN ON RETURNING.
WHAT HAVE YOU DONE TO ME?

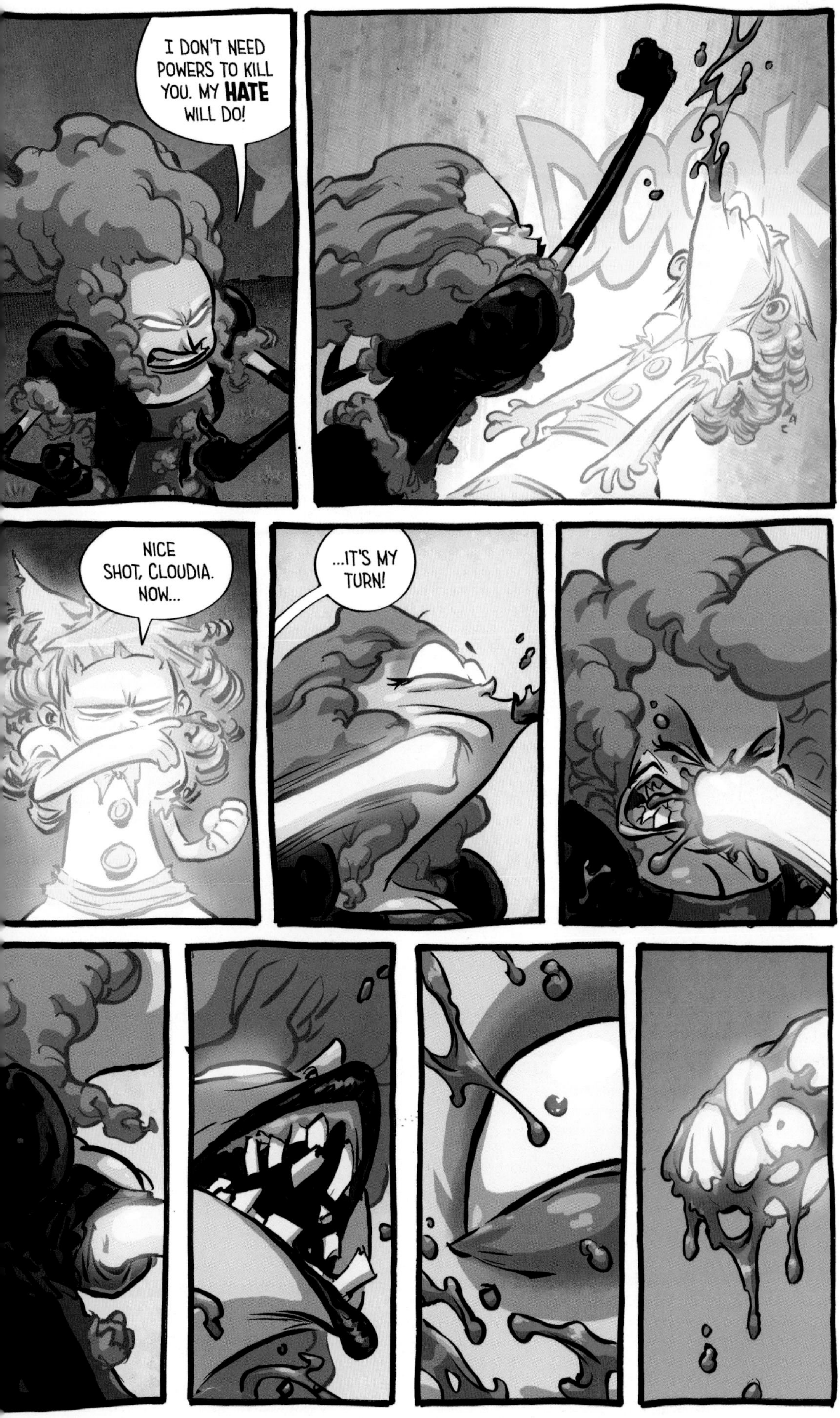
I DON'T NEED POWERS TO KILL YOU. MY **HATE** WILL DO!
NICE SHOT, CLOUDIA. NOW...
...IT'S MY TURN!

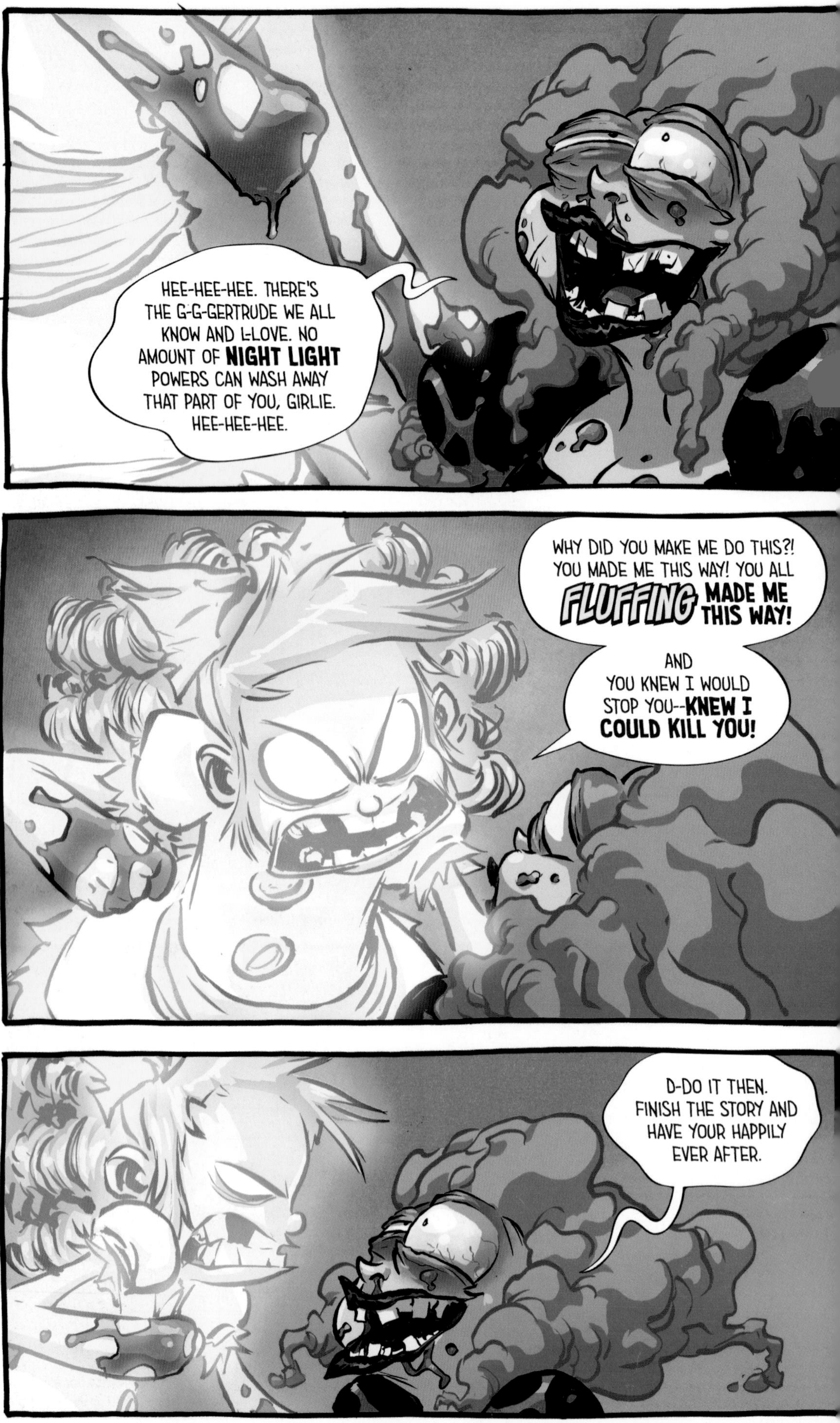
HEE-HEE-HEE. THERE'S THE G-G-GERTRUDE WE ALL KNOW AND L-LOVE. NO AMOUNT OF **NIGHT LIGHT** POWERS CAN WASH AWAY THAT PART OF YOU, GIRLIE. HEE-HEE-HEE.
WHY DID YOU MAKE ME DO THIS?! YOU MADE ME THIS WAY! YOU ALL **FLUFFING MADE ME THIS WAY!**
AND YOU KNEW I WOULD STOP YOU--**KNEW I COULD KILL YOU!**
D-DO IT THEN. FINISH THE STORY AND HAVE YOUR HAPPILY EVER AFTER.

FINE...!

...HAVE IT YOUR WAY!

YOU DON'T HAVE TO KILL ANYONE. YOU UNDERSTAND THAT, RIGHT?

IF I WANT THE COUNCIL TO SEND ME HOME, I DO. I HAVE TO DEFEAT CLOUDIA.

YES, THEY SAID **DEFEAT**... NOT KILL.

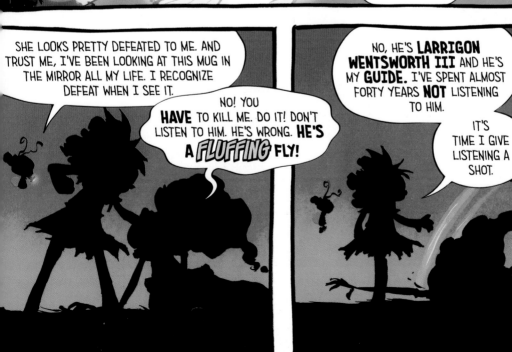

SHE LOOKS PRETTY DEFEATED TO ME. AND TRUST ME, I'VE BEEN LOOKING AT THIS MUG IN THE MIRROR ALL MY LIFE. I RECOGNIZE DEFEAT WHEN I SEE IT.

NO! YOU **HAVE** TO KILL ME. DO IT! DON'T LISTEN TO HIM. HE'S WRONG. **HE'S A _FLUFFING_ FLY!**

NO, HE'S **LARRIGON WENTSWORTH III** AND HE'S MY **GUIDE.** I'VE SPENT ALMOST FORTY YEARS **NOT** LISTENING TO HIM.

IT'S TIME I GIVE LISTENING A SHOT.

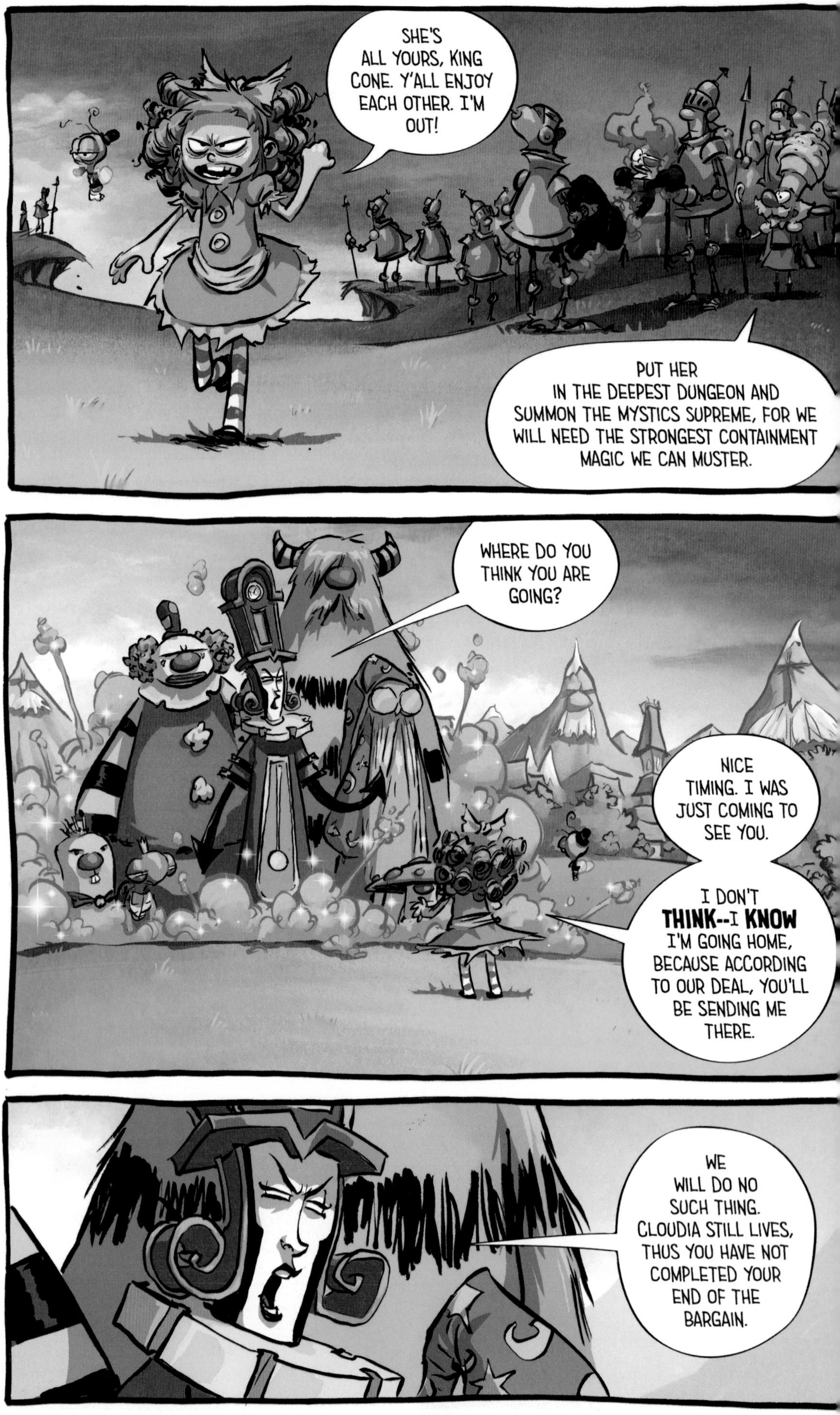
SHE'S ALL YOURS, KING CONE. Y'ALL ENJOY EACH OTHER. I'M OUT!
PUT HER IN THE DEEPEST DUNGEON AND SUMMON THE MYSTICS SUPREME, FOR WE WILL NEED THE STRONGEST CONTAINMENT MAGIC WE CAN MUSTER.
WHERE DO YOU THINK YOU ARE GOING?
NICE TIMING. I WAS JUST COMING TO SEE YOU.
I DON'T **THINK**--I **KNOW** I'M GOING HOME, BECAUSE ACCORDING TO OUR DEAL, YOU'LL BE SENDING ME THERE.
WE WILL DO NO SUCH THING. CLOUDIA STILL LIVES, THUS YOU HAVE NOT COMPLETED YOUR END OF THE BARGAIN.

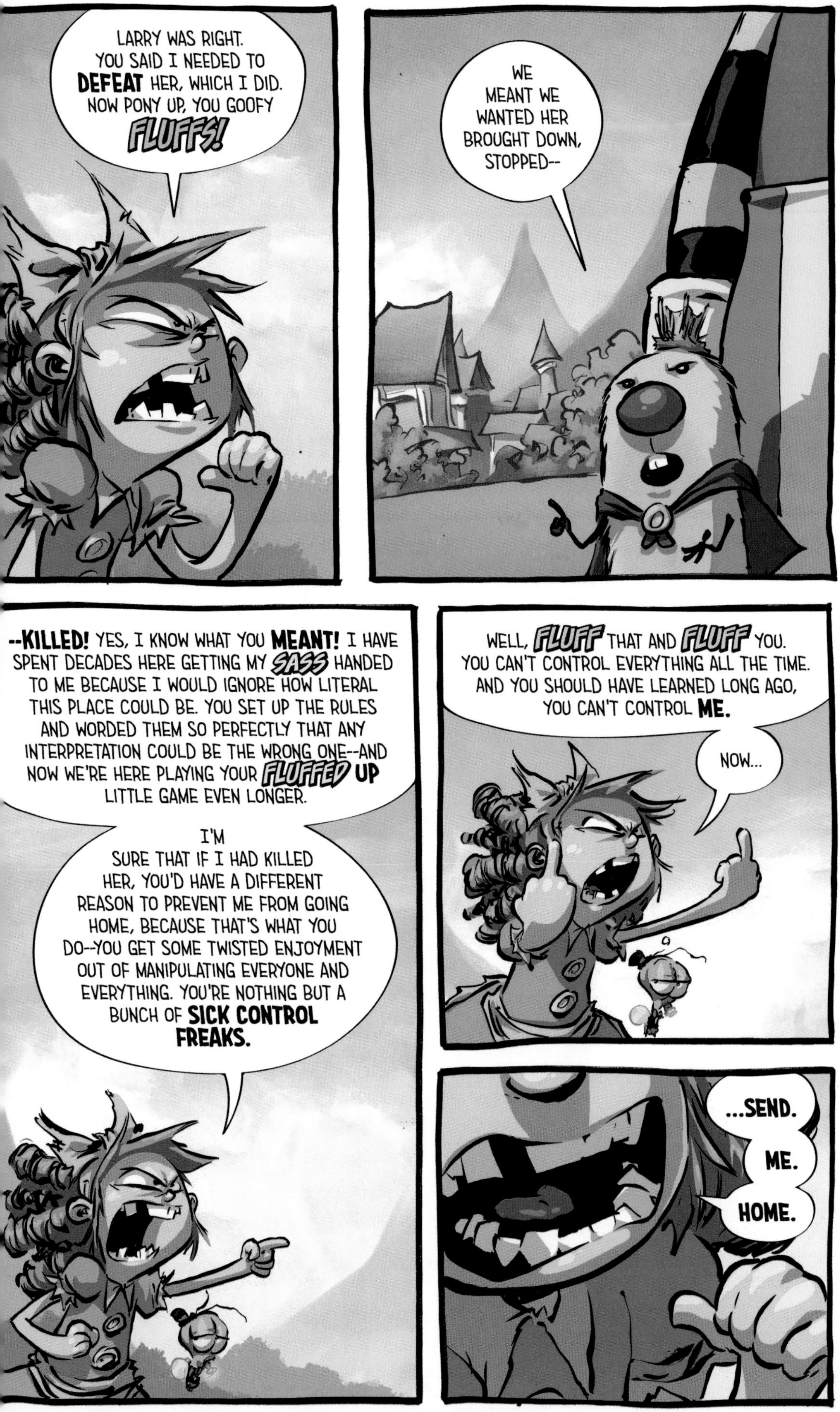

LARRY WAS RIGHT. YOU SAID I NEEDED TO DEFEAT HER, WHICH I DID. NOW PONY UP, YOU GOOFY FLUFFS!
WE MEANT WE WANTED HER BROUGHT DOWN, STOPPED--
--KILLED! YES, I KNOW WHAT YOU MEANT! I HAVE SPENT DECADES HERE GETTING MY SASS HANDED TO ME BECAUSE I WOULD IGNORE HOW LITERAL THIS PLACE COULD BE. YOU SET UP THE RULES AND WORDED THEM SO PERFECTLY THAT ANY INTERPRETATION COULD BE THE WRONG ONE--AND NOW WE'RE HERE PLAYING YOUR FLUFFED UP LITTLE GAME EVEN LONGER.
I'M SURE THAT IF I HAD KILLED HER, YOU'D HAVE A DIFFERENT REASON TO PREVENT ME FROM GOING HOME, BECAUSE THAT'S WHAT YOU DO--YOU GET SOME TWISTED ENJOYMENT OUT OF MANIPULATING EVERYONE AND EVERYTHING. YOU'RE NOTHING BUT A BUNCH OF SICK CONTROL FREAKS.
WELL, FLUFF THAT AND FLUFF YOU. YOU CAN'T CONTROL EVERYTHING ALL THE TIME. AND YOU SHOULD HAVE LEARNED LONG AGO, YOU CAN'T CONTROL ME.
NOW...
...SEND.
ME.
HOME.

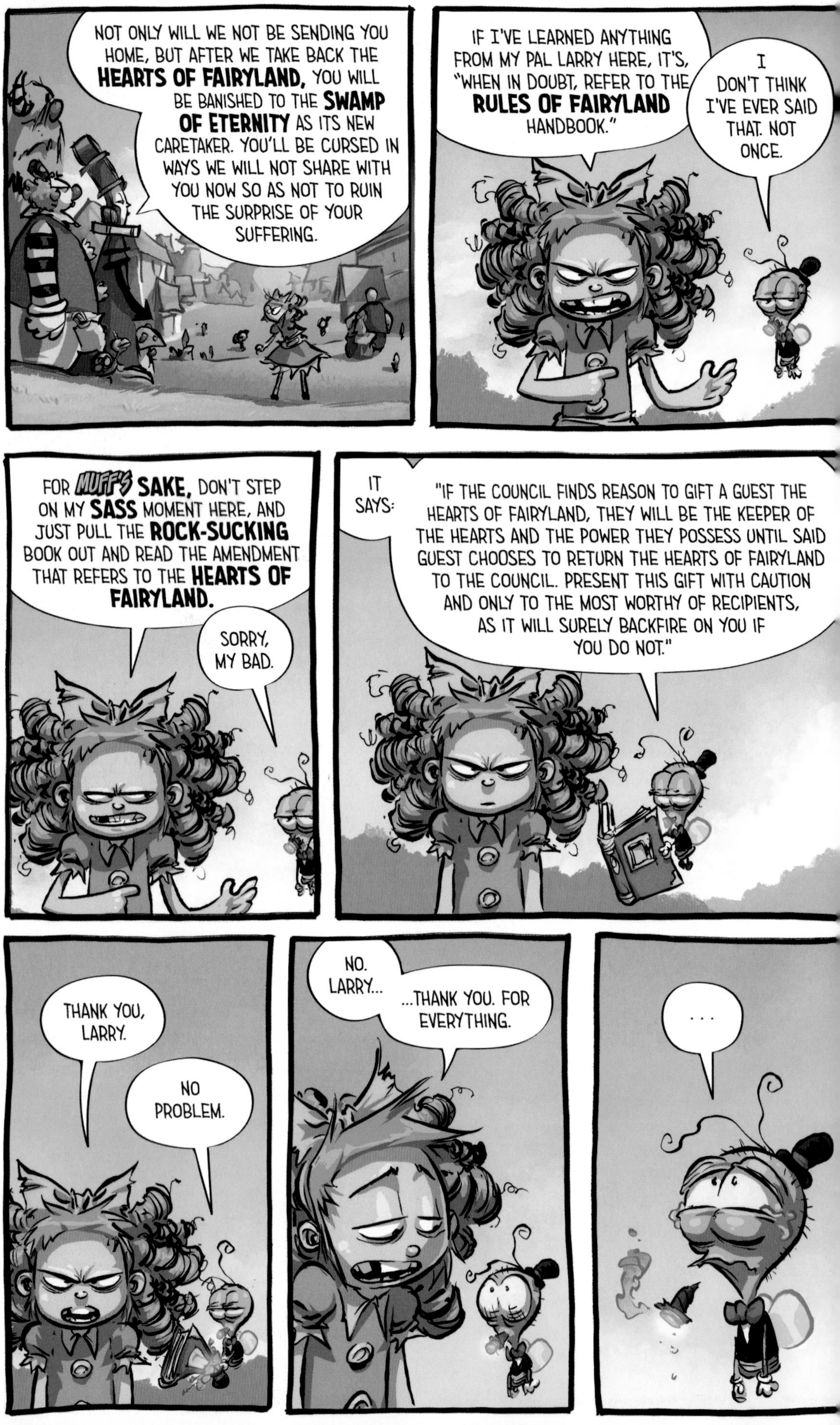
NOT ONLY WILL WE NOT BE SENDING YOU HOME, BUT AFTER WE TAKE BACK THE HEARTS OF FAIRYLAND, YOU WILL BE BANISHED TO THE SWAMP OF ETERNITY AS ITS NEW CARETAKER. YOU'LL BE CURSED IN WAYS WE WILL NOT SHARE WITH YOU NOW SO AS NOT TO RUIN THE SURPRISE OF YOUR SUFFERING.
IF I'VE LEARNED ANYTHING FROM MY PAL LARRY HERE, IT'S, "WHEN IN DOUBT, REFER TO THE RULES OF FAIRYLAND HANDBOOK."
I DON'T THINK I'VE EVER SAID THAT. NOT ONCE.
FOR MUFF'S SAKE, DON'T STEP ON MY SASS MOMENT HERE, AND JUST PULL THE ROCK-SUCKING BOOK OUT AND READ THE AMENDMENT THAT REFERS TO THE HEARTS OF FAIRYLAND.
SORRY, MY BAD.
IT SAYS:
"IF THE COUNCIL FINDS REASON TO GIFT A GUEST THE HEARTS OF FAIRYLAND, THEY WILL BE THE KEEPER OF THE HEARTS AND THE POWER THEY POSSESS UNTIL SAID GUEST CHOOSES TO RETURN THE HEARTS OF FAIRYLAND TO THE COUNCIL. PRESENT THIS GIFT WITH CAUTION AND ONLY TO THE MOST WORTHY OF RECIPIENTS, AS IT WILL SURELY BACKFIRE ON YOU IF YOU DO NOT."
THANK YOU, LARRY.
NO PROBLEM.
NO. LARRY...
...THANK YOU. FOR EVERYTHING.
. . .

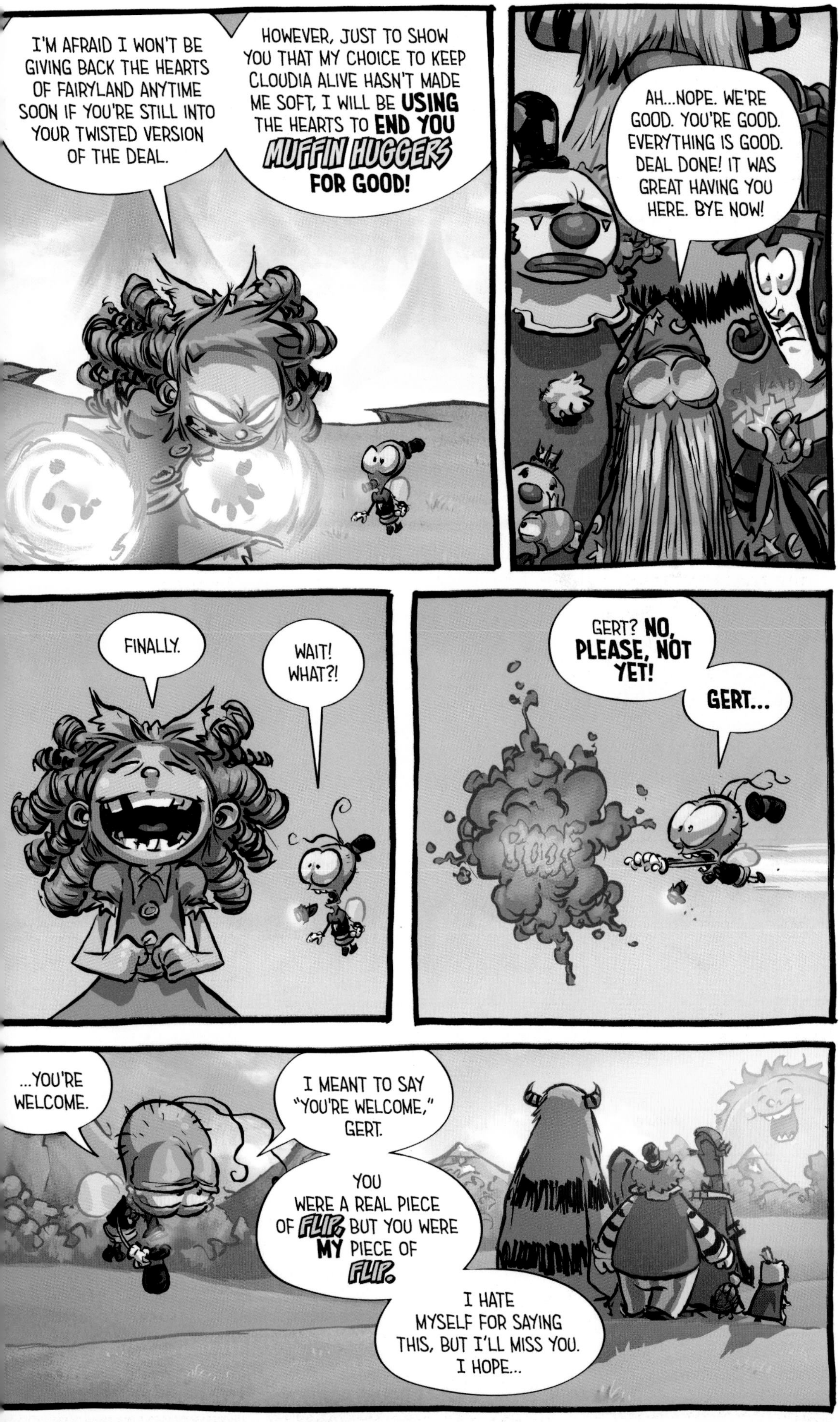
I'M AFRAID I WON'T BE GIVING BACK THE HEARTS OF FAIRYLAND ANYTIME SOON IF YOU'RE STILL INTO YOUR TWISTED VERSION OF THE DEAL.
HOWEVER, JUST TO SHOW YOU THAT MY CHOICE TO KEEP CLOUDIA ALIVE HASN'T MADE ME SOFT, I WILL BE USING THE HEARTS TO END YOU MUFFIN HUGGERS FOR GOOD!
AH...NOPE. WE'RE GOOD. YOU'RE GOOD. EVERYTHING IS GOOD. DEAL DONE! IT WAS GREAT HAVING YOU HERE. BYE NOW!
FINALLY.
WAIT! WHAT?!
GERT? NO, PLEASE, NOT YET!
GERT...
...YOU'RE WELCOME.
I MEANT TO SAY "YOU'RE WELCOME," GERT.
YOU WERE A REAL PIECE OF FLIP, BUT YOU WERE MY PIECE OF FLIP.
I HATE MYSELF FOR SAYING THIS, BUT I'LL MISS YOU. I HOPE...

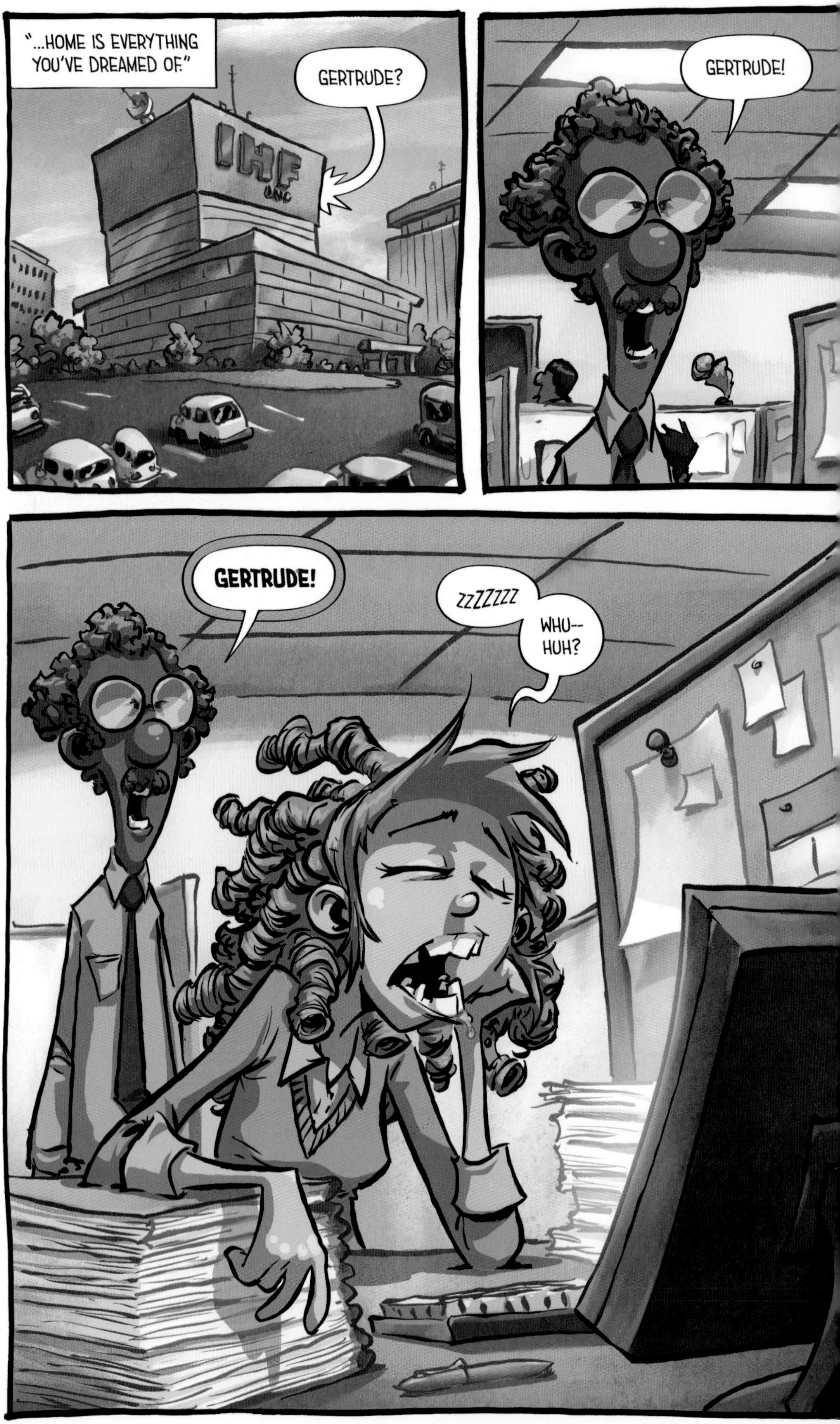
"...HOME IS EVERYTHING YOU'VE DREAMED OF."
IHF INC
GERTRUDE?
GERTRUDE!
GERTRUDE!
zzZZZZZ
WHU-- HUH?

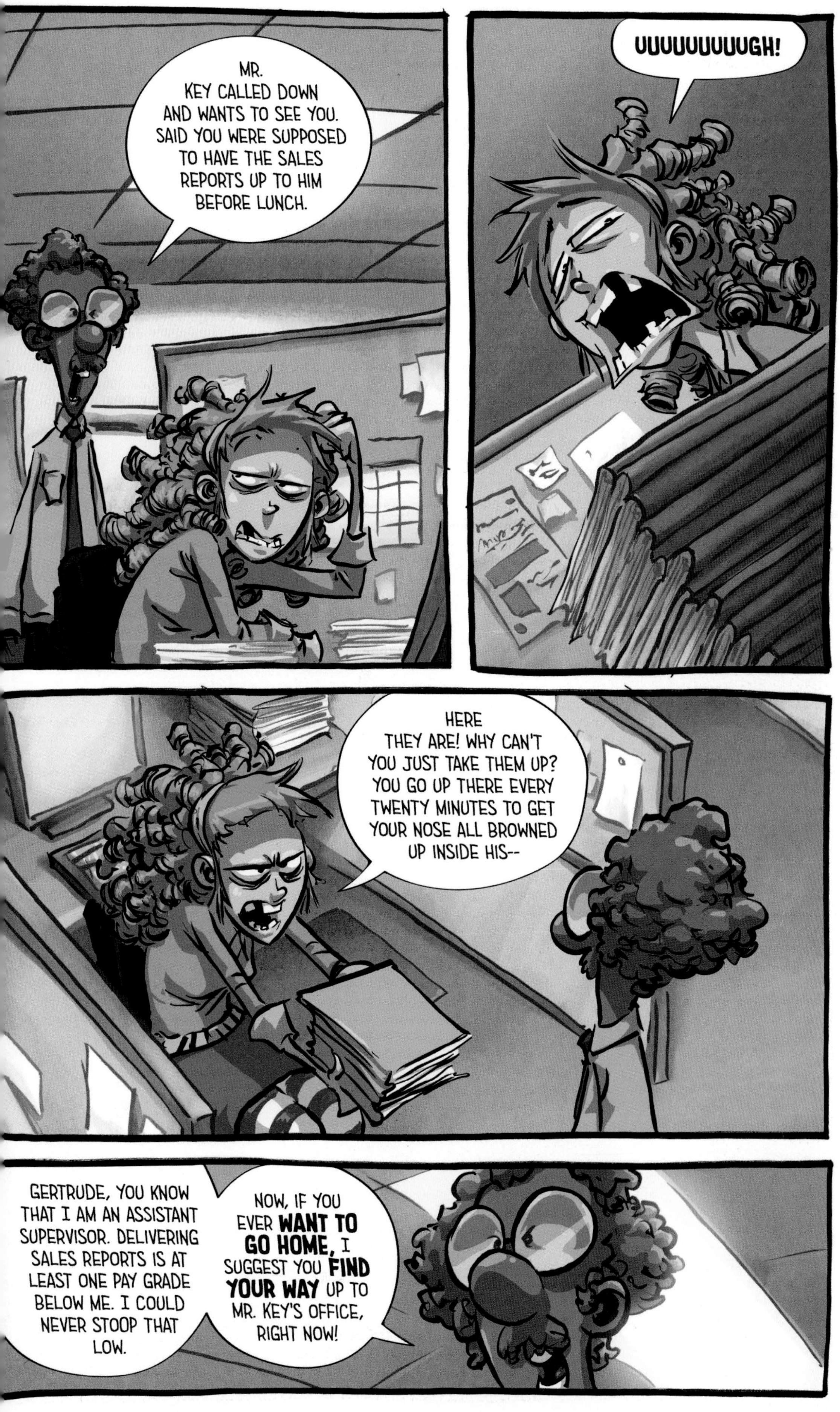
MR. KEY CALLED DOWN AND WANTS TO SEE YOU. SAID YOU WERE SUPPOSED TO HAVE THE SALES REPORTS UP TO HIM BEFORE LUNCH.
UUUUUUUUUGH!
HERE THEY ARE! WHY CAN'T YOU JUST TAKE THEM UP? YOU GO UP THERE EVERY TWENTY MINUTES TO GET YOUR NOSE ALL BROWNED UP INSIDE HIS--
GERTRUDE, YOU KNOW THAT I AM AN ASSISTANT SUPERVISOR. DELIVERING SALES REPORTS IS AT LEAST ONE PAY GRADE BELOW ME. I COULD NEVER STOOP THAT LOW.
NOW, IF YOU EVER **WANT TO GO HOME,** I SUGGEST YOU **FIND YOUR WAY** UP TO MR. KEY'S OFFICE, RIGHT NOW!

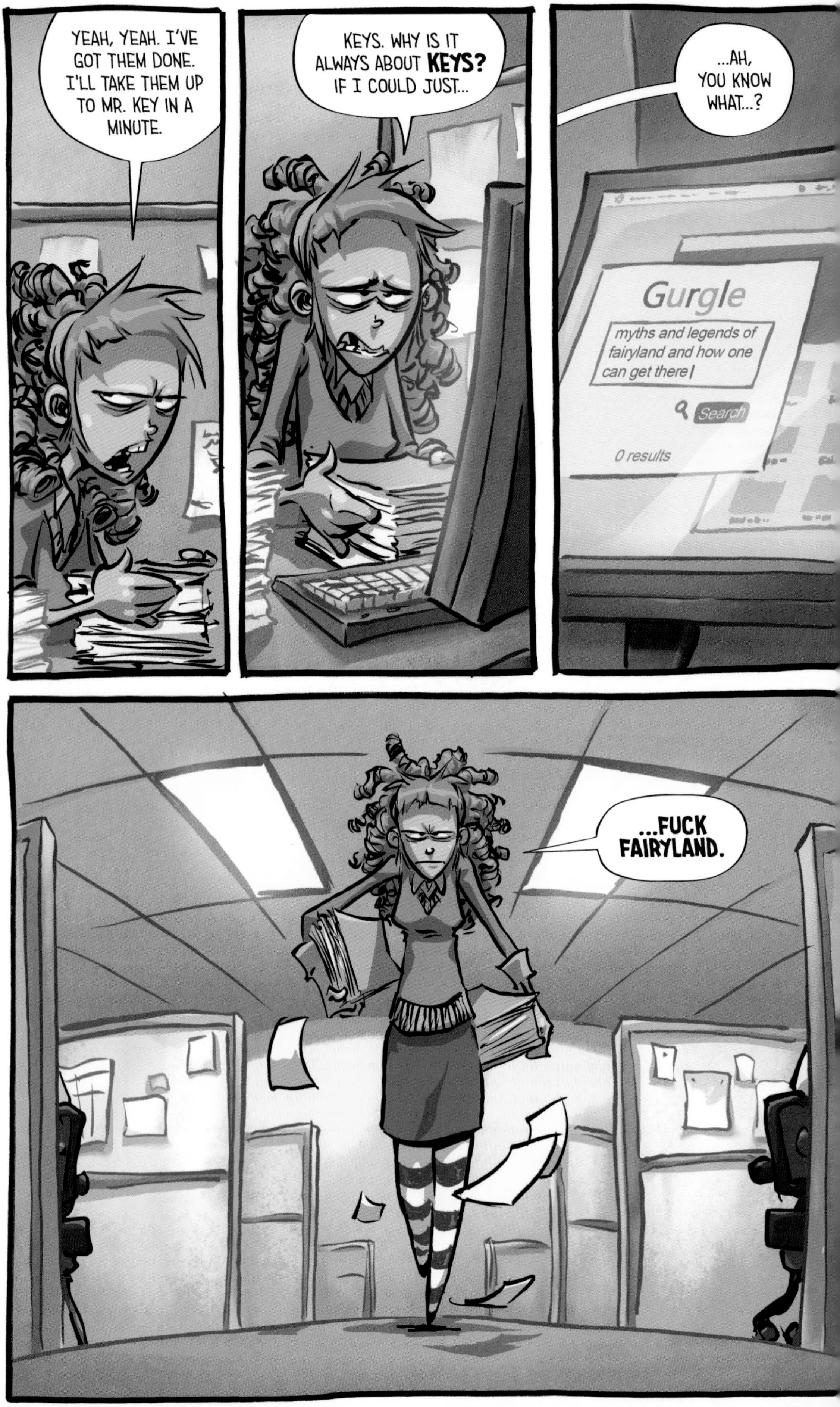
YEAH, YEAH. I'VE GOT THEM DONE. I'LL TAKE THEM UP TO MR. KEY IN A MINUTE.
KEYS. WHY IS IT ALWAYS ABOUT KEYS? IF I COULD JUST...
...AH, YOU KNOW WHAT...?
Gurgle
myths and legends of fairyland and how one can get there
Search
0 results
...FUCK FAIRYLAND.

SKOTTIE YOUNG

...is the *New York Times* bestselling, Eisner Award-winning artist on Marvel's WIZARD OF OZ graphic novel adaptions, writer and artist on ROCKET RACOON, writer on DEADPOOL, MIDDLEWEST and BULLY WARS and, you know, cartoonist on the widely popular I HATE FAIRYLAND series that you just finished reading. Oh yeah, he's also done somewhere in ballpark of three million baby covers over at Marvel. You love 'em and you buy all the pins, moving on. Skottie fled Illinois like most other residents of that state in the last few years and now lives in Kansas City, KS with his wife, two boys, and two very large dogs. Oh, and Jason Aaron. So three very large dogs.

JEAN-FRANCOIS BEAULIEU

...is the acclaimed colorist behind Marvel's WIZARD OF OZ graphic novel adaptations, ROCKET RACCOON, GIANT-SIZE LITTLE MARVEL, NEW WARRIORS, NEW X-MEN, and probably other books that Skottie Young didn't draw but since Skottie Young is writing this we'll keep it to mostly Skottie Young books. Okay, fine, INVINCIBLE. Happy? Jean and Skottie have been working together for over a decade. (Which sounds way more epic than saying te years.) Jean is considered one of the industry's top colorists and also holds the record for most people who don't know how to pronounce his last name. He lives somewhere in the Canadian wilderness with his fiancé, three dogs, nine cats, and an unknown amour of dope robot model kits.

NATE PIEKOS

...is the founder of Blambot.com, a company with a much cooler name than any of us could probably come up with. Good job, Nate! He has created some of the industry's most popular fonts and has used them to letter comic books for Image Comics (REBORN, HUCK), Marvel Comics (X-STATIX, X-MEN FIRST CLASS), DC Comics (GREEN ARRO SUICIDE SQUAD), Dark Horse Comics (STRANGER THINGS, FIGHT CLUB 2, UMBRELLA ACADEMY). and all of the other companies that end with the wo "Comics." Nate has more guitars in his studio than an other letterer on the planet. (That was not fact-checked, but I'm going with it.) He lives in Rhode Isla with his wife and the previously mentioned guitars.